Cambridge School Shakespeare

中文详注剑桥莎士比亚精选

HAMLET

哈慕雷

原版创始主编：[英] 瑞克斯·吉布森（Rex Gibson）

原版主编：[英] 瑞查德·安褚斯（Richard Andrews）

[英] 维姬·维南德（Vicki Wienand）

原版编注：[英] 瑞查德·安褚斯（Richard Andrews）

总主编：陈国华

分册主编：潘铁楠 陈国华

社图号 21211

图书在版编目（CIP）数据

中文详注剑桥莎士比亚精选. 哈慕雷 / 陈国华总主编 ; 潘铁楠，陈国华分册主编. -- 北京 : 北京语言大学出版社，2021.11

书名原文：Cambridge School Shakespeare：Hamlet
ISBN 978-7-5619-6035-6

Ⅰ. ①中… Ⅱ. ①陈… ②潘… Ⅲ. ①悲剧－剧本－英国－中世纪 Ⅳ. ①I561.33

中国版本图书馆 CIP 数据核字（2021）第 237530 号

中文详注剑桥莎士比亚精选：哈慕雷

ZHONGWEN XIANG ZHU JIANQIAO SHASHIBIYA JINGXUAN: HAMULEI

项目策划：李　亮　　责任编辑：孙冠群　李　亮
封面设计：乔　剑　　排版制作：北京创艺涵文化发展有限公司
责任印制：周　燚

出版发行：北京语言大学出版社
社　　址：北京市海淀区学院路 15 号，100083
网　　址：www.blcup.com
电子信箱：service@blcup.com
电　　话：编 辑 部　8610-82301019/0178
　　　　　发 行 部　8610-82303650/3591/3648
　　　　　北语书店　8610-82303653
　　　　　网购咨询　8610-82303908
印　　刷：北京博海升彩色印刷有限公司

版　　次：2021 年 11 月第 1 版　　印　　次：2021 年 11 月第 1 次印刷
开　　本：787 毫米 × 1092 毫米　1/16　　印　　张：18.75
字　　数：480 千字
定　　价：109.00 元

PRINTED IN CHINA

序

由于观察角度不同，评判标准不同，关于哪个国家哪位诗人或小说家的成就最大，世人可能难以达成一致；可是说到剧作家，大家的共识是，莎士比亚不仅是英语国家有史以来最伟大的剧作家，也是全世界最伟大的剧作家，在知名度、影响力和传世作品的数量上，没有任何一位剧作家可以与之比肩。正是由于其公认的文学成就和人文精神，在过去400多年里，莎士比亚戏剧的演出在英语国家和许多非英语国家经久不衰，莎剧的阅读和鉴赏已成为这些国家英文教学的必选内容。

莎剧进入中国，已经有100多年历史，莎士比亚全集已经有了四个中文译本。不懂英文的人可以通过译本来欣赏莎士比亚剧作。然而文学作品的语言，尤其是诗歌的语言，具有相当程度的不可译性，而几乎所有莎剧的大部分台词都是素体诗（blank verse）。例如《哈慕雷》（*Hamlet*）里主人公的名言“To be, or not to be, that is the question”，不论怎样译，都难以完全再现原文的深刻内涵和形式特点。要想真正欣赏莎士比亚的语言和戏剧艺术，还得阅读其英文原作。最早由剑桥大学出版社出版的这套莎剧精选，收录了最受读者和观众喜爱的14部剧目，涵盖莎剧的各个类别，以其独具匠心的设计和编排，成为所有英文原版莎剧中最适合英语学习者阅读、最适合戏剧爱好者排演的莎剧选集。

本选集的创始主编瑞克斯·吉布森（Rex Gibson）在本书引言（Introduction）里指出：“不论做什么，都要记住，莎士比亚写下他的剧本是为了演出、观看和享受的。”秉承这一宗旨，这一新版莎剧选集有四个鲜明的区别性特点：

一、书的开本和页面的宽高比例特别适合学校的老师和学生以及剧团的导演和演员在排练莎剧时把书打开，拿在手里，随时参阅，而且左边页面上有许多有关排演活动的建议。

二、书中配有大量世界各国莎剧演出的彩色剧照，为莎剧爱好者和剧团排演莎剧提供了灵感。

三、书的正文部分打开后，右页是未经删减、原汁原味的剧本原文，左页是多种不同栏目，包括导演技巧（Stagecraft）、剧中语言（Language in the play）、人物分析（Characters）、主题分析（Themes）、写作练习（Write about it）及词语注释等。每幕之间（本幕回顾）和最后一幕后（本剧回顾）有与剧情相关的各种思考题。

四、在剧本之后有各种针对全剧的专题论述，以《哈慕雷》为例，包括视角与主题（Perspectives and themes）、人物分析（Characters）、《哈慕雷》的语言（The language of *Hamlet*）、《哈慕雷》的演出（*Hamlet* in performance）、笔论莎士比亚（Writing about Shakespeare）、笔论《哈慕雷》（Writing about *Hamlet*），还有一份莎翁年表（William Shakespeare 1564–1616）。

左页上的栏目对于解读和排演莎剧特别有帮助，剧本后面的专题论述对于撰写有关莎士比亚的文章特别有帮助，而参加莎剧排演、背诵台词、撰写论文，又是提高英语水平的极好途径。

为了方便更多的中国读者阅读、欣赏、排演莎士比亚原作，北京语言大学出版社携手剑桥大学出版社，将这套莎剧精选引入中国。我有幸应邀担任这套书的中文版总主编，组织起一个团队，对原版进行一定程度的改编和汉化，以适应中国读者的需求。我们不仅将原版提供的关键注释基本译成了中文，而且针对中国英语学习者和莎剧爱好者阅读理解上的难点，主要做了以下四件事：

一、参考*The Oxford Dictionary of Original Shakespearean Pronunciation* (David Crystal 2016)、*Oxford Dictionary of Pronunciation for Current English* (Clive Upton 2003) 和 *Shakespeare's Names: A Pronouncing Dictionary* (Helge Kökeritz 1950)，给每个剧本前面人物表里的人名加上了国际音标。为了便于读者识别，我们将第一本发音词典里一般中国读者不认识的个别音标替换成了大家熟悉的近似音标。

二、为左页顶端的剧情简介添加中文译文。

三、左页中以及剧本后面论文部分里有一些具有挑战性的词和术语（如tableau），我们为其中的大部分添加了相应的中文释义。

四、适当增加了原版里没有的词语注释。

给剧中人物的名字加了国际音标之后，我们发现，现有莎剧中文译本里一些人名的中文译名与原文的读音差别较大且互不相同。根据定名不咎、译音循本、音义兼顾、音系对应的原则，我们给出了新译名。根据前两个原则，我们将剧本 *Julius Caesar* /ˈdʒuːlɪəs ˈsiːzə(r)/ 译成《儒略・恺撒》，而没有采用《尤利/力乌斯・恺撒》《裘利/力斯・凯撒》《居里厄斯・恺撒》等现成译名中的任何一个，因为从公元前1世纪到公元16世纪西方使用的儒略历（Julian calendar）就是以这位 Julius Caesar（拉丁文读音是 /ˈjuːlɪ.ʊs ˈkae̯sar/）命名的。根据音义兼顾的原则，我们将剧本 *Hamlet* /ˈ(h)amlət/ 译成《哈慕雷》而不是《哈姆莱特》或《哈姆雷特》，因为“慕雷”比“姆莱”或“姆雷”更适合用来给男子起名，结尾的辅音 /t/ 在实际说话中往往不发音。根据音系对应的原则，我们借鉴了曹禺的译法，将剧本 *Romeo and Juliet* 译成《柔密欧与茱丽叶》，没有将 Romeo 译成更常见的“罗密欧”，因为“柔 /rou/”比“罗 /luo/”更接近原名 Romeo /ˈroːmɪoː/ 的读音；同时我们将 Juliet /ˈdʒuːlɪət/ 译成“茱丽叶”而不是“朱丽叶”，因为这样做不容易让人误以为这个女孩姓“朱”。

这套经过改编并且带中文注释的《中文详注剑桥莎士比亚精选》不仅可以用作中国高中和大学的英文教材，而且适合中国所有具有较高英语能力的莎剧爱好者阅读和欣赏，将戏剧从书中提升到自己心中，将剧本从课堂搬演到戏台。

相信《中文详注剑桥莎士比亚精选》会带给中国广大英语爱好者一个惊喜。

陈国华

2020年5月于英国剑桥家中

Contents 目录

Introduction 引言

This *Hamlet* is part of the **Cambridge School Shakespeare** series. Like every other play in the series, it has been specially prepared to help all students in schools and colleges.

The **Cambridge School Shakespeare** *Hamlet* aims to be different. It invites you to lift the words from the page and to bring the play to life in your classroom, hall or drama studio. Through enjoyable and focused activities, you will increase your understanding of the play. Actors have created their different interpretations of the play over the centuries. Similarly, you are invited to make up your own mind about *Hamlet*, rather than having someone else's interpretation handed down to you.

Cambridge School Shakespeare does not offer you a cut-down or simplified version of the play. This is Shakespeare's language, filled with imaginative possibilities. You will find on every left-hand page: a summary of the action, an explanation of unfamiliar words, and a choice of activities on Shakespeare's stagecraft, characters, themes and language.

Between each act and in the pages at the end of the play, you will find notes, illustrations and activities. These will help to encourage reflection after every act and give you insights into the background and context of the play as a whole.

This edition will be of value to you whether you are studying for an examination, reading for pleasure or thinking of putting on the play to entertain others. You can work on the activities on your own or in groups. Many of the activities suggest a particular group size, but don't be afraid to make up larger or smaller groups to suit your own purposes. Please don't think you have to do every activity: choose those that will help you most.

Although you are invited to treat *Hamlet* as a play, you don't need special dramatic or theatrical skills to do the activities. By choosing your activities, and by exploring and experimenting, you can make your own interpretations of Shakespeare's language, characters and stories.

Whatever you do, remember that Shakespeare wrote his plays to be acted, watched and enjoyed.

Rex Gibson
Founding editor

This new edition contains more photographs, more diversity and more supporting material than previous editions, whilst remaining true to Rex's original vision. Specifically, it contains more activities and commentary on stagecraft and writing about Shakespeare, to reflect contemporary interest. The glossary has been enlarged too. Finally, this edition aims to reflect the best teaching and learning possible, and to represent not only Shakespeare through the ages, but also the relevance and excitement of Shakespeare today.

Richard Andrews and Vicki Wienand
Series editors

This edition of *Hamlet* uses the text of the play established by Philip Edwards in **The New Cambridge Shakespeare**.

Hamlet dramatises the tragic story of the young prince of Denmark. His country is threatened with invasion by Norway, but Hamlet is obsessed with the recent death of his father and the marriage of his mother, Gertrude, to his uncle, Claudius, who has become king.

Hamlet's first appearance, dressed in black, conveys his isolation from the court. His unhappiness about Gertrude's relationship with Claudius is evident. The outcome will be the destruction of two families: Hamlet's (Gertrude and Claudius) and royal counsellor Polonius's (Laertes and Ophelia).

Hamlet learns the truth from his father's ghost: Claudius murdered old Hamlet. Hamlet desires revenge, but is not sure if the Ghost has spoken honestly.

To test the truth of the Ghost's story, Hamlet puts on 'an antic disposition'. His strange behaviour arouses the suspicion of Claudius.

Claudius sends for Hamlet's old schoolfriends, Rosencrantz and Guildenstern, to spy on his stepson. Hamlet greets them joyfully, but then discovers they are Claudius's agents.

Hamlet plans to discover Claudius's guilt. He orders a group of players to stage a play showing a king murdered by his brother, who then marries the queen.

Hamlet's plan succeeds, and Claudius acknowledges his guilt as he prays. Hamlet is about to kill Claudius, but decides to wait until he can choose a moment when Claudius's soul will go straight to hell.

▲ Polonius has concealed himself, wishing to overhear what Hamlet says to Gertrude. But Hamlet mistakes the hidden Polonius for Claudius, and kills him.

◀ Hamlet rages at his mother, begging her to give up Claudius. But Claudius, wanting to be rid of his dangerous stepson, sends Hamlet to England, secretly ordering his execution there.

▶ (top) Claudius and Gertrude watch appalled as Ophelia's songs recall Hamlet's rejection and his killing of her father, Polonius. Her madness will shortly result in her death.

▶ (bottom) Hamlet has escaped execution in England, but has sent Rosencrantz and Guildenstern to their deaths there. In the graveyard, the sight of Yorick's skull prompts him to reflect on mortality.

Hamlet duels with Laertes, Polonius's son, who seeks revenge for his father's and sister's deaths.

Claudius and Laertes have conspired to kill Hamlet by deceit. But their plot descends into chaos: Gertrude drinks the poison intended for Hamlet, and Laertes, Claudius and Hamlet are all fatally wounded by the poisoned sword.

List of characters 人物表

The Royal House of Denmark 丹麦王室

HAMLET /ˈhamlət/ (哈慕雷) Prince of Denmark
CLAUDIUS /ˈklɔːdɪəs/ (克劳迭) King of Denmark, Hamlet's uncle
GERTRUDE /ˈgɜː(r)truːd/ (葛楚德) Queen of Denmark, Hamlet's mother
GHOST of King Hamlet, Hamlet's father

The Court of Denmark 丹麦宫廷

POLONIUS /pəˈloːnɪəs/ (珀娄涅) Counsellor to the king
OPHELIA /ɒˈfiːljə/ (奥菲丽叶) Polonius's daughter
LAERTES /leɪˈəː(r)tiːz/ (雷厄提) Polonius's son
REYNALDO /reɪˈnaldoː/ (瑞纳尔窦) Polonius's servant

OSRIC /ˈɒsrɪk/ (奥斯睿), LORDS, GENTLEMAN — Courtiers
MESSENGER and ATTENDANTS

VOLTEMAND /ˈvɒltɪmand/ (沃尔提曼), CORNELIUS /kɔː(r)ˈniːlɪəs/ (考尼列) — Ambassadors to Norway
MARCELLUS /mɑː(r)ˈseləs/ (玛塞勒), BARNARDO /bə(r)ˈnɑː(r)doː/ (博纳窦), FRANCISCO /franˈsɪskoː/ (伏冉希斯寇) — Officers of the Watch
SOLDIERS and GUARDS

Former fellow students of Hamlet 哈慕雷以前的同学

HORATIO /həˈreɪsɪoː/ (何瑞修) Hamlet's friend
ROSENCRANTZ /ˈroːzenˌkrants/ (柔森克阮茨), GUILDENSTERN /ˈgɪldənˌstəː(r)n/ (吉尔顿斯登) — Sent for by Claudius to inform on Hamlet

Norway 挪威

FORTINBRAS /ˈfɔː(r)tɪnˌbras/ (福庭布拉) Prince of Norway
CAPTAIN in Fortinbras's army

Other characters in the play 剧中其他角色

First PLAYER, Other players — actors visiting Elsinore
English AMBASSADORS
SAILORS
CLOWN gravedigger and sexton (教堂司事)
SECOND CLOWN Clown's assistant
PRIEST at Ophelia's funeral

The action of the play is set in and around the Danish royal palace at Elsinore*.

* 埃尔悉诺，即赫尔辛格（丹麦文写作*Helsingør*），北距哥本哈根约30千米，位于丹麦西兰岛最东北端，扼守连接波罗的海和大西洋的松德海峡的出海口，让丹麦王室得以对过往船只征收巨额通行费。本剧第一幕的场景设在埃尔悉诺克隆堡城堡（Kronborg Castle）的城墙上，该城堡建于15世纪初，是当时的王宫，如今是世界遗产。

Francisco is on sentry duty on the gun platform of Elsinore. It is midnight and freezing cold. Barnardo comes to relieve Francisco. Horatio and Marcellus arrive to join Barnardo.

剧情简介：午时分夜，天寒地冻，埃尔悉诺的炮台上，伏冉希斯寇正在站岗。博纳窦来换岗，接着何瑞修和玛塞勒也到了，他们三人站同一班岗。

Stagecraft 导演技巧

To experience the tense and uneasy atmosphere of the play's opening, the best thing to do is take parts and act out the first nineteen lines. As you rehearse, talk together about the following points. Remember, your aim is to make the opening moments of the play gripping and dramatic.

- What will be the first thing the audience sees? For example, is Francisco on sentry duty, patrolling the stage, before the first members of the audience enter?
- Barnardo, the newcomer, challenges Francisco. This is contrary to military practice (Francisco should challenge him). How can you use that error to intensify the nervous atmosphere?
- What effect do the short, staccato ('rapid fire') verbal exchanges have?
- How can you show the audience that the night is bitterly cold?
- Francisco is never seen again in the play, but his remark 'And I am sick at heart' forecasts the troubled melancholy that Hamlet feels when he appears in the next scene. How might Francisco speak and behave during his brief time on stage? What would be the effect if Hamlet and Francisco were played by the same actor?
- In Shakespeare's day, plays were staged in broad daylight. Identify all the words and phrases in the script that help create the impression of night and darkness.

1 Horatio

This is the first time we meet Horatio, who will turn out to be an important character in the play.

- Look at Horatio's lines in the script opposite and on the following page, and start making notes on his character, based on the attitude he takes towards the Watch and the Ghost. Write down the range of emotions he displays. As you progress through the play, your first impressions of his character will inform your notes on Horatio, and the role he plays in relation to Hamlet.

1 Nay answer me 不对，你回答我（发问的应该是我）（nay用于反驳或否定）

2 unfold yourself 报上名来

3 Long live the King! 吾王万岁！（这是当晚口令。后面剧情透露哈慕雷王已死，让此句具有反讽意味。）

4 most carefully upon your hour 您一刻不差，踩着点上岗

5 'Tis now struck twelve 钟声响了十二下

6 relief 换岗，换班

7 sick at heart 心情郁闷

8 rivals of my watch 我这班岗的搭档

9 Stand ho! 站住！停下！（这里的ho是马车夫让马停下的用语，= hold）

10 Friends to this ground 这地方的朋友；自家人

11 liegemen to the Dane 效忠丹麦王的人

12 Give you = May God give you 祝您

13 A piece of him 他的一部分（演员说此话时将一只手伸出去，由此可见何瑞修的严谨和幽默）

Hamlet, Prince of Denmark

Act 1 Scene 1

A gun platform on the battlements of Elsinore Castle

Enter BARNARDO *and* FRANCISCO, *two* sentinels

BARNARDO Who's there?
FRANCISCO Nay answer me[1]. Stand and unfold yourself[2].
BARNARDO Long live the king![3]
FRANCISCO Barnardo?
BARNARDO He.
FRANCISCO You come most carefully upon your hour[4].
BARNARDO 'Tis now struck twelve[5], get thee to bed Francisco.
FRANCISCO For this relief[6] much thanks, 'tis bitter cold
And I am sick at heart[7].
BARNARDO Have you had quiet guard?
FRANCISCO Not a mouse stirring.
BARNARDO Well, good night.
If you do meet Horatio and Marcellus,
The rivals of my watch[8], bid them make haste.
FRANCISCO I think I hear them.

Enter HORATIO *and* MARCELLUS

Stand ho![9] Who is there?
HORATIO Friends to this ground[10].
MARCELLUS And liegemen to the Dane[11].
FRANCISCO Give you[12] good night.
MARCELLUS Oh farewell honest soldier,
Who hath relieved you?
FRANCISCO Barnardo hath my place.
Give you good night. *Exit Francisco*
MARCELLUS Holla, Barnardo!
BARNARDO Say,
What, is Horatio there?
HORATIO A piece of him[13].

Marcellus reports that he and Barnardo have seen the Ghost twice. Horatio doesn't believe them, but is struck with fear and amazement when the Ghost of Hamlet's father appears.

剧情简介：玛塞勒通报说，他和博纳窦见过那个鬼魂两次了。何瑞修不信，但他看到哈慕雷父亲的鬼魂出现时，又惊又怕。

Stagecraft 导演技巧

'Enter GHOST' – dead King Hamlet appears (in pairs)

The entry of the Ghost of Hamlet's father is a thrilling moment in the theatre. Each new production attempts to ensure that the entrance is as electrifying and memorable as possible. Imagine you are directing the play. You will keep a Director's Journal in which you consider stagecraft, how to advise the actors, tone and other features of the production.

a Talk with your partner and write notes on each of the following:

- What does the Ghost look like? Horatio gives a clue in lines 47–9 (and see the pictures in the photo gallery and on pp. 10 and 48).
- Suggest how the Ghost might enter. Slowly or suddenly? From which direction? Decide whether he makes any gestures, what sound effects you might use and how he leaves the stage.
- Sometimes, as the Ghost appears, the bell strikes. Would you have it strike if you were directing the play? Why, or why not?

b In some productions, the Ghost does not appear physically. The audience has to imagine its presence through lighting, sound and characters' reactions. How effective do you think this style of presenting the Ghost would be? Have two groups present the scene, one with the Ghost on stage and the other with him off stage, to compare dramatic effect.

1 An inner ghost? (in pairs)

In a production at the Royal Court Theatre in London in 1980, the actor Jonathan Pryce played Hamlet, with the Ghost appearing to speak from inside him. At times he was bent double with the pain of the Ghost's voice coming through him; at other times the Ghost appeared to speak in a horrible voice that cut through Hamlet's own voice, bubbling up in an uncontrolled fashion. Discuss the following points:

- What are the advantages and disadvantages of having the Ghost come from within a character?
- How could this first scene be presented if the Ghost is an internal rather than an external presence?
- What does an inner Ghost imply about the nature of ghosts, and the purpose of this particular Ghost in the play as a whole?

1 but our fantasy 不过是我们的幻觉
2 Touching 关于
3 entreated 央求，好说歹说
4 watch … night 守望今夜的每时每刻
5 apparition 幽灵
6 approve our eyes 证实我们所见
7 Tush 啧
8 assail … story 攻打您那修了工事、抵御我们故事的耳朵
9 yond 彼处，远处
10 pole 北极星
11 t'illume = to illume 照亮
12 scholar 读书人（会拉丁文，可直接跟说拉丁文的鬼魂对话）
13 a = he
14 harrows 折磨
15 usurp'st 僭用
16 buried Denmark 已下葬的丹麦王
17 sometimes 以前
18 charge 命令
19 stalks 昂首阔步

BARNARDO Welcome Horatio, welcome good Marcellus.
MARCELLUS What, has this thing appeared again tonight?
BARNARDO I have seen nothing.
MARCELLUS Horatio says 'tis but our fantasy[1],
And will not let belief take hold of him
Touching[2] this dreaded sight, twice seen of us.
Therefore I have entreated[3] him along
With us to watch the minutes of this night[4],
That if again this apparition[5] come
He may approve our eyes[6], and speak to it.
HORATIO Tush[7], tush, 'twill not appear.
BARNARDO Sit down awhile,
And let us once again assail your ears,
That are so fortified against our story[8],
What we two nights have seen.
HORATIO Well, sit we down,
And let us hear Barnardo speak of this.
BARNARDO Last night of all,
When yond[9] same star that's westward from the pole[10]
Had made his course t'illume[11] that part of heaven
Where now it burns, Marcellus and myself,
The bell then beating one –

Enter GHOST

MARCELLUS Peace, break thee off. Look where it comes again.
BARNARDO In the same figure, like the king that's dead.
MARCELLUS Thou art a scholar[12], speak to it Horatio.
BARNARDO Looks a[13] not like the king? Mark it Horatio.
HORATIO Most like. It harrows[14] me with fear and wonder.
BARNARDO It would be spoke to.
MARCELLUS Question it Horatio.
HORATIO What art thou that usurp'st[15] this time of night,
Together with that fair and warlike form
In which the majesty of buried Denmark[16]
Did sometimes[17] march? By heaven I charge[18] thee speak.
MARCELLUS It is offended.
BARNARDO See, it stalks[19] away.
HORATIO Stay! Speak, speak, I charge thee speak!

Exit Ghost

Horatio agrees that the Ghost is the exact image of the dead King Hamlet. He thinks it foretells disasters for Denmark. Horatio begins to explain why there are so many urgent preparations for war.

剧情简介：何瑞修认同那鬼魂与已故哈慕雷王一模一样，认为这预示着丹麦将有大祸。何瑞修开始解释为何到处都在加紧战备。

1 A battle? Or an angry gesture? (in small groups)

Do lines 62–3 tell of Denmark's king defeating the Polish army ('Polacks') in a battle on the ice ('sledded' = on sledges)? Or do they mean that the king, in an angry discussion ('parle') with the Norwegians, struck his battle-axe on the ice like a sledgehammer (= 'sledded'). Sometimes the word 'Polacks' is printed as 'polax' (poleaxe).

- Stage two tableaux (定格；活人画) (frozen pictures) showing each interpretation. Decide which version is more imaginative and dramatic.

Write about it 写作练习

Denmark prepares for war (in pairs)

In lines 70–9, Marcellus questions why Denmark is feverishly preparing for war. Guards are mounted everywhere. 'Brazen' (brass) cannons roll off the production line daily. Weapons are bought in foreign countries and imported ('foreign mart for implements of war'). Ships are being built by forced labour ('impress'), working night and day, even on Sundays (unusual in a Christian country).

- Write six additional lines, in Shakespearean verse or in modern prose, listing more of Denmark's frantic war preparations. Use the same urgent style as Marcellus does.

Language in the play 剧中语言

'Doubling' – a feature of the play

In the script opposite there are several examples of a language device that recurs through the play. It is the use of 'and' between two verbs, nouns or noun phrases, or between adjectives, to achieve a 'doubling' effect: 'tremble and look pale', 'sensible and true avouch', 'gross and scope', 'strict and most observant'.

a As you read on, list other examples (there are at least seven in Horatio's lines 80–107). The technical term is **hendiadys** (一语二体，重言法) (pronounced 'hen-die-a-dees'). You will find information about its dramatic importance on page 267.

b What is the linguistic and dramatic effect of such doubling?

1 on't = of it

2 sensible and true avouch 切实的证据

3 Norway 挪威王

4 parle 谈判；舌战

5 smote the sledded Polacks 痛击乘坐雪橇的波兰人

6 jump 就（在），恰好

7 martial stalk 威武的步态；大摇大摆

8 In … work 具体往什么事上去想

9 in … opinion 我朦朦胧胧的直觉告诉我

10 bodes … state 预示着咱们国家要突发某种异乎寻常的事

11 Good 好朋友

12 mart = market

13 impress 征用，强征

14 toward 即将来临

15 emulate 妒忌

16 sealed compact 签下的条约

17 ratified 批准

18 by law and heraldy = by the law of heraldry 根据交战的礼仪规矩（heraldy = heraldry）

19 forfeit 丧失

MARCELLUS 'Tis gone and will not answer.

BARNARDO How now Horatio? you tremble and look pale.
Is not this something more than fantasy?
What think you on't[1]?

HORATIO Before my God, I might not this believe
Without the sensible and true avouch[2]
Of mine own eyes.

MARCELLUS Is it not like the king?

HORATIO As thou art to thyself.
Such was the very armour he had on
When he th'ambitious Norway[3] combated;
So frowned he once, when in an angry parle[4]
He smote the sledded Polacks[5] on the ice.
'Tis strange.

MARCELLUS Thus twice before, and jump[6] at this dead hour,
With martial stalk[7] hath he gone by our watch.

HORATIO In what particular thought to work[8] I know not,
But in the gross and scope of mine opinion[9]
This bodes some strange eruption to our state[10].

MARCELLUS Good[11] now sit down, and tell me he that knows,
Why this same strict and most observant watch
So nightly toils the subject of the land,
And why such daily cast of brazen cannon,
And foreign mart[12] for implements of war,
Why such impress[13] of shipwrights, whose sore task
Does not divide the Sunday from the week.
What might be toward[14], that this sweaty haste
Doth make the night joint-labourer with the day?
Who is't that can inform me?

HORATIO That can I –
At least the whisper goes so. Our last king,
Whose image even but now appeared to us,
Was as you know by Fortinbras of Norway,
Thereto pricked on by a most emulate[15] pride,
Dared to the combat; in which our valiant Hamlet –
For so this side of our known world esteemed him –
Did slay this Fortinbras; who by a sealed compact[16],
Well ratified[17] by law and heraldy[18],
Did forfeit[19] (with his life) all those his lands
Which he stood seized of, to the conqueror;

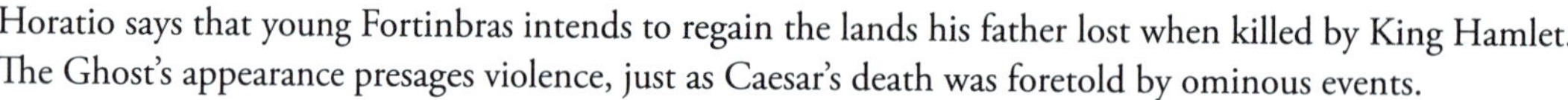

Horatio says that young Fortinbras intends to regain the lands his father lost when killed by King Hamlet. The Ghost's appearance presages violence, just as Caesar's death was foretold by ominous events.

剧情简介：何瑞修说小福庭布拉意欲夺回父亲被哈慕雷王杀死后失去的土地。鬼魂出现预示着暴力冲突，就像恺撒死前就有许多不祥之兆一样。

1 Act out Horatio's story (in groups of six or more)

In lines 80–107, Horatio explains why Denmark is preparing for war. The king of Norway (old Fortinbras) had challenged King Hamlet (Hamlet's father) to personal combat. Both men wagered ('gagèd') large areas of land on the outcome of the duel. King Hamlet killed Fortinbras and so took over his territory, which was passed on to his son, Hamlet, when he died. Now young Fortinbras, with an army of mercenaries ('landless resolutes'), seeks to recover his father's lost lands. The Danes are hastily preparing to defend themselves against the imminent invasion.

- Bring Horatio's story to life. One person narrates while the others enact each episode. The lines contain over twenty-five separate actions that can be shown. (For instance, 'Sharked up' is a vivid **image** of a shark feeding indiscriminately.)

Write about it 写作练习

Predicting disasters

'A mote it is to trouble the mind's eye' says Horatio (line 112): the appearance of the Ghost is an irritant ('mote') to the imagination. It suggests that disasters lie ahead. Shakespeare had written *Julius Caesar* shortly before *Hamlet*. The sinister omens that preceded the death of Caesar were fresh in his mind. Horatio lists them: the living dead, comets, bloody rain, sunspots, an eclipse of the moon ('the moist star'). Horatio uses the language of classical **allusion** (典故) (referencing), which gives the speech a lofty, important style.

a Compare Horatio's style here (lines 112–39) with that of his speech at lines 148–56 in this scene. Why does he use the more florid style in the script opposite?

b Find a copy of *The Elizabethan World Picture* by E.M.W. Tillyard (first published in 1943) and write up a paragraph or two of background information on how the Elizabethans and Jacobeans (people living under the reign of James I, 1603–25) saw the universe and its influence on humanity. You could also compare Gloucester and Edmond's lines in *King Lear* (Act 1 Scene 2, 91–116). Present your research to the rest of the class. You might wish to develop these short presentations into a wall display or some other resource that everyone in the group can refer to.

1 a moiety competent / Was gagèd 押上了相等的一份土地
2 which … vanquisher = which would have gone to the inheritance of King Fortinbras if he had been the winner
3 by … Hamlet = by the same agreement and by carrying out the article designated in the agreement, his part fell to King Hamlet
4 unimprovèd mettle hot and full 锋芒未试，血气方刚
5 skirts of Norway 挪威的外围
6 Sharked … resolutes 纠集了一帮无田无地的亡命之徒
7 hath a stomach in't 对此有胃口
8 recover … compulsatory 用强硬手腕，并根据强制条款，从我方收回……
9 head 源头
10 post-haste and romage 匆忙和慌乱（romage = rummage）
11 Well may it sort that 这很可能可以解释为什么
12 portentous figure 不祥的人形
13 question = cause
14 mote 尘埃
15 palmy 昌盛
16 ere = before
17 stood tenantless 空无住客
18 sheeted dead 裹尸布包裹的死尸
19 trains of fire 拖着火尾（如彗星那样）
20 Neptune's empire 海神涅普顿的帝国（即大海，Neptune是罗马神话里的海神，对应希腊神话里的海神波塞冬［Poseidon，又译作波塞顿］）
21 precurse 预兆
22 harbingers 先行官
23 climatures 地域，国土

Against the which a moiety competent
Was gagèd[1] by our king, which had returned
To the inheritance of Fortinbras
Had he been vanquisher[2]; as by the same comart
And carriage of the article design,
His fell to Hamlet[3]. Now sir, young Fortinbras,
Of unimprovèd mettle hot and full[4],
Hath in the skirts of Norway[5] here and there
Sharked up a list of landless resolutes[6]
For food and diet to some enterprise
That hath a stomach in't[7]; which is no other,
As it doth well appear unto our state,
But to recover of us by strong hand
And terms compulsatory[8] those foresaid lands
So by his father lost. And this, I take it,
Is the main motive of our preparations,
The source of this our watch, and the chief head[9]
Of this post-haste and romage[10] in the land.

[BARNARDO I think it be no other but e'en so.
Well may it sort that[11] this portentous figure[12]
Comes armèd through our watch so like the king
That was and is the question[13] of these wars.

HORATIO A mote[14] it is to trouble the mind's eye.
In the most high and palmy[15] state of Rome,
A little ere[16] the mightiest Julius fell,
The graves stood tenantless[17] and the sheeted dead[18]
Did squeak and gibber in the Roman streets;
As stars with trains of fire[19], and dews of blood,
Disasters in the sun; and the moist star,
Upon whose influence Neptune's empire[20] stands,
Was sick almost to doomsday with eclipse.
And even the like precurse[21] of feared events,
As harbingers[22] preceding still the fates
And prologue to the omen coming on,
Have heaven and earth together demonstrated
Unto our climatures[23] and countrymen.]

Horatio five times demands that the reappearing Ghost speak to him. The cock crows and the Ghost vanishes without reply. Horatio says it cannot be harmed, but that it behaved like a criminal summoned to justice.

剧情简介：何瑞修五次要求再次出现的鬼魂与他说话。鸡鸣传来，鬼魂消失，且并未答话。何瑞修说，鬼魂是无法受到伤害的，但它的举止像一个受到传唤的罪犯。

Characters 人物分析

Horatio's response to the Ghost (in pairs)

a Look back at Horatio's lines in this scene, and refer to your notes on the activity about Horatio on page 2. Make a list of the different characteristics Horatio has shown, then compare them with a partner and build up a list that includes your combined ideas. Share this list with the class as a whole.

b Try reading out lines 112–25 and lines 126–39, experimenting with different styles of delivery. The two sections are clearly different, but in how many ways could you present each of the sections? Which combination works best?

c Stage an interview with Horatio, questioning him about his different reactions to the Ghost. Questions could include: what was your first reaction to hearing the reports of Marcellus and Barnardo? Have you changed your position since seeing the Ghost? What do you think its presence portends (signifies)?

d Extend your notes on Horatio from the page 2 activity by writing up what you have learnt about his character from the activities on this page.

◀ In what ways does this Ghost match your own conceptions of how he might look?

1 soft, behold, lo 安静，睁大眼，看（lo = look）

2 cross … me 截住它，哪怕它毁了我

3 privy to 知道……的内情

4 uphoarded 积累起来

5 Extorted 搜刮

6 oft = often

7 partisan 长矛

8 invulnerable 无法受到伤害

9 vain blows 徒劳的攻击

10 started 吓一跳

11 a guilty … summons 罪犯听到令他胆战的传唤

12 extravagant and erring 在外游荡，漂泊不定

13 hies / To his confine 赶回他的斗室

14 present object 刚才那东西

15 made probation 就是证明

Enter GHOST

But soft, behold, lo[1] where it comes again!
I'll cross it though it blast me[2]. Stay, illusion.
It spreads his arms
If thou hast any sound or use of voice,
Speak to me.
If there be any good thing to be done
That may to thee do ease, and grace to me,
Speak to me.
If thou art privy to[3] thy country's fate,
Which happily foreknowing may avoid,
Oh speak.
Or if thou hast uphoarded[4] in thy life
Extorted[5] treasure in the womb of earth,
For which they say you spirits oft[6] walk in death, *The cock crows*
Speak of it. Stay and speak! Stop it Marcellus.

MARCELLUS Shall I strike at it with my partisan[7]?

HORATIO Do if it will not stand.

BARNARDO 'Tis here.

HORATIO 'Tis here.

MARCELLUS 'Tis gone.

Exit Ghost

We do it wrong being so majestical
To offer it the show of violence,
For it is as the air invulnerable[8],
And our vain blows[9] malicious mockery.

BARNARDO It was about to speak when the cock crew.

HORATIO And then it started[10] like a guilty thing
Upon a fearful summons[11]. I have heard,
The cock, that is the trumpet to the morn,
Doth with his lofty and shrill-sounding throat
Awake the god of day; and at his warning,
Whether in sea or fire, in earth or air,
Th'extravagant and erring[12] spirit hies
To his confine[13]. And of the truth herein
This present object[14] made probation[15].

Marcellus claims that the cockerel crows all night long at Christmas, a time when no harm can be done. Horatio seems to agree. He proposes that they tell Hamlet about the Ghost.

剧情简介：玛塞勒声称圣诞节一到，公鸡整夜啼叫，此时任何危害都无法发生。何瑞修似乎同意这一点。他提议把鬼魂的事告知哈慕雷。

1 Daybreak after darkness: a change of mood

(in pairs)

Dawn is breaking. The mood of fear, tension and apprehension gives way to a different emotional climate. Lyrical, poetic language creates a sense of religious awe and wonder. To experience the atmosphere of these closing moments of Scene 1, try the activities below:

a Talk together about non-verbal ways in which the change of mood could be conveyed in the theatre (lighting, sound, posture and so on).

b Marcellus is a soldier. He may be dressed in armour for his night's vigil (守夜), but he speaks eloquently. His words are filled with poetic wonderment, and do not sound like the language of a no-nonsense military man. Experiment with ways of speaking lines 157–64: full of religious awe; bluntly and factually; conspiratorially, as a great secret. Decide how you think the lines should be spoken on stage.

c After Marcellus's eloquent description of how Christmastime prevents any evil, Horatio responds with 'So have I heard, and do in part believe it.' His remark seems tinged with scepticism. Speak line 165, emphasising 'in part'. See if you can agree on whether the actor should use the line to show that Horatio does not really believe what Marcellus says.

Themes 主题分析

Disorder, death and the afterlife (in pairs)

The first scene in *Hamlet* provides us with an atmospheric and dramatic start to the play. The Watch is nervous, having seen the Ghost twice already. There is a tense political situation – Denmark is in dispute with Norway over lands that have been awarded to Hamlet, following the killing of the king of Norway by Hamlet's father. The Ghost's appearance seems to foreshadow a number of disturbing themes.

a Note down as many themes as you can identify in this opening scene. Remember that a 'theme' can be captured by more than a single word. So, as well as 'fear', 'anxiety' and 'politics', for example, you can characterise a theme in a more complex way, such as 'the relationship between reason and the imagination'.

b Arrange the themes you have identified in a diagram that shows how they relate to each other.

1 ever … celebrated = always just before that season comes, in which our Saviour's birth is celebrated 总是在我们庆祝救世主生日的季节

2 bird of dawning 报晓的公鸡

3 stir abroad 在外游荡

4 no planets strike （人们认为行星不时会相撞，给世界带来灾难）

5 fairy takes 精灵偷换婴儿

6 hallowed = holy

7 russet mantle 红褐色斗篷（可能是血污的颜色）

8 yon = that/those ... over there

9 impart 告诉

10 acquaint him with it 让他知道这事儿

11 *Exeunt* （两个以上演员）退场，下场

MARCELLUS It faded on the crowing of the cock.
Some say that ever 'gainst that season comes
Wherein our Saviour's birth is celebrated[1],
This bird of dawning[2] singeth all night long,
And then, they say, no spirit dare stir abroad[3],
The nights are wholesome, then no planets strike[4],
No fairy takes[5], nor witch hath power to charm,
So hallowed[6] and so gracious is that time.

HORATIO So have I heard, and do in part believe it.
But look, the morn in russet mantle[7] clad
Walks o'er the dew of yon[8] high eastward hill.
Break we our watch up, and by my advice
Let us impart[9] what we have seen tonight
Unto young Hamlet, for upon my life
This spirit, dumb to us, will speak to him.
Do you consent we shall acquaint him with it[10],
As needful in our loves, fitting our duty?

MARCELLUS Let's do't I pray, and I this morning know
Where we shall find him most conveniently.

Exeunt[11]

Claudius announces to the court that, although he grieves for his dead brother, he has, with joy, married Gertrude. He turns his attention to the political situation: young Fortinbras is threatening Denmark.

剧情简介：克劳迭向宫中人宣布，尽管他仍为死去的哥哥感到哀痛，却已经愉快地跟葛楚德结为夫妻，接着他把注意力转移到政治局势上：小福庭布拉正在威胁丹麦的安全。

1 Claudius: honest or devious? (in small groups)

King Hamlet has recently died. Claudius, his brother, has become king of Denmark and has married Gertrude. Claudius now possesses his dead brother's throne and his widow. He explains his marriage to his sister-in-law so soon after her first husband's death (lines 1–16), and then turns to political affairs (lines 17–39).

a **Stage the entrance** Explore different stagings of Claudius's entrance. One version could show Claudius respected by the courtiers. Another might show he is feared: his courtiers suspect he may become a tyrant.

b **Honest or devious?** Some critics argue that Claudius's eloquence is appropriate to the occasion. His long, carefully constructed sentences suggest he is self-assured and honest. But other critics argue that the speech reveals his insincerity. Its fluency makes it sound rehearsed and false. His constant references to himself using the royal 'we', 'us', 'our' suggest he is anxious about whether his kingship is legal. Take turns to speak lines 1–39 to show Claudius as, alternately: confident and in control, uneasy and insecure, devious and crafty, honest and sincere. Afterwards, talk together about what you feel Claudius's language reveals about his character.

c **Oppositions** Lines 10–14 display another characteristic of the play's language: **antithesis** (对偶) (setting words against each other, for example 'defeated' versus 'joy', 'mirth' versus 'funeral', see p. 265). Speak the lines using an action to accompany each antithesis.

Characters 人物分析

Claudius

a After you have done some or all of the activities above, start making notes on Claudius as a character. There is much in this opening speech for you to include. Collect what you see as the key lines in Claudius's speech. Then annotate each quotation with comments about Claudius's character. As the activities above suggest, you can gauge his character through his actions, his words and his manner of speaking.

b Compare your notes with others to see if you are coming to the same initial conclusions about Claudius.

1 our 朕的（克劳迭巧妙地在our和us的御用复数用法、包括听者在内的兼称用法［如第2行的us befitted］和第一人称复数用法［如第16行的our thanks］之间来回切换，以获得听众对他以及他的行为的认同）

2 green 新鲜

3 contracted … woe 皱成一个悲伤的眉头

4 our sometime sister 朕以前的嫂子

5 imperial … state 我们这个可能遇上战祸的国家的王后

6 auspicious 喜庆

7 dirge 挽歌

8 weighing delight and dole 平衡喜悦与哀伤

9 Taken to wife 娶为妻子

10 barred 不考虑

11 Holding … worth 低估了咱的国力

12 by = because of

13 disjoint and out of frame 分崩离析，一片混乱

14 Colleaguèd … advantage 加之他幻想自己具有优势

15 Importing 关于，涉及

16 bands of law 条约的约束

17 writ = written

Act 1 Scene 2

The Great Hall of Elsinore Castle

Trumpet Call *Enter* CLAUDIUS *King of Denmark*, GERTRUDE *the Queen*, HAMLET, POLONIUS, LAERTES, OPHELIA, VOLTEMAND, CORNELIUS, LORDS *attendant*

CLAUDIUS
Though yet of Hamlet our[1] dear brother's death
The memory be green[2], and that it us befitted
To bear our hearts in grief, and our whole kingdom
To be contracted in one brow of woe[3],
Yet so far hath discretion fought with nature
That we with wisest sorrow think on him,
Together with remembrance of ourselves.
Therefore our sometime sister[4], now our queen,
Th'imperial jointress to this warlike state[5],
Have we, as 'twere with a defeated joy,
With one auspicious[6] and one dropping eye,
With mirth in funeral and with dirge[7] in marriage,
In equal scale weighing delight and dole[8],
Taken to wife[9]; nor have we herein barred[10]
Your better wisdoms, which have freely gone
With this affair along – for all, our thanks.
Now follows that you know: young Fortinbras,
Holding a weak supposal of our worth[11],
Or thinking by[12] our late dear brother's death
Our state to be disjoint and out of frame[13],
Colleaguèd with this dream of his advantage[14],
He hath not failed to pester us with message
Importing[15] the surrender of those lands
Lost by his father, with all bands of law[16],
To our most valiant brother. So much for him.
Now for ourself and for this time of meeting
Thus much the business is: we have here writ[17]
To Norway, uncle of young Fortinbras,

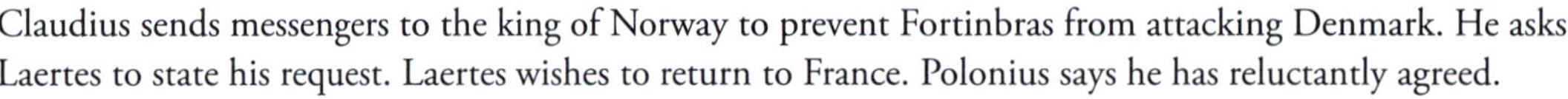

Claudius sends messengers to the king of Norway to prevent Fortinbras from attacking Denmark. He asks Laertes to state his request. Laertes wishes to return to France. Polonius says he has reluctantly agreed.

剧情简介：克劳迭派信使送信给挪威王，试图阻止福庭布拉进犯丹麦。他还问雷厄提有什么请求。雷厄提说他希望回法国。珀娄涅说自己已经勉强同意了。

1 Claudius's manliness?

The king of Norway is, like Claudius, a man who has succeeded to his brother's throne. Claudius describes him as 'impotent and bed-rid' (line 29).

- Suggest a way of speaking the line to give the audience an insight into Claudius's character. For example, might he embrace Gertrude as he speaks, to stress his own virility and manhood? Emphasise the linguistic power of his speeches: Claudius's use of imperatives, the royal 'we', his referring to himself as 'the Dane' and the insistent questioning.

2 Social superiority (in eights)

Everyone takes a part: Claudius, Gertrude, Hamlet, Polonius, Laertes, Ophelia, Cornelius and Voltemand. Line up in order of social status in Denmark. You can look back at the character list on page 1 to help you decide. Do you all agree on who is socially superior to whom? Argue any differences in view. As you work through the play, you can use this ranking activity in other ways (order of dramatic importance, or age, or most moral to least moral and so on).

Themes 主题分析

The political dimension

Old Norway is Fortinbras's uncle, and present ruler of Norway. Cornelius and Voltemand are dispatched to Norway to deliver the 'dilated articles' (clear, full statements) that no doubt concern the matters raised in the first scene: Hamlet and Denmark's right to appropriate lands that formerly belonged to Norway.

a Compare and contrast the first scene with the opening of this second scene. How could they be linked?

b Hamlet is King Hamlet's son; Claudius is his uncle and the former king's brother. What parallels can you see with the situation in Norway, and why do you think Shakespeare is setting up a comparison here?

c Add to the list of themes you began compiling on page 12.

d Look at Laertes's speech in lines 50–6. What impression do you get of his character, and of his position in the Danish court?

1 impotent 虚弱无力
2 further gait herein 进一步的举动或进展
3 in that 因为
4 the levies … proportions 派的捐，征的兵，全部的兵力
5 subject 臣民，百姓
6 dilated articles 详细列出的条款
7 suit 请求
8 speak of reason 提出合理的请求
9 the Dane 丹麦王
10 native 亲密
11 instrumental 好使，趁手
12 dread lord 尊敬的主公
13 leave and favour 恩准
14 bend 折回
15 bow them 使之乞求
16 pardon 宽恕
17 hath my lord wrung = has, my lord, wrung（wrung：死缠，硬磨）
18 slow leave 不情愿的允许
19 laboursome petition 软磨硬泡
20 Upon … consent 给他的恳请勉强加盖同意的印章
21 beseech 恳请

Who, impotent[1] and bed-rid, scarcely hears
Of this his nephew's purpose, to suppress
His further gait herein[2], in that[3] the levies,
The lists, and full proportions[4], are all made
Out of his subject[5]; and we here dispatch
You, good Cornelius, and you, Voltemand,
For bearers of this greeting to old Norway,
Giving to you no further personal power
To business with the king, more than the scope
Of these dilated articles[6] allow.
Farewell, and let your haste commend your duty.

CORNELIUS, VOLTEMAND In that and all things will we show our duty.

CLAUDIUS We doubt it nothing, heartily farewell.

Exeunt Voltemand and Cornelius

And now Laertes, what's the news with you?
You told us of some suit[7], what is't Laertes?
You cannot speak of reason[8] to the Dane[9]
And lose your voice. What wouldst thou beg Laertes,
That shall not be my offer, not thy asking?
The head is not more native[10] to the heart,
The hand more instrumental[11] to the mouth,
Than is the throne of Denmark to thy father.
What wouldst thou have Laertes?

LAERTES My dread lord[12],
Your leave and favour[13] to return to France,
From whence though willingly I came to Denmark
To show my duty in your coronation,
Yet now I must confess, that duty done,
My thoughts and wishes bend[14] again toward France,
And bow them[15] to your gracious leave and pardon[16].

CLAUDIUS Have you your father's leave? What says Polonius?

POLONIUS He hath my lord wrung[17] from me my slow leave[18]
By laboursome petition[19], and at last
Upon his will I sealed my hard consent[20].
I do beseech[21] you give him leave to go.

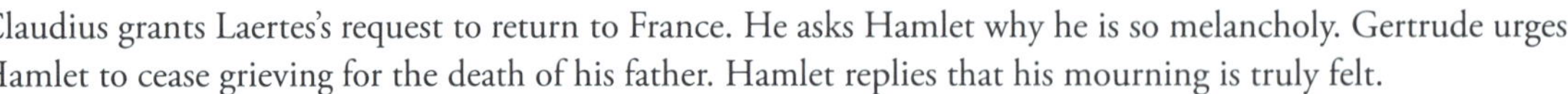
Claudius grants Laertes's request to return to France. He asks Hamlet why he is so melancholy. Gertrude urges Hamlet to cease grieving for the death of his father. Hamlet replies that his mourning is truly felt.

剧情简介：克劳迭批准雷厄提返回法国，然后又问哈慕雷为什么如此郁郁寡欢。葛楚德劝哈慕雷不要再为死去的父王伤心。哈慕雷回答说，他的悲哀发自内心。

1 Hamlet: the listener (in pairs)

You will discover that everything Hamlet says throughout the play reveals his acute alertness to language. He listens carefully to everything that is said to him, and often plays or **puns** (双关) on the words he has heard, giving them different meaning and significance (see p. 254).

Hamlet immediately picks up the implications of Claudius's use of 'cousin' and 'son'. He detests the close kinship that Claudius's marriage to his mother has created. His first line puns on 'kin' and 'kind', saying in effect that he feels too closely related, and does not have the same nature as his new stepfather. His second line plays on 'sun' and 'son', again rejecting any close relationship to Claudius.

a Talk together, and then write notes in your Director's Journal (see p. 4) for the actor playing Hamlet about how to speak line 65. Is he speaking to himself? To the audience? In a sardonic tone, or bitterly? Or some other way? The line is an **aside** (旁白), not heard by other characters. Also give advice on line 67: which word or words might Hamlet stress to question his kinship to Claudius, for example?

b Read aloud the script opposite, one person as Hamlet and one as Claudius/Gertrude. Play with emphasis and intonation on key words in the short exchanges Hamlet has with Claudius and Gertrude to show how characterisation can be shaped?

▼ Does this image of Hamlet, from an all-male Japanese production, fit your impression of Hamlet the listener? Why, or why not?

1 thy best graces 你的大好年华

2 cousin 侄子（当时这个词可以用来称呼侄子、侄女或外甥、外甥女）

3 A little … kind 略微胜过亲戚，何尝有过亲情（英语中有句成语是：The nearer in kin, the less in kindness.［亲戚越近，亲情越少。］）

4 nighted 铁青；阴沉

5 vailèd lids 目光低垂

6 common 人所共知；人之常情

7 nature 人生；世间

8 inky 墨色

9 windy suspiration 长吁短叹

10 fruitful river in the eye 眼中的滚滚大河

11 haviour of the visage 脸上的表情

12 denote 代表，表现

13 passes show 超出外表

14 but … woe 仅是悲伤的装饰和外衣

15 That father lost, lost his = That father, who was lost, lost his father

16 bound / In filial obligation 受到孝道的约束

17 obsequious 规规矩矩

18 persever / In obstinate condolement 沉溺于固而不化的哀伤（persever = persevere）

19 impious 不敬（大道）

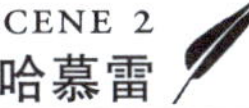

CLAUDIUS Take thy fair hour Laertes, time be thine,
And thy best graces[1] spend it at thy will.
But now my cousin[2] Hamlet, and my son –
HAMLET (*Aside*) A little more than kin, and less than kind[3].
CLAUDIUS How is it that the clouds still hang on you?
HAMLET Not so my lord, I am too much i'th'sun.
GERTRUDE Good Hamlet cast thy nighted[4] colour off,
And let thine eye look like a friend on Denmark.
Do not forever with thy vailèd lids[5]
Seek for thy noble father in the dust.
Thou know'st 'tis common[6], all that lives must die,
Passing through nature[7] to eternity.
HAMLET Ay madam, it is common.
GERTRUDE If it be,
Why seems it so particular with thee?
HAMLET Seems madam? nay it is, I know not seems.
'Tis not alone my inky[8] cloak, good mother,
Nor customary suits of solemn black,
Nor windy suspiration[9] of forced breath,
No, nor the fruitful river in the eye[10],
Nor the dejected haviour of the visage[11],
Together with all forms, moods, shapes of grief,
That can denote[12] me truly. These indeed seem,
For they are actions that a man might play,
But I have that within which passes show[13] –
These but the trappings and the suits of woe[14].
CLAUDIUS 'Tis sweet and commendable in your nature Hamlet,
To give these mourning duties to your father;
But you must know, your father lost a father,
That father lost, lost his[15], and the survivor bound
In filial obligation[16] for some term
To do obsequious[17] sorrow; but to persever
In obstinate condolement[18] is a course
Of impious[19] stubbornness, 'tis unmanly grief,

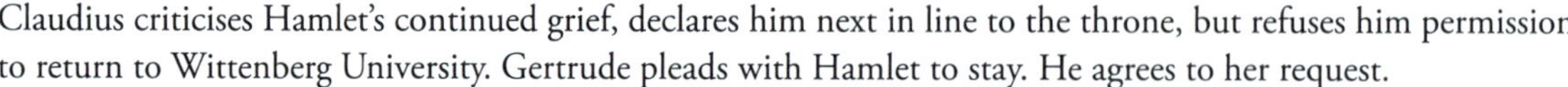

Claudius criticises Hamlet's continued grief, declares him next in line to the throne, but refuses him permission to return to Wittenberg University. Gertrude pleads with Hamlet to stay. He agrees to her request.

剧情简介：克劳迭批评哈慕雷无休止地悲痛，并宣布他是自己的王位继承人，但不同意让他回维滕堡大学去。葛楚德央求哈慕雷留下来，哈慕雷同意了她的请求。

Stagecraft 导演技巧

Rebuke, assurance and refusal (in small groups)

In an extended speech, Claudius first delivers a long criticism of Hamlet's grief. Next, he briefly pleads with Hamlet to abandon his mourning and declares him heir to the throne. Then, he abruptly refuses Hamlet permission to return to Wittenberg. Claudius's speech offers opportunities for the actor to establish the king's character and his attitude to his stepson. Take turns to speak the three sections:

- **The rebuke** (lines 87–106, to 'This must be so') Use a commanding tone. Emphasise repetitions ('fathers', 'father', 'father'; 'a fault', 'A fault', 'a fault'), and the critical expressions ('persever', 'obstinate condolement' and so on).
- **The assurance** (lines 106–12, to 'toward you') Use a cordial tone, and make much of declaring Hamlet as 'most immediate to our throne' (the next king).
- **The refusal** (lines 112–17) Be abrupt and sharp, but end using a seemingly friendly, reassuring tone.

Do you agree with the division of the speech into these categories? Discuss, then work on how the speech could be delivered on stage.

Language in the play 剧中语言

Key words

So far in this scene, at least three key words have been used: 'nature', 'will' and 'sense'.

a First, scour the pages of the play up to this point, and see if you can identify other key words that have more than one meaning and that seem central to the preoccupations of the characters.

b By yourself or in pairs, research the meanings of these key words in a dictionary and/or on the Internet. In particular, look for past or obsolete meanings that will give an indication of the history of the word. In what ways are these words significant to the play so far?

c Present your findings to the rest of the class in pairs, or play a game of 'Call My Bluff' where each member of a team of three presents one of the meanings, trying to persuade the rest of the class or another team that their definition is the 'right' one.

1 a will … heaven 最有违上天的意志
2 heart unfortified 不坚强的内心
3 vulgar thing to sense 能想到的平常事
4 peevish 愚蠢
5 fault 冒犯
6 corse = corpse
7 unprevailing 无用，无效
8 nobility of love 纯粹的爱
9 impart 给予
10 intent 打算
11 going back to school 回去上学（这里的“学”指维滕堡大学［University of Wittenberg］。该校由神圣罗马帝国萨克森选帝侯［Elector of Saxony］腓特烈三世［Frederick III，1443—1525年］于1502年出资建立，1508年聘马丁•路德［Martin Luther，1483—1546年］为其神学系教师。马丁•路德1512年获该校博士学位，同年晋升为教授和神学系主任，1517年发起抗议罗马教廷种种恶行的新教改革［Protest Reformation］，为教廷所不容，腓特烈三世为他提供了庇护。）
12 Wittenberg 维滕堡（又译作威登贝格，位于柏林西南90千米处，从11世纪起就是欧洲最古老的贵族之一维滕家族的领地。15世纪，维滕家族的家长成为萨克森公国［Duchy of Saxony］的公爵和神圣罗马帝国的选帝侯，维滕堡随即成为该国的政治和文化中心。）
13 retrograde 相反
14 bend you 委屈您
15 Why 哎呀，呦，嗨（表示惊讶、不耐烦、愤怒等）
16 accord 顺服
17 in grace whereof 为感谢此事
18 No … drinks 丹麦王不喝喜酒
19 rouse 举杯痛饮
20 bruit 大声宣布
21 Re-speaking = Echoing
22 *Flourish* 奏花腔

It shows a will most incorrect to heaven[1],
A heart unfortified[2], a mind impatient,
An understanding simple and unschooled.
For what we know must be, and is as common
As any the most vulgar thing to sense[3],
Why should we in our peevish[4] opposition
Take it to heart? Fie, 'tis a fault[5] to heaven,
A fault against the dead, a fault to nature,
To reason most absurd, whose common theme
Is death of fathers, and who still hath cried,
From the first corse[6] till he that died today,
'This must be so.' We pray you throw to earth
This unprevailing[7] woe, and think of us
As of a father, for let the world take note
You are the most immediate to our throne,
And with no less nobility of love[8]
Than that which dearest father bears his son,
Do I impart[9] toward you. For your intent[10]
In going back to school[11] in Wittenberg[12],
It is most retrograde[13] to our desire,
And we beseech you bend you[14] to remain
Here in the cheer and comfort of our eye,
Our chiefest courtier, cousin, and our son.

GERTRUDE Let not thy mother lose her prayers Hamlet.
I pray thee stay with us, go not to Wittenberg.

HAMLET I shall in all my best obey you madam.

CLAUDIUS Why[15], 'tis a loving and a fair reply.
Be as ourself in Denmark. Madam, come.
This gentle and unforced accord[16] of Hamlet
Sits smiling to my heart, in grace whereof[17],
No jocund health that Denmark drinks[18] today
But the great cannon to the clouds shall tell,
And the king's rouse[19] the heaven shall bruit[20] again,
Re-speaking[21] earthly thunder. Come away.

Flourish[22]. Exeunt all but Hamlet

Hamlet longs for death but knows that suicide is forbidden by God. He is disgusted that his mother has married so soon after his father's death, but feels he must keep silent. He greets Horatio and Marcellus.

剧情简介：哈慕雷想死，但是知道上帝不允许自杀。他十分反感母亲在父亲死后没多久就再嫁，又觉得自己必须保持沉默。他向何瑞修和玛塞勒打招呼。

1 A soliloquy (独白)

A **soliloquy** is spoken by a character who is alone (or thinks he or she is alone) on stage. It reveals the speaker's true thoughts and feelings. Hamlet's soliloquy exposes his deep depression. In turn he expresses weariness, despair, grief, anger, nausea, loathing and disgust, and resignation. He has no thoughts about political matters, about becoming king, or about being forbidden to return to Wittenberg. His troubled mind is obsessed solely with family matters: his father, his uncle and – above all – his mother.

- First, read the soliloquy to yourself. Then listen to it read aloud by someone else.
- On another copy of the speech, mark what you think are the key breaks (shifts of thought) in the speech.
- Discuss these breaks as a whole class, and agree on what you think are the main breaks – thus defining the structure of the speech.
- In small groups, take a section of the speech each and explore it in detail, teasing out its meaning(s). Also work out how you would deliver the section aloud.
- Each group now speaks their section (using individual and/or choral voices). The whole speech is delivered, section by section.
- In your groups, reflect on what you learnt by dealing with the speech in this way.
- Finally, note down words and phrases in the speech that you think are pivotal to Hamlet's thought and moral development as a character.

1 too too solid 结结实实（也有版本作sullied ［肮脏］或sallied ［受围攻］）
2 resolve 化解
3 Everlasting … canon 永生不灭者没有定好其戒律
4 self-slaughter 自戕
5 all the uses of 一切风俗习惯
6 grows to seed 滋生不息
7 merely = completely
8 But = Only
9 Hyperion 许珀里翁（希腊神话中的第一代日神、地神盖娅［Gaia］和天神乌拉诺［Uranus］所生12个名叫提坦［Titan］的巨人之一）
10 satyr 萨提若（又译作“萨提尔”或“羊男”，希腊神话里一种半人半羊的神，头上有羊角和羊耳，身后有羊尾巴，下身是羊腿、羊蹄和羊的生殖器，生性贪婪淫荡）
11 beteem = allow
12 would hang on him 本应对他魂牵梦绕
13 frailty 脆弱
14 Niobe 妮娥波（希腊神话里的一个女性人物，底比斯城［Thebes］的缔造者安菲翁［Amphion］之妻，曾向仅有一双儿女的女提坦勒佗［Leto］夸耀自己生了7男7女，勒佗心生嫉妒，派儿子阿波罗［Apollo］和女儿阿尔媞弥［Artemis］将其孩子全部杀死。孩子死后，妮娥波伤心过度，化为石头，仍泪流不止。）
15 wants discourse of reason 没有思维能力
16 Hercules 赫丘力（罗马神话中主神朱庇特［Jupiter］的儿子，力大无比，完成了12项常人无法完成的伟绩）
17 gallèd 哭肿
18 post 赶往
19 dexterity 迅捷，麻利
20 incestuous sheets 乱伦的床单

HAMLET O that this too too solid[1] flesh would melt,
Thaw and resolve[2] itself into a dew,
Or that the Everlasting had not fixed
His canon[3] 'gainst self-slaughter[4]. O God, God,
How weary, stale, flat and unprofitable
Seem to me all the uses of[5] this world!
Fie on't, ah fie, 'tis an unweeded garden
That grows to seed[6], things rank and gross in nature
Possess it merely[7]. That it should come to this!
But[8] two months dead – nay not so much, not two –
So excellent a king, that was to this
Hyperion[9] to a satyr[10], so loving to my mother
That he might not beteem[11] the winds of heaven
Visit her face too roughly – heaven and earth,
Must I remember? why, she would hang on him[12]
As if increase of appetite had grown
By what it fed on, and yet within a month –
Let me not think on't; frailty[13], thy name is woman –
A little month, or ere those shoes were old
With which she followed my poor father's body
Like Niobe[14], all tears, why she, even she –
O God, a beast that wants discourse of reason[15]
Would have mourned longer – married with my uncle,
My father's brother, but no more like my father
Than I to Hercules[16] – within a month,
Ere yet the salt of most unrighteous tears
Had left the flushing in her gallèd[17] eyes,
She married. Oh most wicked speed, to post[18]
With such dexterity[19] to incestuous sheets[20].
It is not, nor it cannot come to good.
But break, my heart, for I must hold my tongue.

Enter HORATIO, MARCELLUS *and* BARNARDO

HORATIO Hail to your lordship.
HAMLET I am glad to see you well.
Horatio – or I do forget myself.
HORATIO The same, my lord, and your poor servant ever.
HAMLET Sir, my good friend, I'll change that name with you.
And what make you from Wittenberg, Horatio?
Marcellus.

Hamlet does not believe Horatio returned to Denmark as a truant or to attend King Hamlet's funeral, but to see Gertrude's marriage. Horatio reports that he thinks he saw Hamlet's father the previous night.

剧情简介：哈慕雷认为何瑞修回丹麦不是为了逃学或者参加自己父王的葬礼，而是为了看葛楚德结婚。何瑞修说前一天晚上他好像看到哈慕雷的父亲了。

Characters 人物分析

Hamlet and Horatio (in pairs)

Take parts and read the exchange between Hamlet and Horatio. Try it in different ways:

- with Hamlet as consistently disbelieving Horatio
- with Hamlet changing mood frequently, or once or twice
- as close friends, or as past friends that have moved away from each other and are more cautious about their relationship.

What does your reading of the dialogue suggest to you about the relationship and about the differences between the two characters?

▼ In a production, would you have Horatio consistently 'lower' than Hamlet in staging and positioning, as in the image below, or do you see him as older and wiser (and possibly taking the upper moral ground)?

1 Good even = Good evening
2 make you from 使您离开
3 truant disposition 逃学的秉性
4 truster = believer
5 followed hard upon 紧跟着就来了
6 Thrift 节省
7 coldly furnish forth 当成凉菜摆上
8 Would = I wish
9 Or ever = Before ever
10 all in all 总体来说
11 Season your admiration 缓一缓您的惊讶
12 attent 集中注意力

MARCELLUS My good lord.
HAMLET I am very glad to see you. (*To Barnardo*) Good even[1] sir.
But what in faith make you from[2] Wittenberg.
HORATIO A truant disposition[3], good my lord.
HAMLET I would not hear your enemy say so,
Nor shall you do my ear that violence
To make it truster[4] of your own report
Against yourself. I know you are no truant.
But what is your affair in Elsinore?
We'll teach you to drink deep ere you depart.
HORATIO My lord, I came to see your father's funeral.
HAMLET I pray thee do not mock me fellow student,
I think it was to see my mother's wedding.
HORATIO Indeed my lord, it followed hard upon[5].
HAMLET Thrift[6], thrift, Horatio. The funeral baked meats
Did coldly furnish forth[7] the marriage tables.
Would[8] I had met my dearest foe in heaven
Or ever[9] I had seen that day, Horatio.
My father, methinks I see my father –
HORATIO Where my lord?
HAMLET In my mind's eye, Horatio.
HORATIO I saw him once, a was a goodly king.
HAMLET A was a man, take him for all in all[10].
I shall not look upon his like again.
HORATIO My lord, I think I saw him yesternight.
HAMLET Saw? Who?
HORATIO My lord, the king your father.
HAMLET The king my father!
HORATIO Season your admiration[11] for a while
With an attent[12] ear, till I may deliver
Upon the witness of these gentlemen
This marvel to you.
HAMLET For God's love let me hear.

Horatio reports the sightings of the Ghost: how it was clad in armour and how it vanished at daybreak. Hamlet is troubled by what he hears. He closely questions Marcellus and Barnardo.

剧情简介：何瑞修报告他看到鬼魂的经过：鬼魂如何身披盔甲，如何在破晓时消失。哈慕雷对听到的事情感到困惑，向玛塞勒和博纳窦追问细节。

▲ This image is from the 1948 movie of *Hamlet*, starring Laurence Olivier.

1 dead waste 死一般寂静
2 Armèd at point exactly 全副武装，分毫不差
3 cap-a-pe 从头到脚
4 solemn march 轩昂步伐
5 oppressed 被震慑
6 Within his truncheon's length 他一伸军杖就能够到
7 distilled / Almost to jelly 几乎化成了果冻
8 act 作用
9 as they had delivered 正如他们讲述的那样
10 These … like 我的左手和右手彼此都没那么像
11 platform 炮台
12 answer made it none = it made no answer
13 methought = I thought
14 it = its
15 did … as 确实做出了好像……的样子
16 even then = just then
17 writ down in our duty 我们的职责里规定
18 Hold you the watch tonight? 今晚你们值岗吗？

1 Creating atmosphere in the theatre

One of the challenges of theatre, as opposed to film, is how to create atmospheric scenes such as the one depicted above.

a Imagine you were the director of a staged play, and you had your choice of setting for *Hamlet*. Would you set it in an actual building that you know, or recreate the scene within a theatre?

b Write notes in your Director's Journal for how you would create an atmospheric setting for the battlement scenes.

HORATIO Two nights together had these gentlemen,
Marcellus and Barnardo, on their watch
In the dead waste[1] and middle of the night,
Been thus encountered. A figure like your father,
Armèd at point exactly[2], cap-a-pe[3],
Appears before them, and with solemn march[4]
Goes slow and stately by them. Thrice he walked
By their oppressed[5] and fear-surprisèd eyes
Within his truncheon's length[6], whilst they, distilled
Almost to jelly[7] with the act[8] of fear,
Stand dumb and speak not to him. This to me
In dreadful secrecy impart they did,
And I with them the third night kept the watch,
Where, as they had delivered[9], both in time,
Form of the thing, each word made true and good,
The apparition comes. I knew your father,
These hands are not more like[10].

HAMLET But where was this?

MARCELLUS My lord, upon the platform[11] where we watched.

HAMLET Did you not speak to it?

HORATIO My lord, I did,
But answer made it none[12]. Yet once methought[13]
It lifted up it[14] head and did address
Itself to motion like as[15] it would speak;
But even then[16] the morning cock crew loud,
And at the sound it shrunk in haste away
And vanished from our sight.

HAMLET 'Tis very strange.

HORATIO As I do live my honoured lord 'tis true,
And we did think it writ down in our duty[17]
To let you know of it.

HAMLET Indeed, indeed sirs, but this troubles me.
Hold you the watch tonight?[18]

MARCELLUS, BARNARDO We do, my lord.

HAMLET Armed say you?

MARCELLUS, BARNARDO Armed my lord.

HAMLET From top to toe?

Hamlet continues his close questioning about the Ghost. He resolves to join the others on watch that night and to speak to the Ghost. He commands the others not to talk about what they've seen.

剧情简介：哈慕雷继续追问鬼魂的事情。他决心当晚要和其他人一同去值岗，去和鬼魂说话。他命令其他人不得透露所见之事。

Stagecraft 导演技巧

Very fast exchanges? (in fours)

Take parts and speak lines 224–42, in which Hamlet questions the three men. Theatrical convention is that when speeches follow each other in single lines, or when a line is shared between speakers, the dialogue should be spoken very quickly, without pauses (in a staccato or 'rat-a-tat-tat' style).

a Read the exchanges in this manner, then experiment with using pauses. Afterwards, discuss whether the actors should follow dramatic custom here, or use pauses.

b Without knowing what is to follow in the play, what can you gather from the dramatic foreshadowing (suggestion that something is about to happen) that occurs on this page?

Write about it 写作练习

Choose one of the following activities:

a **Marcellus and Barnardo compare notes** Marcellus and Barnardo have seen the Ghost three times. They have told their news to Hamlet. Imagine they have returned to their quarters. They talk about their sightings of the Ghost and about Hamlet's response. Write the script of their conversation, using your knowledge of Scenes 1 and 2.

b **Hamlet writes about his day's experience** Hamlet's final four lines express surprise, apprehension, suspicion, impatience and the certainty that evil actions cannot remain concealed. As you will discover in Scene 5, Hamlet keeps a notebook ('tables') in which he writes down what he learns. Write Hamlet's notebook entry for this day. It should describe his behaviour at the court, his feelings about Claudius and Gertrude and his own moodiness, what he makes of Horatio's story, and his speculations about why his father's Ghost appears to be haunting Elsinore.

c **A more distanced look** Write a paragraph or two giving your initial impressions of the impact of the Ghost on Horatio, the Watch and Hamlet. Bear in mind the context (Denmark is at war with Norway), Hamlet's position as Prince of Denmark, the nature and form of the Ghost, and the different reactions of the characters. Include quotations in your text.

1 beaver （头盔上带的）面罩
2 countenance 表情
3 with moderate haste might tell 不快不慢数到
4 grizzled 花白
5 sable silvered 银黑
6 Perchance 也许
7 warrant 保证
8 assume 假扮
9 concealed 隐瞒
10 tenable 守住
11 hap = happen
12 Give … tongue 放在心里，别放嘴上
13 requite 回报
14 loves 情义
15 'twixt = betwixt = between
16 doubt some foul play 怀疑有人捣鬼
17 Though … eyes 哪怕用全世界的土埋住它不让人看见

MARCELLUS
BARNARDO } My lord, from head to foot.
HAMLET Then saw you not his face?
HORATIO Oh yes my lord, he wore his beaver[1] up.
HAMLET What, looked he frowningly?
HORATIO A countenance[2] more in sorrow than in anger.
HAMLET Pale, or red?
HORATIO Nay very pale.
HAMLET And fixed his eyes upon you?
HORATIO Most constantly.
HAMLET I would I had been there.
HORATIO It would have much amazed you.
HAMLET Very like, very like. Stayed it long?
HORATIO While one with moderate haste might tell[3] a hundred.
MARCELLUS
BARNARDO } Longer, longer.
HORATIO Not when I saw 't.
HAMLET His beard was grizzled[4], no?
HORATIO It was as I have seen it in his life,
A sable silvered[5].
HAMLET I will watch tonight,
Perchance[6] 'twill walk again.
HORATIO I warrant[7] it will.
HAMLET If it assume[8] my noble father's person,
I'll speak to it though hell itself should gape
And bid me hold my peace. I pray you all,
If you have hitherto concealed[9] this sight,
Let it be tenable[10] in your silence still,
And whatsomever else shall hap[11] tonight,
Give it an understanding but no tongue[12].
I will requite[13] your loves[14]. So fare you well:
Upon the platform 'twixt[15] eleven and twelve
I'll visit you.
ALL Our duty to your honour.
HAMLET Your loves, as mine to you. Farewell.
Exeunt all but Hamlet
My father's spirit, in arms! All is not well.
I doubt some foul play[16]. Would the night were come.
Till then sit still my soul. Foul deeds will rise
Though all the earth o'erwhelm them to men's eyes[17]. *Exit*

Laertes warns Ophelia against Hamlet's love, saying it is merely youthful infatuation. As a prince, Hamlet is not free to choose his own wife; he must marry in the interest of the state.

剧情简介：雷厄提告诫奥菲丽叶不要与哈慕雷产生恋情，说那不过是年少时的痴迷。哈慕雷身为王子，婚事无法自主，必须服从国家利益。

1 Advice to a sister (in pairs)

Laertes hands out much advice to his sister. His elaborate style may make him sound pompous (言辞浮夸), even overbearing.

a **Young love won't last** In lines 5–10, Laertes stresses Hamlet's youth and the fickleness of young love. It won't last, he tells Ophelia, and he makes comparisons with short-lived things: 'fashion' (passing mood), 'toy in blood' (whim of passionate youth), 'violet' (a flower of early spring) and so on. One person reads lines 5–10, pausing at each punctuation mark. In the pause, the other person repeats what has just been said, but with scornful emphasis. How many comparisons with short-lasting love does Laertes make?

b **Maturity comes with age** When Ophelia questions Laertes's assertion that Hamlet's love will be short-lived, he replies very formally: the body ('this temple') does not only increase ('waxes') in sinews (肌腱) and size ('thews and bulk'), but in wisdom too. Take turns reading Laertes's lines 10–14 to each other. Use actions to bring out the meaning.

c **Princes can't choose** Can a prince choose to marry whomever he wants? Laertes doesn't think so. He tells Ophelia that 'his [Hamlet's] will is not his own'. In lines 17–28, he gives reasons why a prince, unlike an ordinary person, is not free to marry anyone he chooses; he must bear in mind the needs and interests of his country. Discuss whether you think what Laertes says was true in past times – and whether it is true for princes and other royalty today.

Language in the play 剧中语言

Laertes's diction (措辞，用词)

A character's **diction** signifies (among other meanings) a selection of the wider language that the character uses, repeated to the extent that it becomes distinctive.

a Make a note of three or four phrases that typify Laertes's diction. For example, one feature of Laertes's speech is that he uses 'doubling' (see p. 6) frequently, as in 'no soil nor cautel'.

b Make a comparison between Laertes and his father, Polonius, when the latter shortly arrives in this scene. What similarities and differences are there in their dictions?

1 necessaries 行李
2 convoy is assistant 有船运送邮件
3 trifling of his favour 他的那些小恩小惠
4 the youth of primy nature 青春年华
5 suppliance 消遣
6 crescent … bulk 自然成长并非仅是长个子
7 at this temple waxes 随着这座庙宇长大
8 no … besmirch 没有污垢、没有欺骗可以丑化
9 unvalued persons 平民百姓
10 Carve for himself 自作主张
11 circumscribed 局限
12 peculiar sect and force 独特身份地位
13 give his saying deed 将他的话付诸行动
14 main … withal 多数丹麦人遵循的老生常谈

Act 1 Scene 3

Elsinore A private room

Enter LAERTES *and his sister* OPHELIA

LAERTES My necessaries[1] are embarked, farewell.
And sister, as the winds give benefit
And convoy is assistant[2], do not sleep
But let me hear from you.

OPHELIA Do you doubt that?

LAERTES For Hamlet, and the trifling of his favour[3],
Hold it a fashion, and a toy in blood,
A violet in the youth of primy nature[4],
Forward, not permanent, sweet, not lasting,
The perfume and suppliance[5] of a minute,
No more.

OPHELIA No more but so?

LAERTES Think it no more.
For nature crescent does not grow alone
In thews and bulk[6], but as this temple waxes[7]
The inward service of the mind and soul
Grows wide withal. Perhaps he loves you now,
And now no soil nor cautel doth besmirch[8]
The virtue of his will; but you must fear,
His greatness weighed, his will is not his own,
For he himself is subject to his birth.
He may not, as unvalued persons[9] do,
Carve for himself[10], for on his choice depends
The sanctity and health of this whole state,
And therefore must his choice be circumscribed[11]
Unto the voice and yielding of that body
Where of he is the head. Then if he says he loves you,
It fits your wisdom so far to believe it
As he in his peculiar sect and force[12]
May give his saying deed[13], which is no further
Than the main voice of Denmark goes withal[14].

Laertes continues to warn Ophelia not to trust Hamlet, because young women are vulnerable and face many dangers. She reminds him to follow his own advice. Polonius urges Laertes to leave.

剧情简介：雷厄提继续告诫奥菲丽叶不要相信哈慕雷，因为年轻女子易受伤害，并面临重重险境。奥菲丽叶提醒哥哥说，给别人的忠告自己要先做到。珀娄涅催促雷厄提出发。

1 Is Laertes pompous, or sincerely caring? (in pairs)

In the script opposite, Laertes uses images of treasure, war, masks and disease to warn Ophelia against losing her virginity to Hamlet. How does Laertes speak all his advice to his sister? Pompously? Lovingly? Imploringly? And how does Ophelia react as her brother lectures her on the briefness of young love, Hamlet's high status and the dangers that face young women?

a Take parts and experiment with different ways of speaking lines 1–44, and of showing Ophelia's reactions.

b Afterwards, jointly write a paragraph saying what you think is Laertes's attitude to his sister. For example, is he genuinely affectionate or is he sexist and condescending? Bear in mind what you know about family relationships then and now.

2 First impressions of Ophelia (in pairs)

In lines 45–51, Ophelia agrees to follow Laertes's advice, but then reminds him to practise what he preaches. Is her first sentence (agreeing) spoken ironically or submissively?

- Experiment with speaking the lines and decide which style best fits your view of Ophelia's character and of the relationship between her and her brother.

▶What does this photograph suggest about Ophelia's character?

1 credent 轻信
2 list his songs 听他的甜言蜜语
3 chaste treasure 宝贵的贞洁
4 unmastered importunity 无节制的纠缠
5 keep … affection 将你的感情压在心底
6 chariest 最小心谨慎
7 prodigal 放荡不羁
8 scapes = escapes
9 calumnious strokes 毁谤的摧残
10 canker 蛀虫
11 galls the infants 残害花蕾
12 buttons be disclosed 花苞开放
13 morn = morning
14 Contagious blastments 传染性病害
15 Whiles = Whilst
16 puffed and reckless libertine 自大又莽撞的浪荡公子
17 dalliance 嬉戏调笑
18 recks not his own rede 不管他自己的劝诫
19 The wind … sail 正好顺风
20 stayed for 等着

Then weigh what loss your honour may sustain
If with too credent[1] ear you list his songs[2],
Or lose your heart, or your chaste treasure[3] open
To his unmastered importunity[4].
Fear it Ophelia, fear it my dear sister,
And keep you in the rear of your affection[5],
Out of the shot and danger of desire.
The chariest[6] maid is prodigal[7] enough
If she unmask her beauty to the moon.
Virtue itself scapes[8] not calumnious strokes[9].
The canker[10] galls the infants[11] of the spring
Too oft before their buttons be disclosed[12],
And in the morn[13] and liquid dew of youth
Contagious blastments[14] are most imminent.
Be wary then, best safety lies in fear:
Youth to itself rebels, though none else near.

OPHELIA I shall th'effect of this good lesson keep
As watchman to my heart. But good my brother,
Do not as some ungracious pastors do,
Show me the steep and thorny way to heaven,
Whiles[15] like a puffed and reckless libertine[16]
Himself the primrose path of dalliance[17] treads,
And recks not his own rede[18].

LAERTES Oh fear me not.

Enter POLONIUS

I stay too long – But here my father comes.
A double blessing is a double grace;
Occasion smiles upon a second leave.

POLONIUS Yet here Laertes? Aboard, aboard for shame!
The wind sits in the shoulder of your sail[19],
And you are stayed for[20]. There, my blessing with thee,

Polonius gives Laertes fatherly advice on speech, friendship, quarrelling, judgement, dress, money and consistency. He questions Ophelia about her relationship with Hamlet, saying she has met him often.

剧情简介：珀娄涅从言谈、交友、争吵、判断力、衣着、金钱、自洽等各方面忠告雷厄提，尽显父爱。他问奥菲丽叶与哈慕雷是什么关系，为何二人频繁见面。

Characters 人物分析

A father gives advice to his son (in pairs)

How does Polonius deliver his advice to his son? So far, his style has been variously comic, authoritarian, lovingly sincere and pompous.

a Try speaking lines 58–81 in these styles, then talk together about what the lines and various modes of delivery suggest about Polonius's character.

b How do Laertes and Ophelia react? In some productions, Polonius's children listen dutifully and respectfully. In others they make faces behind Polonius's back, mocking his advice. In yet others they silently mouth his words, showing they have heard it all many times before. In your Director's Journal, advise Laertes and Ophelia how to react to each sentence of counsel.

1 Ophelia's broken promise

In lines 85–6, Ophelia promises to keep Laertes's advice secret. But three lines later she begins to tell Polonius what the advice was about.

- Suggest to the rest of the class one or two reasons why she so quickly breaks her promise.

Themes 主题分析

Father/daughter and mother/son (whole class)

We have already seen the beginnings of a relationship between son and father (Hamlet and his father's Ghost); and a very different father/son relationship in Polonius and Laertes. Here, we see the beginnings of a father/daughter relationship – and we have already seen Hamlet's response to his mother (one that will develop further in the play).

a Compare and contrast any two of these inter-generational relationships. Follow them through the play. This particular theme could develop into a piece of extended writing later on.

b Discuss in class the nature of parental relationships. Are sons closer to their mothers and daughters to their fathers? Or do gender divides rule more strongly within families? How do your conclusions apply to this play?

1 **precepts** 准则，规矩

2 **character** 牢记

3 **unproportioned** 未经深思

4 **familiar** 友好

5 **adoption tried** 考验过，值得结交

6 **dull thy palm with entertainment** 见人就握手，让手失去知觉

7 **unfledged courage** 未经考验的交情

8 **censure** 意见，批评

9 **habit** 着装

10 **gaudy** 花哨

11 **husbandry** 精打细算

12 **my … thee** 愿我的祝福让你牢记这一切

13 **Marry** 圣母马利亚

14 **audience** 见面的时间

15 **so 'tis put on me** （别人）告诉我的

And these few precepts[1] in thy memory
Look thou character[2]. Give thy thoughts no tongue,
Nor any unproportioned[3] thought his act.
Be thou familiar[4], but by no means vulgar.
Those friends thou hast, and their adoption tried[5],
Grapple them unto thy soul with hoops of steel,
But do not dull thy palm with entertainment[6]
Of each new-hatched, unfledged courage[7]. Beware
Of entrance to a quarrel, but being in,
Bear't that th'opposèd may beware of thee.
Give every man thy ear, but few thy voice;
Take each man's censure[8], but reserve thy judgement.
Costly thy habit[9] as thy purse can buy,
But not expressed in fancy: rich, not gaudy[10].
For the apparel oft proclaims the man,
And they in France of the best rank and station
Are of a most select and generous chief in that.
Neither a borrower nor a lender be,
For loan oft loses both itself and friend,
And borrowing dulls the edge of husbandry[11].
This above all, to thine own self be true,
And it must follow, as the night the day,
Thou canst not then be false to any man.
Farewell, my blessing season this in thee[12].

LAERTES Most humbly do I take my leave, my lord.

POLONIUS The time invites you. Go, your servants tend.

LAERTES Farewell Ophelia, and remember well
What I have said to you.

OPHELIA 'Tis in my memory locked,
And you yourself shall keep the key of it.

LAERTES Farewell. *Exit Laertes*

POLONIUS What is't Ophelia he hath said to you?

OPHELIA So please you, something touching the Lord Hamlet.

POLONIUS Marry[13], well bethought.
'Tis told me he hath very oft of late
Given private time to you, and you yourself
Have of your audience[14] been most free and bounteous.
If it be so, as so 'tis put on me[15],
And that in way of caution, I must tell you
You do not understand yourself so clearly

Polonius, scornful of Hamlet's love, remonstrates with Ophelia. He orders her not to believe Hamlet's love-talk. She must give up seeing him because of his royal position and his merely lustful desire.

剧情简介：珀娄涅对哈慕雷的示爱嗤之以鼻。他责备奥菲丽叶，要她别信哈慕雷的情话，也不得再去见他，因为他是王子，他的感情不过是一时的欲望。

Polonius picks up words Ophelia uses and interprets them differently: 'affection' (love/lust), 'tenders' (offers/look after/make), 'fashion' (manner/pretence). But does he speak harshly and/or affectionately?

1 **behooves** 相称，相配
2 **He … affection** = He has, my lord, of late made many tenders of his affection 父亲大人，他近来多次向我表达爱意（这里tender 的意思是offer）
3 **green girl** 黄毛丫头
4 **Unsifted** 未经历练，不谙世事
5 **tane … pay** = taken these tenders for true money 把代金券当成了真钱（这里tender的意思是token；tane = taken）
6 **sterling** 真金白银
7 **Tender yourself more dearly** 把自己的价位定得高一些（这里tender的意思是treat）
8 **crack … phrase** 让这个词累得喘不过气（这里crack的意思是break，wind的意思是breath，the poor phrase指tender这个词）
9 **Roaming** 转悠，遛（这里把tender这个词当作一匹马，先前把它累得喘不过气，现在再遛遛它）
10 **tender me a fool** 给我献出个傻瓜来（这里又回到这段对话里出现的第一个tender的意思上）
11 **importuned** 再三恳求
12 **Go to** 得了吧（表示批评或无可奈何）
13 **countenance** 支持
14 **springes to catch woodcocks** 抓笨鸟的套儿
15 **prodigal** 大手大脚
16 **blazes** 辞令的火花
17 **scanter** 吝惜
18 **entreatments** 谈判
19 **command to parley** 谈情说爱的邀请函
20 **larger tedder** = longer tether 更长的狗带（喻指主子给予奴仆的自由）
21 **In few** 总之
22 **brokers** 中介，经纪人
23 **investments** 外衣
24 **implorators of unholy suits** 有着肮脏追求的说客
25 **sanctified and pious bonds** 神圣虔诚的誓约
26 **The better to beguile** 欺骗好人
27 **Have … leisure** 允许你如此浪费任何闲暇时间

Characters 人物分析

Polonius

a Compare Polonius's advice to Laertes with his advice to Ophelia. What are the main points he makes in each case?

b Build a portrait of Polonius from these two speeches. Use it as a foundation to explore his character in more depth as the play progresses. Highlight and collect key quotations from the speeches and from elsewhere in this act, to provide evidence of his character and of his language.

c Compose an entry in Ophelia's diary, written after this advice from her father. How does she feel about the treatment from her brother and father? And how does she feel about Hamlet's 'tenders / Of … affection'?

As it behooves[1] my daughter, and your honour.
What is between you? Give me up the truth.

OPHELIA He hath my lord of late made many tenders
Of his affection[2] to me.

POLONIUS Affection? Puh! You speak like a green girl[3],
Unsifted[4] in such perilous circumstance.
Do you believe his tenders as you call them?

OPHELIA I do not know my lord what I should think.

POLONIUS Marry I'll teach you. Think yourself a baby
That you have tane these tenders for true pay[5],
Which are not sterling[6]. Tender yourself more dearly[7],
Or – not to crack the wind of the poor phrase[8],
Roaming[9] it thus – you'll tender me a fool[10].

OPHELIA My lord, he hath importuned[11] me with love
In honourable fashion.

POLONIUS Ay, fashion you may call it. Go to[12], go to.

OPHELIA And hath given countenance[13] to his speech, my lord,
With almost all the holy vows of heaven.

POLONIUS Ay, springes to catch woodcocks[14]. I do know,
When the blood burns, how prodigal[15] the soul
Lends the tongue vows. These blazes[16] daughter,
Giving more light than heat, extinct in both
Even in their promise as it is a-making,
You must not take for fire. From this time
Be something scanter[17] of your maiden presence.
Set your entreatments[18] at a higher rate
Than a command to parley[19]. For Lord Hamlet,
Believe so much in him, that he is young
And with a larger tedder[20] may he walk
Than may be given you. In few[21] Ophelia,
Do not believe his vows, for they are brokers[22],
Not of that dye which their investments[23] show,
But mere implorators of unholy suits[24],
Breathing like sanctified and pious bonds[25],
The better to beguile[26]. This is for all:
I would not in plain terms from this time forth
Have you so slander any moment leisure[27]
As to give words or talk with the Lord Hamlet.
Look to't I charge you. Come your ways.

OPHELIA I shall obey, my lord.

Exeunt

Just after midnight. Trumpets and gun salutes are heard. Hamlet condemns the drunkenness of the Danes and reflects that some men have a particular character fault that overwhelms reason and dignity.

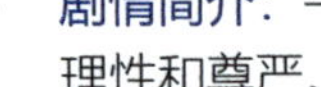

剧情简介：午夜刚过。号角和礼炮声响起。哈慕雷批评丹麦人的醉态，思考一些人的特定性格缺陷会压倒理性和尊严。

1 Danish revelry: a custom best broken?

Hamlet explains that '*A flourish of trumpets and two pieces goes off*' means that Claudius is celebrating with revelry ('wake'), drinking ('rouse', 'wassail') and wild dances ('swaggering up-spring reels'). As Claudius drinks his draughts of 'Rhenish' (German wine), loud music accompanies his toast ('pledge'). In Scene 2, lines 125–8, Claudius had promised such noisy revelry. Hamlet deplores this tradition of the Danes, saying more honour results from not following the custom ('More honoured in the breach than the observance').

- In your Director's Journal, write down, giving reasons, the tone in which you think Hamlet speaks lines 8–22.

2 Fatal flaw: 'some vicious mole of nature'

In lines 23–36, Hamlet reflects on how a single character flaw ('complexion') can corrupt a person entirely. One way of looking at Shakespeare's plays is to emphasise the destructive effect of such a character defect: Macbeth is destroyed by ambition, Othello by jealousy, Coriolanus by pride. Laurence Olivier began his film of *Hamlet* (see pp. 26 and 276) with lines 23–36 as a voice-over, and added: 'This is the tragedy of a man who could not make up his mind.'

Aristotle, in the *Poetics*, says that the most important element of tragedy is plot, i.e. what happens. But he also mentions four types of tragedy: complex tragedy, depending on reversal and recognition; the tragedy of suffering; the tragedy of character; and simple tragedy. *Hamlet* is probably a tragedy of character, with elements of all the other types woven into the whole. There is reversal and recognition: a straightforward revenge plot, but also a complex interrelationship of the personal and political, the parent–child relationship, and meditations on love, existence and death. For more information about Hamlet as a tragic hero, see pages 258–9.

a Research the nature of classical and Shakespearean tragedy.

b As you read on in the play, keep a record of the types of tragic action that you see emerging. Collect quotations as evidence of the progress of this action.

c One key question to think about, and perhaps write about later, is whether Hamlet's tragedy could be avoided or whether he was impelled toward his end.

1 shrewdly 凶狠，要命
2 lacks of 不到
3 held his wont 按他的习惯
4 *two pieces* 两门炮
5 drains … down 喝下他那一杯杯的莱茵酒（Rhenish：德国莱茵地区产的葡萄酒）
6 bray out 嗷嗷喊出
7 to the manner born 生于这种生活方式中
8 breach 打破，违反
9 heavy-headed 昏了头
10 traduced and taxed of 被……非议、指责
11 clepe （管……）叫，称（……为）
12 Soil our addition 玷污我们的名声
13 pith … attribute 我们名声的精华和骨髓
14 complexion 性情（人体内四种体液的组合决定人的性情）
15 pales 藩篱
16 o'erleavens … manners 侵蚀优良品行（o'erleavens的意思是"过度发酵"）

Act 1 Scene 4

The gun platform

Enter HAMLET, HORATIO *and* MARCELLUS

HAMLET The air bites shrewdly[1], it is very cold.
HORATIO It is a nipping and an eager air.
HAMLET What hour now?
HORATIO I think it lacks of[2] twelve.
MARCELLUS No, it is struck.
HORATIO Indeed? I heard it not. It then draws near the season
Wherein the spirit held his wont[3] to walk.
A flourish of trumpets and two pieces[4] goes off
What does this mean, my lord?
HAMLET The king doth wake tonight and takes his rouse,
Keeps wassail, and the swaggering up-spring reels,
And as he drains his draughts of Rhenish down[5],
The kettle-drum and trumpet thus bray out[6]
The triumph of his pledge.
HORATIO Is it a custom?
HAMLET Ay marry is't,
But to my mind, though I am native here
And to the manner born[7], it is a custom
More honoured in the breach[8] than the observance.
[This heavy-headed[9] revel east and west
Makes us traduced and taxed of[10] other nations.
They clepe[11] us drunkards, and with swinish phrase
Soil our addition[12]; and indeed it takes
From our achievements, though performed at height,
The pith and marrow of our attribute[13].
So, oft it chances in particular men,
That for some vicious mole of nature in them,
As in their birth, wherein they are not guilty,
Since nature cannot choose his origin,
By their o'ergrowth of some complexion[14],
Oft breaking down the pales[15] and forts of reason,
Or by some habit that too much o'erleavens
The form of plausive manners[16] – that these men,

The Ghost appears, interrupting Hamlet's reflections on human nature. Hamlet addresses it as his dead father, asking why it has returned from the grave. Marcellus urges Hamlet not to follow the Ghost.

剧情简介：鬼魂出现，打断了哈慕雷对人性的思考。哈慕雷称鬼魂为先父，问他为什么从坟墓回到人间。玛塞勒力劝哈慕雷不要跟鬼魂走。

1 'The dram of eale'

In lines 36–8, the meaning of 'The dram of eale … scandal' might be that a small quantity ('dram') of 'eale' (some kind of rotting agent) corrupts the whole of a noble enterprise, bringing discredit on a man, however good he may be.

a Write about how you might edit these three lines (you can change the words if you think it sensible; for example, 'eale' might become 'evil').

b Think more broadly about editing the script, as some directors do. Is there anything in the first four scenes that you would edit out, to make the play more engaging to the audience? Decide on which lines you would cut, bearing in mind that you need to maintain the flow of the action. Then discuss your selections with the rest of the class.

c As a whole class, discuss whether you think editing of this sort is justifiable, or whether it would be better to leave Shakespeare's script as it stands.

Language in the play 剧中语言

A good spirit? Or an evil goblin? (in pairs)

Hamlet is unsure about what type of apparition he sees. Is it a good spirit from heaven or an evil goblin from hell, tempting him to eternal damnation? He expresses his uncertainty in vivid antitheses (see p. 265):

'spirit of health' versus 'goblin damned'
'airs from heaven' versus 'blasts from hell'
'wicked' versus 'charitable'.

The problem of knowing whether the Ghost is good or bad will preoccupy Hamlet for much of the play. You will find notes on pages 249–50 to help you understand why Hamlet speaks of 'Angels', 'goblin damned', 'heaven' and 'hell' here.

- Take turns to read lines 39–57 to each other. Emphasise the antitheses, and try different pacings: fast, slow, varied. Experiment with different tones: amazed, questioning, fearful and pleading.

1 stamp 印记
2 livery 服饰
3 fortune's star 命里带来的瑕疵
4 be they = even if they are
5 The dram … scandal 一星半点儿的恶就让人对他所有的善都起疑心，让他声名狼藉
6 canonised 追封为圣徒
7 hearsèd 入棺
8 cerements 寿衣
9 enurned 下葬
10 oped = opened
11 ponderous 沉重
12 complete steel 全身铠甲
13 glimpses of the moon 时隐时现的月光
14 disposition 镇定
15 wherefore = why
16 impartment 交流，有话要说
17 wafts 招手
18 removèd ground 隐秘的地方

Carrying I say the stamp[1] of one defect,
Being nature's livery[2] or fortune's star[3],
His virtues else be they[4] as pure as grace,
As infinite as man may undergo,
Shall in the general censure take corruption
From that particular fault. The dram of eale
Doth all the noble substance of a doubt
To his own scandal[5].]

Enter GHOST

HORATIO Look my lord, it comes!

HAMLET Angels and ministers of grace defend us!
Be thou a spirit of health, or goblin damned,
Bring with thee airs from heaven or blasts from hell,
Be thy intents wicked or charitable,
Thou com'st in such a questionable shape
That I will speak to thee. I'll call thee Hamlet,
King, father, royal Dane. Oh answer me.
Let me not burst in ignorance, but tell
Why thy canonised[6] bones, hearsèd[7] in death,
Have burst their cerements[8]; why the sepulchre,
Wherein we saw thee quietly enurned[9],
Hath oped[10] his ponderous[11] and marble jaws
To cast thee up again. What may this mean,
That thou, dead corse, again in complete steel[12]
Revisits thus the glimpses of the moon[13],
Making night hideous, and we fools of nature
So horridly to shake our disposition[14]
With thoughts beyond the reaches of our souls?
Say, why is this? wherefore[15]? What should we do?

Ghost beckons Hamlet

HORATIO It beckons you to go away with it,
As if it some impartment[16] did desire
To you alone.

MARCELLUS Look with what courteous action
It wafts[17] you to a more removèd ground[18].
But do not go with it.

HORATIO No, by no means.

Horatio tries to persuade Hamlet not to follow the Ghost. Hamlet is determined to follow. He threatens Horatio and Marcellus with death if they try to restrain him. He follows the Ghost.

剧情简介：何瑞修试图劝说哈慕雷不要跟鬼魂走。哈慕雷决意要去，他警告何瑞修和玛塞勒不要拦他，否则死路一条。他跟随鬼魂而去。

1 Hamlet defends himself

Below is an image of Mel Gibson as Hamlet in a 1990 film by Franco Zeffirelli. A strong tradition has developed of Hamlet following the Ghost while using his sword hilt as a cross to defend himself against evil. That gesture, the ambiguous nature of the Ghost, and Marcellus's line 90 ('Something is rotten in the state of Denmark') create a sense of corruption that grows increasingly through the play.

- Can you think of any other props (道具) or gestures that Hamlet could use to try and protect himself at this point in the scene?

1 a pin's fee 一根针的价钱
2 flood 海
3 beetles 高悬在……之上
4 sovereignty 自主或自控能力
5 toys of desperation 绝望的冲动
6 petty arture 微小血管
7 hardy 强韧
8 Nemean lion 尼米亚狮（刀枪不入，后被赫丘力勒死）
9 I'll … me 谁拦我，我就要他的命
10 waxes 变大
11 Have after 跟上去
12 issue 结果，后果
13 Something … Denmark （见第243—245页和第264页）

HAMLET It will not speak. Then I will follow it.
HORATIO Do not my lord.
HAMLET Why, what should be the fear?
I do not set my life at a pin's fee[1],
And for my soul, what can it do to that,
Being a thing immortal as itself?
It waves me forth again. I'll follow it.
HORATIO What if it tempt you toward the flood[2] my lord,
Or to the dreadful summit of the cliff
That beetles[3] o'er his base into the sea,
And there assume some other horrible form
Which might deprive your sovereignty[4] of reason,
And draw you into madness? Think of it.
[The very place puts toys of desperation[5],
Without more motive, into every brain
That looks so many fathoms to the sea
And hears it roar beneath.]
HAMLET It wafts me still. Go on, I'll follow thee.
MARCELLUS You shall not go my lord.
HAMLET Hold off your hands.
HORATIO Be ruled, you shall not go.
HAMLET My fate cries out,
And makes each petty arture[6] in this body
As hardy[7] as the Nemean lion's[8] nerve.
Still am I called. Unhand me gentlemen!
By heaven I'll make a ghost of him that lets me[9].
I say away! – Go on, I'll follow thee.
Exit Ghost and Hamlet
HORATIO He waxes[10] desperate with imagination.
MARCELLUS Let's follow, 'tis not fit thus to obey him.
HORATIO Have after[11]. To what issue[12] will this come?
MARCELLUS Something is rotten in the state of Denmark[13].
HORATIO Heaven will direct it.
MARCELLUS Nay let's follow him.
Exeunt

The Ghost says it must shortly return to its suffering but is forbidden to tell mortals of the horrors it endures. Otherwise it would speak of appalling torments. The Ghost commands Hamlet to revenge.

剧情简介：鬼魂说他很快就得回去受罪了，他想告诉给世间的人他受的罪有多么可怕，但这是不允许的。鬼魂命哈慕雷复仇。

1 An agent of the devil? (in small groups)

The Ghost hints at the terrors of its suffering. It cannot go to heaven because it died before it could confess its sins. So it must suffer dreadfully in purgatory (炼狱). According to medieval (Catholic) Christian belief, purgatory is the place where unconfessed sinners experience indescribable remorse as their sins are burnt and purged away before they can see God in heaven (see pp. 249–50). But the Ghost says it is forbidden to tell of its terrifying ordeal ('this eternal blazon must not be').

The majority of Shakespeare's audiences were Protestants, and they would have two reasons for suspecting that the Ghost was an evil agent of the devil. First, because Protestantism had abolished the notion of purgatory. Second, because the Protestant Church judged revenge as a sin, for which the revenger's soul was damned. But the Ghost's words make thrilling theatre.

- Experiment with readings of lines 9–22 that will make the audience shrink back in their seats. The lines are packed with vivid phrases suggesting horrors and torments. Make the most of them! Add sound effects as you think appropriate. You might also wish to construct a tableau to show how the Ghost and Hamlet appear in line 25.

▼ Search in the library or on the Internet for further pictures by Hieronymus Bosch (1450–1516), whose image of Hell is shown here. Bosch painted haunting scenes of the torments of the dead. They will help you imagine what Shakespeare's audience might have pictured the Ghost enduring.

1 Whither = Where
2 Mark me 听我说
3 My hour 我的时间
4 sulph'rous 硫黄（当时人们认为地狱里的火是难闻的硫黄之火）
5 render up myself 投案自首；自我返回
6 unfold 透露
7 bound 一定要
8 term 时段
9 fast 挨饿
10 But that 要不是
11 harrow up 撕裂
12 start 跳出
13 combinèd locks 打了结、编成辫的头发
14 stand an end = stand on end 立起来
15 quills upon the fretful porpentine 毛了的豪猪身上的刺（porpentine = porcupine）
16 eternal blazon 永不熄灭的火焰
17 List = Listen

Act 1 Scene 5

The walls of Elsinore Castle

Enter GHOST *and* HAMLET

HAMLET Whither[1] wilt thou lead me? Speak, I'll go no further.
GHOST Mark me[2].
HAMLET I will.
GHOST My hour[3] is almost come
When I to sulph'rous[4] and tormenting flames
Must render up myself[5].
HAMLET Alas poor ghost!
GHOST Pity me not, but lend thy serious hearing
To what I shall unfold[6].
HAMLET Speak, I am bound[7] to hear.
GHOST So art thou to revenge, when thou shalt hear.
HAMLET What?
GHOST I am thy father's spirit,
Doomed for a certain term[8] to walk the night,
And for the day confined to fast[9] in fires,
Till the foul crimes done in my days of nature
Are burnt and purged away. But that[10] I am forbid
To tell the secrets of my prison house,
I could a tale unfold whose lightest word
Would harrow up[11] thy soul, freeze thy young blood,
Make thy two eyes like stars start[12] from their spheres,
Thy knotted and combinèd locks[13] to part
And each particular hair to stand an end[14]
Like quills upon the fretful porpentine[15].
But this eternal blazon[16] must not be
To ears of flesh and blood. List[17], list, oh list!
If thou didst ever thy dear father love –
HAMLET O God!
GHOST Revenge his foul and most unnatural murder.
HAMLET Murder?

Hamlet is eager to take immediate revenge for his father's murder. The Ghost reveals he was killed by Claudius, and expresses disgust that Gertrude now sleeps with his brother.

剧情简介：哈慕雷急不可待要替被害的父亲报仇。鬼魂透露说他是被克劳迭杀害的，并对葛楚德现在跟他弟弟同床共枕表示恶心。

Write about it 写作练习

Family matters again

Like Hamlet (in his soliloquy in Scene 2, lines 129–59), the Ghost seems little concerned with affairs of state. His mind is full of family matters. He expresses revulsion at the thought of Gertrude's sexual relationship with Claudius ('that incestuous, that adulterate beast'). He is sickened at the thought of his betrayal by his 'seeming virtuous queen', and speaks bitterly of 'lust' and 'garbage'.

Actors often speculate about the past lives of their characters. Join in the speculation by writing a paragraph or two on these two questions:

- Had Gertrude been unfaithful while her husband was alive?
- Had Hamlet earlier suspected that Claudius had killed his father (when he says 'O my prophetic soul! / My uncle?')?

Language in the play 剧中语言

Portray the vivid images (in small groups)

The script opposite is full of strikingly imaginative images. Here are just four:

Lines 29–31 'I with wings as swift / As meditation or the thoughts of love / May sweep to my revenge.'

Lines 39–40 'The serpent that did sting thy father's life / Now wears his crown.'

Line 42 'that incestuous, that adulterate beast'

Lines 53–7 'But virtue as it never will be moved, / Though lewdness court it in a shape of heaven, / So lust, though to a radiant angel linked, / Will sate itself in a celestial bed, / And prey on garbage.'

a Choose one of these images (or another of your choice from the script opposite). Talk together about each element in the image – for example, in lines 29–31 how can you relate 'wings as swift / As meditation' and 'thoughts of love' to 'revenge'?

b Decide on a way of presenting your understanding of the image to the rest of the class. Ideas include: a mime, a drawing, a reading of the line(s) with sound effects.

c Consider what effect the images here have on the themes and characterisation of the play.

1 Murder … is 谋杀无比邪恶，哪怕谋划得再好

2 meditation 念头

3 apt 准备好

4 duller … weed 会比粗大的芦苇还麻木

5 Lethe 忘川（希腊神话中的阴界河流；亡魂饮河水后，生前一切即遗忘净尽）

6 Wouldst … this 你要是竟然对此事无动于衷

7 'Tis given out 有人放出消息说

8 whole ear of Denmark 所有丹麦人的耳朵

9 forgèd process of my death 编造的我死亡的过程

10 Rankly abused 完全蒙蔽了

11 decline 堕落

12 court 勾引

13 sate 迎合，满足

GHOST Murder most foul, as in the best it is[1],
But this most foul, strange, and unnatural.
HAMLET Haste me to know't, that I with wings as swift
As meditation[2] or the thoughts of love
May sweep to my revenge.
GHOST I find thee apt[3],
And duller shouldst thou be than the fat weed[4]
That rots itself in ease on Lethe[5] wharf,
Wouldst thou not stir in this[6]. Now Hamlet, hear.
'Tis given out[7] that, sleeping in my orchard,
A serpent stung me. So the whole ear of Denmark[8]
Is by a forgèd process of my death[9]
Rankly abused[10]; but know, thou noble youth,
The serpent that did sting thy father's life
Now wears his crown.
HAMLET O my prophetic soul!
My uncle?
GHOST Ay, that incestuous, that adulterate beast,
With witchcraft of his wits, with traitorous gifts –
O wicked wit and gifts that have the power
So to seduce – won to his shameful lust
The will of my most seeming virtuous queen.
O Hamlet, what a falling off was there,
From me whose love was of that dignity
That it went hand in hand even with the vow
I made to her in marriage, and to decline[11]
Upon a wretch whose natural gifts were poor
To those of mine.
But virtue as it never will be moved,
Though lewdness court[12] it in a shape of heaven,
So lust, though to a radiant angel linked,
Will sate[13] itself in a celestial bed,
And prey on garbage.
But soft, methinks I scent the morning air;

The Ghost tells how Claudius murdered him by pouring poison in his ear. He died with no chance to confess his sins. He urges Hamlet to revenge, but without harming Gertrude.

剧情简介：鬼魂讲述克劳迭是如何将毒药灌进他耳朵里将他杀害的。他来不及忏悔这一生的罪孽就死了。他叮嘱哈慕雷一定要复仇，但不要伤害葛楚德。

1 Act out the Ghost's story (in fours)

Take parts as narrator, Hamlet's father, Claudius and Gertrude. The narrator reads lines 59–80, pausing often. The others act what is described. This type of 'dumb-show', or mimed version of a play, will prepare you for the play-within-a-play in Act 3.

▼ Compare this ghost to the one shown on page 10. Which do you prefer, and why?

1 Brief let me be 我长话短说
2 Upon my secure hour 趁我不备
3 stole 溜了进来
4 juice … vial 一小瓶该死的天仙子汁（hebenon很可能是henbane［天仙子，一种有毒植物］的别称）
5 porches 耳道
6 leperous distilment 造成麻风溃烂的毒剂
7 Holds such an enmity 对……破坏力极强
8 quicksilver 水银
9 courses through 流遍
10 posset 凝结
11 eager droppings 酸水滴（eager源自法文*aigre*，本身就有"酸"的意思）
12 thin and wholesome 鲜活又健康
13 tetter barked about 全身起红疹，像裹了层树皮
14 lazar-like 麻风病人似的
15 dispatched 被夺去
16 even … sin 正值我罪孽达到巅峰之时
17 Unhouseled 未领圣餐
18 disappointed 未准备好见上帝
19 unaneled 未受涂油礼
20 reckoning 清点（自己的罪孽，即忏悔）
21 account （上帝的）审判
22 luxury 淫欲
23 contrive 谋划
24 matin 黎明
25 gins = begins
26 couple = join
27 distracted globe 被弄糊涂了的脑壳

Brief let me be[1]. Sleeping within my orchard,
My custom always of the afternoon,
Upon my secure hour[2] thy uncle stole[3],
With juice of cursèd hebenon in a vial[4],
And in the porches[5] of my ears did pour
The leperous distilment[6], whose effect
Holds such an enmity[7] with blood of man
That swift as quicksilver[8] it courses through[9]
The natural gates and alleys of the body,
And with a sudden vigour it doth posset[10]
And curd, like eager droppings[11] into milk,
The thin and wholesome[12] blood. So did it mine,
And a most instant tetter barked about[13],
Most lazar-like[14], with vile and loathsome crust,
All my smooth body.
Thus was I, sleeping, by a brother's hand,
Of life, of crown, of queen, at once dispatched[15];
Cut off even in the blossoms of my sin[16],
Unhouseled[17], disappointed[18], unaneled[19];
No reckoning[20] made, but sent to my account[21]
With all my imperfections on my head –
Oh horrible, oh horrible, most horrible!
If thou hast nature in thee bear it not;
Let not the royal bed of Denmark be
A couch for luxury[22] and damnèd incest.
But howsomever thou pursues this act
Taint not thy mind, nor let thy soul contrive[23]
Against thy mother aught. Leave her to heaven
And to those thorns that in her bosom lodge
To prick and sting her. Fare thee well at once.
The glow-worm shows the matin[24] to be near,
And gins[25] to pale his uneffectual fire.
Adieu, adieu, adieu. Remember me. *Exit*

HAMLET O all you host of heaven! O earth! what else?
And shall I couple[26] hell? Oh fie! Hold, hold, my heart,
And you my sinews grow not instant old
But bear me stiffly up. Remember thee?
Ay thou poor ghost, whiles memory holds a seat
In this distracted globe[27]. Remember thee?

Hamlet determines to remember only the Ghost's commandment to revenge. He writes in his notebook. When Horatio and Marcellus find him, he avoids telling them what he knows.

剧情简介：哈慕雷决定记忆中只留下鬼魂让他复仇这个敕命，于是把它记在笔记本里。何瑞修和玛塞勒来找他，他没有告诉他们自己知道的事。

Characters 人物分析

Claudius as a 'smiling damnèd villain!'

Shakespeare's imagination was haunted by the image of the smiling villain. He used it to express the theme of deceptive appearances:

'There's daggers in men's smiles' (*Macbeth*)
'I can smile, and murder whiles I smile' (*King Henry VI, Part 3*)
'Some that smile have in their hearts, I fear, millions of mischief' (*Julius Caesar*)
'I did but smile till now' (false Angelo in *Measure for Measure*)
'one may smile, and smile, and be a villain' (line 108 opposite).

- Would playing Claudius as a 'smiler' add to or lessen dramatic impact? Write a paragraph giving your views and reasons.

Themes 主题分析

Madness: real or false?

There is much debate as to whether Hamlet is really mad, or feigning madness in order to disguise his true intent to revenge his father's death. Although most of the evidence points towards his pretending to be mad, there are strong arguments that the encounter with his father's Ghost has seriously disturbed him.

a Look at the opening lines of Hamlet's interplay with Horatio and Marcellus in the script opposite and in the rest of this scene. What evidence can you find for the real onset of madness on the one hand, and feigned madness on the other?

b Research 'madness' in Elizabethan and Jacobean culture. In particular, look up Robert Burton's *Anatomy of Melancholy*.

c Begin a set of notes on madness in the play. You will be able to use these notes both in a discussion of the themes of the play, and in relation to Hamlet's character.

d Look further into the pattern of behaviour by heroes in revenge plays of the period, such as Thomas Kyd's *The Spanish Tragedy*. How many of these contemporary heroes show signs of madness in their words and actions, and what do your conclusions suggest about Hamlet and revenge?

e Does the fact that Hamlet appears to be keeping a record ('table') add to the sense that he is truly mad?

1 table of my memory （引用了心智白板说［拉丁文是 *tabula rasa*］，这种理论最早起源于亚里士多德，他认为人的大脑起初是块未经写字的石板［blank slate］）
2 fond 愚蠢
3 saws of books 书本里的格言
4 forms 印象
5 pressures 印迹
6 baser 没什么价值
7 pernicious 恶毒
8 tables 笔记本
9 meet 合适，恰当
10 word 誓言
11 Illo, ho, ho 咦喽，吼，吼（Illo = Hillo = Hello，驯鹰人唤鹰的叫声）
12 arrant knave 彻头彻尾的傻子

Yea, from the table of my memory[1]
I'll wipe away all trivial fond[2] records,
All saws of books[3], all forms[4], all pressures[5] past,
That youth and observation copied there,
And thy commandment all alone shall live
Within the book and volume of my brain,
Unmixed with baser[6] matter: yes, by heaven!
O most pernicious[7] woman!
O villain, villain, smiling damnèd villain!
My tables[8] – meet[9] it is I set it down
That one may smile, and smile, and be a villain;
At least I'm sure it may be so in Denmark. [*Writing*]
So uncle, there you are. Now to my word[10]:
It is 'Adieu, adieu, remember me.'
I have sworn't.

HORATIO (*Within*) My lord, my lord!

MARCELLUS (*Within*) Lord Hamlet!

Enter HORATIO *and* MARCELLUS

HORATIO Heavens secure him!

HAMLET So be it.

MARCELLUS Illo, ho, ho[11], my lord!

HAMLET Hillo, ho, ho, boy! Come bird, come.

MARCELLUS How is't, my noble lord?

HORATIO What news my lord?

HAMLET Oh, wonderful!

HORATIO Good my lord, tell it.

HAMLET No, you will reveal it.

HORATIO Not I my lord, by heaven.

MARCELLUS Nor I my lord.

HAMLET How say you then, would heart of man once think it –
But you'll be secret?

HORATIO, MARCELLUS Ay, by heaven, my lord.

HAMLET There's ne'er a villain dwelling in all Denmark
But he's an arrant knave[12].

HORATIO There needs no ghost, my lord, come from the grave,
To tell us this.

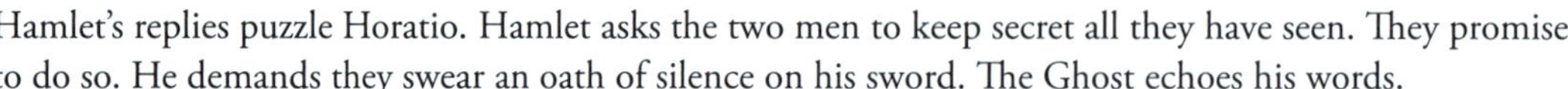
Hamlet's replies puzzle Horatio. Hamlet asks the two men to keep secret all they have seen. They promise to do so. He demands they swear an oath of silence on his sword. The Ghost echoes his words.

剧情简介：哈慕雷的回答让何瑞修摸不着头脑。哈慕雷要他二人保守秘密，不得将看到的事情说出去。他们答应后，哈慕雷又要求他们手按他的佩剑，发誓保守秘密。他每说一句，鬼魂就跟着重复一句。

Stagecraft 导演技巧

'wild and whirling words' (in threes)

In performance, Hamlet usually delivers lines 126–32 very quickly indeed, shaking hands vigorously, then making to go off and pray. Horatio expresses puzzlement at the hectic pace and seeming meaninglessness of Hamlet's words.

a To gain a sense of the rapid changes in Hamlet's language, take parts as Hamlet, Marcellus and Horatio and read lines 115–52. As you read, move around the room, with Hamlet frequently changing direction. The other two try to keep up with him.

b Afterwards, talk together about how the physical movement gives additional meaning to Horatio's claim of 'wild and whirling words'. Also discuss what the activity reveals about the state of Hamlet's mind.

1 Does only Hamlet hear the Ghost?

In most productions only Hamlet hears the Ghost. But what would be the dramatic effect if Marcellus and Horatio also heard the Ghost's demand 'Swear' (line 149)?

a Imagine you are directing the play. Write a set of notes listing the dramatic gains and losses if all three characters hear the Ghost's 'Swear'.

b Decide how you would like to play this part of the scene, and instruct the three actors how best to exploit the dramatic gains of the decision you have made. You can write this up in your Director's Journal, and/or act out the lines in a group.

2 Swearing the oath of silence (in pairs)

- Imagine the hilt of Hamlet's sword is shaped like a cross (see p. 42). Work out how he would hold it so the other two men could swear their promise of silence upon it. Decide whether you think Horatio and Marcellus are willing or unwilling to swear the oath (see line 147).
- In what other ways might Hamlet use his sword to encourage Marcellus and Horatio to swear?

1 circumstance 多说
2 desire 欲求
3 whirling words 疯话
4 by Saint Patrick 向圣派翠克发誓（圣派翠克，约385—461年，罗马不列颠人，最早将基督教传入爱尔兰。传说他是炼狱［purgatory］的看守，将炼狱中的罪人放了出来。）
5 O'ermaster't as you may = You may overcome it 你们可以克制一下（指your desire）
6 Give me one poor 答应我一个小小的
7 Nay = Now
8 truepenny 值得信赖的人（16世纪英国首部喜剧*Ralph Roister Doister*中一个老实仆人叫Truepenie）
9 in the cellarage 在地窖里（指戏台下面）

HAMLET Why right, you are i'th'right,
And so without more circumstance[1] at all
I hold it fit that we shake hands and part –
You as your business and desire[2] shall point you,
For every man hath business and desire,
Such as it is, and for my own poor part,
Look you, I'll go pray.
HORATIO These are but wild and whirling words[3], my lord.
HAMLET I'm sorry they offend you, heartily,
Yes faith, heartily.
HORATIO There's no offence my lord.
HAMLET Yes by Saint Patrick[4] but there is Horatio,
And much offence too. Touching this vision here,
It is an honest ghost, that let me tell you.
For your desire to know what is between us,
O'ermaster't as you may[5]. And now good friends,
As you are friends, scholars, and soldiers,
Give me one poor[6] request.
HORATIO What is't my lord? we will.
HAMLET Never make known what you have seen tonight.
HORATIO / MARCELLUS My lord we will not.
HAMLET Nay[7] but swear't.
HORATIO In faith
My lord not I.
MARCELLUS Nor I my lord in faith.
HAMLET Upon my sword.
MARCELLUS We have sworn my lord already.
HAMLET Indeed, upon my sword, indeed.
GHOST Swear. *Ghost cries under the stage*
HAMLET Ha, ha, boy, sayst thou so? art thou there truepenny[8]?
Come on, you hear this fellow in the cellarage[9],
Consent to swear.
HORATIO Propose the oath my lord.
HAMLET Never to speak of this that you have seen,
Swear by my sword.
GHOST Swear.

Hamlet demands that Horatio and Marcellus swear they will not reveal what has happened. They must also promise not to put on a show of knowing the true nature of any future strange behaviour by Hamlet.

剧情简介：哈慕雷要求何瑞修、玛塞勒二人发誓不会将发生的事说出去，还得答应以后看到哈慕雷的任何奇怪行为不能表现出知道内情的样子。

Stagecraft 导演技巧

Stage directions for Hamlet

Hamlet shifts position to swear the oath as the Ghost's voice is again heard from beneath the stage. Often in the theatre this 'swearing' episode results in audience laughter.

Hamlet then orders his friends not to look knowing if they see him behaving oddly (lines 173–9). His instructions contain detailed stage directions about how he could behave as he speaks. There are more stage directions in Hamlet's final speech as he expresses friendship, again orders the two men to keep silent, and ends with 'let's go together'.

Imagine you are about to play Hamlet. Write detailed notes about how you will behave as you speak all the lines in the script opposite. Add reasons to justify that behaviour. Ensure you cover these points:

- Should I attempt to make the audience laugh as I order the others to move around the stage to 'swear'?
- What actions should accompany my instructions in lines 173–9 and 188?
- How might I show friendship in my final line?

1 *Hic et ubique?* （拉丁文）= Here and everywhere?

2 **old mole** 老鼹鼠（表演时鬼魂是在戏台下面说话，就像鼹鼠在地下潜行）

3 **worthy pioneer** 挖坑道的好手

4 **put an antic disposition on** 换一副古怪的性情

5 **doubtful phrase** 令人生疑的话

6 **list** 想，愿

7 **giving out** 说漏

8 **aught** = anything

9 **commend** 托付

10 **still** 一直，永远

11 **out of joint** 大乱

12 **cursèd spite** 该死的命运

▲ In this production, the Ghost wore a fencing mask and carried a thin epée (重剑).

HAMLET *Hic et ubique?*[1] then we'll shift our ground.
Come hither gentlemen,
And lay your hands again upon my sword.
Never to speak of this that you have heard,
Swear by my sword.

GHOST Swear.

HAMLET Well said old mole[2], canst work i'th'earth so fast?
A worthy pioneer[3]. Once more remove, good friends.

HORATIO O day and night, but this is wondrous strange.

HAMLET And therefore as a stranger give it welcome.
There are more things in heaven and earth, Horatio,
Than are dreamt of in your philosophy.
But come –
Here as before, never so help you mercy,
How strange or odd some'er I bear myself,
As I perchance hereafter shall think meet
To put an antic disposition on[4] –
That you at such times seeing me never shall,
With arms encumbered thus, or this head-shake,
Or by pronouncing of some doubtful phrase[5],
As 'Well, well, we know,' or 'We could and if we would,'
Or 'If we list[6] to speak,' or 'There be and if they might,'
Or such ambiguous giving out[7], to note
That you know aught[8] of me: this not to do,
So grace and mercy at your most need help you,
Swear.

GHOST Swear.

HAMLET Rest, rest, perturbèd spirit. So gentlemen,
With all my love I do commend[9] me to you,
And what so poor a man as Hamlet is
May do t'express his love and friending to you,
God willing shall not lack. Let us go in together,
And still[10] your fingers on your lips I pray. –
The time is out of joint[11]: O cursèd spite[12],
That ever I was born to set it right. –
Nay come, let's go together.

Exeunt

Looking back at Act 1 第1幕回顾

Activities for groups or individuals

1 'Who's there?' – Does appearance match reality?

The opening line of the play is the first of many anxious questions that establish the tone of uncertainty that runs throughout. It symbolises the search for personal identity, and for the reality that lies behind outward appearance.

a Write down one example from each of the five scenes in Act 1 where you feel that appearance does not match reality. In each case, write a commentary exploring what aspects of appearance and reality are being addressed.

b Examine the notion of duplicity (deceitfulness) in Act 1. How does this idea contribute to the questioning of identity?

2 Disordered society, disturbed individuals

Recurring dramatic motifs of the disordered state of society and of individuals run through Act 1: 'Something is rotten in the state of Denmark' (Scene 4, line 90); 'The time is out of joint' (Scene 5, line 189).

- Look in more depth at *The Elizabethan World Picture* by E.M.W Tillyard (see p. 8). Divide into groups. Each group takes a chapter of the book and works on a presentation about how the Elizabethan and Jacobean ideology in that chapter are relevant to Hamlet.

3 Political matters – family matters

Hamlet begins as if it will be a play centrally concerned with politics and affairs of state (descriptions of feverish preparations for war; Claudius's dispatch of ambassadors to old Fortinbras). But Hamlet, Laertes, Polonius and the Ghost appear to be obsessed with family matters, particularly the sexuality of Gertrude and Ophelia.

- Create two columns: head one column 'Political matters' and the other 'Family matters'. Work through Act 1, noting in the appropriate column the events and quotations relevant to the heading. Which column contains most entries? What are the connections between family and politics in the play so far?

4 Horatio's point of view

Horatio has come to Denmark from Wittenberg University. He appears in four of the five scenes in Act 1, and seems to know a great deal about state affairs. Yet, in Act 1 Scene 5, lines 166–7, Hamlet says in response to Horatio's amazement at the Ghost: 'There are more things in heaven and earth, Horatio, / Than are dreamt of in your philosophy.'

a Look back through Act 1 and trace the way in which Horatio responds to the Watch, to the Ghost and to Hamlet. What qualities and types of response does he show? As part of a character study, write down quotations that reveal Horatio's reactions and motivations.

b Horatio appears to be a 'foil' or counterpart to Hamlet. Compare the two characters. What qualities does Horatio have that contrast with Hamlet's?

5 Summarising the action

a Imagine that a daily court circular is issued, recording the activities of the royal family in this play. Write the court circular for one day in Act 1. You can find an example of a court circular, focused on the British royal family, in a copy of *The Times*.

b Write and present a two-minute version of Act 1. Be prepared to defend your inclusions, compressions and omissions.

Which of these images of Claudius, Gertrude and Hamlet best fits your conception of the characters – and why?

Polonius gives Reynaldo money for Laertes in Paris. He orders Reynaldo to spy on Laertes's behaviour using devious, indirect methods. Even lies may be used to discover what Laertes is doing.

剧情简介：珀娄涅让瑞纳尔窦给在巴黎的雷厄提送钱。他命瑞纳尔窦打探雷厄提的行为，打探方式要狡猾、迂回。为了套出雷厄提干了什么，编瞎话也可以。

1 Polonius's approach

Polonius (right) tells Reynaldo that indirect ways of questioning will yield better information than direct approaches.

- How would you advise an actor to speak Polonius's lines in this scene in order to suggest his character and his role in the Danish court?

1 inquire = inquiry 打听
2 well said 说得对
3 Danskers 丹麦人
4 means 家境
5 keep 光顾
6 encompassment and drift 拐弯抹角
7 particular demands 具体问题
8 Take you 您装作
9 distant knowledge 略有耳闻
10 Addicted 沾染（恶习）
11 forgeries 编造
12 wanton 放荡
13 gaming 赌博
14 drabbing 嫖

Act 2 Scene 1

A state room in the castle

Enter POLONIUS *and* REYNALDO

POLONIUS Give him this money, and these notes, Reynaldo.
REYNALDO I will my lord.
POLONIUS You shall do marvellous wisely, good Reynaldo,
Before you visit him, to make inquire[1]
Of his behaviour.
REYNALDO My lord, I did intend it.
POLONIUS Marry well said[2], very well said. Look you sir,
Inquire me first what Danskers[3] are in Paris,
And how, and who, what means[4], and where they keep[5],
What company, at what expense; and finding
By this encompassment and drift[6] of question
That they do know my son, come you more nearer
Than your particular demands[7] will touch it.
Take you[8] as 'twere some distant knowledge[9] of him,
As thus, 'I know his father and his friends,
And in part him' – do you mark this Reynaldo?
REYNALDO Ay, very well, my lord.
POLONIUS 'And in part him, but' – you may say – 'not well,
But if't be he I mean, he's very wild,
Addicted[10] so and so' – and there put on him
What forgeries[11] you please; marry, none so rank
As may dishonour him, take heed of that,
But sir, such wanton[12], wild, and usual slips
As are companions noted and most known
To youth and liberty.
REYNALDO As gaming[13] my lord?
POLONIUS Ay, or drinking, fencing, swearing,
Quarrelling, drabbing[14] – you may go so far.
REYNALDO My lord, that would dishonour him.

Polonius continues to advise Reynaldo to use indirect methods to find out whether Laertes is guilty of improper behaviour in Paris. But Polonius loses the thread of his argument.

剧情简介：珀娄涅继续教瑞纳尔窦怎么用迂回的方式来调查雷厄提在巴黎有没有不端行为。可他忘了自己说到哪儿了。

1 Reynaldo – the fox? (in pairs)

This is Reynaldo's only appearance in the play. The actor playing him will wish to establish his character, even though he has such a small part. He might be guided by the knowledge that Reynaldo (Reynard) means 'the fox', an animal with a reputation for cunning. Take parts and read lines 1–72 in several ways to discover which works best:

- Reynaldo is an experienced secret agent
- Reynaldo thinks that Polonius is a rambling old fool
- Reynaldo is genuinely puzzled about what he's being asked to do, but wishes to be a loyal servant.

2 Losing the drift of his argument

Identify the line where Polonius begins to lose the thread of his argument. Advise the actor on how he should play this 'forgetful' episode to help establish the character of Polonius. For example, should he try to win audience sympathy for an old man's failing memory, or should he aim to get a laugh at Polonius's expense? In performance, the forgetfulness is often played for laughs.

Language in the play 剧中语言

Polonius's diction

Polonius's language (specifically, his individual diction or 'idiolect') is distinctive, as it is for many Shakespearean characters. He is a serious character in the play, but is also a figure of fun and ridicule – largely because of his language.

a Look over Polonius's speeches so far in this scene and identify the characteristics of his diction. Collect quotations to provide evidence of the different ways in which Polonius uses language to instruct Reynaldo. You might also look at his speeches to Laertes and Ophelia in Act 1 Scene 3. Why do you think Shakespeare makes Polonius appear so ridiculous?

b Write a short speech as Polonius, using the characteristic elements of his diction that you have identified. Read the speech aloud in a small group, in character as Polonius. Think about the tone, emphasis and gestures that you could use to bring the speech to life.

1 as … charge 那就看您的指控怎么措辞了
2 incontinency 纵欲无度
3 breathe his faults so quaintly 巧妙地说出他的缺点
4 taints of liberty 自由过多造成的瑕疵
5 savageness in unreclaimèd blood 气血旺盛引发的撒野
6 Of general assault 人人都有的毛病
7 drift 打算
8 fetch of warrant 管保有效的策略
9 sullies 污点
10 party 对方
11 converse 交谈（也有“反过来”的意思）
12 prenominate 前面提到的
13 closes … consequence 结果就会这样跟您掏心窝子
14 addition 称呼，尊称
15 o'ertook in's rouse 喝得酩酊大醉
16 falling out at tennis 打网球时大打出手
17 Videlicet 也就是

POLONIUS Faith no, as you may season it in the charge[1].
You must not put another scandal on him,
That he is open to incontinency[2],
That's not my meaning. But breathe his faults so quaintly[3]
That they may seem the taints of liberty[4],
The flash and outbreak of a fiery mind,
A savageness in unreclaimèd blood[5],
Of general assault[6].

REYNALDO But my good lord –

POLONIUS Wherefore should you do this?

REYNALDO Ay my lord,
I would know that.

POLONIUS Marry sir, here's my drift[7],
And I believe it is a fetch of warrant[8].
You laying these slight sullies[9] on my son,
As 'twere a thing a little soiled i'th'working,
Mark you,
Your party[10] in converse[11], him you would sound,
Having ever seen in the prenominate[12] crimes
The youth you breathe of guilty, be assured
He closes with you in this consequence[13],
'Good sir', or so, or 'friend', or 'gentleman',
According to the phrase and the addition[14]
Of man and country.

REYNALDO Very good my lord.

POLONIUS And then sir does a this – a does – what was I about to say?
By the mass I was about to say something. Where did I leave?

REYNALDO At 'closes in the consequence', at 'friend, or so', and 'gentleman'.

POLONIUS At 'closes in the consequence' – ay marry,
He closes with you thus: 'I know the gentleman,
I saw him yesterday, or th'other day,
Or then, or then, with such or such, and as you say,
There was a gaming, there o'ertook in's rouse[15],
There falling out at tennis[16]', or perchance,
'I saw him enter such a house of sale' –
Videlicet[17], a brothel – or so forth. See you now,
Your bait of falsehood takes this carp of truth,

Polonius dispatches Reynaldo on his spying mission to Paris. Ophelia comes to report that she has been frightened by Hamlet's strange appearance. His clothing was dishevelled and his behaviour odd.

剧情简介：珀娄涅打发瑞纳尔窦去巴黎执行打探任务。奥菲丽叶过来说哈慕雷奇怪的样子吓到她了。他衣衫不整，行为古怪。

1 Act Hamlet's 'antic disposition' (in threes)

One film of the play added a scene showing Ophelia's encounter with Hamlet, and included lines 75–98 as a voice-over to Hamlet's behaviour.

- Act out your own version of this 'absent scene'. As one person slowly narrates the lines, the other two mime them.

2 Points of view on Hamlet's madness (in fours)

Lines 76–82 describe the first physical manifestation of Hamlet's madness.

- Take parts as Claudius, Gertrude, Polonius and Ophelia. In role, offer your explanation of Hamlet's appearance at this point in the play from your character's point of view. Begin by saying whether you think Hamlet is really mad or just putting on an act. Then go on to say why you think he is behaving as he is. Are there any points on which all four characters agree?

▶ **As a director, how would you portray Hamlet and Ophelia as described by Ophelia opposite? Would you show their encounter, or leave it to the imagination of the audience?**

1 **of wisdom and of reach** 聪明睿智的人

2 **windlasses** 绕着弯儿

3 **assays of bias** 旁敲侧击

4 **God buy ye** = God be with you = Goodbye

5 **Observe his inclination in yourself** 您自己也要留心观察他

6 **ply his music** 练习他的音乐（即顺着他来）

7 **closet** 内室，密室

8 **doublet** 小双衣（一种有短下摆的紧身衣）

9 **down-gyvèd** 滑到脚踝（成了脚镣）

10 **in purport** 这么说吧

11 **perusal** 细看，研究

And thus do we of wisdom and of reach[1],
With windlasses[2] and with assays of bias[3],
By indirections find directions out.
So, by my former lecture and advice,
Shall you my son. You have me, have you not?

REYNALDO My lord, I have.

POLONIUS God buy ye[4], fare ye well.

REYNALDO Good my lord.

POLONIUS Observe his inclination in yourself[5].

REYNALDO I shall my lord.

POLONIUS And let him ply his music[6].

REYNALDO Well my lord.

POLONIUS Farewell.

Exit Reynaldo

Enter OPHELIA

How now Ophelia, what's the matter?

OPHELIA Oh my lord, my lord, I have been so affrighted.

POLONIUS With what, i'th'name of God?

OPHELIA My lord, as I was sewing in my closet[7],
Lord Hamlet with his doublet[8] all unbraced,
No hat upon his head, his stockings fouled,
Ungartered, and down-gyvèd[9] to his ankle,
Pale as his shirt, his knees knocking each other,
And with a look so piteous in purport[10]
As if he had been loosèd out of hell
To speak of horrors – he comes before me.

POLONIUS Mad for thy love?

OPHELIA My lord I do not know,
But truly I do fear it.

POLONIUS What said he?

OPHELIA He took me by the wrist, and held me hard;
Then goes he to the length of all his arm,
And with his other hand thus o'er his brow
He falls to such perusal[11] of my face
As a would draw it. Long stayed he so;

Ophelia says how strangely Hamlet behaved. Polonius guesses that Hamlet has been driven mad by Ophelia's rejection of his love. He decides to tell all to Claudius.

剧情简介：奥菲丽叶讲了哈慕雷的举止有多怪异。珀娄涅猜测哈慕雷是因为奥菲丽叶拒绝了他的爱才发了疯。他决定把这一切都禀告克劳迭。

Stagecraft 导演技巧

'I am sorry' (in pairs)

a These three words from line 104 could have different meanings. Decide which of the following you prefer, based on your view of Polonius:

- Polonius is genuinely sorry for his daughter
- he feels sorry for Hamlet
- he doesn't care at all about Ophelia's or Hamlet's feelings
- he is worried about his own position as a state official who should know about such matters.

b Try a reading of the dialogue, from line 73 to the end of the scene, in which you make clear your view of how Polonius reacts to the fact that Hamlet has been visiting (in her private chambers – her 'closet') and writing to Ophelia. Does the mention of 'jealousy' at line 111 have any bearing on your portrayal?

Write about it 写作练习

A letter from Hamlet

From what you know of the relationship between Hamlet and Ophelia so far, compose a letter from Hamlet to her. It should reveal some of the concerns, suspicions and melancholy that Hamlet has exhibited, but also touch on other aspects of their relationship. Be prepared to defend your letter by reference to the script. You might also compose one from Ophelia in return.

1 More references to madness

Look back at the 'Themes' box on madness on page 50. There is more talk of Hamlet's madness in the script opposite.

- Write a psychiatrist's preliminary report on the suggestion that Hamlet is mad. What evidence is there to support the notion, and what is the evidence against it? Include quotations from the play to support your evidence. How would you clinically describe this madness? In crafting your diagnosis, you could refer to the literature on love and madness that you found in the earlier activity, looking further into Robert Burton's *Anatomy of Melancholy* and also researching more widely.

1 bulk 身子
2 to the last 一直到最后
3 bended their light on me 把目光投向我
4 ecstasy 痴狂
5 property 本质，性质
6 fordoes 害了，毁了
7 undertakings 举动
8 repel 退回
9 heed 注意，留心
10 quoted 观察
11 trifle 玩弄
12 wrack 毁掉
13 beshrew 让……见鬼去吧
14 jealousy 多疑
15 proper to 是……的特点
16 cast beyond ourselves 操心过头儿
17 being kept close 瞒下去的话
18 move … love 可能往后隐瞒的悲哀要多于不愿说出的爱情

At last, a little shaking of mine arm,
And thrice his head thus waving up and down,
He raised a sigh so piteous and profound
As it did seem to shatter all his bulk[1],
And end his being. That done, he lets me go,
And with his head over his shoulder turned
He seemed to find his way without his eyes,
For out-a-doors he went without their helps
And to the last[2] bended their light on me[3].

POLONIUS Come, go with me, I will go seek the king.
This is the very ecstasy[4] of love,
Whose violent property[5] fordoes[6] itself,
And leads the will to desperate undertakings[7]
As oft as any passion under heaven
That does afflict our natures. I am sorry.
What, have you given him any hard words of late?

OPHELIA No my good lord; but as you did command,
I did repel[8] his letters, and denied
His access to me.

POLONIUS That hath made him mad.
I am sorry that with better heed[9] and judgement
I had not quoted[10] him. I feared he did but trifle[11],
And meant to wrack[12] thee, but beshrew[13] my jealousy[14].
By heaven, it is as proper to[15] our age
To cast beyond ourselves[16] in our opinions
As it is common for the younger sort
To lack discretion. Come, go we to the king.
This must be known, which being kept close[17], might move
More grief to hide than hate to utter love[18].
Come.

Exeunt

Claudius has sent for Hamlet's fellow students. They are to find out the cause of Hamlet's strange behaviour. Gertrude promises Rosencrantz and Guildenstern they will be royally rewarded if they stay.

剧情简介：克劳迭派人找来哈慕雷的同学，要他们调查哈慕雷行为怪异的原因。葛楚德向柔森克阮茨和吉尔顿斯登许诺，如果他二人愿意留下来，将会得到王室的重赏。

Themes 主题分析

A state of surveillance (监视)

The arrival of Rosencrantz and Guildenstern in the Danish court helps to build the sense not only that 'Denmark's a prison' (see line 234) but also that Hamlet will be under surveillance.

a Look back at Act 2 Scene 1 to find evidence of how Polonius might play a part in watching Hamlet. Use this evidence, and more from Scene 2, to build up a case that surveillance is part of the Danish state – and perhaps part of how Hamlet sees himself.

b In your Director's Journal, make notes on how you would use staging techniques to show the theme of surveillance in a production of *Hamlet*. Include details on the set design, props, costumes, lighting and actors' gestures.

1 Moreover = In addition to
2 provoke 引发
3 Sith = Since 既然，因为
4 should 究竟
5 entreat 恳请
6 vouchsafe your rest 答应住下来
7 companies 陪伴
8 occasion 机会
9 glean 搜集
10 adheres 亲近
11 gentry 绅士风度
12 expend 花（费）
13 supply and profit 助益
14 fits 合乎
15 more … entreaty 更多当作命令而不是请求

▼ How do you envisage Rosencrantz and Guildenstern? In this 2010 National Theatre production they wore suits like Claudius and Polonius.

Act 2 Scene 2

The Great Hall of Elsinore Castle

Trumpet Call *Enter* KING *and* QUEEN, ROSENCRANTZ *and* GUILDENSTERN, *with others*

CLAUDIUS Welcome dear Rosencrantz and Guildenstern!
Moreover[1] that we much did long to see you,
The need we have to use you did provoke[2]
Our hasty sending. Something have you heard
Of Hamlet's transformation – so call it,
Sith[3] nor th'exterior nor the inward man
Resembles that it was. What it should[4] be,
More than his father's death, that thus hath put him
So much from th'understanding of himself,
I cannot dream of. I entreat[5] you both,
That being of so young days brought up with him,
And sith so neighboured to his youth and haviour,
That you vouchsafe your rest[6] here in our court
Some little time, so by your companies[7]
To draw him on to pleasures, and to gather
So much as from occasion[8] you may glean[9],
Whether aught to us unknown afflicts him thus,
That opened lies within our remedy.

GERTRUDE Good gentlemen, he hath much talked of you,
And sure I am, two men there is not living
To whom he more adheres[10]. If it will please you
To show us so much gentry[11] and good will
As to expend[12] your time with us a while,
For the supply and profit[13] of our hope,
Your visitation shall receive such thanks
As fits[14] a king's remembrance.

ROSENCRANTZ Both your majesties
Might by the sovereign power you have of us
Put your dread pleasures more into command
Than to entreaty[15].

Guildenstern promises that he and Rosencrantz will do whatever Claudius commands. Polonius announces the ambassadors' return. He says he has discovered the cause of Hamlet's madness.

剧情简介：吉尔顿斯登许诺说，他和柔森克阮茨将听从克劳迭的命令做任何事。珀娄涅宣布使者回来了。他说他找到了哈慕雷发疯的原因。

Stagecraft 导演技巧

Rosencrantz or Guildenstern?! (in threes)

Many directors seize on Gertrude's line 34 as an opportunity to make the audience laugh and to make a point about the similarity between Rosencrantz and Guildenstern. These directors advise Gertrude to speak the line in one of two ways:

- She is unable to distinguish which man is which, and so speaks the line as an uncertain question, unsure whether she is addressing the right person.
- She corrects a mistake by Claudius, who has misidentified the two courtiers.

a How would you advise Gertrude to speak line 34? Would you want to get a laugh on the line by having the king or queen (or both) unable to differentiate between the two men? Take the parts of Gertrude, Rosencrantz and Guildenstern. Perform lines 19–39 in two ways: first comically, then seriously. Then try to combine the two approaches.

b Why do you think Shakespeare introduces the idea of their similarity or interchangeability? What other forms of 'doubling' have you noticed so far in the play?

Themes 主题分析

Public and private (in pairs)

Gertrude and Claudius share a brief private moment together in lines 54–8. How would you stage the lines to emphasise the difference between their public life (as king and queen) and their domestic life (as mother and stepfather, and wife and husband)? Remember, the rest of the court on stage will be watching their every move, and hoping to overhear what they are saying.

a How significant is the distinction between private and public life in *Hamlet*? Why might this be an important theme of the play?

b Compare the notes you made on the theme of surveillance on page 66 to the emerging theme of public and private selves and responsibilities. Are the two themes related?

1 give … bent 尽我们最大之力（本义是“把弓拉满”）

2 practices 所作所为（也有“骗局”之意）

3 still = always

4 or else = otherwise

5 trail of policy 国家大事的蛛丝马迹

6 admittance 接见

7 fruit （餐后）甜点

8 do grace to 迎接

9 head and source 根源

10 distemper 失常

11 main 主因

12 sift him 细细查问他

13 brother Norway 挪威王兄弟

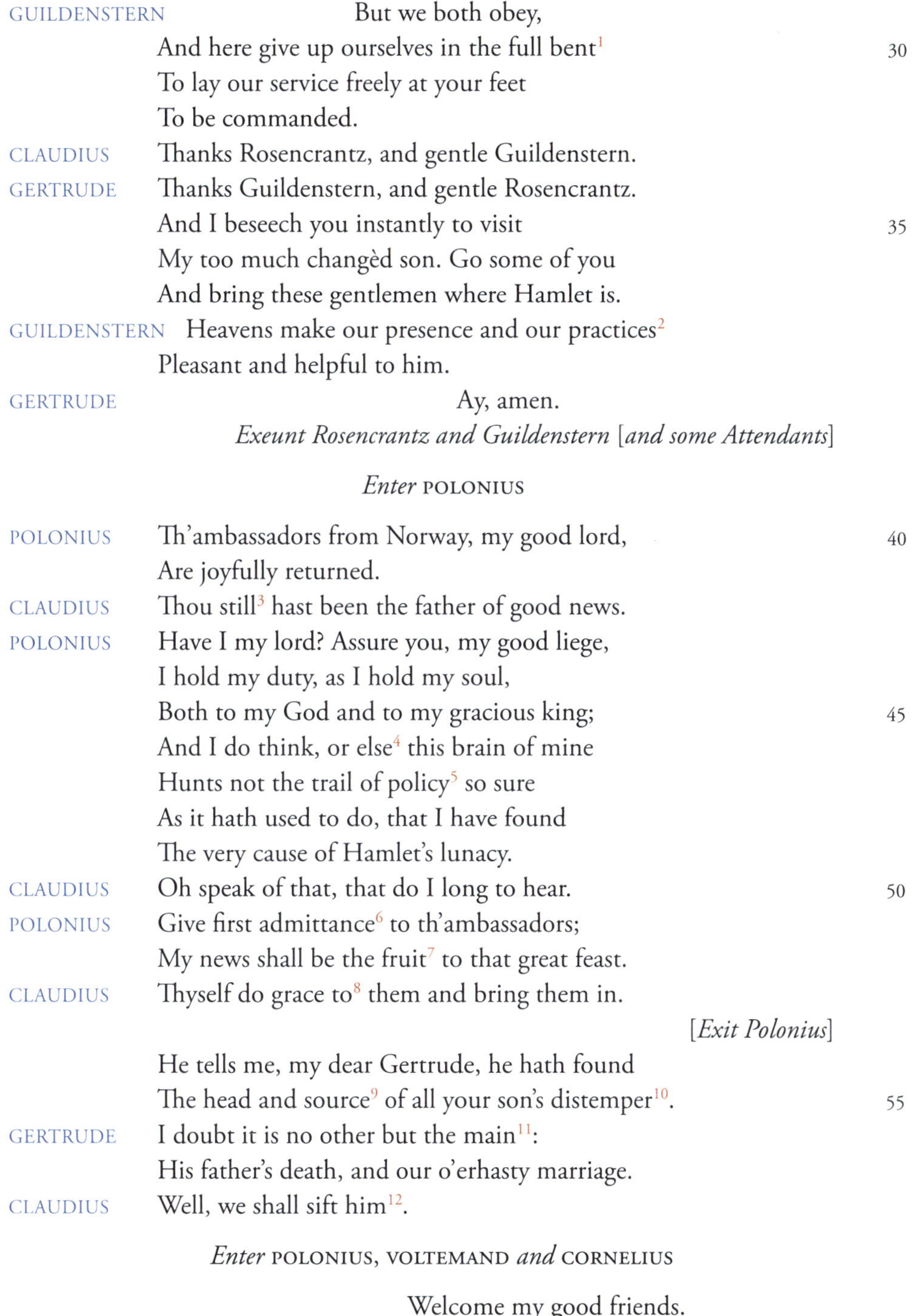

GUILDENSTERN But we both obey,
And here give up ourselves in the full bent[1]
To lay our service freely at your feet
To be commanded.

CLAUDIUS Thanks Rosencrantz, and gentle Guildenstern.

GERTRUDE Thanks Guildenstern, and gentle Rosencrantz.
And I beseech you instantly to visit
My too much changèd son. Go some of you
And bring these gentlemen where Hamlet is.

GUILDENSTERN Heavens make our presence and our practices[2]
Pleasant and helpful to him.

GERTRUDE Ay, amen.

Exeunt Rosencrantz and Guildenstern [*and some Attendants*]

Enter POLONIUS

POLONIUS Th'ambassadors from Norway, my good lord,
Are joyfully returned.

CLAUDIUS Thou still[3] hast been the father of good news.

POLONIUS Have I my lord? Assure you, my good liege,
I hold my duty, as I hold my soul,
Both to my God and to my gracious king;
And I do think, or else[4] this brain of mine
Hunts not the trail of policy[5] so sure
As it hath used to do, that I have found
The very cause of Hamlet's lunacy.

CLAUDIUS Oh speak of that, that do I long to hear.

POLONIUS Give first admittance[6] to th'ambassadors;
My news shall be the fruit[7] to that great feast.

CLAUDIUS Thyself do grace to[8] them and bring them in.

[*Exit Polonius*]

He tells me, my dear Gertrude, he hath found
The head and source[9] of all your son's distemper[10].

GERTRUDE I doubt it is no other but the main[11]:
His father's death, and our o'erhasty marriage.

CLAUDIUS Well, we shall sift him[12].

Enter POLONIUS, VOLTEMAND *and* CORNELIUS

Welcome my good friends.
Say Voltemand, what from our brother Norway[13]?

Voltemand reports that the king of Norway has prevented Fortinbras from attacking Denmark, sending him instead to invade Poland. Polonius embarks on a long-winded explanation of Hamlet's madness.

剧情简介：沃尔提曼汇报说挪威王已阻止福庭布拉进犯丹麦，派他去攻打波兰了。珀娄涅开始长篇大论地解释哈慕雷的疯病。

1 Voltemand's report (in small groups)

Much political activity has taken place. To help your understanding of Voltemand's report, try one or more of the following activities.

a One person slowly reads aloud lines 60–85 (to 'Most welcome home.'). At every mention of a person, everyone in the group points to a group member as that person (allocate parts as you read). It sounds complicated, but you will very quickly pick it up and find it helps you understand who's who. The first 'point' is in line 61, 'our' (Voltemand and Cornelius); the next is on 'he' (king of Norway). If you do not have enough group members for everyone mentioned, just point to objects (e.g. a chair or table) to represent characters.

b One person reads aloud, pausing at each punctuation mark. The others act out each section of Voltemand's speech.

c What do you notice about Voltemand's language in this report? There are three sentences in the speech. Identify them, and discuss their structure.

d The king of Norway has sent a formal letter to Claudius. Among other things, it asks for safe passage through Denmark for Fortinbras's army as it marches to invade Poland. Write the document in full.

Characters 人物分析

Polonius

Polonius has appeared in several scenes so far. He often speaks up at inappropriate moments or without due propriety.

a Look back at Polonius's speeches, so far and at those on the following page, and list his characteristics as evidenced by his words. In particular, look for contradictions in his character. What do his duplicity and obsequiousness (谄媚) suggest about the state of Denmark?

b Read lines 85–94 to yourself, thinking about how you would express them. Then work in pairs or threes to decide how you would share out the lines for maximum effect. Have a pair or group of three in the class perform the lines, justifying (and answering questions from others in the class) as to why they split up the speech in the way that they did.

1 desires 祝愿
2 Upon our first 我们刚一提（这事）
3 levies 部队
4 whereat grieved / That so 明白这一点之后，他十分恼怒
5 age … hand 年老体弱被利用了
6 in fine 最后
7 th'assay of arms against 武力挑战
8 quiet pass 安全通行
9 dominions 国土
10 allowance 准许
11 It likes us well 甚合朕意（us为御用复数）
12 more considered time 更合适的时间
13 expostulate 论说
14 flourishes 华饰

VOLTEMAND Most fair return of greetings and desires[1].
Upon our first[2], he sent out to suppress
His nephew's levies[3], which to him appeared
To be a preparation 'gainst the Polack;
But better looked into, he truly found
It was against your highness; whereat grieved
That so[4] his sickness, age and impotence
Was falsely borne in hand[5], sends out arrests
On Fortinbras, which he in brief obeys,
Receives rebuke from Norway, and in fine[6]
Makes vow before his uncle never more
To give th'assay of arms against[7] your majesty.
Whereon old Norway, overcome with joy,
Gives him three thousand crowns in annual fee,
And his commission to employ those soldiers,
So levied as before, against the Polack;
With an entreaty, herein further shown,
That it might please you to give quiet pass[8]
Through your dominions[9] for this enterprise,
On such regards of safety and allowance[10]
As therein are set down.

[*Gives a document*]

CLAUDIUS It likes us well[11],
And at our more considered time[12] we'll read,
Answer, and think upon this business.
Meantime, we thank you for your well-took labour.
Go to your rest; at night we'll feast together.
Most welcome home.

Exeunt Ambassadors

POLONIUS This business is well ended.
My liege, and madam, to expostulate[13]
What majesty should be, what duty is,
Why day is day, night night, and time is time,
Were nothing but to waste night, day, and time.
Therefore, since brevity is the soul of wit
And tediousness the limbs and outward flourishes[14],
I will be brief. Your noble son is mad.

Polonius rambles on, even though Gertrude urges him to come to the point. He reads aloud Hamlet's letter to Ophelia, and says his daughter has told him all about Hamlet's attempts to woo her.

剧情简介：尽管葛楚德催他说重点，珀娄涅仍啰唆个没完。他大声读着哈慕雷写给奥菲丽叶的信，并说他女儿把哈慕雷试图追求她的事情全部告诉他了。

▲ **How do Polonius's words in this scene help to develop your understanding of his relationship with Ophelia?**

1 More matter with less art 多说实的，少来花里胡哨的
2 figure 修辞
3 Perpend 请细想
4 mark 注意
5 gather and surmise 请各位自己判断
6 *et cetera* = etc. 等等
7 stay 等
8 ill 不擅长
9 numbers 诗
10 reckon my groans 尽数我的悲愁
11 whilst … him 只要这皮囊还属于他
12 solicitings 追求
13 fell out 发生

Write about it 写作练习

Hamlet's letter

Polonius reads out part of the letter from Hamlet that Ophelia has given him, and mocks it in front of Claudius and Gertrude (lines 109–12 and lines 115–22).

a Do you believe Hamlet could have written in this florid and elaborate style? Is this a fabricated letter that Polonius has made up in order to degrade and frame Hamlet?

b Whether the letter is real or fake, try your hand at writing the middle part of it that Polonius indicates at line 112, with '*et cetera*'. Start with the words given in lines 109–12, and finish with lines 115–22. You can insert as many lines as you like in between, but try to capture the same style.

Mad call I it, for to define true madness,
What is't but to be nothing else but mad?
But let that go.

GERTRUDE More matter with less art[1].

POLONIUS Madam, I swear I use no art at all.
That he is mad, 'tis true; 'tis true 'tis pity,
And pity 'tis 'tis true – a foolish figure[2],
But farewell it, for I will use no art.
Mad let us grant him then, and now remains
That we find out the cause of this effect,
Or rather say, the cause of this defect,
For this effect defective comes by cause.
Thus it remains, and the remainder thus.
Perpend[3].
I have a daughter – have while she is mine –
Who in her duty and obedience, mark[4],
Hath given me this. Now gather and surmise[5].

Reads the letter

'To the celestial, and my soul's idol, the most beautified Ophelia,' – That's an ill phrase, a vile phrase, 'beautified' is a vile phrase – but you shall hear. Thus:
'In her excellent white bosom, these, *et cetera*[6].'

GERTRUDE Came this from Hamlet to her?

POLONIUS Good madam stay[7] awhile, I will be faithful.
'Doubt thou the stars are fire,
Doubt that the sun doth move,
Doubt truth to be a liar,
But never doubt I love.
'O dear Ophelia, I am ill[8] at these numbers[9], I have not art to reckon my groans[10]; but that I love thee best, O most best, believe it. Adieu.
'Thine evermore, most dear lady, whilst this machine is to him[11], Hamlet.'
This in obedience hath my daughter shown me,
And, more above, hath his solicitings[12],
As they fell out[13], by time, by means, and place,
All given to mine ear.

CLAUDIUS But how hath she
Received his love?

POLONIUS What do you think of me?

CLAUDIUS As of a man faithful and honourable.

Polonius reports that he ordered Ophelia to reject Hamlet's love, so causing the prince's madness. Polonius suggests a plan: he and Claudius will spy on an arranged meeting between Ophelia and Hamlet.

剧情简介：珀娄涅汇报他命奥菲丽叶拒绝哈慕雷的追求，如此才使得王子发疯。珀娄涅想出一条计策：给哈慕雷和奥菲丽叶安排一次见面，他和克劳迭暗中观察。

Stagecraft 导演技巧

Show what happened (in small groups)

a Shakespeare often builds stage directions into his language. In lines 141–9, Polonius describes at least eleven distinct actions. One person slowly narrates the lines while the others act out each event.

b 'Take this from this': what does Polonius do at line 154? Does he touch his head and shoulder ('chop off my head')? Or does he touch his official staff of office and his hand ('dismiss me')? Work out an appropriate action to accompany the line.

c With what movement would you accompany the final words of the short speech in lines 154–7: 'Within the centre'? What do you think is the significance of that phrase?

Themes 主题分析

'I'll loose my daughter to him'

Themes in *Hamlet* and in other Shakespeare plays are often closely associated with – indeed suggested by – imagery (意象). In this case, the image of release is associated with entrapment, the notion that 'Denmark's a prison' and the suppression of feelings and energies and ideas, perhaps resulting in forms of madness.

a 'Loose' sounds like the act of releasing a farmyard or wild animal. Reflect on what line 160 suggests about Polonius's view of Ophelia. Consider also how he refers to her in line 138.

b How does the theme of entrapment and release relate to other themes that have been mentioned so far: surveillance, identity and the personal/public and inner/outer self? As you build up your thoughts about emerging themes and the way they interrelate, highlight your notes with evidence of imagery in the quotations you are collecting.

c As you read on, identify and record further images of entrapment and release in the play.

1 fain 乐意
2 on the wing 迅速升温
3 played the desk 装成桌子
4 given my heart a winking 睁一只眼闭一只眼
5 went round 二话不说就去
6 out of thy star 非你命中所有（star：命）
7 prescripts 规定，命令
8 from his resort 不让他找见
9 tokens 信物
10 took the fruits 得到益处
11 watch 失眠
12 lightness 精神恍惚
13 declension 每况愈下
14 arras 挂毯

POLONIUS I would fain[1] prove so. But what might you think,
When I had seen this hot love on the wing[2] –
As I perceived it, I must tell you that,
Before my daughter told me – what might you,
Or my dear majesty your queen here, think,
If I had played the desk[3], or table-book,
Or given my heart a winking[4], mute and dumb,
Or looked upon this love with idle sight –
What might you think? No, I went round[5] to work,
And my young mistress thus I did bespeak:
'Lord Hamlet is a prince out of thy star[6].
This must not be.' And then I prescripts[7] gave her,
That she should lock herself from his resort[8],
Admit no messengers, receive no tokens[9].
Which done, she took the fruits[10] of my advice,
And he, repulsed – a short tale to make –
Fell into a sadness, then into a fast,
Thence to a watch[11], thence into a weakness,
Thence to a lightness[12], and by this declension[13]
Into the madness wherein now he raves,
And all we mourn for.

CLAUDIUS Do you think 'tis this?

GERTRUDE It may be, very like.

POLONIUS Hath there been such a time, I'ld fain know that,
That I have positively said, 'tis so,
When it proved otherwise?

CLAUDIUS Not that I know.

POLONIUS Take this from this, if this be otherwise.
If circumstances lead me, I will find
Where truth is hid, though it were hid indeed
Within the centre.

CLAUDIUS How may we try it further?

POLONIUS You know sometimes he walks four hours together
Here in the lobby.

GERTRUDE So he does indeed.

POLONIUS At such a time I'll loose my daughter to him.
Be you and I behind an arras[14] then.

Claudius agrees to Polonius's plan to spy on Hamlet. Polonius tries to make sense of Hamlet's puzzling replies and questions.

剧情简介：克劳迭同意珀娄涅暗中观察哈慕雷的计策。珀娄涅尝试着理解哈慕雷那令人捉摸不透的回答和提问。

Write about it 写作练习

'Enter HAMLET *reading on a book'*

Each new production of the play takes decisions on the following questions. Write a paragraph in your Director's Journal in response to each, explaining the dramatic effect of your decisions.

- Does Hamlet see Polonius plotting with Claudius?
- How is Hamlet dressed, and how does he behave? (This is his first appearance since he was reported to be mad.)
- Is Hamlet aware of others on stage before Polonius greets him?
- Why, and to whom, does Polonius say 'Oh give me leave' (line 168)? To Claudius? Gertrude? The Attendants? Hamlet?

1 Cross-talk comics? (in pairs)

Some critics argue that Hamlet treats Polonius as the 'straight man' in a comic duo (表演搭档). Take parts and read lines 169–212 in a variety of ways to discover if Hamlet and Polonius really do sound like a pair of comedians.

2 'kissing carrion'

Shakespeare sometimes uses a seemingly throwaway (脱口而出的) phrase that is packed with meaning. In this case (line 180), the literal meaning of the statement is clear: dead dogs provide good carrion (dead meat) for birds, like carrion crows. But the yoking together of 'kissing carrion' with his next statement – 'Have you a daughter?' – suggests that Hamlet (who knows that Polonius has a daughter!) is associating death with love, kissing and flesh.

Elizabethan and Jacobean revenge dramatists were obsessed with the connection between love and death, often assuming that sexuality and physicality were closely linked with decay, sin and putrefaction (腐朽).

- What further evidence can you find for an obsession with the physicality of love and of existence in the character of Hamlet?

1 thereon 因此事

2 assistant for a state 国之辅臣

3 carters 马车夫

4 board him presently 这就招呼他（presently = immediately）

5 God-a-mercy = God have mercy 上帝宽宏

6 fishmonger 卖鱼的（也指拉皮条的）

7 carrion 死尸

8 Conception 有孕

9 harping on 念念不忘，念叨

Mark the encounter: if he love her not,
And be not from his reason fallen thereon[1],
Let me be no assistant for a state[2],
But keep a farm and carters[3].

CLAUDIUS We will try it.

Enter HAMLET *reading on a book*

GERTRUDE But look where sadly the poor wretch comes reading.

POLONIUS Away, I do beseech you both, away.
I'll board him presently[4].

Exeunt Claudius and Gertrude [and Attendants]

Oh give me leave.
How does my good Lord Hamlet?

HAMLET Well, God-a-mercy[5].

POLONIUS Do you know me, my lord?

HAMLET Excellent well, y'are a fishmonger[6].

POLONIUS Not I my lord.

HAMLET Then I would you were so honest a man.

POLONIUS Honest my lord?

HAMLET Ay sir. To be honest, as this world goes, is to be one man picked out of ten thousand.

POLONIUS That's very true my lord.

HAMLET For if the sun breed maggots in a dead dog, being a good kissing carrion[7] – Have you a daughter?

POLONIUS I have my lord.

HAMLET Let her not walk i'th'sun. Conception[8] is a blessing, but as your daughter may conceive – Friend, look to't.

POLONIUS (*Aside*) How say you by that? Still harping on[9] my daughter. Yet he knew me not at first, a said I was a fishmonger – a is far gone, far gone. And truly, in my youth I suffered much extremity for love, very near this. I'll speak to him again. – What do you read my lord?

HAMLET Words, words, words.

POLONIUS What is the matter, my lord?

HAMLET Between who?

POLONIUS I mean the matter that you read, my lord.

Hamlet insults Polonius who none the less persists in finding good sense in Hamlet's words. Polonius leaves, and Hamlet welcomes Rosencrantz and Guildenstern, exchanging sexual puns with them.

剧情简介：哈慕雷侮辱珀娄涅，而珀娄涅仍在努力解读哈慕雷话里的理智。珀娄涅离场，哈慕雷欢迎柔森克阮茨和吉尔顿斯登，他们互相说着荤笑话。

1 'the satirical rogue'

To ridicule Polonius, Hamlet quotes the author of the book he is reading. Two well-known writers mocked the handicaps of old age. Juvenal, a Roman satirist of the first century AD, ridiculed folly. Erasmus (1466–1536) was a Dutch Christian humanist who wrote *In Praise of Folly*.

- Research either Juvenal or Erasmus. Report on whether you think their writings would appeal to Hamlet, and why.

2 Young men joking together (in pairs)

Hamlet greets Rosencrantz and Guildenstern warmly. He joins in the wordplay and sexual innuendo. Fortune is **personified** (拟人化) as a female prostitute. So 'her privates we' might mean her genitals (private parts), but it could simply mean 'we are intimate with Fortune'. Similarly, 'favours' and 'secret parts' could also be **double entendres** (双关语) (words or phrases that have double meanings, one of which is usually risqué), though their surface meanings are 'help' and 'private affairs' respectively.

- Shakespeare often indulges in such wordplay for fun. What are the dramatic purposes of its inclusion here, do you think?

Characters 人物分析

The presentation of self in everyday life

One of the reasons that Hamlet is an attractive character to adolescent or young adults is that he appears to have a number of different selves. In the script opposite, he is putting on a humorous front to deal with Polonius, and then (differently) Rosencrantz and Guildenstern. Personal and public engagement is one of the major themes of the play – and perhaps it is most obviously seen in Hamlet himself.

a In role as Hamlet, tell an audience (e.g. a psychiatrist or a friend) your difficulties so far in the play. You might wish to refer to your relationship with Gertrude, Claudius, your dead father, Ophelia, Polonius, Rosencrantz and Guildenstern.

b Is there a 'true self' emerging in the soliloquies, or is Hamlet a reflection of his relationships with the other characters? Identify any lines in the play so far where you think he is speaking as his true self, then debate your view with the rest of the class.

1 Slanders 胡言乱语
2 purging 流出
3 amber and plumtree gum 松香和李子树的胶
4 hams 大腿
5 out of the air 进来避避风
6 pregnant 意味深长
7 prosperously 滔滔不绝
8 suddenly 立即
9 withal = with
10 indifferent 平平常常
11 button 帽顶纽
12 strumpet 婊子

HAMLET Slanders[1] sir, for the satirical rogue says here that old men have grey beards, that their faces are wrinkled, their eyes purging[2] thick amber and plumtree gum[3], and that they have a plentiful lack of wit, together with most weak hams[4]. All which sir, though I most powerfully and potently believe, yet I hold it not honesty to have it thus set down. For yourself sir shall grow old as I am, if like a crab you could go backward.

POLONIUS (*Aside*) Though this be madness, yet there is method in't. – Will you walk out of the air[5], my lord?

HAMLET Into my grave?

POLONIUS Indeed that's out of the air. (*Aside*) How pregnant[6] sometimes his replies are! a happiness that often madness hits on, which reason and sanity could not so prosperously[7] be delivered of. I will leave him, and suddenly[8] contrive the means of meeting between him and my daughter. – My honourable lord, I will most humbly take my leave of you.

HAMLET You cannot sir take from me anything that I will more willingly part withal[9]; except my life, except my life, except my life.

POLONIUS Fare you well my lord.

HAMLET These tedious old fools!

Enter GUILDENSTERN *and* ROSENCRANTZ

POLONIUS You go to seek the Lord Hamlet, there he is.

ROSENCRANTZ God save you sir.

[*Exit Polonius*]

GUILDENSTERN My honoured lord!

ROSENCRANTZ My most dear lord!

HAMLET My excellent good friends! How dost thou Guildenstern? Ah, Rosencrantz. Good lads, how do you both?

ROSENCRANTZ As the indifferent[10] children of the earth.

GUILDENSTERN Happy in that we are not over-happy; on Fortune's cap we are not the very button[11].

HAMLET Nor the soles of her shoe?

ROSENCRANTZ Neither, my lord.

HAMLET Then you live about her waist, or in the middle of her favours?

GUILDENSTERN Faith, her privates we.

HAMLET In the secret parts of Fortune? Oh most true, she is a strumpet[12]. What news?

Hamlet, Rosencrantz and Guildenstern continue their banter, but Hamlet becomes more serious. He challenges the courtiers about why they have come to Elsinore. Have they come freely or been sent for?

剧情简介：哈慕雷、柔森克阮茨和吉尔顿斯登继续开玩笑，但哈慕雷严肃了起来。他质问二侍臣为何到埃尔悉诺来。他们此行是自愿的还是受人指使？

Stagecraft 导演技巧

'Denmark's a prison' (in groups)

Some productions of *Hamlet* take up the line, 'Denmark's a prison', and build the design of the whole play around the image (and the theme of confinement). Stage sets have included heavy prison doors, chains and warders. Costume designs have included dark, prisoner-like clothes. Sound effects have been used to suggest the clanking, claustrophobic (引起幽闭恐怖的) nature of prison life.

Work on a full design for *Hamlet*, either taking the **metaphor** (隐喻) (see p. 264) of the prison and confinement as your principal idea, or using another unifying image or theme. Split into four groups.

- Group 1 works on stage and set design, perhaps building a model of what the set would look like.
- Group 2 works on sound, identifying a range of sound effects that will accompany a reading or production of the play.
- Group 3 works on costume design, designing a set of clothes for any number of the characters in the play.
- Group 4 works on lighting.

1 True or false? (in small groups)

Hamlet says 'for there is nothing either good or bad but thinking makes it so' (lines 239–40).

- Do you believe that? Talk together about whether you agree with Hamlet's claim. Use practical examples from your own experience.

2 Verbal fencing (in threes)

On three or four occasions in lines 241–9, Rosencrantz and Guildenstern try to encourage Hamlet to talk about 'ambition'. Presumably they are following Claudius's instructions to discover what afflicts Hamlet. If they can get him to talk about his ambition, they will have something of real importance to report to the king.

- Take parts and experiment with ways of speaking the lines. Try to bring out how Rosencrantz and Guildenstern are attempting to get Hamlet to reveal his secret thoughts (for example, they might stress 'ambition'). Show how Hamlet warily fends them off. Keep the image of a sword-fencing match in your mind as you speak.

1 doomsday 审判日
2 Fortune 命运女神
3 confines, wards 监牢
4 be bounded in 关在……里
5 bodies 躯体（与头脑相对）
6 outstretched heroes 抻长的英雄
7 fay = faith
8 sort 划归
9 am most dreadfully attended 受着最惨的伺候
10 in … friendship 像有着历经千锤百炼的交情
11 my … halfpenny 我连半便士的感谢都付不起（半便士相当于一镑钱的1/480；这句话也可以理解为“我连半便士的感谢都舍不得付”）
12 modesties 羞耻心
13 craft enough to colour 狡猾到面不改色（colour：掩饰）

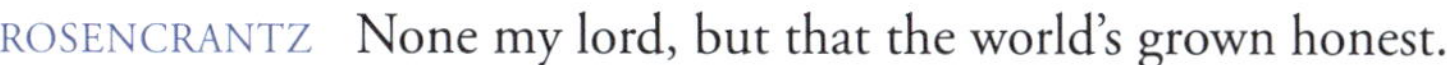

ROSENCRANTZ None my lord, but that the world's grown honest.

HAMLET Then is doomsday[1] near – but your news is not true. Let me question more in particular. What have you, my good friends, deserved at the hands of Fortune[2], that she sends you to prison hither?

GUILDENSTERN Prison, my lord?

HAMLET Denmark's a prison.

ROSENCRANTZ Then is the world one.

HAMLET A goodly one, in which there are many confines, wards[3], and dungeons; Denmark being one o'th'worst.

ROSENCRANTZ We think not so my lord.

HAMLET Why then 'tis none to you, for there is nothing either good or bad but thinking makes it so. To me it is a prison.

ROSENCRANTZ Why then your ambition makes it one; 'tis too narrow for your mind.

HAMLET O God, I could be bounded in[4] a nutshell, and count myself a king of infinite space, were it not that I have bad dreams.

GUILDENSTERN Which dreams indeed are ambition, for the very substance of the ambitious is merely the shadow of a dream.

HAMLET A dream itself is but a shadow.

ROSENCRANTZ Truly, and I hold ambition of so airy and light a quality that it is but a shadow's shadow.

HAMLET Then are our beggars bodies[5], and our monarchs and out-stretched heroes[6] the beggars' shadows. Shall we to th'court? for by my fay[7] I cannot reason.

BOTH We'll wait upon you.

HAMLET No such matter. I will not sort[8] you with the rest of my servants; for to speak to you like an honest man, I am most dreadfully attended[9]. But in the beaten way of friendship[10], what make you at Elsinore?

ROSENCRANTZ To visit you my lord, no other occasion.

HAMLET Beggar that I am, I am even poor in thanks, but I thank you – and sure, dear friends, my thanks are too dear a halfpenny[11]. Were you not sent for? Is it your own inclining? Is it a free visitation? Come, deal justly with me. Come, come. Nay, speak.

GUILDENSTERN What should we say my lord?

HAMLET Why, anything but to the purpose. You were sent for – and there is a kind of confession in your looks which your modesties[12] have not craft enough to colour[13]. I know the good king and queen have sent for you.

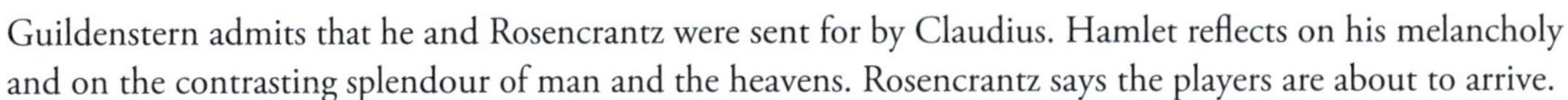
Guildenstern admits that he and Rosencrantz were sent for by Claudius. Hamlet reflects on his melancholy and on the contrasting splendour of man and the heavens. Rosencrantz says the players are about to arrive.

剧情简介：吉尔顿斯登承认他和柔森克阮茨是克劳迭派来的。哈慕雷思考着自己的忧郁，又想到人类和天堂对照形成的壮观景象。柔森克阮茨说剧团演员们就要到了。

1 From friendship to suspicion (in threes)

Hamlet becomes increasingly suspicious of his two friends. Why have they come to Denmark? He decides to 'conjure' (seriously ask) them to tell, appealing to their 'consonancy' (youthful friendship).

- Take parts and read lines 215–77. Identify where you feel Hamlet's suspicions begin, and explain the reasons for your choices of line(s).

Characters 人物分析

Hamlet's melancholy

In lines 280–90, Hamlet reflects that he has 'lost all my mirth'. He speaks of the wonderful nature both of the world and of humankind, but says that nothing now gives him pleasure. Earth seems 'a sterile promontory' (贫瘠的海角); the heavens 'a foul and pestilent (致命，有害) congregation of vapours'; and humankind, though the 'paragon' (ideal of excellence) of animals, is merely 'dust', offering him no delight. It is possible that Shakespeare is referring ironically to the Globe Theatre: 'majestical roof' = the painted canopy over the stage; 'foul and pestilent ... vapours' = the audience (see p. 272).

Every actor who plays Hamlet spends many hours deciding how to speak the lines. Is Hamlet's tone sincere, ironical, sarcastic, bitter, awe-struck (肃然起敬) – or does the mood vary from line to line?

a There is no single 'right' way to deliver these lines, so explore ways of speaking, then write notes on the version that you would recommend.

b Use these notes in your build-up of material on Hamlet's character (see p. 78). Note that these lines are in prose rather than Hamlet's usual verse. Does that make a difference?

c Research melancholy (sadness, depression) in some depth by looking not only at Robert Burton's *Anatomy of Melancholy*, but at early twentieth-century studies by Freud, such as his 1917 essay 'Mourning and Melancholy'. On page 78 you were asked to speak from Hamlet's point of view about his various selves. Here, turn the tables and write the psychiatrist's report on Hamlet's problems, and on the particular kind of depression from which he seems to be suffering.

1 what more dear 什么更有意义
2 a better proposer 更会说话的人
3 hold not off 别瞒着了
4 anticipation 先于你们说出来
5 discovery 身份暴露
6 moult no feather 不掉一根羽毛（保全无虞）
7 goodly frame 美好的架构（演员可以指着剧场说话）
8 fretted with 饰有
9 congregation 集会；弥撒
10 express 精美
11 apprehension 理解力
12 paragon 灵长
13 quintessence of dust 泥土之精粹（《旧约·创世纪》里说，人类是上帝用泥土按照自己的形象造成的）
14 lenten （斋戒般）简陋
15 coted 超过
16 foil and target 剑和盾
17 gratis 白白地
18 humorous man 喜怒无常的人（humour指人体内的四种液体，四种液体均衡则人的性格正常，某种液体过多便会造成性格失常）
19 lungs are tickle o'th'sere 容易逗笑（sere：枪的扳机）
20 Even those you were wont 就是那些您平常
21 tragedians 悲惨剧演员
22 How chances it = How come
23 their residence 他们驻剧院演出

ROSENCRANTZ To what end my lord?

HAMLET That you must teach me. But let me conjure you, by the rights of our fellowship, by the consonancy of our youth, by the obligation of our ever-preserved love, and by what more dear[1] a better proposer[2] can charge you withal, be even and direct with me, whether you were sent for or no.

ROSENCRANTZ (*To Guildenstern*) What say you?

HAMLET (*Aside*) Nay then I have an eye of you. – If you love me, hold not off[3].

GUILDENSTERN My lord, we were sent for.

HAMLET I will tell you why. So shall my anticipation[4] prevent your discovery[5], and your secrecy to the king and queen moult no feather[6]. I have of late, but wherefore I know not, lost all my mirth, forgone all custom of exercises; and indeed it goes so heavily with my disposition that this goodly frame[7], the earth, seems to me a sterile promontory; this most excellent canopy the air, look you, this brave o'erhanging firmament, this majestical roof fretted with[8] golden fire – why, it appeareth no other thing to me but a foul and pestilent congregation[9] of vapours. What a piece of work is a man! How noble in reason, how infinite in faculties, in form and moving how express[10] and admirable, in action how like an angel, in apprehension[11] how like a god! The beauty of the world, the paragon[12] of animals – and yet to me, what is this quintessence of dust[13]? Man delights not me – no, nor woman neither, though by your smiling you seem to say so.

ROSENCRANTZ My lord, there was no such stuff in my thoughts.

HAMLET Why did ye laugh then, when I said man delights not me?

ROSENCRANTZ To think, my lord, if you delight not in man, what lenten[14] entertainment the players shall receive from you. We coted[15] them on the way, and hither are they coming to offer you service.

HAMLET He that plays the king shall be welcome, his majesty shall have tribute of me; the adventurous knight shall use his foil and target[16], the lover shall not sigh gratis[17], the humorous man[18] shall end his part in peace, the clown shall make those laugh whose lungs are tickle o'th'sere[19], and the lady shall say her mind freely – or the blank verse shall halt for't. What players are they?

ROSENCRANTZ Even those you were wont[20] to take such delight in, the tragedians[21] of the city.

HAMLET How chances it[22] they travel? their residence[23], both in reputation and profit, was better both ways.

Hamlet asks many questions about the travelling actors. Rosencrantz explains that the popularity of a company of child actors has forced the players to travel. Hamlet reflects on the fickleness of fashion.

剧情简介：哈慕雷问了很多关于巡演戏班的问题。柔森克阮茨解释说一个儿童戏班太受欢迎，逼得这个戏班不得不踏上旅途。哈慕雷思考着时尚的多变。

1 The players

The arrival of the players is sudden, and enables Rosencrantz and Guildenstern to divert Hamlet from his musings on the world. Compare the players in this image with their appearance on pages 90 and 118.

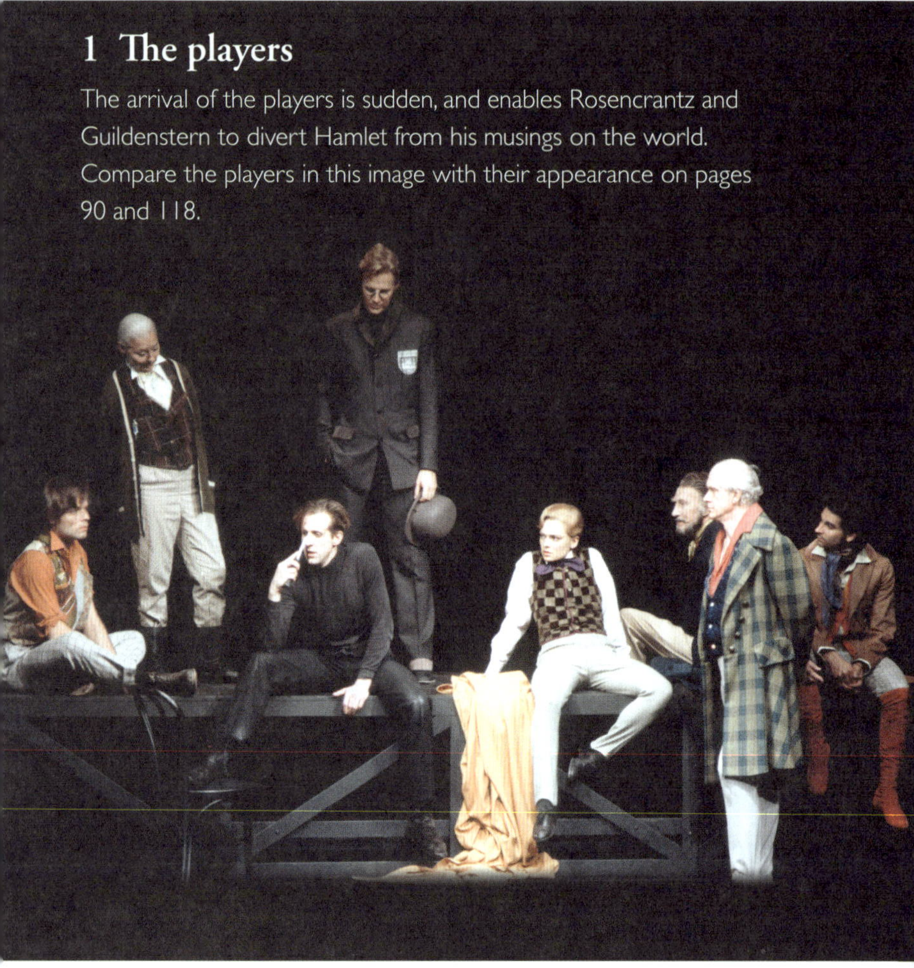

▲ The arrival of the players. Rosencrantz refers to the 'war of the theatres' in 1600, when the success of a company of boy actors threatened the adult acting companies in London. The boys specialised in bitter satire. Some noblemen were afraid to visit the theatre for fear of mockery ('many wearing rapiers are afraid of goose-quills').

2 Hamlet's questions

Note that almost the entire dialogue in the script opposite is driven by Hamlet's questions about the players. Identify the turning point where Hamlet uses the dialogue to make a point about Claudius and Denmark. Does he say anything before then to indicate that he was leading to this challenge to Rosencrantz?

1 inhibition 限令
2 late innovation 近来的新招数
3 estimation 名气
4 rusty 生涩，生疏
5 wonted pace 一贯的水平
6 an eyrie … eyases 一窝娃娃，小鹰雏
7 rapiers 护手刺剑（一种剑柄带有护手装置的开刃轻剑）
8 thither 到那里，向那里
9 escoted 资助
10 pursue the quality 从事演艺（事业）
11 no … sing 到变声期为止（戏班只重视男童演员变声之前的嗓音）
12 exclaim against their own succession 吵嚷着自毁前程
13 tar 煽风点火
14 went to cuffs 大打出手
15 carry it away 获胜
16 Hercules and his load 赫丘力背负的世界（暗指环球剧场）
17 make mouths 撇嘴嘲弄
18 ducats 金达克（一种金币）
19 picture in little 微缩像
20 'Sblood = God's blood 以上帝之血发誓
21 Th'appurtenance of 合适的礼仪
22 comply … garb 按惯例以这种方式欢迎你们
23 lest … players 以免我向演员们表示的欢迎

ROSENCRANTZ I think their inhibition[1] comes by the means of the late innovation[2].

HAMLET Do they hold the same estimation[3] they did when I was in the city? Are they so followed?

ROSENCRANTZ No indeed are they not.

HAMLET How comes it? Do they grow rusty[4]?

ROSENCRANTZ Nay, their endeavour keeps in the wonted pace[5], but there is sir an eyrie of children, little eyases[6], that cry out on the top of question and are most tyrannically clapped for't. These are now the fashion, and so be-rattle the common stages (so they call them) that many wearing rapiers[7] are afraid of goose-quills, and dare scarce come thither[8].

HAMLET What, are they children? Who maintains 'em? How are they escoted[9]? Will they pursue the quality[10] no longer than they can sing[11]? Will they not say afterwards, if they should grow themselves to common players – as it is most like if their means are no better, their writers do them wrong to make them exclaim against their own succession[12]?

ROSENCRANTZ Faith, there has been much to do on both sides, and the nation holds it no sin to tar[13] them to controversy. There was for a while no money bid for argument unless the poet and the player went to cuffs[14] in the question.

HAMLET Is't possible?

GUILDENSTERN Oh there has been much throwing about of brains.

HAMLET Do the boys carry it away[15]?

ROSENCRANTZ Ay that they do my lord, Hercules and his load[16] too.

HAMLET It is not very strange, for my uncle is king of Denmark, and those that would make mouths[17] at him while my father lived give twenty, forty, fifty, a hundred ducats[18] apiece for his picture in little[19]. 'Sblood[20], there is something in this more than natural, if philosophy could find it out.

A flourish

GUILDENSTERN There are the players.

HAMLET Gentlemen, you are welcome to Elsinore. Your hands, come then. Th'appurtenance of[21] welcome is fashion and ceremony. Let me comply with you in this garb[22], lest my extent to the players[23], which I tell you must show fairly outwards, should more appear like entertainment than yours. You are welcome – but my uncle-father and aunt-mother are deceived.

Polonius enters to tell Hamlet of the players' arrival. Hamlet mocks him. Polonius praises the actors in high-flown language. Hamlet taunts Polonius about his daughter.

剧情简介：珀娄涅上场，告诉哈慕雷说戏班子到了。哈慕雷讽刺他。珀娄涅用浮夸的语言称赞戏班的演员。哈慕雷拿珀娄涅的女儿戏弄他。

1 Appearance versus reality – and hawks (苍鹰) and handsaws

The talk about the players (lines 295–345) may seem to have little to do with the concerns of the play. But it is important because acting reflects the key theme of appearance versus reality (and Hamlet will shortly devise a scheme using the players to expose Claudius's guilt). Hamlet uses the change in acting fashions to make a barbed comment on Denmark: courtiers now buy Claudius's picture (lines 334–6). He ends with an enigmatic comment: 'I know a hawk from a handsaw' (line 348). A 'hawk' might be a bird of prey, or a plasterer's board for mortar (灰泥板). A 'handsaw' could be a 'hernshaw' (苍鹭), or a carpenter's saw. Hamlet might be saying, 'I know the difference between one thing and another – I'm not mad.'

a Suggest what you think Hamlet's words might mean. For example, 'I can recognise a bird of prey [Guildenstern?] when I see one.' Trying out hand gestures to accompany the lines will help you explore the possible meanings.

b How does Hamlet's statement, 'I am but mad north-north-west. When the wind is southerly, I know a hawk from a handsaw' contribute to your understanding of his madness? You might like to add this quotation and your interpretation of it to the evidence you are collecting on Hamlet's state of mind and behaviour. Is it important to take the context of each quotation into account?

Stagecraft 导演技巧

A question of pace (in pairs)

The arrival of the players appears to excite Hamlet. Some productions play the lines with Polonius at a fast pace to emphasise Hamlet's state of mind and his very sane (or crazed?) command of wit.

- Try the dialogue between Hamlet and Polonius with both characters speaking at a fast pace; then try it again with one of the characters speaking slowly, and the other faster; finally, slow it down for both characters. What does this variation in pace tell you about the characters? Which of the versions worked best?

1 I am but mad north-north-west 我仅在刮北西北风的时候发疯（north-north-west指"北"与"西北"之间的方位）

2 Well be with you 大家好

3 swaddling clouts 襁褓（clouts = clothes）

4 Happily = Perhaps

5 You say right sir 您说得对（哈慕雷假装正跟柔森克阮茨说事情）

6 Roscius 若修（Quintus Roscius，约前126—约前62年，古罗马的一位著名演员）

7 Buzz, buzz! 得，得！（哈慕雷在讽刺珀娄涅叽叽地说个没完）

8 scene individable 独幕戏

9 Seneca/Plautus 塞涅卡/普劳图（两位古罗马剧作家）

10 For … liberty 就戏剧创作的法则和自由而言

11 Jephtha 耶弗他（《旧约•士师记》中以色列的一位军事领袖和审判官。为赢得战争的胜利，他发誓如果凯旋，会将第一个出门迎接他的人作为牺牲献给上帝。结果出来的是他的独生女，他只好履行誓言。）

12 One … well 一个漂亮闺女，天下无双，/是他心肝宝贝，最为珍贵（这句歌谣显然与耶弗他的故事有关）

13 As by lot God wot 全是碰巧，上帝知道

14 row 诗行

15 pious chanson 圣歌

16 abridgement 消遣；打断我的事情

GUILDENSTERN In what my dear lord?

HAMLET I am but mad north-north-west[1]. When the wind is southerly, I know a hawk from a handsaw.

Enter POLONIUS

POLONIUS Well be with you[2] gentlemen.

HAMLET Hark you Guildenstern, and you too – at each ear a hearer. That great baby you see there is not yet out of his swaddling clouts[3].

ROSENCRANTZ Happily[4] he's the second time come to them, for they say an old man is twice a child.

HAMLET I will prophesy: he comes to tell me of the players, mark it. – You say right sir[5], a Monday morning, 'twas then indeed.

POLONIUS My lord, I have news to tell you.

HAMLET My lord, I have news to tell you. When Roscius[6] was an actor in Rome –

POLONIUS The actors are come hither my lord.

HAMLET Buzz, buzz![7]

POLONIUS Upon my honour.

HAMLET Then came each actor on his ass –

POLONIUS The best actors in the world, either for tragedy, comedy, history, pastoral, pastoral-comical, historical-pastoral, tragical-historical, tragical-comical-historical-pastoral, scene individable[8] or poem unlimited. Seneca[9] cannot be too heavy, nor Plautus[9] too light. For the law of writ and the liberty[10], these are the only men.

HAMLET O Jephtha[11] judge of Israel, what a treasure hadst thou!

POLONIUS What a treasure had he my lord?

HAMLET Why –
'One fair daughter and no more,
The which he lovèd passing well.'[12]

POLONIUS Still on my daughter.

HAMLET Am I not i'th'right, old Jephtha?

POLONIUS If you call me Jephtha my lord, I have a daughter that I love passing well.

HAMLET Nay, that follows not.

POLONIUS What follows then my lord?

HAMLET Why –
'As by lot God wot,'[13]
And then you know –
'It came to pass, as most like it was,' –
the first row[14] of the pious chanson[15] will show you more, for look where my abridgement[16] comes.

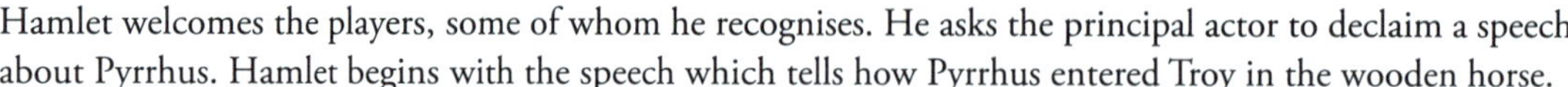

Hamlet welcomes the players, some of whom he recognises. He asks the principal actor to declaim a speech about Pyrrhus. Hamlet begins with the speech which tells how Pyrrhus entered Troy in the wooden horse.

剧情简介：哈慕雷欢迎演员们到来，还认出了其中的几位。他让戏班的台柱子说一段皮若士的词。哈慕雷起了个头，从皮若士如何藏身于木马进入特洛伊城说起。

Write about it 写作练习

A soliloquy

a List as many reasons as you can for Hamlet's enthusiasm over the arrival of the players.

b Work this list into a soliloquy or an aside in which Hamlet reveals his inner thoughts on the arrival of the players.

c It is at this time that Hamlet begins to formulate his plan for revenge on Claudius. Think about how you would include details of the plan in the soliloquy or aside, and where in the scene you would insert this speech.

Stagecraft 导演技巧

Hamlet's memory of the speech (in pairs)

Hamlet begins his recollection of the speech about Pyrrhus in stuttering style, as he tries to remember the words.

a Try reading the speech yourself. Be hesitant at the start, then move to a more assured flow as the speech (and memory) gains momentum. Do you think Hamlet is an accomplished actor, or an amateur having trouble with the lines?

b Reflect on the shift from prose to highly formal – and indeed, elaborate – verse at line 407. To achieve a sense of the difference, translate the previous ten lines of prose into Shakespearean verse, and rewrite the verse as prose. Read them out, and then discuss the difference with a partner. Finally, look again at the original script and discuss the qualities of each style.

1 The story of Pyrrhus

Pyrrhus, like Hamlet, was a son who vowed to avenge his dead father. Lines 404–6 refer to Virgil's *Aeneid*, in which Aeneas tells Queen Dido the story of Pyrrhus, whose father Achilles was killed at the siege of Troy. Pyrrhus was one of the Greek warriors in the wooden horse ('the ominous horse') that was used to defeat the Trojans. Hamlet begins the tale of how the 'rugged' (long-haired) Pyrrhus, like a savage tiger ('th'Hyrcanian beast'), clad in black armour ('sable arms'), but covered in blood ('total gules', 'o'er-sized with coagulate gore'), sought out Priam, king of Troy, to kill him in revenge for his own father.

- On a copy of the script opposite, highlight the words and phrases that Hamlet uses to enhance the drama and violence.

1 valanced 挂了毛帘（戏称蓄了胡子）
2 beard 挑战
3 byrlady = by Our Lady 向圣母发誓
4 altitude of a chopine （台上穿的）高跟鞋的高度
5 uncurrent gold 不流通的硬币（元首头像有裂缝的硬币）
6 e'en to't = even to it 这就来试试
7 fly at anything we see 看见什么都撒鹰
8 caviary = caviar 鱼子酱（在当时是一般人吃不惯的珍稀美味）
9 the general 老百姓，一般人
10 cried … mine 超过我
11 sallets = salads （隐喻荤话）
12 indict 起诉；指责
13 more handsome than fine 与其说漂亮，不如说好看
14 Aeneas' tale to Dido 埃涅阿对荻朵讲的故事（在古罗马诗人维吉尔的长诗《埃涅阿记》中，埃涅阿是特洛伊保卫战的英雄；特洛伊被希腊联军攻陷后，埃涅阿逃到迦太基；迦太基女王荻朵接见他的时候，他向荻朵讲了特洛伊战争的始末）
15 Priam 普瑞阿摩（特洛伊战争时的特洛伊王）
16 Pyrrhus 皮若士（希腊神话中第一勇士阿喀琉斯［Achilles］的儿子，本名是Neoptolemus，意思是“新武士”，Pyrrhus是其别名，意思是“红头发”。在特洛伊战争中，他是藏在木马中的武士之一，杀死了特洛伊国王普瑞阿摩，因野蛮而闻名。）
17 th'Hyrcanian beast 希尔卡尼亚（古代里海东南的一个地区，传说那里有凶猛的狮子出没）的野兽
18 sable 黝黑
19 complexion 容貌
20 tricked 饰有（和sable、arms、gules均为纹章学用语）
21 impasted 结成硬壳
22 coagulate gore 凝结的血
23 carbuncles 石榴石（一种红色宝石）

Enter the PLAYERS

Y'are welcome masters, welcome all. I am glad to see thee well. Welcome good friends. Oh, my old friend! why, thy face is valanced[1] since I saw thee last; com'st thou to beard[2] me in Denmark? What, my young lady and mistress – byrlady[3], your ladyship is nearer to heaven than when I saw you last by the altitude of a chopine[4]. Pray God your voice like a piece of uncurrent gold[5] be not cracked within the ring. Masters, you are all welcome. We'll e'en to't[6] like French falconers, fly at anything we see[7]: we'll have a speech straight. Come give us a taste of your quality: come, a passionate speech.

I PLAYER What speech, my good lord?

HAMLET I heard thee speak me a speech once, but it was never acted, or if it was, not above once, for the play I remember pleased not the million: 'twas caviary[8] to the general[9]. But it was, as I received it, and others whose judgements in such matters cried in the top of mine[10], an excellent play, well digested in the scenes, set down with as much modesty as cunning. I remember one said there were no sallets[11] in the lines to make the matter savoury, nor no matter in the phrase that might indict[12] the author of affectation, but called it an honest method, as wholesome as sweet and by very much more handsome than fine[13]. One speech in't I chiefly loved, 'twas Aeneas' tale to Dido[14], and thereabout of it especially where he speaks of Priam's[15] slaughter. If it live in your memory, begin at this line, let me see, let me see –

'The rugged Pyrrhus[16], like th'Hyrcanian beast'[17] –

'Tis not so, it begins with Pyrrhus –

'The rugged Pyrrhus, he whose sable[18] arms,
Black as his purpose, did the night resemble
When he lay couchèd in the ominous horse,
Hath now this dread and black complexion[19] smeared
With heraldy more dismal. Head to foot
Now is he total gules, horridly tricked[20]
With blood of fathers, mothers, daughters, sons,
Baked and impasted[21] with the parching streets,
That lend a tyrannous and a damnèd light
To their lord's murder. Roasted in wrath and fire,
And thus o'er-sizèd with coagulate gore[22],
With eyes like carbuncles[23], the hellish Pyrrhus
Old grandsire Priam seeks –'

So, proceed you.

The first player continues the speech from where Hamlet leaves off. He declaims how Pyrrhus finds Priam, pauses for a long moment, then slays him. The player is interrupted by Polonius, but Hamlet urges him on.

剧情简介：演员甲接着哈慕雷的词往下说，讲述皮若士如何找到普瑞阿摩，又等了好一会儿才杀他。演员的朗诵被珀娄涅打断，哈慕雷催他继续。

1 Bombast (in pairs)

Shakespeare may be 'sending up' an older stage tradition of acting and speaking. He gives the player a speech full of high-flown language.

- Work out a dramatic way of reading aloud the Player's lines 426–55 and Hamlet's lines 410–22. Try a bombastic, over-the-top, declamatory style, to match the highly coloured language. Add exaggerated gestures and formal movements to match the style. One of you plays Hamlet and the other directs.

2 'Did nothing': Pyrrhus and Hamlet both delay

Both Hamlet and Pyrrhus are sons who seek revenge for the killing of their fathers. The player's speech contains another parallel. Pyrrhus stood still and 'Did nothing' (line 440). His inability to act forecasts Hamlet's own inaction as he delays avenging his father's murder. Some productions heavily emphasise this moment, and Hamlet echoes 'Did nothing'.

- Explain the dramatic effect of that echo.

▼ Can you explain Hamlet's fascination and reverence for the players? (In this photograph, Hamlet is the character kneeling.)

1 good discretion 准确把握
2 Anon 很快
3 Repugnant to command 抗命不遵
4 fell 凶残
5 unnervèd 精疲力竭
6 senseless Ilium 没有知觉的伊利昂（特洛伊的别称）
7 Stoops to his base 轰然倒地
8 Takes prisoner Pyrrhus' ear 震得皮若士耳鸣
9 milky 白发苍苍
10 as a painted tyrant 如同一幅暴君的画像
11 like … matter 就像一个无法按照其意志和想法行动的人（neutral to = unable to act according to）
12 rack 流云
13 orb 地球
14 Cyclops 赛克洛普（希腊神话中的独眼巨人，以打铁为生）
15 Mars 玛尔斯（希腊神话里的战神）
16 proof eterne 永远保护（刀枪不入）
17 synod 会集
18 fellies 轮辋
19 nave 轮毂
20 Prithee 请你
21 Hecuba 赫喀芭（特洛伊战争时期普瑞阿摩的妻子）
22 mobled 蒙面

POLONIUS 'Fore God my lord, well spoken, with good accent and good discretion[1].

I PLAYER 'Anon[2] he finds him,
Striking too short at Greeks; his antique sword,
Rebellious to his arm, lies where it falls,
Repugnant to command[3]. Unequal matched,
Pyrrhus at Priam drives, in rage strikes wide,
But with the whiff and wind of his fell[4] sword
Th'unnervèd[5] father falls. Then senseless Ilium[6],
Seeming to feel this blow, with flaming top
Stoops to his base[7], and with a hideous crash
Takes prisoner Pyrrhus' ear[8]; for lo, his sword,
Which was declining on the milky[9] head
Of reverend Priam, seemed i'th'air to stick.
So, as a painted tyrant[10], Pyrrhus stood,
And like a neutral to his will and matter[11],
Did nothing.
But as we often see against some storm,
A silence in the heavens, the rack[12] stand still,
The bold winds speechless, and the orb[13] below
As hush as death, anon the dreadful thunder
Doth rend the region; so after Pyrrhus' pause,
A rousèd vengeance sets him new a-work,
And never did the Cyclops'[14] hammers fall
On Mars's[15] armour, forged for proof eterne[16],
With less remorse than Pyrrhus' bleeding sword
Now falls on Priam.
Out, out, thou strumpet Fortune! All you gods,
In general synod[17] take away her power,
Break all the spokes and fellies[18] from her wheel,
And bowl the round nave[19] down the hill of heaven
As low as to the fiends.'

POLONIUS This is too long.

HAMLET It shall to th' barber's with your beard. Prithee[20] say on. He's for a jig or a tale of bawdry, or he sleeps. Say on, come to Hecuba[21].

I PLAYER 'But who – ah woe! – had seen the mobled[22] queen –'

HAMLET The mobled queen?

POLONIUS That's good, 'mobled queen' is good.

The player, with tears in his eyes, ends his tale of Hecuba. Hamlet orders Polonius to treat the actors hospitably. He asks the player to perform a play the next night, including a specially written speech.

剧情简介：这位演员含泪讲完了赫喀芭的故事。哈慕雷命珀娄涅热情招待戏班演员。他让戏班演员第二天晚上演一出戏，戏中包含一段专门创作的台词。

Language in the play 剧中语言

The shift from high poetry to prose

The players speak in a formalised, high-flown diction and style; much of the rest of *Hamlet* is in freer **blank verse** (无韵诗，素体诗), and there is a good deal of prose in the play (see p. 266).

- Using examples from the script opposite, prepare director's notes for an actor on how he or she should speak the different types of lines. Look particularly at transitions between verse and prose, as at line 476.

Write about it 写作练习

Pyrrhus

a An outline of the story of Pyrrhus is provided on page 88. Using this as a start, read through Hamlet's speech again and write a 100–200 word summary of the speech in prose.

b Rewrite the speech in one of the following styles:

- a sonnet
- a question-and-answer format (e.g. an interrogation)
- the blurb of a novel
- a news item.

c Once you have experimented with, and attained a good understanding of, the speech and its story, make comparisons between Pyrrhus and Hamlet.

1 'according to their desert'

Polonius appears to have strict notions of propriety in terms of how the actors should be welcomed: they are of lower social class, and therefore will be treated accordingly. Hamlet is more generous.

a Look at Hamlet's reaction to Polonius in lines 485–8. What does this tell us about Hamlet's character, and how does it fit with what we know about him so far?

b Read line 497 in various ways: tongue-in-cheek, forcefully, as a genuine warning, or in some other tone. Decide which seems most appropriate to match what is in Hamlet's mind at this moment.

1 bisson rheum 模糊视线的泪水
2 a clout 一块布
3 diadem 冠冕
4 lank and all o'er-teemèd 生养了过多孩子而干瘪（赫喀芭生了19个孩子）
5 milch = milky 落泪
6 burning eyes （指星辰）
7 passion in the gods 诸神的同情
8 bestowed 招待
9 be well used 受到妥善款待
10 the abstract and brief chronicles 浓缩的编年史书
11 epitaph 墓志铭
12 their desert 他们应得的
13 bodkin 粗针，锥子
14 bounty 慷慨
15 for a need 需要

I PLAYER 'Run barefoot up and down, threat'ning the flames
With bisson rheum[1], a clout[2] upon that head
Where late the diadem[3] stood, and, for a robe,
About her lank and all o'er-teemèd[4] loins
A blanket, in th'alarm of fear caught up –
Who this had seen, with tongue in venom steeped
'Gainst Fortune's state would treason have pronounced.
But if the gods themselves did see her then,
When she saw Pyrrhus make malicious sport
In mincing with his sword her husband's limbs,
The instant burst of clamour that she made,
Unless things mortal move them not at all,
Would have made milch[5] the burning eyes[6] of heaven,
And passion in the gods[7].

POLONIUS Look where he has not turned his colour, and has tears in's eyes. Prithee no more.

HAMLET 'Tis well, I'll have thee speak out the rest of this soon. – Good my lord, will you see the players well bestowed[8]? Do you hear, let them be well used[9], for they are the abstract and brief chronicles[10] of the time. After your death you were better have a bad epitaph[11] than their ill report while you live.

POLONIUS My lord, I will use them according to their desert[12].

HAMLET God's bodkin[13] man, much better. Use every man after his desert, and who shall scape whipping? Use them after your own honour and dignity; the less they deserve, the more merit is in your bounty[14]. Take them in.

POLONIUS Come sirs. *Exit Polonius*

HAMLET Follow him friends, we'll hear a play tomorrow. – Dost thou hear me old friend, can you play *The Murder of Gonzago*?

I PLAYER Ay my lord.

HAMLET We'll ha't tomorrow night. You could for a need[15] study a speech of some dozen or sixteen lines, which I would set down and insert in't, could you not?

I PLAYER Ay my lord.

HAMLET Very well. Follow that lord, and look you mock him not.

Exeunt Players

My good friends, I'll leave you till night. You are welcome to Elsinore.

ROSENCRANTZ Good my lord.

Exeunt Rosencrantz and Guildenstern

Hamlet wonders at the player's ability to weep for a fictional character. He berates himself for doing nothing, even though he has real reasons for revenge. He curses Claudius, and cries for vengeance.

剧情简介：哈慕雷惊讶于这位演员竟然能为一个虚构的角色而流泪。他责备自己明明身负血海深仇却没有任何行动。他咒骂克劳迭，大喊要复仇。

1 Self-reproach: 'And all for nothing?' (in pairs)

'What's Hecuba to him, or he to Hecuba … ?' demands Hamlet as he sees the player weeping for the sufferings of Hecuba. Faced with an actor who can cry at the imagined torments of a fictional character in a play, Hamlet reproaches himself for his own lack of action. The actor can weep 'for nothing', but Hamlet, with a murdered father, is incapable of taking revenge ('unpregnant of my cause'). Like a day-dreamer ('John-a-dreams'), he does nothing.

a Do you think that Hamlet is being too hard on himself? Consider in turn each of the things he calls himself and decide if they are true ('rogue', 'peasant slave', 'dull and muddy-mettled rascal', 'John-a-dreams', 'coward', 'pigeon-livered'). Why does he level these accusations at himself?

b Consider each of the seven things Hamlet calls Claudius in lines 532–3 and discuss how justified you think each description is.

c Shakespeare often inserts lists into his plays (a literary device called **copiousness** [词语堆砌]). The accumulation of items helps to increase the intensity of the mood being created. Pick out the following lists: the player's reactions (lines 506–9); what the player would do if he played Hamlet (lines 514–18); what Hamlet imagines a bully would do to him (lines 524–7); what Hamlet calls Claudius (lines 532–3). Write a new list to insert into the soliloquy opposite (for example, a list concerning his mother, or his false friends).

Themes 主题分析

Procrastination (拖延，耽搁) and revenge

Hamlet is, for most of the play, delaying his revenge of his father's death. There are good reasons for this, as he wishes to be sure that what the Ghost has told him and his intuition about Claudius are correct. He can be fairly said to procrastinate (delay) but not to prevaricate (搪塞，推诿) (to straddle an issue, to act in collusion, to waver).

a Follow up your research on revenge plays (see page 50) and discuss to what extent *Hamlet* is the same as, and different from, a typical revenge tragedy.

b Now think about Hamlet as a revenge tragedy hero or protagonist (see 'Hamlet: a tragic hero?', p. 258). What are his heroic qualities? How do these interfere with his drive to revenge?

1 conceit 想象
2 visage wanned 苍白的脸色
3 in's aspect 他的表情上
4 function 一举一动
5 cleave 劈开
6 the free 无罪之人
7 Confound 震惊
8 muddy-mettled 烂泥扶不上墙
9 peak 无所事事；无动于衷
10 John-a-dreams 白日做梦的约翰
11 unpregnant of my cause 空怀一腔仇恨
12 pate 脑壳
13 gives … i'th'throat 狠狠指责我说谎
14 'swounds = God's wounds 向上帝的伤口发誓
15 gall 胆气
16 should … kites 早就喂肥了这地方的所有黑鸢
17 offal 杂碎
18 kindless 没人性

HAMLET
Ay so, God bye to you. Now I am alone.
O what a rogue and peasant slave am I!
Is it not monstrous that this player here,
But in a fiction, in a dream of passion,
Could force his soul so to his own conceit[1]
That from her working all his visage wanned[2],
Tears in his eyes, distraction in's aspect[3],
A broken voice, and his whole function[4] suiting
With forms to his conceit? And all for nothing?
For Hecuba!
What's Hecuba to him, or he to Hecuba,
That he should weep for her? What would he do,
Had he the motive and the cue for passion
That I have? He would drown the stage with tears,
And cleave[5] the general ear with horrid speech,
Make mad the guilty and appal the free[6],
Confound[7] the ignorant, and amaze indeed
The very faculties of eyes and ears. Yet I,
A dull and muddy-mettled[8] rascal, peak[9]
Like John-a-dreams[10], unpregnant of my cause[11],
And can say nothing – no, not for a king,
Upon whose property and most dear life
A damned defeat was made. Am I a coward?
Who calls me villain, breaks my pate[12] across,
Plucks off my beard and blows it in my face,
Tweaks me by th'nose, gives me the lie i'th'throat[13]
As deep as to the lungs? Who does me this?
Ha, 'swounds[14], I should take it, for it cannot be
But I am pigeon-livered, and lack gall[15]
To make oppression bitter, or ere this
I should ha' fatted all the region kites[16]
With this slave's offal[17]. Bloody, bawdy villain!
Remorseless, treacherous, lecherous, kindless[18] villain!
Oh, vengeance!

Hamlet rebukes himself for his emotional outburst. He resolves to stage a play showing a murder similar to his father's. If the watching Claudius reveals his guilt, it will prove that the Ghost has spoken truly.

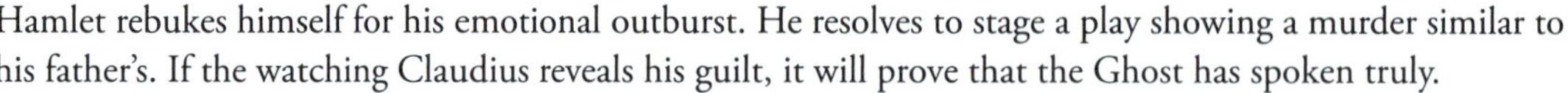

剧情简介：哈慕雷责备自己没有控制自己的情绪爆发。他决定排演一出戏，戏中表现出他父亲遭遇的那种谋杀。如果克劳迭看戏时暴露出他有罪，就证明鬼魂说的话是真的。

1 Changing moods (in threes or fours)

Hamlet goes through several changes of mood in lines 501–58. His soliloquy contains the following sections:

- **Line 501** dismissing Rosencrantz and Guildenstern
- **Line 502** self-criticism
- **Lines 503–12** wondering at the player's tears for Hecuba
- **Lines 512–18** imagining the player's reactions to real grievances
- **Lines 518–32** deepening self-disgust
- **Lines 532–4** rage against Claudius
- **Lines 535–40** self-reproach for his emotional outburst
- **Lines 541–51** working out a plan to test the Ghost's word
- **Lines 551–6** fear that the Ghost may be a devil, telling lies to tempt him to eternal damnation by killing Claudius
- **Lines 557–8** elation at the thought that he will prove Claudius's guilt.

a Make notes on each section, advising Hamlet on how to communicate his changes of mood through tone, pace, rhythm, volume, movement and gesture. Then speak your own version of the soliloquy. You may wish to use more than one voice to do so.

b Print out this soliloquy and cut it into the sections listed above. Without looking back at this text, see if you can put together the speech in the same order. Compare notes with other groups, and justify your sequence. Then look back at the book to discuss why Shakespeare puts it in the order in which it appears in the script.

2 'The play's the thing' (in pairs)

a Is theatre as powerful as Hamlet claims? Talk together about whether you think a criminal, watching a play with a similar theme to his or her own crime, will feel guilty and remorseful or will cry out and admit their guilt.

b Try to think of instances you have experienced or have read about when a play literally moves an audience to act, inciting demonstrations, violence or other actions. Use the library and the Internet to research some examples.

c Hamlet is planning a play within the play. Other instances of this device are in Thomas Kyd's *The Spanish Tragedy* and Shakespeare's *A Midsummer Night's Dream* and *The Taming of the Shrew*. A more recent example is Brecht's *Caucasian Chalk Circle*. Find the play-within-a-play in each of these examples.

1 the dear murderèd 尊贵的被害人
2 drab/scullion 下等奴才
3 malefactions 恶行
4 organ 器官；声音
5 tent 探测
6 quick 痛处
7 If a do blench = If he do blink 万一他眨一眨眼（被触动）
8 grounds 根据
9 relative 切实相关
10 conscience 愧疚

Why, what an ass am I! This is most brave,
That I, the son of the dear murderèd[1],
Prompted to my revenge by heaven and hell,
Must like a whore unpack my heart with words,
And fall a-cursing like a very drab[2],
A scullion[2]!
Fie upon't, foh! About, my brains. Hum, I have heard
That guilty creatures sitting at a play
Have by the very cunning of the scene
Been struck so to the soul, that presently
They have proclaimed their malefactions[3];
For murder, though it have no tongue, will speak
With most miraculous organ[4]. I'll have these players
Play something like the murder of my father
Before mine uncle. I'll observe his looks,
I'll tent[5] him to the quick[6]. If a do blench[7],
I know my course. The spirit that I have seen
May be a devil – and the devil hath power
T'assume a pleasing shape. Yea, and perhaps,
Out of my weakness and my melancholy,
As he is very potent with such spirits,
Abuses me to damn me. I'll have grounds[8]
More relative[9] than this. The play's the thing
Wherein I'll catch the conscience[10] of the king. *Exit*

Looking back at Act 2 第2幕回顾

Activities for groups or individuals

1 Players within a play

One of the activities on page 96 suggests that you look at plays within a play. Here, consider what players arriving on stage means for *Hamlet* as a whole. In watching a movie or theatre production of *Hamlet*, or reading it, we are engaged in a 'suspension of disbelief' and enter the fictional world of Elsinore. To then be presented with players is to be challenged yet further: is fictionality relative, with figures we take as fictional becoming 'real' as another dimension of fictionality is introduced? The notion of 'metatheatre' or 'theatre about theatre' is one way of looking at this issue; another is that of *mise en abyme* or 'standing between two mirrors'.

a Is the players' presence further emphasis on the theme of appearance and reality? If so, why is that theme so prevalent in Shakespeare's plays and *Hamlet* in particular?

b Looking at Activity 2 on this page, see if you can identify a unifying theme for the play as a whole. Is it appearance and reality or is there a further general theme in the play that unites all the others, such as the nature of existence and identity?

c Write a short essay on what you take to be the central themes in *Hamlet*. Be prepared to adapt your views as you explore further in the following acts.

2 The development of themes in Act 2

Several interconnected themes have been developed in Act 2: spying and surveillance; the notion of confinement and escape; distinctions between appearance and reality; personal and public engagement, and the formation of identity; the nature of madness; duplicity and delay; and the nature of love, including physicality.

a Add to the diagram of themes that you began on page 12. Try to include all the various themes that have been developed through Act 2. Provide quotations to illustrate each of the themes and the connections between them.

b Present a poster to the rest of the class showing how you see the emerging and related themes in the play.

3 Nine episodes

A great deal happens in Scene 2. You will find that new events begin at the following lines: 1, 40, 85, 166, 213, 295, 339, 490 and 501.

a Use these lines to identify the separate events in the scene, and write a single sentence or create a storyboard about each.

b Choose one line from each section that you think best expresses the dramatic action. Then use your chosen lines to work out a very short enactment of the whole scene.

4 Character development

Take one of the characters in the play and follow his or her progress through Acts 1 and 2. Almost all the main characters in *Hamlet* develop throughout the play. Can you identify the different sides of the character you have chosen, and provide evidence in the form of quotations to back up your ideas?

Can you identify the characters in these images from Act 2? Rank these character representations in order of preference and justify your choice to the rest of the class.

Rosencrantz and Guildenstern report Hamlet's unwillingness to talk about the reasons for his madness, and his joy at news of the players. Claudius asks them to encourage Hamlet's theatrical interests.

剧情简介：柔森克阮茨和吉尔顿斯登汇报说，哈慕雷不愿谈他为什么发疯，他对戏班子的到来很高兴。克劳迭便让他二人去鼓励哈慕雷发展他对戏剧的兴趣。

1 Rosencrantz and Guildenstern's report

Rosencrantz and Guildenstern report on their meeting with Hamlet. But how truthfully do they describe that conversation?

- Turn back to Act 2 Scene 2 and refresh your memory by quickly reading lines 215–348. Then read aloud what Rosencrantz and Guildenstern say in the script opposite and decide if they give Claudius a true and full account of their meeting.

▼ Rosencrantz with Hamlet in a National Theatre production from 2010.

Characters 人物分析

Claudius

Claudius begins this third act with a thorough investigation of Hamlet's behaviour. He seems keen to find out the cause of Hamlet's madness, and is delighted that Hamlet is engaged by the arrival of the players.

- It appears that Claudius has been checking up on Hamlet's behaviour. Write an entry in Claudius's private diary to reflect his understanding of Hamlet's state.

1 drift of circumstance 旁敲侧击
2 confusion 疯癫
3 Grating 不安稳
4 distracted 精神失常
5 forward 愿意
6 sounded 询问
7 Niggard 很少，几乎不
8 assay 试探（意向）
9 o'er-raught 超过
10 about 在附近
11 order 命令，任务
12 a further edge 继续鼓励

Act 3 Scene 1

The Great Hall of Elsinore Castle

Enter KING, QUEEN, POLONIUS, OPHELIA, ROSENCRANTZ, GUILDENSTERN, LORDS

CLAUDIUS And can you by no drift of circumstance[1]
Get from him why he puts on this confusion[2],
Grating[3] so harshly all his days of quiet
With turbulent and dangerous lunacy?

ROSENCRANTZ He does confess he feels himself distracted[4],
But from what cause a will by no means speak.

GUILDENSTERN Nor do we find him forward[5] to be sounded[6],
But with a crafty madness keeps aloof
When we would bring him on to some confession
Of his true state.

GERTRUDE Did he receive you well?

ROSENCRANTZ Most like a gentleman.

GUILDENSTERN But with much forcing of his disposition.

ROSENCRANTZ Niggard[7] of question, but of our demands
Most free in his reply.

GERTRUDE Did you assay[8] him
To any pastime?

ROSENCRANTZ Madam, it so fell out that certain players
We o'er-raught[9] on the way; of these we told him,
And there did seem in him a kind of joy
To hear of it. They are about[10] the court,
And as I think, they have already order[11]
This night to play before him.

POLONIUS 'Tis most true,
And he beseeched me to entreat your majesties
To hear and see the matter.

CLAUDIUS With all my heart, and it doth much content me
To hear him so inclined.
Good gentlemen, give him a further edge[12],
And drive his purpose on to these delights.

ROSENCRANTZ We shall my lord.

Exeunt Rosencrantz and Guildenstern

Claudius and Polonius prepare to spy on Hamlet to discover if his love for Ophelia has really driven him mad. Claudius's guilty conscience surfaces and reminds him of the murder of King Hamlet.

剧情简介：克劳迭和珀娄涅打算暗中观察哈慕雷，以便搞清楚他是否真的因为对奥菲丽叶的爱而发疯。克劳迭的内疚苏醒，让他想起自己杀了老国王哈慕雷。

Stagecraft 导演技巧

Do Polonius and/or Ophelia overhear? (in pairs or threes)

Every production must decide whether Ophelia and/or Polonius overhear Claudius's lines 28–37.

a Imagine that Ophelia does overhear. One person slowly reads Claudius's lines, pausing frequently. In each pause, the other person, as Ophelia, speaks her thoughts. Change roles and repeat. Then discuss whether you would have Ophelia overhear if you were directing the play. Consider the dramatic implications of each alternative.

b Now add Polonius into the mix. Does he hear, and how does it affect him? Would he acknowledge to Ophelia that he had heard?

c Starting from 'Madam, I wish it may', enact lines 42–55, showing how you would position yourselves as Claudius, Ophelia and Polonius. Compare your interpretation with that of other groups.

1 closely 悄悄
2 Affront 撞上
3 Lawful espials 合法的监视
4 bestow 藏
5 is behaved 行为表现
6 To both your honours 托您二位的福
7 Gracious 陛下
8 this book （一本祈祷书）
9 colour / Your loneliness 掩饰您为何独自一人
10 devotion's visage 专心的样子
11 sugar o'er 裹上糖衣
12 smart 钻心疼
13 plastering art 化妆术
14 painted 粉饰过

1 Catching the conscience of the king

Line 50 reveals that the Ghost's story is true – Claudius is guilty of murder. Claudius's conscience pricks him as he hears Polonius say that a pious (虔诚) appearance often covers evil.

a Design a mask that represents the disguises described in lines 47–9 or lines 51–3. As you read on, think about where masks might be appropriate in other parts of the play. How would masks help or hinder the interpretation in each case?

b Look through the rest of the play for other examples of asides. Divide the instances you find across the class, and work out individually or in pairs how you would present the aside to the audience. Would it be spoken directly to the audience; speaking to oneself, as if reflecting; to another character; or in some other way?

CLAUDIUS Sweet Gertrude, leave us too,
For we have closely[1] sent for Hamlet hither,
That he, as 'twere by accident, may here
Affront[2] Ophelia. Her father and myself,
Lawful espials[3],
Will so bestow[4] ourselves, that seeing unseen,
We may of their encounter frankly judge,
And gather by him, as he is behaved[5],
If't be th'affliction of his love or no
That thus he suffers for.

GERTRUDE I shall obey you.
And for your part Ophelia, I do wish
That your good beauties be the happy cause
Of Hamlet's wildness. So shall I hope your virtues
Will bring him to his wonted way again,
To both your honours[6].

OPHELIA Madam, I wish it may.

[Exit Gertrude with Lords]

POLONIUS Ophelia walk you here. – Gracious[7], so please you,
We will bestow ourselves. – Read on this book[8],
That show of such an exercise may colour
Your loneliness[9]. – We are oft to blame in this:
'Tis too much proved, that with devotion's visage[10],
And pious action, we do sugar o'er[11]
The devil himself.

CLAUDIUS *(Aside)* Oh, 'tis too true.
How smart[12] a lash that speech doth give my conscience!
The harlot's cheek, beautied with plastering art[13],
Is not more ugly to the thing that helps it
Than is my deed to my most painted[14] word.
O heavy burden!

POLONIUS I hear him coming. Let's withdraw, my lord.

Exeunt Claudius and Polonius

Hamlet reflects on death. Is it better to live or die, to endure suffering or to fight against it? The fear of what might happen after death makes us bear with life. Thought prevents us from acting.

剧情简介：哈慕雷思考生死这一问题。活着好还是死了好？忍受苦痛还是奋力抗争？对死后未知世界的恐惧让我们苟且活着。瞻前顾后，人就行动不起来。

1 Advising Hamlet (in pairs)

a Imagine you are a director working with the actor playing Hamlet on his speech opposite. Divide the speech into sections. You might agree or disagree with the following:

- **Line 56** Hamlet wonders whether to commit suicide.
- **Lines 57–60** He wonders whether to endure or fight.
- **Lines 60–4** He looks forward to the sleep of death.
- **Lines 64–8** He is troubled with thoughts of what happens after death.
- **Lines 68–82** He believes that what stops people committing suicide, in spite of all oppressions in this life, is the fear of terrors that await the dead.
- **Lines 83–8** He decides that thinking stops us from acting.

b Choose one or more of the following activities on the soliloquy:

- **An exercise in persuasion** Aim to build up the soliloquy as a developing argument, each speaking in turn one of the sections.
- **Speak it aloud in different ways** Examples could be: as if Hamlet has only suicide in mind; as if Hamlet has only killing Claudius in mind; as a philosophy lecture to a group of students.
- **A dramatic reading for radio** Use sound effects, music, and short phrases from elsewhere in the play to enhance the soliloquy.

c Afterwards, write director's notes on how best to speak the soliloquy on stage. You might also like to watch/listen to two or three different film or radio versions to inform your ideas.

Language in the play 剧中语言

'To be, or not to be': the metaphorical dimension

This is a speech often quoted or cited. Its language is rich, driven by the thought processes explored in the activities above. It says much about some of the themes (existence and death, identity and injustice, the relationship between thought and action); and Hamlet's character (the depth of his conscious reflection on his position, his dilemma).

- Focus on the metaphors that are used in this speech. Map them in thematic clusters, and draw links to show how they relate to each other and to the ideas expressed in the speech. The metaphors could also be sketched in order to understand them visually.

1 slings 石弹
2 arms 武器
3 is heir to 继承下来；躲不掉
4 consummation 完满
5 rub 难点
6 shuffled off this mortal coil 摆脱了这副肉身
7 give us pause 让我们迟疑
8 respect 方面
9 the whips and scorns 鞭笞和嘲讽
10 contumely 侮辱
11 disprized 被人轻贱
12 office 官员
13 the spurns … takes 老实的君子遭受小人的欺辱
14 his quietus make 自我了断
15 bare bodkin 仅一把尖刀
16 fardels 负重
17 bourn = boundary 地界
18 native hue of resolution 决心的自然色（血红色）
19 sicklied o'er 浑身是病
20 of great pitch and moment 规模大且意义重
21 turn awry 出错，出岔子
22 Soft you 您别说话
23 Nymph （希腊、罗马神话中居于山林水泽的）仙女
24 orisons 祈祷

Enter HAMLET

HAMLET To be, or not to be, that is the question –
Whether 'tis nobler in the mind to suffer
The slings[1] and arrows of outrageous fortune,
Or to take arms[2] against a sea of troubles,
And by opposing end them. To die, to sleep –
No more; and by a sleep to say we end
The heart-ache and the thousand natural shocks
That flesh is heir to[3] – 'tis a consummation[4]
Devoutly to be wished. To die, to sleep –
To sleep, perchance to dream. Ay, there's the rub[5],
For in that sleep of death what dreams may come,
When we have shuffled off this mortal coil[6],
Must give us pause[7]. There's the respect[8]
That makes calamity of so long life,
For who would bear the whips and scorns[9] of time,
Th'oppressor's wrong, the proud man's contumely[10],
The pangs of disprized[11] love, the law's delay,
The insolence of office[12], and the spurns
That patient merit of th'unworthy takes[13],
When he himself might his quietus make[14]
With a bare bodkin[15]? Who would fardels[16] bear,
To grunt and sweat under a weary life,
But that the dread of something after death,
The undiscovered country from whose bourn[17]
No traveller returns, puzzles the will,
And makes us rather bear those ills we have
Than fly to others that we know not of?
Thus conscience does make cowards of us all,
And thus the native hue of resolution[18]
Is sicklied o'er[19] with the pale cast of thought,
And enterprises of great pitch and moment[20]
With this regard their currents turn awry[21]
And lose the name of action. Soft you[22] now,
The fair Ophelia. – Nymph[23], in thy orisons[24]
Be all my sins remembered.

OPHELIA Good my lord,
How does your honour for this many a day?

Ophelia attempts to return Hamlet's gifts. Hamlet taunts her, saying that he once loved her, then denying it. He orders her to a nunnery and self-loathingly accuses himself of vices. Ophelia lies about her father.

剧情简介：奥菲丽叶要把礼物还给哈慕雷。哈慕雷羞辱她，说以前爱过她，接着又否认爱过。他命她出家去修道院，又厌恶地数着自己的罪过。奥菲丽叶说到父亲时没说实话。

1 Different stresses = different meanings (in pairs)

Try five different ways of speaking line 96 ('I never gave you aught.'). Each time, heavily stress a different word. Talk together about how each version results in different possible interpretations.

2 Three decisions – no 'right' answers!

a Draw up a list of possible reasons that might explain Hamlet's bitter treatment of Ophelia. Put them in order of 'most likely' to 'least likely'. What is your evidence?

b Does Hamlet urge Ophelia to go to a convent (女修道院) because there she will be safe from (or renounce) the temptations and corruption of the world? Or is Hamlet being sarcastic, and by 'nunnery' means 'brothel'? Which interpretation seems more likely to you, and why? Does Hamlet think she is lying when she says 'At home, my lord'? How might such a belief colour his future actions?

c Beauty will corrupt virtue more easily than virtue can make beautiful people virtuous or pure, asserts Hamlet (lines 111–14). Is he thinking mainly of Ophelia or of Gertrude at this moment? Is his pessimism characteristic? Give evidence for your decisions.

Themes 主题分析

Sin and virtue; surveillance and power; and appearance and reality (in groups)

These three themes are manifest in the dialogue between Hamlet and Ophelia in the script opposite.

a In small groups, take one of these themes and identify lines where it is expressed. How does your theme and its expression here relate to the same theme elsewhere in the play? Present your case to the whole class.

b To bring the three themes together, draw a mind map of the themes and how (and where in the text) they interrelate.

c Identify any further themes in the dialogue between Hamlet and Ophelia, here and up to the end of this scene, and include them in the map.

1 remembrances 礼物，信物
2 wax 变得
3 honest 真心；纯洁
4 discourse to 与……交往
5 commerce 结合
6 inoculate our old stock 嫁接到我们的老树桩上
7 relish of it 保有它的味道
8 indifferent 相当，在某种程度上
9 at my beck 听我招呼

HAMLET I humbly thank you, well, well, well.

OPHELIA My lord, I have remembrances[1] of yours
That I have longèd long to re-deliver.
I pray you now receive them.

HAMLET No, not I,
I never gave you aught.

OPHELIA My honoured lord, you know right well you did,
And with them words of so sweet breath composed
As made the things more rich. Their perfume lost,
Take these again, for to the noble mind
Rich gifts wax[2] poor when givers prove unkind.
There my lord.

HAMLET Ha, ha, are you honest[3]?

OPHELIA My lord?

HAMLET Are you fair?

OPHELIA What means your lordship?

HAMLET That if you be honest and fair, your honesty should admit no discourse to[4] your beauty.

OPHELIA Could beauty, my lord, have better commerce[5] than with honesty?

HAMLET Ay truly, for the power of beauty will sooner transform honesty from what it is to a bawd, than the force of honesty can translate beauty into his likeness. This was sometime a paradox, but now the time gives it proof. I did love you once.

OPHELIA Indeed my lord you made me believe so.

HAMLET You should not have believed me, for virtue cannot so inoculate our old stock[6] but we shall relish of it[7]. I loved you not.

OPHELIA I was the more deceived.

HAMLET Get thee to a nunnery – why wouldst thou be a breeder of sinners? I am myself indifferent[8] honest, but yet I could accuse me of such things, that it were better my mother had not borne me. I am very proud, revengeful, ambitious, with more offences at my beck[9] than I have thoughts to put them in, imagination to give them shape, or time to act them in. What should such fellows as I do crawling between earth and heaven? We are arrant knaves all, believe none of us. Go thy ways to a nunnery. Where's your father?

OPHELIA At home my lord.

HAMLET Let the doors be shut upon him, that he may play the fool nowhere but in's own house. Farewell.

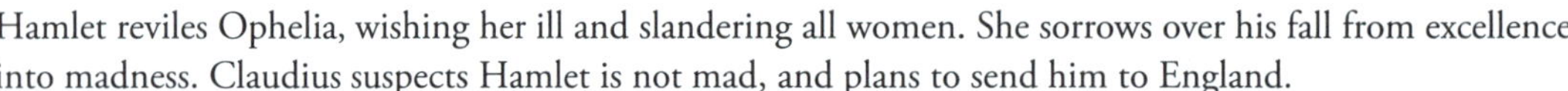

Hamlet reviles Ophelia, wishing her ill and slandering all women. She sorrows over his fall from excellence into madness. Claudius suspects Hamlet is not mad, and plans to send him to England.

剧情简介：哈慕雷辱骂奥菲丽叶，诅咒她，并咒骂所有女人。她心痛哈慕雷这样的人中龙凤变得疯癫痴狂。克劳迭怀疑哈慕雷没有疯，并打算送他去英格兰。

1 Experiencing a tongue-lashing (in large groups)

This activity helps bring out the devastating power of Hamlet's verbal assault on Ophelia.

- One person volunteers to take the part of Ophelia. The others surround her as Hamlet. The 'Hamlets' select short extracts from lines 103–43 (e.g. 'are you honest?' 'Get thee to a nunnery', 'marry a fool'). The Hamlets hurl their insults at Ophelia, who tries to get away from them, saying 'What means your lordship?' It can be a very cruel experience for Ophelia – so don't force anyone to take on the role.

Characters 人物分析

Ophelia and Hamlet

a **How should Ophelia be played?** There is debate about how to play Ophelia: as a meek, passive victim of Hamlet's anger, or as a stronger character. Try lines 144–55 in both ways.

b **Hamlet: Renaissance man – or idealised prince?** In lines 145–8, Ophelia paints a picture of the ideal prince. Hamlet exemplified the ideal qualities of the courtier, soldier and scholar. He was the hope and crowning glory of Denmark. He was the very mirror and model of behaviour and taste, looked up to as an ideal example by everyone.

- To what extent is Hamlet aware of his shortcomings as a person and as a prince? Do you think his inaction is a result of his sense of himself as a perfectionist and 'man of contemplation'? Write a paragraph or two about the complexities of his character as demonstrated here. You might like to compare him to Fortinbras and/or Laertes.

1 dowry 陪嫁，嫁妆
2 chaste 贞洁
3 calumny 诽谤
4 paintings 描眉画脸，涂脂抹粉
5 jig 跳吉格舞（一种快节奏的舞蹈）
6 amble 慢步起舞（以撩人的方式）
7 lisp 打情骂俏
8 nickname God's creatures 给生灵取昵称或外号
9 make your wantonness your ignorance 假装放荡来自你们的天真
10 mo = more
11 expectancy 期望
12 glass 镜子
13 blown 盛放
14 lacked form a little 有些失常
15 on brood 沉思；孵蛋
16 hatch 破壳，孵出
17 disclose 结果
18 for to 为了
19 I have in quick determination 我已迅速下决心
20 tribute 进贡

OPHELIA Oh help him you sweet heavens!

HAMLET If thou dost marry, I'll give thee this plague for thy dowry[1]: be thou as chaste[2] as ice, as pure as snow, thou shalt not escape calumny[3]. Get thee to a nunnery, go. Farewell. Or if thou wilt needs marry, marry a fool, for wise men know well enough what monsters you make of them. To a nunnery go, and quickly too. Farewell.

OPHELIA O heavenly powers, restore him!

HAMLET I have heard of your paintings[4] too, well enough. God hath given you one face and you make yourselves another. You jig[5], you amble[6], and you lisp[7], you nickname God's creatures[8], and make your wantonness your ignorance[9]. Go to, I'll no more on't, it hath made me mad. I say we will have no mo[10] marriages. Those that are married already, all but one shall live, the rest shall keep as they are. To a nunnery, go. *Exit*

OPHELIA
Oh what a noble mind is here o'erthrown!
The courtier's, soldier's, scholar's, eye, tongue, sword,
Th'expectancy[11] and rose of the fair state,
The glass[12] of fashion and the mould of form,
Th'observed of all observers, quite, quite down,
And I of ladies most deject and wretched,
That sucked the honey of his music vows,
Now see that noble and most sovereign reason,
Like sweet bells jangled, out of time and harsh;
That unmatched form and feature of blown[13] youth
Blasted with ecstasy. Oh woe is me
T'have seen what I have seen, see what I see.

Enter KING *and* POLONIUS

CLAUDIUS
Love? His affections do not that way tend;
Nor what he spake, though it lacked form a little[14],
Was not like madness. There's something in his soul
O'er which his melancholy sits on brood[15],
And I do doubt the hatch[16] and the disclose[17]
Will be some danger; which for to[18] prevent,
I have in quick determination[19]
Thus set it down: he shall with speed to England
For the demand of our neglected tribute[20].

Polonius agrees with Claudius's plan to send Hamlet to England. He proposes to spy on Gertrude's meeting with Hamlet. In Scene 2, Hamlet instructs the players on acting style.

剧情简介：珀娄涅赞成克劳迭将哈慕雷派往英格兰的计划，提议暗中观察葛楚德与哈慕雷的会面。在第二场，哈慕雷就表演风格问题指导演员。

1 A loving father? (in small groups)

'How now Ophelia? / You need not tell us what Lord Hamlet said, / We heard it all.' These are the last words spoken by Polonius to his daughter in the play.

- Just how does he speak them? Remember that she has been on the receiving end of a brutal tongue-lashing from Hamlet. Is Polonius sympathetic, officious, uncaring or something else? Experiment with styles to see if you can agree on how he should speak the lines to match his character and the occasion.

2 'must not unwatched go'

Once again the theme of surveillance is given verbal expression in Claudius's final line in the scene.

- Suggest how Ophelia and Polonius react to it, and how they leave the stage.

Write about it 写作练习

A framed scene (in fives)

Act 3 Scene 1 starts and ends with Claudius, who is engineering the surveillance of Hamlet. In the middle of the scene is Hamlet's soliloquy, 'To be or not to be'.

a Act out a symposium (小型讨论会), chaired by a director, TV host or chairperson, who comments on all four characters and reacts to comments from each of the characters. Such enactment will enable an interrogation of the actions and motives of each character.

b Write about this scene from the point of view of one or more of the four main characters in it: Claudius, Hamlet, Polonius and Ophelia. The aim of the writing activity is to try a different genre from the essay: to speak in different voices, both from the point of view of the character, and perhaps also from the view of an actor playing the part. Make close reference to the text to support your views, as you would in a conventional essay.

c When you have explored the action and motivation from the 'inside', through the characters' voices, step back and consider again: why is the scene framed by Claudius?

1 Haply 也许
2 variable objects 不一样的风物
3 something-settled matter 搁在心里的什么事
4 puts … himself 这样就将他与自己的行为方式对立起来
5 commencement 开端
6 fit 合适
7 be round with him 跟他单刀直入
8 trippingly 轻快
9 as lief the town-crier 情愿让镇上的告示员（手里拿着铃铛，一边摇铃，一边宣读告示）
10 saw the air 挥来挥去（好像在用力劈空气）
11 temperance 克制
12 robustious 声嘶力竭
13 periwig-pated 头戴假发的
14 groundlings 凭站票看戏的人
15 are capable of 懂……
16 o'erdoing Termagant 把河东狮演过火了
17 out-Herods Herod 比希律王还希律（希律，前74—前4年，耶稣童年时代犹太地区的统治者，既是了不起的建设者，又是残忍的暴君）

Haply[1] the seas, and countries different,
With variable objects[2], shall expel
This something-settled matter[3] in his heart,
Whereon his brains still beating puts him thus
From fashion of himself[4]. What think you on't?

POLONIUS
It shall do well. But yet do I believe
The origin and commencement[5] of his grief
Sprung from neglected love. How now Ophelia?
You need not tell us what Lord Hamlet said,
We heard it all. My lord, do as you please,
But if you hold it fit[6], after the play,
Let his queen mother all alone entreat him
To show his grief. Let her be round with him[7],
And I'll be placed, so please you, in the ear
Of all their conference. If she find him not,
To England send him; or confine him where
Your wisdom best shall think.

CLAUDIUS
It shall be so.
Madness in great ones must not unwatched go.

Exeunt

Act 3 Scene 2

The Great Hall of Elsinore Castle

Enter HAMLET *and two or three of the* PLAYERS

HAMLET
Speak the speech I pray you as I pronounced it to you, trippingly[8] on the tongue; but if you mouth it as many of our players do, I had as lief the town-crier[9] spoke my lines. Nor do not saw the air[10] too much with your hand thus, but use all gently; for in the very torrent, tempest, and, as I may say, whirlwind of your passion, you must acquire and beget a temperance[11] that may give it smoothness. Oh, it offends me to the soul to hear a robustious[12] periwig-pated[13] fellow tear a passion to totters, to very rags, to split the ears of the groundlings[14], who for the most part are capable of[15] nothing but inexplicable dumb-shows and noise. I would have such a fellow whipped for o'erdoing Termagant[16] – it out-Herods Herod[17]. Pray you avoid it.

Hamlet urges moderation in acting. He defines theatre as the mirror of nature and society. He criticises bad actors and overambitious clowns. Preparations for the play begin.

剧情简介：哈慕雷力主表演要克制含蓄，称戏剧为反映人性和社会的镜子。他批判演技差的演员和野心过大的小丑。这出戏的准备工作开始了。

Themes 主题分析

'some necessary question of the play'

Every play has a set of 'necessary questions' (lines 34–5): central themes or issues. In the 'Themes' boxes in this book, you will have identified a number of themes already. Another 'necessary question' of this play is revenge. But there is an irony in Hamlet's advice, because his delay in taking his revenge can be seen as his own continued refusal to consider that 'necessary question'.

a What are the 'necessary questions' in *Hamlet*? Make a list of what you consider these to be. Compare your list with those of other students and those discussed on pages 242–53. Remember that themes may not always be characterised by single words such as 'revenge' or 'death', but can be more complex; for example, 'the relationship between physicality and the soul'.

- If revenge is a theme, it is also a way of constructing the plot and positioning the characters in relation to the plot/theme.
- One further theme that is emerging in this central part of the play is via the device of the 'play-within-a-play'. Shakespeare uses the device in a number of plays, as we have seen, but he is also fascinated by the 'idea of the play'. Part of the idea seems to be to make the audience conscious of the artifice (奸计) of the action.

b Update your themes mind map from Act 3 Scene 1 in the light of the themes of revenge and its relation to natural and formal justice; and the notion of 'the idea of the play'. How do these themes relate to those identified so far?

c Hold a forum in class in six groups, each of which argues that their theme is the dominant one in the play to date. Use these themes as a starting point:

- revenge and justice
- appearance and reality
- the notion of the play; or 'the play's the thing'
- physicality and the soul, and their relation to identity and existence
- death, sin, love and lust
- honour, duty and the individual in relation to the state.

1 warrant 向……保证（照做）
2 modesty 适度，节制
3 from the purpose 背离宗旨
4 scorn 鄙夷
5 the very … pressure 描绘一个时代的风貌和烙印
6 come tardy off 表演得不到位
7 censure 评判
8 profanely 不敬
9 gait 仪态
10 journeymen 雇工
11 indifferently 马马虎虎，差不多
12 barren 不戴帽子（的普通大众）；外行
13 presently 立马
14 just 正派
15 As … withal 我打过交道的

1 PLAYER I warrant[1] your honour.

HAMLET Be not too tame neither, but let your own discretion be your tutor. Suit the action to the word, the word to the action, with this special observance, that you o'erstep not the modesty[2] of nature. For anything so o'erdone is from the purpose[3] of playing, whose end both at the first and now, was and is, to hold as 'twere the mirror up to nature; to show virtue her own feature, scorn[4] her own image, and the very age and body of the time his form and pressure[5]. Now this overdone, or come tardy off[6], though it makes the unskilful laugh, cannot but make the judicious grieve, the censure[7] of the which one must in your allowance o'erweigh a whole theatre of others. Oh, there be players that I have seen play, and heard others praise and that highly, not to speak it profanely[8], that neither having th'accent of Christians, nor the gait[9] of Christian, pagan, nor man, have so strutted and bellowed that I have thought some of nature's journeymen[10] had made men, and not made them well, they imitated humanity so abominably.

1 PLAYER I hope we have reformed that indifferently[11] with us, sir.

HAMLET Oh reform it altogether. And let those that play your clowns speak no more than is set down for them, for there be of them that will themselves laugh, to set on some quantity of barren[12] spectators to laugh too, though in the meantime some necessary question of the play be then to be considered. That's villainous, and shows a most pitiful ambition in the fool that uses it. Go make you ready.

Exeunt Players

Enter POLONIUS, ROSENCRANTZ *and* GUILDENSTERN

How now my lord, will the king hear this piece of work?

POLONIUS And the queen too, and that presently[13].

HAMLET Bid the players make haste.

Exit Polonius

Will you two help to hasten them?

ROSENCRANTZ Ay my lord.

Exeunt Rosencrantz and Guildenstern

HAMLET What ho, Horatio!

Enter HORATIO

HORATIO Here sweet lord, at your service.

HAMLET Horatio, thou art e'en as just[14] a man
As e'er my conversation coped withal[15].

Hamlet praises Horatio's well-balanced character and criticises obsequious flatterers. He urges Horatio to watch Claudius closely for any guilty reaction during the play.

剧情简介：哈慕雷夸何瑞修的正派品格，批评那些巴结逢迎的小人。他叮嘱何瑞修在看戏时密切观察克劳迭是否有任何心虚的反应。

Language in the play 剧中语言

Vivid images: flattery and fortune (in pairs)

Lines 50–2 describe the sweet-tongued courtier ('candied tongue') who flatters vain people in high positions ('lick absurd pomp'), and bows and scrapes readily ('crook the pregnant … knee') for profit ('thrift'). Lines 57–8 and 60–1 turn Fortune into a woman, buffeting and rewarding human beings, or treating them like a musical instrument ('pipe') on which she can play any tune she pleases ('sound what stop she please').

- Identify other images in Hamlet's speech opposite, and write down the quotations that contain them.
- Discuss the meaning of the images.
- How do these images, and those of sickly sweetness and fortune mentioned above, relate to the themes of the play you have explored so far?

1 Hamlet's speech (in pairs)

Hamlet's speech is not a soliloquy, but simply a speech as part of a conversational exchange with Horatio. Nevertheless, it has the weight of an extended reflection on human nature and fortune. It also includes a set of instructions about the observing of Claudius at the forthcoming play.

a The speech appears to fall into two halves. Can you identify where? Why do you think this is?

b Prepare a performance of the speech by deciding:

- how you will vary the pace throughout
- whether Horatio reacts to the questions posed in the first half (and how)
- which lines have a more public import, and which are intended for Horatio's ears only.

1 advancement 帮忙
2 revenue 财产
3 fawning 巴结逢迎
4 election 选择
5 Sh'ath sealed 她已选定
6 commeddled 融合起来
7 stop 音符
8 circumstance 详情
9 afoot 开场，开演
10 very comment 细致观察
11 occulted 深藏的
12 unkennel 暴露，显露
13 Vulcan's stithy 沃尔坎的铁砧（沃尔坎是罗马神话中的火神，职业是铁匠）
14 rivet to 牢牢盯在
15 censure of his seeming 判断他的神情
16 If a steal aught = If he steal anything 假如他逃避了什么
17 pay the theft 为丢失负责
18 must be idle 得装没事人

HORATIO Oh my dear lord.

HAMLET Nay, do not think I flatter,
For what advancement[1] may I hope from thee,
That no revenue[2] hast but thy good spirits
To feed and clothe thee? Why should the poor be flattered?
No, let the candied tongue lick absurd pomp
And crook the pregnant hinges of the knee
Where thrift may follow fawning[3]. Dost thou hear?
Since my dear soul was mistress of her choice,
And could of men distinguish her election[4],
Sh'ath sealed[5] thee for herself, for thou hast been
As one in suffering all that suffers nothing,
A man that Fortune's buffets and rewards
Hast tane with equal thanks. And blest are those
Whose blood and judgement are so well commeddled[6]
That they are not a pipe for Fortune's finger
To sound what stop[7] she please. Give me that man
That is not passion's slave, and I will wear him
In my heart's core, ay in my heart of heart,
As I do thee. Something too much of this.
There is a play tonight before the king:
One scene of it comes near the circumstance[8]
Which I have told thee of my father's death.
I prithee when thou seest that act afoot[9],
Even with the very comment[10] of thy soul
Observe my uncle. If his occulted[11] guilt
Do not itself unkennel[12] in one speech,
It is a damnèd ghost that we have seen,
And my imaginations are as foul
As Vulcan's stithy[13]. Give him heedful note,
For I mine eyes will rivet to[14] his face,
And after we will both our judgements join
In censure of his seeming[15].

HORATIO Well my lord.
If a steal aught[16] the whilst this play is playing
And scape detecting, I will pay the theft[17].

Sound a flourish

HAMLET They are coming to the play. I must be idle[18].
Get you a place.

Hamlet revels in wordplay. He puns on what Claudius and Polonius say to him, and subjects Ophelia to much sexual innuendo. He comments bitterly on Gertrude's appearance.

剧情简介：哈慕雷兴致勃勃地玩着文字游戏。克劳迭和珀娄涅跟他说的话，他也拿来做双关语。说到奥菲丽叶时，他的话里充满性暗示；说到葛楚德的外表时，他的评价很刻薄。

1 Hamlet's wordplay: insulting and obsessive?

(in fives)

Hamlet has just promised to be 'idle' – perhaps to appear mad. His words now are deliberately disconcerting as he seizes on meanings that neither Claudius nor Polonius nor Ophelia intends. Claudius's line 82 means 'How are you?' but Hamlet interprets 'fares' as meaning 'feeds', so he replies as if Claudius had asked him what he has eaten.

Hamlet mocks Claudius about his earlier promise (that Hamlet should succeed him), suggesting that it is just empty air. He also mocks Polonius, punning on 'Brutus' and 'Capitol' with 'brute' and 'capital'. For Shakespeare's company, this was also a theatrical in-joke, because Shakespeare wrote *Julius Caesar* shortly before *Hamlet*, and the same pair of actors probably played Brutus/Caesar and Hamlet/Polonius.

a Take parts as Hamlet, Claudius, Polonius, Gertrude and Ophelia. Read the script opposite several times. Stress Hamlet's puns. Then, in role, say how you think each character regards Hamlet at this moment.

b There is a theatrical tradition that when Shakespeare's dialogue is set out as opposite (each speech in a single line) the lines are spoken rapidly, with no pauses between speeches. Experiment with that style of delivery, then speak again using pauses. Which style seems more effective dramatically?

c Notice that Hamlet ends by returning to his obsession: his mother's sexuality and marriage to Claudius. Explore ways of speaking lines 111–20 to express Hamlet's intense feelings.

d The dialogue is rapid here, reflecting perhaps Hamlet's excitement as the play is about to begin. Variations in pace are characteristic of productions of *Hamlet*, especially by Hamlet himself. Look through Act 3 Scene 2 and then, on a copy for your Director's Journal, mark it up for variations in pace. Why are some sections better played faster than others?

e Do you think Hamlet's lines to Ophelia are private or are they meant to be heard by the others present? What difference does that make to our understanding of their relationship and Hamlet's motive here? Is the exchange merely light sexual banter between two people who have a history of physical intimacy, or is it intended to humiliate Ophelia by publicly addressing her as if she was a whore?

1 fares = does（又有“进食”之意）

2 chameleon 变色龙

3 capons 阉鸡（育肥后供食用）

4 have nothing with = have nothing to do with

5 i'th'Capitol = in the Capitol 在卡比托利乌山（the Capitol的拉丁文是*Capitolium*，全称是*Mons Capitolinus*，即位于罗马市中心的卡比托利乌山，特指建于山顶的朱庇特神庙及其周边建筑。该庙最早建于公元前509年，公元前83年毁于大火，公元前69年重建。由于国家元老们开会议政的场所元老院［Senate House］也建在山顶，这座山也可被理解为议会或国会山。）

6 Brutus 布鲁图（Marcus Junius Brutus，前85—前42年，古罗马共和国元老院的一名元老，组织并参与了谋杀恺撒）

7 It … calf 野兽布鲁图“屠”杀了首都的头号牛犊（brute与Brutus谐音；capital与Capitol谐音；capital和Capitol同源，都有“头，首；顶”的意思）

8 metal 金属（双关mettle［气概，气度］）

9 country matters 乡野之事（双关cunt）

10 only jig-maker 唯一的搞笑大师

Danish march (trumpets and kettle-drums). Enter KING, QUEEN, POLONIUS, OPHELIA, ROSENCRANTZ, GUILDENSTERN *and other* LORDS *attendant, with his* GUARD *carrying torches*

CLAUDIUS How fares[1] our cousin Hamlet?

HAMLET Excellent i'faith, of the chameleon's[2] dish: I eat the air, promise-crammed. You cannot feed capons[3] so.

CLAUDIUS I have nothing with[4] this answer Hamlet, these words are not mine.

HAMLET No, nor mine now. – My lord, you played once i'th'university, you say.

POLONIUS That did I my lord, and was accounted a good actor.

HAMLET And what did you enact?

POLONIUS I did enact Julius Caesar. I was killed i'th'Capitol[5]. Brutus[6] killed me.

HAMLET It was a brute part of him to kill so capital a calf[7] there. – Be the players ready?

ROSENCRANTZ Ay my lord, they stay upon your patience.

GERTRUDE Come hither my dear Hamlet, sit by me.

HAMLET No good mother, here's metal[8] more attractive.

POLONIUS Oh ho, do you mark that?

HAMLET Lady, shall I lie in your lap?

OPHELIA No my lord.

HAMLET I mean, my head upon your lap?

OPHELIA Ay my lord.

HAMLET Do you think I meant country matters[9]?

OPHELIA I think nothing my lord.

HAMLET That's a fair thought to lie between maids' legs.

OPHELIA What is, my lord?

HAMLET Nothing.

OPHELIA You are merry my lord.

HAMLET Who, I?

OPHELIA Ay my lord.

HAMLET O God, your only jig-maker[10]. What should a man do but be merry? for look you how cheerfully my mother looks, and my father died within's two hours.

OPHELIA Nay, 'tis twice two months my lord.

Hamlet comments bitterly on his mother's hasty second marriage. The dumb-show presents a mirror-image of the murder of Hamlet's father. Hamlet again vents his cynicism on Ophelia.

剧情简介：哈慕雷语气刻薄地评说他母亲的匆忙再婚。哑剧情节影射哈慕雷父亲的被害。哈慕雷又对奥菲丽叶冷嘲热讽。

▲ **Hamlet and the court watch the dumb-show. How would you arrange the onstage audience if you were directing this scene?**

1 sables 紫貂大衣（也有“丧服”之意）
2 a must … on 他得盖个教堂，不然没人记得他了
3 hobby-horse 任人骑的马
4 *Hoboys* = Oboes 双簧管
5 *makes show of protestation* 做发誓状
6 *declines* （往下）放
7 *passionate action* 呼天抢地
8 *mutes* （哑剧）演员
9 *condole* 哀悼
10 *harsh* 抗拒
11 miching mallecho 恶毒阴谋
12 imports 传递出
13 the argument 主旨
14 keep counsel 保守机密
15 naught 讨厌
16 clemency 宽宏
17 posy of a ring 戒指上的箴言

1 The dumb-show (in groups of four or five)

In Elizabethan drama, a dumb-show (mime) often preceded the play, summarising the action ('imports the argument'). In *Hamlet*, this mimed performance prefigures the play-within-a-play to come. The dumb-show presents a sleeping king being murdered by a man who steals both his crown and queen. It is a mirror-image of what Claudius did to his brother.

a Following the stage directions carefully, enact the mime, making it clear that the action is intended to mirror the death of Hamlet's father at the hands of Claudius.

b Discuss how you think Claudius will behave as he sees his own villainy being acted out in front of him. Might he ignore it altogether (as he talks lovingly to Gertrude)? Or does he gradually realise what it means, reacting in one of a variety of ways (with fear, suspicion, anger or in some other way)? Or do you think he might watch it imperturbably, utterly calm? Take turns in acting out different reactions from Claudius, and decide which you find the most convincing given the situation and what you know of Claudius's character.

HAMLET So long? Nay then let the devil wear black, for I'll have a suit of sables[1]. O heavens! die two months ago, and not forgotten yet? Then there's hope a great man's memory may outlive his life half a year, but byrlady a must build churches then, or else shall a suffer not thinking on[2], with the hobby-horse[3], whose epitaph is, 'For O, for O, the hobby-horse is forgot.'

Hoboys[4] play. The dumb-show enters

Enter a KING *and a* QUEEN, *very lovingly, the Queen embracing him. She kneels and makes show of protestation[5] unto him. He takes her up, and declines[6] his head upon her neck. He lies him down upon a bank of flowers. She, seeing him asleep, leaves him. Anon comes in another man, takes off his crown, kisses it, pours poison in the sleeper's ears, and leaves him. The Queen returns, finds the King dead, and makes passionate action[7]. The poisoner, with some two or three mutes[8], comes in again, seeming to condole[9] with her. The dead body is carried away. The poisoner woos the Queen with gifts. She seems harsh[10] awhile, but in the end accepts his love. Exeunt*

OPHELIA What means this my lord?

HAMLET Marry this is miching mallecho[11], it means mischief.

OPHELIA Belike this show imports[12] the argument[13] of the play?

Enter PROLOGUE

HAMLET We shall know by this fellow; the players cannot keep counsel[14], they'll tell all.

OPHELIA Will a tell us what this show meant?

HAMLET Ay, or any show that you'll show him. Be not you ashamed to show, he'll not shame to tell you what it means.

OPHELIA You are naught[15], you are naught. I'll mark the play.

PROLOGUE For us and for our tragedy,
Here stooping to your clemency[16],
We beg your hearing patiently.

HAMLET Is this a prologue, or the posy of a ring[17]?

OPHELIA 'Tis brief my lord.

HAMLET As woman's love.

The Player King speaks of thirty years of loving and holy marriage. The Player Queen expresses worries about his health, but vows not to marry again. He replies that vows are often broken.

剧情简介：剧中国王诉说着三十年的恩爱和神圣婚姻。剧中王后表示担心国王的身体健康，但发誓不会再嫁。国王却回答誓言常常落空。

Stagecraft 导演技巧

The 'masque' (in pairs)

The play-within-a-play takes the form of a 'masque', a popular type of entertainment in aristocratic circles in the Elizabethan period. Such masques were often short plays in highly ornate verse, concerning mythological or legendary figures or, in the case of the play in *Hamlet*, containing references to classical Greek and Roman mythology. They were not dynamic in form, like Shakespeare's own plays, but relatively static. Their energy, therefore, comes from the language and often from costume and setting.

- Research Elizabethan masques, and use the research either to write up a study of masques as background to your emerging writing on *Hamlet*, or to inform your own performance of the masque presented here.

Characters 人物分析

Gertrude's reactions

Much of the attention in Act 3 so far has been on Claudius, but here the players' performance sheds as much light on her as it does on her new husband.

- One person reads the Player Queen's speeches, pausing after each unit of meaning (usually about two or three lines). In each pause, the others, in role, suggest what Gertrude thinks as she hears and sees herself portrayed on stage with her first husband.

1 A difference in style? (in small groups)

Place ten to fifteen lines from the players' speeches (e.g. lines 142–53) alongside roughly the same number of lines of Hamlet's (e.g. Act 2 Scene 2, lines 511–23). Compare the movement of the lines, the flow across line endings, the feeling(s) expressed and the length of the sentences. Discuss the differences you discover.

1 Phoebus' cart 福玻斯的车子；太阳（Phoebus是希腊神话里太阳神Apollo的别名）
2 Neptune's salt wash 尼普顿的咸洪水；大海
3 Tellus' orbèd ground 忒勒斯的地球；大地母亲（Tellus = Tellus Mater或Terra Mater，罗马神话里的大地女神；terra的意思即“大地”）
4 borrowed sheen 借来 / 反射的光
5 Hymen 亥门（希腊神话里的婚姻之神）
6 Unite … bands 用最神圣的纽带结在一起
7 distrust you 放心不下您
8 hold quantity 成正比
9 operant … do 感知力逐渐丧失
10 wormwood 苦蒿，苦艾
11 instances 原因，动机
12 base respects of thrift 钱财这些低层次的考虑

Enter the PLAYER KING *and* QUEEN

PLAYER KING Full thirty times hath Phoebus' cart[1] gone round
Neptune's salt wash[2] and Tellus' orbèd ground[3],
And thirty dozen moons with borrowed sheen[4]
About the world have times twelve thirties been,
Since love our hearts, and Hymen[5] did our hands,
Unite commutual in most sacred bands[6].

PLAYER QUEEN So many journeys may the sun and moon
Make us again count o'er ere love be done.
But woe is me, you are so sick of late,
So far from cheer and from your former state,
That I distrust you[7]. Yet though I distrust,
Discomfort you my lord it nothing must.
For women's fear and love hold quantity[8],
In neither aught, or in extremity.
Now what my love is, proof hath made you know;
And as my love is sized, my fear is so.
[Where love is great, the littlest doubts are fear;
Where little fears grow great, great love grows there.]

PLAYER KING Faith, I must leave thee love, and shortly too:
My operant powers their functions leave to do[9];
And thou shalt live in this fair world behind,
Honoured, beloved; and haply one as kind
For husband shalt thou –

PLAYER QUEEN Oh confound the rest!
Such love must needs be treason in my breast.
In second husband let me be accurst:
None wed the second but who killed the first.

HAMLET That's wormwood[10], wormwood.

PLAYER QUEEN The instances[11] that second marriage move
Are base respects of thrift[12], but none of love.
A second time I kill my husband dead
When second husband kisses me in bed.

PLAYER KING I do believe you think what now you speak,
But what we do determine oft we break.

The Player King argues that strong intentions don't last, because time makes us forget. Changing social conditions change the emotions. But the Player Queen swears she will never remarry.

剧情简介：剧中国王说强烈的意愿不长久，因为时间会让人忘记。社会境况的变化也会让情感发生变化。可是剧中王后发誓永不再嫁。

1 Editing *Hamlet*

Editors as well as directors sometimes cut parts of the play in order to fit their own conception of the unity of action and theme.

a Putting yourself in the role of an editor, and a contemporary of Shakespeare helping him to produce the first printed edition of the play, edit either this speech, this scene, Act 3 or the play as a whole. Working either in electronic format or on paper, cut lines and parts of the play that do not fit in to your conception of it. Make sure the cuts you make do not unduly interrupt the flow of the play.

b Justify your cuts to others, and discuss their feedback on your edited version.

c Perform your version, comparing it to the 'full' version as presented here. Observers of your shortened version might like to review your work, again making comparisons with the full script.

1 validity 效力，功效

2 enactures 兑现

3 slender accident 渺茫的概率

4 not for aye 永远不变

5 flies 离去

6 The poor advanced 穷人发了迹

7 not needs 富有无缺

8 in want 穷困

9 seasons him 将他变成

10 devices still 总是算计 / 盘算

11 anchor's cheer 隐修之人的吃穿（贫穷和孤单）

12 scope 限度

13 blanks the face of joy 令笑颜失色

14 here and hence 此生到来世

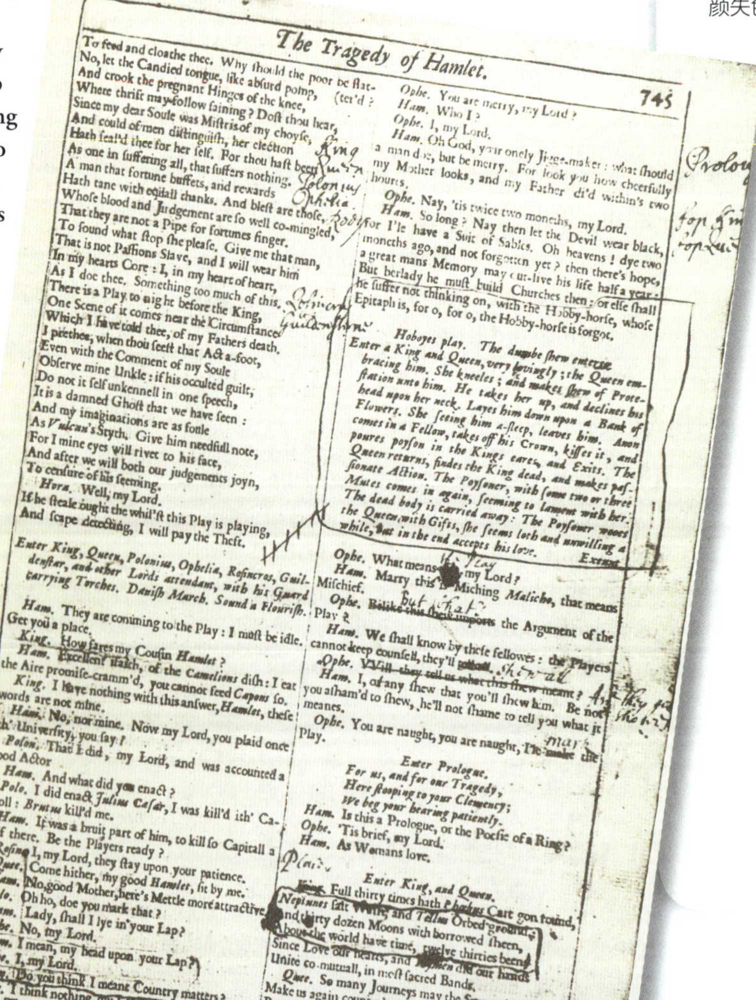

The Tragedy of Hamlet. 745

To feed and cloathe thee. Why ſhould the poor be flat- (ter'd ?
No, let the Candied tongue, like abſurd pomp,
And crook the pregnant Hinges of the knee,
Where thrift may follow faining ? Doſt thou hear,
Since my dear Soule was Miſtris of my choyſe,
And could of men diſtinguiſh, her election
Hath ſeal'd thee for her ſelf. For thou haſt been
As one in ſuffering all, that ſuffers nothing.
A man that fortune buffets, and rewards
Hath tane with eqüall thanks. And bleſt are thoſe,
Whoſe blood and Judgement are ſo well co-mingled,
That they are not a Pipe for fortunes finger.
To ſound what ſtop ſhe pleaſe. Give me that man,
That is not Paſſions Slave, and I will wear him
In my hearts Core : I, in my heart of heart,
As I doe thee. Something too much of this.
There is a Play to night before the King,
One Scene of it comes near the Circumſtance
Which I have told thee, of my Fathers death.
I prethee, when thou ſeeſt that Act a-foot,
Even with the Comment of my Soule
Obſerve mine Unkle : if his occulted guilt,
Do not it ſelf unkennell in one ſpeech,
It is a damned Ghoſt that we have ſeen :
And my imaginations are as foule
As *Vulcan's* Styth. Give him needfull note,
For I mine eyes will rivet to his face,
And after we will both our judgements joyn,
To cenſure of his ſeeming.
Hora. Well, my Lord.
If he ſteale ought the whil'ſt this Play is playing,
And ſcape detecting, I will pay the Theft.

Enter King, Queen, Polonius, Ophelia, Roſincros, Guildenſtar, and other Lords attendant, with his Guard carrying Torches. Daniſh March. Sound a Flouriſh.

Ham. They are comming to the Play : I muſt be idle. Get you a place.
King. How fares my Couſin *Hamlet* ?
Ham. Excellent ifaith, of the *Camelions* diſh : I eat the Aire promiſe-cramm'd, you cannot feed *Capons* ſo.
King. I have nothing with this anſwer, *Hamlet*, theſe words are not mine.
Ham. No, nor mine. Now my Lord, you plaid once ith' Univerſity, you ſay ?
Polon. That I did, my Lord, and was accounted a good Actor
Ham. And what did you enact ?
Polo. I did enact *Julius Caſar*, I was kill'd ith' Capitoll : *Brutus* kill'd me.
Ham. It was a bruit part of him, to kill ſo Capitall a Calf there. Be the Players ready ?
Roſin. I, my Lord, they ſtay upon your patience.
Quee. Come hither, my good *Hamlet*, ſit by me.
Ham. No, good Mother, here's Mettle more attractive.
Polo. Oh ho, doe you mark that ?
Ham. Lady, ſhall I lye in your Lap ?
Ophe. No, my Lord.
Ham. I mean, my head upon your Lap ?
Ophe. I, my Lord.
Ham. Do you think I meant Country matters ?
Ophe. I think nothing, my Lord.

Ophe. You are merry, my Lord ?
Ham. Who I ?
Ophe. I, my Lord.
Ham. Oh God, your onely Jigge-maker : what ſhould a man doe, but be merry. For look you how cheerfully my Mother looks, and my Father di'd within's two houres.
Ophe. Nay, 'tis twice two moneths, my Lord.
Ham. So long ? Nay then let the Devil wear black, for I'le have a Suit of Sables. Oh heavens ! dye two moneths ago, and not forgotten yet ? then there's hope, a great mans Memory may out-live his life half a year : But berlady he muſt build Churches then ; or elſe ſhall he ſuffer not thinking on, with the Hobby-horſe, whoſe Epitaph is, for o, for o, the Hobby-horſe is forgot.

Hoboyes play. The dumbe ſhew enters.
Enter a King and Queen, very lovingly ; the Queen embracing him. She kneeles ; and makes ſhew of Proteſtation unto him. He takes her up, and declines his head upon her neck. Layes him down upon a Bank of Flowers. She ſeeing him a-ſleep, leaves him. Anon comes in a Fellow, takes off his Crown, kiſſes it, and poures poyſon in the Kings eares, and Exits. The Queen returns, findes the King dead, and makes paſſionate Action. The Poyſoner, with ſome two or three Mutes comes in again, ſeeming to lament with her. The dead body is carried away : The Poyſoner wooes the Queen with Gifts, ſhe ſeems loth and unwilling a while, but in the end accepts his love. *Exeunt*

Ophe. What means this, my Lord ?
Ham. Marry this is Miching *Malicho*, that means Miſchief.
Ophe. Belike this ſhew imports the Argument of the Play ?
Ham. We ſhall know by theſe fellowes : the Players cannot keep counſell, they'll tell all.
Ophe. Will they tell us what this ſhew meant ?
Ham. I, or any ſhew that you'll ſhew him. Be not you aſham'd to ſhew, he'll not ſhame to tell you what it meanes.
Ophe. You are naught, you are naught, I'le marke the Play.

Enter Prologue.
For us, and for our Tragedy,
Here ſtooping to your Clemency ;
We beg your hearing patiently.
Ham. Is this a Prologue, or the Poeſie of a Ring ?
Ophe. 'Tis brief, my Lord.
Ham. As Womans love.

Enter King, and Queen.
King. Full thirty times hath *Phœbus* Cart gon round,
Neptunes ſalt Waſh, and *Tellus* Orbed ground,
And thirty dozen Moons with borrowed ſheen,
About the world have time, twelve thirties been,
Since Love our hearts, and *Hymen* did our hands
Unite co-mutuall, in moſt ſacred Bands.
Quee. So many Journeys may the Sun and Moon
Make us again count o're ...

▶ This *Hamlet* prompt book from the seventeenth century has been marked up with notes on staging as well as changes to the script. The page shown here includes line 49 to line 146 of Act 3 Scene 2.

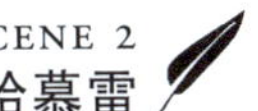

Purpose is but the slave to memory,
Of violent birth but poor validity[1],
Which now like fruit unripe sticks on the tree,
But fall unshaken when they mellow be.
Most necessary 'tis that we forget
To pay ourselves what to ourselves is debt.
What to ourselves in passion we propose,
The passion ending, doth the purpose lose.
The violence of either grief or joy
Their own enactures[2] with themselves destroy.
Where joy most revels, grief doth most lament;
Grief joys, joy grieves, on slender accident[3].
This world is not for aye[4], nor 'tis not strange
That even our loves should with our fortunes change,
For 'tis a question left us yet to prove,
Whether love lead fortune, or else fortune love.
The great man down, you mark his favourite flies[5];
The poor advanced[6] makes friends of enemies,
And hitherto doth love on fortune tend;
For who not needs[7] shall never lack a friend,
And who in want[8] a hollow friend doth try
Directly seasons him[9] his enemy.
But orderly to end where I begun,
Our wills and fates do so contrary run
That our devices still[10] are overthrown;
Our thoughts are ours, their ends none of our own.
So think thou wilt no second husband wed,
But die thy thoughts when thy first lord is dead.

PLAYER QUEEN Nor earth to me give food, nor heaven light,
Sport and repose lock from me day and night,
[To desperation turn my trust and hope,
An anchor's cheer[11] in prison be my scope[12],]
Each opposite that blanks the face of joy[13]
Meet what I would have well, and it destroy;
Both here and hence[14] pursue me lasting strife,
If once a widow, ever I be wife.

HAMLET If she should break it now!

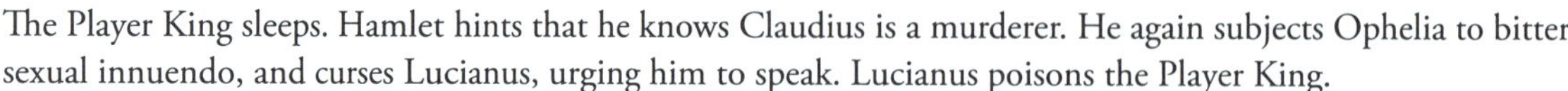

The Player King sleeps. Hamlet hints that he knows Claudius is a murderer. He again subjects Ophelia to bitter sexual innuendo, and curses Lucianus, urging him to speak. Lucianus poisons the Player King.

剧情简介：剧中国王睡去。哈慕雷暗示他知道克劳迭是杀人凶手。他又对奥菲丽叶说起荤话，然后骂鲁先那，催他开口说话。鲁先那给剧中国王下药。

Stagecraft 导演技巧

Gertrude and Lucianus (in pairs)

a Gertrude's judgement on the Player Queen has become a famous saying ('The lady doth protest too much methinks': she is over the top [too rash] with her promises of everlasting love.) Talk together about what lies behind Gertrude's comment. She probably suspects that Hamlet intends her to recognise herself in the Player Queen. So how might she speak line 211?

b Hamlet almost reveals his knowledge of Claudius's guilt when he seizes on the king's 'offence' and turns it into poison, traps and murder. But just how does Hamlet speak lines 214–20? Savagely? Off-handedly? Laughingly? Advise the actor.

c Lucianus speaks the language of melodrama (情节剧，通俗剧). Judging by Hamlet's admonition ('Pox, leave thy damnable faces and begin'), he overacts too. Invent movement, expressions and gestures for lines 231–6.

1 Hamlet's seeming obsession with sex

Hamlet's sexual self seems highly charged, and highly distorted in his engagement with Ophelia in this act as a whole. He chastises her for sexual proclivity (倾向，癖好) ('Get thee to a nunnery'). He seems to want to refer to sexual closeness with her. He frequently makes sexual puns.

a Imagine you are Hamlet's psychiatrist. You can either enact a consultancy with him, where you ask about his seeming obsession with sex and he talks in role, or go straight for a psychiatrist's report on his behaviour. How do you think Hamlet's obsessiveness is related to other aspects of his character?

b How would you play the role of Ophelia in lines 222–30? Coolly and at a polite distance from Hamlet's suggestiveness, or responding to him in kind, with sexual innuendo?

1 fain I would beguile 我很高兴打发……
2 Sleep rock thy brain 你安然入睡吧
3 twain = two
4 offence 犯罪
5 Tropically 打个比方
6 have free souls 心中无鬼
7 galled jade winch 磨痛了（脊背）的马退缩
8 withers 肩颈
9 unwrung 无恙
10 chorus （哑剧）解说员
11 puppets dallying 木偶嬉戏（此处有性暗示）
12 keen 狠，尖酸
13 take off mine edge 让我尽兴
14 Still better and worse 总是时好时坏
15 Pox 遭天花的
16 croaking … revenge 呱呱叫的老鸹叫起来遭报复
17 Confederate season 绝好时机
18 rank 恶心
19 Hecat 赫柯娣（希腊神话中的巫术和魔法女神）
20 usurp 篡夺

PLAYER KING 'Tis deeply sworn. Sweet, leave me here awhile;
My spirits grow dull, and fain I would beguile[1]
The tedious day with sleep.

Sleeps

PLAYER QUEEN Sleep rock thy brain[2],
And never come mischance between us twain[3]. *Exit*

HAMLET Madam, how like you this play?

GERTRUDE The lady doth protest too much methinks.

HAMLET Oh but she'll keep her word.

CLAUDIUS Have you heard the argument? Is there no offence[4] in't?

HAMLET No, no, they do but jest, poison in jest, no offence i'th'world.

CLAUDIUS What do you call the play?

HAMLET The Mousetrap. Marry how? Tropically[5]. This play is the image of a murder done in Vienna. Gonzago is the duke's name, his wife Baptista. You shall see anon. 'Tis a knavish piece of work, but what o' that? Your majesty, and we that have free souls[6], it touches us not. Let the galled jade winch[7], our withers[8] are unwrung[9].

Enter LUCIANUS

This is one Lucianus, nephew to the king.

OPHELIA You are as good as a chorus[10] my lord.

HAMLET I could interpret between you and your love if I could see the puppets dallying[11].

OPHELIA You are keen[12] my lord, you are keen.

HAMLET It would cost you a groaning to take off mine edge[13].

OPHELIA Still better and worse[14].

HAMLET So you mistake your husbands. Begin, murderer. Pox[15], leave thy damnable faces and begin. Come, the croaking raven doth bellow for revenge[16].

LUCIANUS Thoughts black, hands apt, drugs fit, and time agreeing,
Confederate season[17], else no creature seeing.
Thou mixture rank[18], of midnight weeds collected,
With Hecat's[19] ban thrice blasted, thrice infected,
Thy natural magic and dire property
On wholesome life usurp[20] immediately.

Pours the poison in his ears

Claudius abruptly leaves the play, calling for light. Hamlet is delighted that his plot succeeded. He believes the Ghost has told the truth and that Claudius has revealed his guilt.

剧情简介：克劳迭突然离席，命人点灯。哈慕雷很高兴他的计策成功了。他相信鬼魂说的是真话，而克劳迭已经暴露了罪行。

1 Claudius's reaction

Just how does Claudius react to Hamlet's words? Some productions show him terrified and agitated, and his confusion is reflected in his courtiers' behaviour. In other productions, his exit is calm and dignified. Write in your Director's Journal, with reasons, how you would stage lines 237–45.

2 A turning point?

The effect of the play on Claudius is often seen as a turning point for Hamlet. Which one line in the script opposite would you identify as the turning point, if any? When you have read to the end of the play, come back to this point and gauge for yourself whether or not you were right. If so, what is the significance of the turning point?

Themes 主题分析

The fictional and the real (in small groups)

Claudius leaves the play with the telling statement, 'Give me some light. Away!' The fiction presented before him seems to have shocked him into a significant exit from the scene.

a Talk together about any plays, movies or texts that you may have come across that threw you into a reflection on your own life and experience, as if a 'mirror had been held up to nature'?

b Discuss the frames-within-frames that have been presented in the showing of the play: *Hamlet* itself is a fiction, and its lead character is also part of the fiction. Within the fiction, a dumb-show and 'The Mousetrap' have been presented. These have affected Claudius, and, in turn, ourselves as the audience. These frames-within-frames remind the audience of the power of plays and performance, linking to the 'necessary question' discussed on page 112. Update any notes you made then in the light of Claudius's sudden exit.

c How does the theme of fiction and reality link to themes you have already identified, like the relationship of sin to purity of conscience; of death to life; of the public and private; and of appearance and reality?

1 **for's estate** 图他的家产

2 **extant** 现存，存在于世

3 **false fire** 假火情（指编出来的一个故事）

4 **hart ungallèd play** = hart play ungallèd 公鹿安然无恙

5 **Thus runs the world away** = The world runs like this 世界就是这个样子

6 **this … shoes** 这出戏，先生，还有帽子上插满（a forest of）的羽毛，如果我剩下的财富离我而去（turn Turk with me），加上我时髦（razed）皮鞋上的两朵行省（provincial，即法国）蔷薇（哈慕雷想象自己在剧团的装束）

7 **a fellowship** 一个成员

8 **a cry of players** 一个戏班

9 **Half a share** （你能分到）半个股（莎士比亚时代的剧团实行股份制，剧团为股东所有）

10 **Damon** 戴门（希腊传说中的一个人物，愿意为朋友两肋插刀，甚至不惜拿自己的性命冒险）

11 **dismantled was / Of Jove** 被剥夺了乔武（Jove即罗马神话中的主神朱庇特［Jupiter］）

12 **now … pajock** = now a very patchcock rules here 如今一个货真价实身穿百衲衣的公鸡在统治这里（patchcock在口语中读作pajock，patch的意思是“补丁”，小丑穿的花格衣代表用各色补丁或布头做的百衲衣，身穿这种服装的公鸡即指小丑）

13 **recorders** 竖笛

14 **perdy** = by God

15 **vouchsafe** 允许

HAMLET A poisons him i'th'garden for's estate[1]. His name's Gonzago. The story is extant[2], and written in very choice Italian. You shall see anon how the murderer gets the love of Gonzago's wife.

OPHELIA The king rises.

HAMLET What, frighted with false fire[3]?

GERTRUDE How fares my lord?

POLONIUS Give o'er the play.

CLAUDIUS Give me some light. Away!

LORDS Lights, lights, lights!

Exeunt all but Hamlet and Horatio

HAMLET
Why, let the strucken deer go weep,
The hart ungallèd play[4],
For some must watch while some must sleep,
Thus runs the world away[5].

Would not this, sir, and a forest of feathers, if the rest of my fortunes turn Turk with me, with two provincial roses on my razed shoes[6], get me a fellowship[7] in a cry of players[8], sir?

HORATIO Half a share[9].

HAMLET A whole one I.
For thou dost know, O Damon[10] dear,
This realm dismantled was
Of Jove[11] himself, and now reigns here
A very, very – pajock[12].

HORATIO You might have rhymed.

HAMLET O good Horatio, I'll take the ghost's word for a thousand pound. Didst perceive?

HORATIO Very well my lord.

HAMLET Upon the talk of the poisoning?

HORATIO I did very well note him.

Enter ROSENCRANTZ *and* GUILDENSTERN

HAMLET Ah ha! – Come, some music! Come, the recorders[13]!
For if the king like not the comedy,
Why then – belike he likes it not, perdy[14].
Come, some music!

GUILDENSTERN Good my lord, vouchsafe[15] me a word with you.

HAMLET Sir, a whole history.

GUILDENSTERN The king, sir –

HAMLET Ay sir, what of him?

Hamlet disconcerts Guildenstern by deliberately misunderstanding him. He mocks Rosencrantz too, but agrees to visit Gertrude. Hamlet denies any hope of becoming king.

剧情简介：哈慕雷故意曲解吉尔顿斯登，使他难堪 。他嘲弄柔森克阮茨，但同意去见葛楚德。哈慕雷否定了他继位的所有可能。

1 Shaking off old friends (in threes)

Hamlet begins to distance himself from Rosencrantz and Guildenstern as his purpose becomes clearer and he becomes more sure of Claudius's guilt.

- Take parts as Hamlet, Rosencrantz and Guildenstern, and read lines 269–336. Change roles so that everyone has a chance to read Hamlet. Emphasise the words with which Hamlet mocks the two courtiers. Notice particularly that lines 301–2 are the only time in the play that Hamlet uses the royal 'we'. Afterwards, talk together about the ways in which Hamlet clearly shows that their friendship is at an end.

2 Thoughts of kingship

a In line 308, Hamlet says that he lacks 'advancement' (has no ambition – or hope – to rule Denmark). But Rosencrantz assures Hamlet that he will succeed Claudius as king. Hamlet responds (line 311) with a proverb: 'But while the grass grows, the starving horse dies.' Think of one or two reasons why Hamlet makes this reply.

b There are few references in the play to Hamlet's rightful role as prince and successor to the throne of Denmark. Collect those that have been made up to this point (see in Act 1 Scene 2 and Act 1 Scene 5). Add to your list as you read on. When you reach the end of the play, write about the significance of these references.

c When we first meet Hamlet, he seems ill at ease in the Danish court, and more at ease with his friend Horatio and the members of the Watch. His relationship with Ophelia is a complex mix of the personal and public (his position as a prince). As we will see in Act 3 Scene 4, Hamlet's relationship with his mother, the queen, is also a potent mix of the personal and public. Continue to add to your map of the themes in the play, finding quotations to support your claims; or use the present scene as an opportunity to write a few paragraphs on the emerging theme of the personal and the public in *Hamlet*.

1 distempered 发脾气
2 signify 解释
3 purgation 消解
4 discourse 话
5 frame 条理
6 breed 种，类
7 wholesome 头脑正常
8 admiration 惊讶
9 sequel 后续
10 Impart 告诉我
11 trade 事情
12 by these pickers and stealers 向这些小偷和扒手（指双手）发誓
13 musty 发霉；老掉牙

GUILDENSTERN Is in his retirement marvellous distempered[1].

HAMLET With drink sir?

GUILDENSTERN No my lord, rather with choler.

HAMLET Your wisdom should show itself more richer to signify[2] this to his doctor, for, for me to put him to his purgation[3] would perhaps plunge him into far more choler.

GUILDENSTERN Good my lord, put your discourse[4] into some frame[5], and start not so wildly from my affair.

HAMLET I am tame sir, pronounce.

GUILDENSTERN The queen your mother, in most great affliction of spirit, hath sent me to you.

HAMLET You are welcome.

GUILDENSTERN Nay good my lord, this courtesy is not of the right breed[6]. If it shall please you to make me a wholesome[7] answer, I will do your mother's commandment. If not, your pardon and my return shall be the end of my business.

HAMLET Sir, I cannot.

ROSENCRANTZ What, my lord?

HAMLET Make you a wholesome answer; my wit's diseased. But, sir, such answer as I can make, you shall command, or rather, as you say, my mother. Therefore no more, but to the matter. My mother, you say.

ROSENCRANTZ Then thus she says. Your behaviour hath struck her into amazement and admiration[8].

HAMLET O wonderful son that can so stonish a mother! But is there no sequel[9] at the heels of this mother's admiration? Impart[10].

ROSENCRANTZ She desires to speak with you in her closet ere you go to bed.

HAMLET We shall obey, were she ten times our mother. Have you any further trade[11] with us?

ROSENCRANTZ My lord, you once did love me.

HAMLET And do still, by these pickers and stealers[12].

ROSENCRANTZ Good my lord, what is your cause of distemper? You do surely bar the door upon your own liberty if you deny your griefs to your friend.

HAMLET Sir, I lack advancement.

ROSENCRANTZ How can that be, when you have the voice of the king himself for your succession in Denmark?

HAMLET Ay sir, but while the grass grows – the proverb is something musty[13].

Hamlet bitterly accuses Guildenstern of treating him as a mere musical instrument, to be made to say anything at someone else's wish. He demonstrates that process on Polonius.

剧情简介：哈慕雷尖刻地指责吉尔顿斯登拿他当乐器对待，只能发出别人想要的声音。他通过珀娄涅来说明这一点。

Stagecraft 导演技巧

Playing on Polonius (in pairs)

To show Rosencrantz and Guildenstern how they are treating him, Hamlet does the same to Polonius. He plays upon Polonius like a recorder, making him say anything that he, Hamlet, chooses. So Polonius is made to say he sees the imaginary shapes Hamlet suggests are in the clouds.

Some directors and critics challenge this view of Polonius as a silly old man humouring someone he thinks is a lunatic. They argue that Polonius replies in a dignified and tolerant manner, showing that he knows that Hamlet is trying to make fun of him. And certain critics have tried to show that 'camel', 'weasel' and 'whale' are symbols for certain themes of the play.

- One of you plays Polonius while the other takes the role of director and advises the actor on how he should behave in lines 337–47. Swap roles after the actor has read through the lines a few times.

1 withdraw 借一步（说话）

2 recover the wind of me 占我的上风（猎人用占据猎物上风的办法驱赶猎物进入陷阱）

3 toil 陷阱

4 unmannerly 有失分寸，没有礼貌

5 ventages/stops 音孔，按孔

6 discourse 发出

7 mystery 秘密

8 compass 音域

9 organ 笛管

10 fret 按（键、音孔）

11 th'mass 弥撒

12 It … weasel 它的背像黄鼠狼

13 by and by 马上，很快

14 fool … bent 尽最大可能假装傻瓜

Hamlet teases and taunts Polonius. In the production pictured here, he physically intimidates him. Do you think that this side of Hamlet's character is evident in the script?

Enter the PLAYERS *with recorders*

Oh, the recorders. Let me see one. To withdraw[1] with you – Why do you go about to recover the wind of me[2], as if you would drive me into a toil[3]?

GUILDENSTERN O my lord, if my duty be too bold, my love is too unmannerly[4].

HAMLET I do not well understand that. Will you play upon this pipe?

GUILDENSTERN My lord, I cannot.

HAMLET I pray you.

GUILDENSTERN Believe me I cannot.

HAMLET I do beseech you.

GUILDENSTERN I know no touch of it my lord.

HAMLET 'Tis as easy as lying. Govern these ventages[5] with your fingers and thumb, give it breath with your mouth, and it will discourse[6] most eloquent music. Look you, these are the stops[5].

GUILDENSTERN But these cannot I command to any utterance of harmony. I have not the skill.

HAMLET Why look you now how unworthy a thing you make of me. You would play upon me, you would seem to know my stops, you would pluck out the heart of my mystery[7], you would sound me from my lowest note to the top of my compass[8] – and there is much music, excellent voice, in this little organ[9], yet cannot you make it speak. 'Sblood, do you think I am easier to be played on than a pipe? Call me what instrument you will, though you can fret[10] me, you cannot play upon me.

Enter POLONIUS

God bless you sir.

POLONIUS My lord, the queen would speak with you, and presently.

HAMLET Do you see yonder cloud that's almost in shape of a camel?

POLONIUS By th'mass[11], and 'tis like a camel indeed.

HAMLET Methinks it is like a weasel.

POLONIUS It is backed like a weasel[12].

HAMLET Or like a whale?

POLONIUS Very like a whale.

HAMLET Then I will come to my mother by and by[13]. – They fool me to the top of my bent[14]. – I will come by and by.

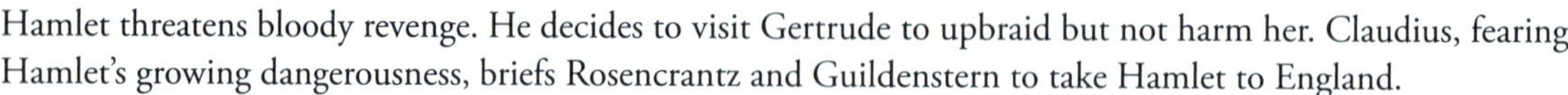

Hamlet threatens bloody revenge. He decides to visit Gertrude to upbraid but not harm her. Claudius, fearing Hamlet's growing dangerousness, briefs Rosencrantz and Guildenstern to take Hamlet to England.

剧情简介：哈慕雷扬言要血腥复仇。他决定去见葛楚德，去斥责但不伤害她。克劳迭担心哈慕雷越来越危险，让柔森克阮茨和吉尔顿斯登把他带往英格兰。

Language in the play 剧中语言

The language of revenge (in pairs)

In lines 349–53, Hamlet uses the language of the traditional revenger in Elizabethan drama (see pp. 245–6). For example, conventional revengers in Elizabethan and Jacobean tragedy – like Hieronimo in *The Spanish Tragedy* and Vindice in *The Revenger's Tragedy* – draw on dark, nightmarish imagery to bolster their causes.

a Talk together about whether you think the lines are out of character with Hamlet's personality, reducing him to a stereotype of traditional revenge tragedy.

b Write ten lines in continuation of lines 349–53. You could refer to Macbeth's speech in Act 3 Scene 2, lines 46–55 (in Cambridge editions), where he invokes darkness, not for revenge, but for murder.

c Look up either Hieronimo's, Vindice's or Macbeth's speeches, and look at them alongside this soliloquy of Hamlet's. Write a critical comparison of their language, concentrating on imagery.

d If you wish to take the idea of revenge tragedy comparisons further, undertake some research on the genre and write a research report on *Hamlet*, discussing the extent to which you think it is a revenge tragedy.

Stagecraft 导演技巧

Work out the scene change (in pairs or threes)

In the Globe Theatre of Shakespeare's time the scenes flowed quickly and smoothly, without long intervals for changing from one to the next. Most modern productions also achieve smooth transitions between scenes.

- Work out how you would stage the change from Scene 2 to Scene 3. Start with Hamlet's soliloquy, deciding how you would have the actor speak it and how you would manage the apparent change of tone at line 353. Might Claudius actually glimpse Hamlet at line 1 of Scene 3?

1 witching time 巫术兴风作浪的时间

2 When churchyards yawn 此时坟墓张开大嘴

3 Contagion 毒气

4 quake 战栗

5 Soft 且住

6 Nero 尼禄（Nero Claudius Caesar，公元37—68年，罗马帝国开国皇帝奥古斯都［Caesar Augustus，前63—公元14年］的玄外孙；2岁时死了父亲；13岁时母亲改嫁，成为罗马帝国第四任皇帝、尼禄的叔父克劳迭［Tiberius Claudius Caesar，前10—前54年］的皇后；克劳迭死后尼禄继位，在宫廷斗争中，先后将自己的养弟［克劳迭的儿子］、皇后和母亲杀死）

7 How … shent 无论我多么狠地骂她

8 seals 落实（行动）

9 commission 委任状

10 The terms of our estate 朕的身份

11 provide 准备妥当

POLONIUS I will say so. *Exit*

HAMLET By and by is easily said. – Leave me, friends.

Exeunt all but Hamlet

'Tis now the very witching time[1] of night,
When churchyards yawn[2], and hell itself breathes out
Contagion[3] to this world. Now could I drink hot blood,
And do such bitter business as the day
Would quake[4] to look on. Soft[5], now to my mother.
O heart, lose not thy nature; let not ever
The soul of Nero[6] enter this firm bosom.
Let me be cruel, not unnatural:
I will speak daggers to her but use none.
My tongue and soul in this be hypocrites,
How in my words somever she be shent[7],
To give them seals[8] never my soul consent. *Exit*

Act 3 Scene 3

The king's private chapel

Enter CLAUDIUS, ROSENCRANTZ *and* GUILDENSTERN

CLAUDIUS I like him not, nor stands it safe with us
To let his madness range. Therefore prepare you:
I your commission[9] will forthwith dispatch,
And he to England shall along with you.
The terms of our estate[10] may not endure
Hazard so near us as doth hourly grow
Out of his brows.

GUILDENSTERN We will ourselves provide[11].
Most holy and religious fear it is
To keep those many many bodies safe
That live and feed upon your majesty.

Rosencrantz contrasts the private individual with a king. Everyone depends upon the ruler: when he dies, everyone suffers. Polonius reports that he will spy on Hamlet and Gertrude.

剧情简介：柔森克阮茨拿百姓个人跟国王对照。大家都依赖统治者：他一死，大家都要受苦。珀娄涅说他会监视哈慕雷和葛楚德。

1 Flattering the king: Rosencrantz

Rosencrantz mouths the flattering belief that all tyrants love to hear: everything and everybody depends on the monarch ('That spirit'). In Tudor England, the ruling class made this the official ideology.

Rosencrantz uses two striking images. First, the king's death ('cess'), like a whirlpool ('gulf'), draws everything in to disaster. The second image is that of a huge ('massy') wheel, with the king at the centre and everybody else firmly attached ('mortised and adjoined'). When the wheel breaks, every tiny part ('annexment') suffers.

a Research the concept of 'the Chain of Being', a harmonious hierarchical society, depending on the king at the top (*The Elizabethan World Picture* by E.M.W. Tillyard is a good place to start). Shakespeare presents the belief clearly in *Troilus and Cressida*, Act 1 Scene 3, lines 77–123. But there, as here, a scheming character (Ulysses) speaks, so you need to be wary of taking this belief to be the truth.

b Advise an actor playing Claudius how to react to Rosencrantz's flattery, especially when he hears the words 'The cess of majesty'. Does Claudius show any signs of guilt at this point?

Characters 人物分析

Polonius – servant and sycophant (谄媚者)

Polonius is going to hide in order to spy on Hamlet and Gertrude. He has a number of motives of his own, as well as carrying out what appears to be an order from Claudius. Think about what you know of Polonius, then carry out the following activities:

a To what degree is Polonius a comic character, and to what degree a mere servant of a 'police state'? Find evidence to support both sides of his character.

b In terms of the relationship between the private and the public, what part does Polonius's suspicion of Hamlet's attitude towards Ophelia play in his actions?

c As well as being pompous, Polonius is a sycophant (a servile and self-serving flatterer). See if you can find other examples of this characteristic in Polonius's speech or actions.

1 single and peculiar 单独个人
2 noyance 伤害
3 weal = welfare 福祉
4 cess （生命的）终止
5 spokes 辐条
6 mortised 榫接
7 annexment 小零件
8 consequence 附件
9 boisterous 地动山摇
10 a general groan 全天下的呻吟
11 Arm you 你们准备好
12 fetters 枷锁
13 process （谈话）过程
14 tax him home 把他痛骂一顿
15 'Tis … mother 最好是他母亲之外的某个人
16 partial 偏心
17 of vantage 从有利位置

ROSENCRANTZ The single and peculiar[1] life is bound
With all the strength and armour of the mind
To keep itself from noyance[2]; but much more
That spirit upon whose weal[3] depends and rests
The lives of many. The cess[4] of majesty
Dies not alone, but like a gulf doth draw
What's near it with it. It is a massy wheel
Fixed on the summit of the highest mount,
To whose huge spokes[5] ten thousand lesser things
Are mortised[6] and adjoined, which when it falls,
Each small annexment[7], petty consequence[8],
Attends the boisterous[9] ruin. Never alone
Did the king sigh, but with a general groan[10].

CLAUDIUS Arm you[11] I pray you to this speedy voyage,
For we will fetters[12] put about this fear
Which now goes too free-footed.

ROSENCRANTZ We will haste us.

Exeunt Rosencrantz and Guildenstern

Enter POLONIUS

POLONIUS My lord, he's going to his mother's closet.
Behind the arras I'll convey myself
To hear the process[13]. I'll warrant she'll tax him home[14],
And as you said, and wisely was it said,
'Tis meet that some more audience than a mother[15],
Since nature makes them partial[16], should o'erhear
The speech of vantage[17]. Fare you well my liege,
I'll call upon you ere you go to bed
And tell you what I know.

CLAUDIUS Thanks, dear my lord.

Exit Polonius

Claudius hopes for divine mercy for his brother's murder. But he knows that pardon is impossible while he retains the fruits of his crime, even though villainy can triumph on Earth. He tries to pray.

剧情简介： 克劳迭希望上天饶恕他的弑兄罪行。但他知道，尽管邪恶能在世间暂时取胜，只要他还保有这罪行带给他的果实，上天是不可能饶恕他的。他想要祈祷。

1 The conscience of the king (in small groups)

Claudius agonises over his dilemma. He has committed murder, yet hopes for heavenly pardon. He knows that although he might escape judgement on Earth, there is no escape for him in heaven, except God's forgiveness through prayer and repentance. He is in too much turmoil to repent, but he calls on angels to help, and kneels to pray.

a Each person speaks a section of the soliloquy, then hands on to the next person. Read around the group in different ways:

- a line at a time
- a sentence at a time
- up to any punctuation mark
- saying only one powerful word from each line.

b Repeat the activity, making your reading sound like a developing argument that Claudius is having with himself. Experiment with whispers, fear, puzzlement and anger. Can you find moments of hope in the soliloquy? After your explorations, decide on the style you prefer and present your version to the class.

2 Heaven and hell: salvation and sin

Research the Christian iconography of heaven and hell as depicted in medieval and Renaissance times. Present your findings to show what bearing Christian morality (which prohibited revenge) has upon the play as a whole. Pages 249–50 will help you. What do they reveal about Hamlet's beliefs and ideology?

Characters 人物分析

Claudius's confession

This is Claudius's most revealing speech in the play and his confession secures the truth of the matter: Claudius did murder his brother, Hamlet's father.

- Look back over Claudius's speeches in the play so far. To prepare for a character study, chart the various sides of his personality and collect quotations to support your depiction. You can present this in note form, or as a collective poster for display.
- What do lines 97–8 at the end of this scene suggest about Claudius?

1 **rank** 发臭
2 **primal eldest curse** 世间最古老的头号诅咒（指《旧约・创世纪》中亚当与夏娃的长子该隐［Cain］因杀死亲弟弟亚伯［Abel］所招致的诅咒）
3 **inclination** 欲望
4 **will** 决心
5 **But … offence** 如若不是直接面对所犯的罪过
6 **forestallèd** 防止
7 **May … th'offence?** 占着罪过带来的好处之人还能得到饶恕吗？
8 **corrupted currents** 腐败的风气
9 **Offence's gilded hand** 穿金戴银的犯罪之人
10 **shove by** 推搡到一边
11 **wicked prize** 用罪恶换来的好处
12 **above** 在天堂
13 **shuffling** 蒙骗
14 **Even … evidence** 只能坦白自己最显而易见的罪行
15 **limèd soul** 被粘住的魂灵（如同鸟被粘鸟胶［birdlime］粘住）
16 **more engaged** 粘得越紧
17 **assay** 试

Oh my offence is rank[1], it smells to heaven;
It hath the primal eldest curse[2] upon't,
A brother's murder. Pray can I not,
Though inclination[3] be as sharp as will[4].
My stronger guilt defeats my strong intent,
And like a man to double business bound,
I stand in pause where I shall first begin,
And both neglect. What if this cursèd hand
Were thicker than itself with brother's blood,
Is there not rain enough in the sweet heavens
To wash it white as snow? Whereto serves mercy
But to confront the visage of offence[5]?
And what's in prayer but this two-fold force,
To be forestallèd[6] ere we come to fall,
Or pardoned being down? Then I'll look up,
My fault is past. But oh, what form of prayer
Can serve my turn? 'Forgive me my foul murder'?
That cannot be, since I am still possessed
Of those effects for which I did the murder,
My crown, mine own ambition, and my queen.
May one be pardoned and retain th'offence?[7]
In the corrupted currents[8] of this world
Offence's gilded hand[9] may shove by[10] justice,
And oft 'tis seen the wicked prize[11] itself
Buys out the law. But 'tis not so above[12];
There is no shuffling[13], there the action lies
In his true nature, and we ourselves compelled
Even to the teeth and forehead of our faults
To give in evidence[14]. What then? What rests?
Try what repentance can. What can it not?
Yet what can it when one cannot repent?
Oh wretched state! Oh bosom black as death!
Oh limèd soul[15] that struggling to be free
Art more engaged[16]! Help, angels! – Make assay[17];
Bow stubborn knees, and heart with strings of steel
Be soft as sinews of the new-born babe.
All may be well.

[*He kneels*]

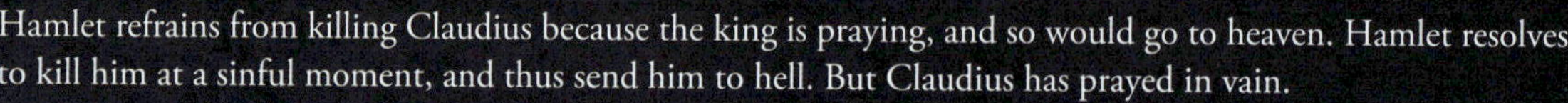

Hamlet refrains from killing Claudius because the king is praying, and so would go to heaven. Hamlet resolves to kill him at a sinful moment, and thus send him to hell. But Claudius has prayed in vain.

剧情简介：克劳迭在祈祷，哈慕雷没有下手杀克劳迭，因为他如果在祈祷时死去就会上天堂。哈慕雷决心在他罪恶之时动手，好送他下地狱。克劳迭的祈祷是没用的。

1 Hamlet delays

Hamlet does not kill Claudius because the king is praying. Hamlet's own father suffers after death because Claudius killed him at a moment when he was unprepared for heaven ('grossly, full of bread' = full of sin, no opportunity to fast), not having confessed his sins. Hamlet therefore decides to wait for a moment when Claudius is committing a sin. Killing Claudius then, when he has no thought of heaven in his mind, will surely send Claudius to hell. Or is Hamlet merely finding another excuse for delay?

a Experiment with dramatic ways of presenting Hamlet's lines. You will find that intercutting Hamlet's lines with Claudius's soliloquy in lines 36–72 can lead to some interesting readings.

b How does the image on this page match your own conception of the moment?

1 pat 立刻

2 would be scanned 得好好考虑

3 hire and salary 雇佣和酬劳；公平交易

4 grossly 冒大不韪

5 broad blown 盛放

6 flush 生机勃勃

7 audit 决算，清算

8 in … thought 照一般认为的那样

9 purging 涤清

10 fit and seasoned 准备得妥妥当当

11 hent 时机，机会

12 At game a-swearing 一边掷骰子一边叫骂时

13 relish of salvation 得享救赎

14 trip him 绊倒他

15 physic 药剂

Enter HAMLET

HAMLET Now might I do it pat[1], now a is a-praying,
And now I'll do't – and so a goes to heaven,
And so am I revenged. That would be scanned[2].
A villain kills my father, and for that,
I his sole son do this same villain send
To heaven.
Why, this is hire and salary[3], not revenge.
A took my father grossly[4], full of bread,
With all his crimes broad blown[5], as flush[6] as May,
And how his audit[7] stands who knows save heaven?
But in our circumstance and course of thought[8]
'Tis heavy with him. And am I then revenged
To take him in the purging[9] of his soul,
When he is fit and seasoned[10] for his passage?
No.
Up sword, and know thou a more horrid hent[11],
When he is drunk asleep, or in his rage,
Or in th'incestuous pleasure of his bed,
At game a-swearing[12], or about some act
That has no relish of salvation[13] in't –
Then trip him[14] that his heels may kick at heaven,
And that his soul may be as damned and black
As hell whereto it goes. My mother stays.
This physic[15] but prolongs thy sickly days. *Exit*

CLAUDIUS My words fly up, my thoughts remain below.
Words without thoughts never to heaven go. *Exit*

Polonius advises Gertrude to speak sharply to her son, and then hides. Hamlet is vehemently critical of Gertrude, making her fear for her life. Her alarm makes Polonius call for help – with fatal results.

剧情简介：珀娄涅建议葛楚德跟哈慕雷把话说得重一些，然后藏了起来。哈慕雷愤慨地批评葛楚德，吓得她以为哈慕雷要杀她。葛楚德的惊吓使得珀娄涅大声呼救——却招来杀身之祸。

Stagecraft 导演技巧

Where is the scene set?

Act 3 Scene 4 is known as 'the closet scene' (a closet was a private room – see also Act 2 Scene 1). But for the last 100 years the stage convention has been to set this scene in Gertrude's bedroom. This heightens the impression of Hamlet having an Oedipus complex (a desire to sleep with his mother – see p. 255). Laurence Olivier's 1948 movie heavily emphasised this Oedipal (恋母情结的) interpretation, as did the 1990 film in which Mel Gibson played Hamlet.

a Imagine you are directing the play and you have a leading Shakespeare scholar as your consultant. They write to you: 'In Shakespeare's day, "closet" meant private room, and the Oedipus complex hadn't been thought of, so I advise you not to bring a bed on stage.' Do you take their advice? Why or why not? Write your reply.

b Compare the two film versions of *Hamlet* mentioned above. Which do you prefer? Why? Which gives the strongest interpretation of the Oedipal theme?

Characters 人物分析

Hamlet's state of mind (in pairs)

What is Hamlet's state of mind as he enters his mother's private room? He has just come from an encounter with Claudius in which he refrained from taking revenge on the king for his father's death. Prior to that, he 'saw off' Rosencrantz and Guildenstern, and Polonius – at least verbally – in the wake of the play-within-a-play.

a Discuss with your partner what you think this rapid sequence of events does for Hamlet's state of mind. In the light of your response to the activity on the Oedipus complex above, what bearing might your interpretation have on your reading of Hamlet's state of mind at this point? Add your thoughts to your collection of notes on Hamlet.

b Write a diary entry for Gertrude in which she reflects on Hamlet's state of mind, his character, and how she sees his development up to this point.

1 A will come straight = He will come straight away
2 lay home 言重
3 pranks have been too broad 行为太出格了
4 your … him 陛下您已经替他遮挡了太多批评
5 with an idle tongue （说话）没大没小
6 rood 十字架
7 I'll … speak 我要找个会说话的人来说你
8 budge 动
9 Dead for a ducat 打赌一个金达克它死定了

Act 3 Scene 4

Gertrude's private room

Enter GERTRUDE *and* POLONIUS

POLONIUS A will come straight[1]. Look you lay home[2] to him.
Tell him his pranks have been too broad[3] to bear with,
And that your grace hath screened and stood between
Much heat and him[4]. I'll silence me e'en here.
Pray you be round with him.

HAMLET (*Within*) Mother, mother, mother!

GERTRUDE I'll warrant you, fear me not. Withdraw, I hear him coming.
[*Polonius hides himself behind the arras*]

Enter HAMLET

HAMLET Now mother, what's the matter?

GERTRUDE Hamlet, thou hast thy father much offended.

HAMLET Mother, you have my father much offended.

GERTRUDE Come, come, you answer with an idle tongue[5].

HAMLET Go, go, you question with a wicked tongue.

GERTRUDE Why, how now Hamlet?

HAMLET What's the matter now?

GERTRUDE Have you forgot me?

HAMLET No by the rood[6], not so.
You are the queen, your husband's brother's wife,
And, would it were not so, you are my mother.

GERTRUDE Nay, then I'll set those to you that can speak[7].

HAMLET Come, come and sit you down, you shall not budge[8].
You go not till I set you up a glass
Where you may see the inmost part of you.

GERTRUDE What wilt thou do? thou wilt not murder me?
Help, help, ho!

POLONIUS (*Behind*) What ho! Help, help, help!

HAMLET (*Draws*) How now, a rat? Dead for a ducat[9], dead.
Kills Polonius

POLONIUS (*Behind*) Oh, I am slain!

Hamlet dismisses the dead Polonius as a meddling fool. He accuses Gertrude of shamefully defiling true love and marriage, making heaven blush with shame.

剧情简介：哈慕雷骂死去的珀娄涅是个爱管闲事的傻子。他指责葛楚德毫无廉耻地玷污了圣洁的真爱和婚姻，令上天都羞愧。

1 Did Gertrude know?

'As kill a king?' echoes Gertrude (line 30). But does she know that Claudius murdered her first husband? On stage, a clue is often given in the way Gertrude behaves as she speaks these four words. Interestingly, there is no further discussion of whether she knows what Claudius did.

- Write notes advising an actor playing Gertrude on how to deliver the line.

2 Did Hamlet know? **(in small groups)**

Hamlet does not seem to know what he is doing, or, rather, he thinks that in thrusting his sword through the arras, he is killing Claudius (line 26). The death of Polonius means little to him. This is the first killing by Hamlet in the play, and appears to come via a moment of hot-headed rashness, or an impulsive sense that the surveillance he is under must stop.

a In your groups, discuss Hamlet's motivation for thrusting his sword through the arras, particularly in the light of his reluctance to avenge his father's death on Claudius in the previous scene.

b How would you stage Polonius's killing? Act out three different mime versions, and decide as a group which one you think works best.

1 thy better 你的上司

2 damnèd custom 万恶的世道

3 brazed 使变硬

4 proof and bulwark against sense 对于感情刀枪不入（字面义：抵御感情的铠甲和堡垒）

5 blurs … modesty 模糊了贞操的优雅和纯真

6 blister 烙印（妓女的额头上打有烙印）

7 dicers 掷骰子的人，赌徒

8 body of contraction 婚姻契约的身体

9 A rhapsody of words 一通胡言乱语

10 glow 脸红

11 solidity and compound mass 坚实广阔的土地

12 tristful visage 阴郁的面容

13 doom 末日审判

14 index 罪孽清单

GERTRUDE Oh me, what hast thou done?
HAMLET Nay I know not, is it the king?
GERTRUDE Oh what a rash and bloody deed is this!
HAMLET A bloody deed? Almost as bad, good mother,
As kill a king and marry with his brother.
GERTRUDE As kill a king?
HAMLET Ay lady, 'twas my word.
[*Lifts up the arras and reveals the body of Polonius*]
Thou wretched, rash, intruding fool, farewell.
I took thee for thy better[1]. Take thy fortune.
Thou find'st to be too busy is some danger. –
Leave wringing of your hands. Peace! Sit you down
And let me wring your heart, for so I shall
If it be made of penetrable stuff,
If damnèd custom[2] have not brazed[3] it so,
That it be proof and bulwark against sense[4].
GERTRUDE What have I done, that thou dar'st wag thy tongue
In noise so rude against me?
HAMLET Such an act
That blurs the grace and blush of modesty[5],
Calls virtue hypocrite, takes off the rose
From the fair forehead of an innocent love
And sets a blister[6] there, makes marriage vows
As false as dicers'[7] oaths. Oh such a deed
As from the body of contraction[8] plucks
The very soul, and sweet religion makes
A rhapsody of words[9]. Heaven's face doth glow[10];
Yea, this solidity and compound mass[11],
With tristful visage[12] as against the doom[13],
Is thought-sick at the act.
GERTRUDE Ay me, what act,
That roars so loud and thunders in the index[14]?

Hamlet compares his father with Claudius: the good man against the bad. He berates Gertrude for not seeing the difference, and deplores her inability to control her sexual desires.

剧情简介： 哈慕雷将自己的父亲跟克劳迭进行对比：一个好人，一个坏人。他痛斥葛楚德看不见二人的区别，谴责她控制不住自己的情欲。

Characters 人物分析

Gertrude's point of view (in pairs)

What does Gertrude feel at being subjected to such a tongue-lashing?

- Write some lines for Gertrude and interject them at key points in Hamlet's verbal attack on her.
- Then perform the speech by Hamlet and the interjections by Gertrude, asking your audience to comment critically on how you have depicted Gertrude.

1 Editing again (in pairs)

Note the lines in square brackets in the script opposite. They suggest that something worse than madness has happened to Gertrude's common sense (and senses). Some argue that these lines were deleted by Shakespeare after the script was first published (see p. 268), perhaps because he thought that they were too complicated. This leaves directors with a decision to make.

a Try the speech in two ways: first, with the bracketed lines included, and then again without them. One of you argues for their inclusion; the other for their exclusion. You might like to bear in mind ideas of sense, language and dramatic impact as you argue your case and make your decision.

b Compare notes with the rest of the class – as a whole, do you think the inclusion of the bracketed lines is justified or not?

2 Gertrude's relationship with Claudius

On page 124, you were asked to consider Hamlet's obsession with sex. In the script opposite, Hamlet questions and challenges his mother on her attitudes towards sex.

a What does Hamlet's attack on Gertrude say about his own attitude and sense of moral propriety? How do you think his diatribe (谴责) to Gertrude relates to the criticism he made of Ophelia?

b Put Hamlet on the psychiatrist's couch once again, to ask him questions about his attitude to his mother. Is his attack on Gertrude a fair one?

c Look at the language in Hamlet's speech opposite. There is something driven, clear and passionate about his words. Is it the 'real' Hamlet coming through, brought to his senses by the killing of Polonius and expressing his concerns directly with his mother? What does the language tell you about him?

1 **counterfeit presentment** 画像
2 **brow** 眉宇
3 **station** 身姿
4 **Mercury** 墨丘利（罗马神话中众神的信使，头戴双翼帽，脚蹬双翅鞋，手握双蛇杖［caduceus］，来去如风）
5 **New-lighted** 刚刚落在
6 **mildewed ear** 霉烂的麦穗
7 **batten** 狼吞虎咽
8 **motion** 移动，动弹（亚里士多德认为一切能自行移动的生物都有感知）
9 **apoplexed** 瘫
10 **madness would not err** 就连疯子也不会犯这种错
11 **Nor … thralled** = Nor sense was never so enthralled to ecstasy 感觉也从不会如此被狂喜奴役
12 **reserved some quantity of choice** 保留一定量的选择余地
13 **serve in such a difference** 用来分辨是与非
14 **cozened you at hoodman-blind** 把您哄得团团转（像戴着眼罩玩捉迷藏）
15 **sans** = without
16 **so mope** 这样糊涂
17 **mutine** = mutiny 叛乱
18 **matron** 老祖母
19 **gives the charge** 发动进攻
20 **panders** 屈服

HAMLET

Look here upon this picture, and on this,
The counterfeit presentment[1] of two brothers.
See what a grace was seated on this brow[2];
Hyperion's curls, the front of Jove himself,
An eye like Mars, to threaten and command;
A station[3] like the herald Mercury[4],
New-lighted[5] on a heaven-kissing hill;
A combination and a form indeed,
Where every god did seem to set his seal
To give the world assurance of a man.
This was your husband. Look you now what follows.
Here is your husband, like a mildewed ear[6]
Blasting his wholesome brother. Have you eyes?
Could you on this fair mountain leave to feed
And batten[7] on this moor? Ha! have you eyes?
You cannot call it love, for at your age
The heyday in the blood is tame, it's humble,
And waits upon the judgement; and what judgement
Would step from this to this? [Sense sure you have,
Else could you not have motion[8], but sure that sense
Is apoplexed[9], for madness would not err[10],
Nor sense to ecstasy was ne'er so thralled[11],
But it reserved some quantity of choice[12]
To serve in such a difference[13].] What devil was't
That thus hath cozened you at hoodman-blind[14]?
[Eyes without feeling, feeling without sight,
Ears without hands or eyes, smelling sans[15] all,
Or but a sickly part of one true sense
Could not so mope[16].]
O shame, where is thy blush? Rebellious hell,
If thou canst mutine[17] in a matron's[18] bones,
To flaming youth let virtue be as wax
And melt in her own fire. Proclaim no shame
When the compulsive ardour gives the charge[19],
Since frost itself as actively doth burn,
And reason panders[20] will.

Hamlet expresses his disgust at Gertrude's sexuality. She pleads with him to stop. He reviles Claudius. The Ghost reminds Hamlet of his mission and urges him to comfort Gertrude. She is amazed by his words.

剧情简介：哈慕雷对葛楚德的情欲表示厌恶。葛楚德求他不要再说了。哈慕雷大骂克劳迭。父亲的鬼魂提醒哈慕雷别忘了自己的任务，并催他安慰葛楚德。葛楚德听到哈慕雷的话很惊讶。

▲ The first published version of *Hamlet* had the stage direction '*Enter the Ghost in his nightgown*'. In the production pictured above, the Ghost was very dominating in his behaviour towards Hamlet, physically demanding his attention as he spoke the lines. Work out how you would stage the Ghost's entry, movement and manner of speech.

1 Why does the Ghost return? (in small groups)

Why does the Ghost return? It appears that Hamlet was getting through to Gertrude ('These words like daggers …').

- Each person in the group suggests several reasons for the Ghost's reappearance at this critical moment. Pool your ideas, arrange them in order of priority, and put them to the class as a whole.
- As a whole class, vote on the reason(s) that you find most convincing.

1 black … tinct 又黑又红的污点，颜色之深，永不会褪（grain既指用红蚧制成的绛红染料，又指染成绛红）

2 rank sweat 油腻床铺的臭汗

3 enseamèd bed 油腻的床铺

4 tithe 十分之一

5 vice 大恶人（又指道德剧中的小丑角色，魔鬼的狗腿子）

6 cutpurse 扒手

7 rule 王位

8 diadem 王冠

9 shreds and patches 褴褛加补丁（小丑的服装）

10 Do … chide = Do you not come to chide your tardy son 您是不是来训斥您迟缓的儿子

11 That … by = Who, lapsed in time and passion, lets go by 他荒废了时间和激情，没有理睬

12 Th'important … command 您要他紧急执行的威严命令

13 whet 磨砺

14 amazement 迷茫

15 Conceit … works = Conceit works strongest in weakest bodies 观念在最柔弱的身体里发挥的作用最强大

16 bend your eye on vacancy 望着虚无缥缈之处

17 th'incorporal 无形

18 Forth … peep = Your spirits wildly peep forth at your eyes 您的精神疯狂地闪现在您的眼光里

GERTRUDE O Hamlet, speak no more.
Thou turn'st my eyes into my very soul,
And there I see such black and grainèd spots
As will not leave their tinct[1].

HAMLET Nay, but to live
In the rank sweat[2] of an enseamèd bed[3],
Stewed in corruption, honeying and making love
Over the nasty sty.

GERTRUDE Oh speak to me no more.
These words like daggers enter in my ears.
No more sweet Hamlet.

HAMLET A murderer and a villain,
A slave that is not twentieth part the tithe[4]
Of your precedent lord, a vice[5] of kings,
A cutpurse[6] of the empire and the rule[7],
That from a shelf the precious diadem[8] stole
And put it in his pocket.

GERTRUDE No more!

Enter GHOST

HAMLET A king of shreds and patches[9] –
Save me and hover o'er me with your wings,
You heavenly guards! – What would your gracious figure?

GERTRUDE Alas he's mad!

HAMLET Do you not come your tardy son to chide[10],
That lapsed in time and passion lets go by[11]
Th'important acting of your dread command[12]? Oh say!

GHOST Do not forget. This visitation
Is but to whet[13] thy almost blunted purpose.
But look, amazement[14] on thy mother sits.
Oh step between her and her fighting soul:
Conceit in weakest bodies strongest works[15].
Speak to her, Hamlet.

HAMLET How is it with you lady?

GERTRUDE Alas, how is't with you,
That you do bend your eye on vacancy[16],
And with th'incorporal[17] air do hold discourse?
Forth at your eyes your spirits wildly peep[18],

Gertrude, unable to see the Ghost, is bewildered by Hamlet's behaviour. Hamlet fears that his impulse to revenge might soften to pity. He says he is not mad, and urges Gertrude to repent.

剧情简介： 葛楚德看不到鬼魂，所以搞不明白哈慕雷的举动。哈慕雷担心自己的复仇决心会被削弱为怜悯。他说自己没有疯，并催葛楚德忏悔。

1 'Do not look upon me' (in threes)

Hamlet says the combination of the Ghost's appearance and plea for justice would make even stones feel pity ('form and cause conjoined … capable'). Hamlet implores the Ghost to turn his gaze away because it weakens his impulse to revenge (lines 126–9).

a Enact lines 115–37, concentrating on facial expression and positioning/movement of the three characters in relation to each other.

b How does Hamlet speak lines 140–56? Does he plead with Gertrude, trying to appeal to her reason with rational argument? Or does he speak vehemently and accusingly, stressing intensely all the words to do with madness and corruption? Experiment with ways of speaking the lines to express Hamlet's emotional state at this point in the play, and adjust Gertrude's reaction accordingly.

Themes 主题分析

Revenge

Look back at your work so far on the theme of revenge. What do the lines opposite add to the development of this theme and its related themes (sexuality, the mother–son relationship)? Add to your map of themes any key quotations you select from the lines opposite, with your own commentary and analysis.

Write about it 写作练习

Why can't Gertrude see the Ghost?

It is clear that Gertrude does not see the Ghost. Write two or three paragraphs about whether you think Gertrude's inability to see the Ghost signifies her moral blindness, and what other possible explanations there might be. Support your writing with quotations.

1 in th'alarm 听到号声
2 bedded 伏贴
3 life in excrements 就像体生之物（毛发、指甲等）有了生命（这些事物通常无知觉）
4 conjoined 加在一起
5 stern effects 激烈行动
6 want true colour 失去其本色（由血变成泪）
7 habit as he lived 生前穿的衣服
8 portal 大门
9 coinage 编造
10 This bodiless … in = Ecstasy is very cunning in this bodiless creation 这种虚无的幻象，人在精神失常时很容易看到
11 temperately 不紧不慢
12 reword 复述
13 gambol 回避（疯子无法复述一段话）
14 unction 油膏
15 trespass 误入歧途
16 but skin and film 只会盖住并遮掩
17 mining 腐蚀
18 compost 肥料
19 ranker 太过茂盛
20 pursy 长满痈疽
21 of vice must pardon beg = must beg vice for pardon
22 curb and woo for leave 屈膝乞求许可

And, as the sleeping soldiers in th'alarm[1],
Your bedded[2] hair, like life in excrements[3],
Start up and stand an end. O gentle son,
Upon the heat and flame of thy distemper
Sprinkle cool patience. Whereon do you look?

HAMLET On him, on him! Look you how pale he glares.
His form and cause conjoined[4], preaching to stones,
Would make them capable. – Do not look upon me,
Lest with this piteous action you convert
My stern effects[5]. Then what I have to do
Will want true colour[6]: tears perchance for blood.

GERTRUDE To whom do you speak this?

HAMLET Do you see nothing there?

GERTRUDE Nothing at all, yet all that is I see.

HAMLET Nor did you nothing hear?

GERTRUDE No, nothing but ourselves.

HAMLET Why, look you there – look how it steals away –
My father in his habit as he lived[7] –
Look where he goes, even now out at the portal[8].

Exit Ghost

GERTRUDE This is the very coinage[9] of your brain.
This bodiless creation ecstasy
Is very cunning in[10].

HAMLET Ecstasy?
My pulse as yours doth temperately[11] keep time,
And makes as healthful music. It is not madness
That I have uttered. Bring me to the test,
And I the matter will reword[12], which madness
Would gambol[13] from. Mother, for love of grace,
Lay not that flattering unction[14] to your soul,
That not your trespass[15] but my madness speaks;
It will but skin and film[16] the ulcerous place,
Whiles rank corruption, mining[17] all within,
Infects unseen. Confess yourself to heaven,
Repent what's past, avoid what is to come,
And do not spread the compost[18] on the weeds
To make them ranker[19]. Forgive me this my virtue,
For in the fatness of these pursy[20] times
Virtue itself of vice must pardon beg[21],
Yea, curb and woo for leave[22] to do him good.

Hamlet pleads with Gertrude not to sleep with Claudius tonight: that abstinence will begin what can become a virtuous habit. He claims to be heaven's agent in killing Polonius.

剧情简介：哈慕雷求葛楚德今晚不要再跟克劳迭同床共眠：这样的禁欲会演变成一种道德习惯。他声称自己杀死珀娄涅是替天行道。

Language in the play 剧中语言

What's the missing word?

No one knows what Shakespeare intended to write in line 170. The word is missing in all the earliest printed editions.

- Which word do you think would fit? Suggestions have been: curb, master, aid, shame, speed, quell, house, lodge and oust. You may come up with some other suggestions.

1 Is Hamlet God's agent? (in pairs)

Traditional revengers do not see themselves as agents for good, but for a type of rough justice in the world. In lines 174–6, Hamlet appears not to blame heaven for the death of Polonius, but rather to see himself as God's agent, as well as being punished for the act of murder.

a Discuss to what extent to which you see Hamlet as a force for good in the play.

b Look back at speeches by Hamlet in this act. How far does this speech reflect the 'true' Hamlet, if we can say there is such a thing? Referring to your developing notes on his character, provide for each of the speeches a few keywords that describe the nature of his character at that point.

c 'heaven hath pleased it so': this phrase suggests that Hamlet feels he is impelled by a force for good, but also that he is in the hands of Fortune, unable to exercise his own will. Do you agree?

d 'I must be cruel only to be kind': this apparent contradiction in terms is central to the notion of revenge and also to the purging of the sickness that Hamlet perceives in Denmark as well as in himself. Find quotations and instances in the play (e.g. Act 1 Scene 3; Act 3 Scene 1) to support this dichotomy of cruelty/kindness (and remember that 'kindness' shares a root with 'kinship').

2 Playing Gertrude

Gertrude has two lines in the script opposite, and speaks little in the face of Hamlet's tirades (批评性的长篇激烈讲话) and persuasions.

- How genuine are Gertrude's responses? Make notes in your Director's Journal as to how an actor should play Gertrude in this scene.

1 cleft my heart in twain 把我的心劈成两半

2 Assume a virtue 装出贞洁的样子

3 That … this = Custom, that monster of evil habits who doth eat all sense, is angel yet in this 习惯，这头吞噬一切良知、让人作起恶来习以为常的怪物，却在另一方面是位天使

4 frock or livery 外衣或制服

5 aptly is put on = is put on aptly 很容易就穿上（指好习惯也容易养成）

6 Refrain 忍耐

7 abstinence 避免房事

8 use … nature 习惯可以磨掉天性加盖的烙印

9 wondrous potency 惊人之力

10 scourge and minister 鞭子和鞭挞者

11 bestow 解决，处理

12 remains behind 还在后头

GERTRUDE Oh Hamlet, thou hast cleft my heart in twain[1].

HAMLET Oh throw away the worser part of it
And live the purer with the other half.
Good night – but go not to my uncle's bed;
Assume a virtue[2] if you have it not.
[That monster custom, who all sense doth eat,
Of habits devil, is angel yet in this[3],
That to the use of actions fair and good
He likewise gives a frock or livery[4]
That aptly is put on[5].] Refrain[6] tonight,
And that shall lend a kind of easiness
To the next abstinence[7], [the next more easy,
For use almost can change the stamp of nature[8],
And either . . . the devil, or throw him out,
With wondrous potency[9].] Once more good night,
And when you are desirous to be blessed,
I'll blessing beg of you. For this same lord,
I do repent; but heaven hath pleased it so,
To punish me with this, and this with me,
That I must be their scourge and minister[10].
I will bestow[11] him, and will answer well
The death I gave him. So again, good night.
I must be cruel only to be kind;
Thus bad begins, and worse remains behind[12].
One word more good lady.

GERTRUDE What shall I do?

Hamlet urges Gertrude not to reveal his pretended madness to Claudius. He threatens her. She promises to keep silent. Hamlet plans to kill Rosencrantz and Guildenstern, who are involved in a plot against him.

剧情简介：哈慕雷极力要求葛楚德别把自己装疯的事透露给克劳迭。他威胁葛楚德，她答应不说。哈慕雷计划杀掉柔森克阮茨和吉尔顿斯登，因为他们卷入了一场谋害自己的阴谋。

1 Irony or sarcasm? (in pairs)

Lines 183–92 are heavily ironic, even sarcastic. Hamlet seems to order Gertrude to reveal his secrets to Claudius. But line 182 makes his intention clear: she is not to do as he commands.

- Advise the actor playing Hamlet on how to speak lines 182–92. Your interpretation of these lines will have a bearing on whether you take Hamlet's 'mad in craft' at face value, or as a poor attempt by Hamlet to explain his actions and inaction.

2 To cut or not to cut?

Lines 203–11, which are in square brackets (see p. 268), suggest that Hamlet already has plans to kill Rosencrantz and Guildenstern. As Act 5 Scene 2 shows, that may not be true.

- Try Hamlet's final speech in two ways: with the bracketed lines and without them. Take it from line 201 to the end of the scene. Which version works best, and why? If you were directing the play, would you cut these lines?

Characters 人物分析

How does Gertrude feel? (in pairs)

Gertrude has been on the receiving end of Hamlet's tirade. What she believes at the end of this scene may not be the same as that which she reports to Claudius at the start of Act 4.

a Before you move on to Act 4, discuss Gertrude's probable feelings and then write a diary entry describing her unspoken thoughts and reactions about Hamlet.

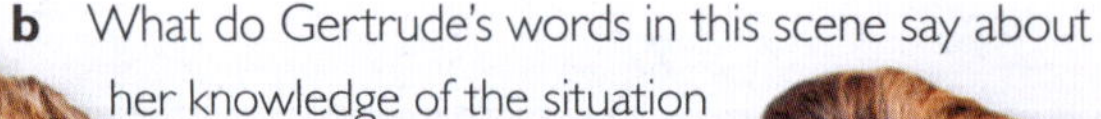

b What do Gertrude's words in this scene say about her knowledge of the situation as a whole?

1 bloat 臃肿
2 Pinch wanton on 肆意捏
3 reechy 肮脏
4 ravel 吐露
5 in craft 伪装
6 paddock/gib 癞蛤蟆 / 公猫（均与巫师关系密切）
7 dear concernings 关系重大的事
8 Unpeg … top 打开房顶鸟笼的门
9 try conclusions 试试什么结果（一个失传的寓言故事：一只猴子摘下房顶的鸟笼，放出里面的鸟，自己钻了进去，试图像鸟那样飞出来，结果掉在地上摔死了）
10 adders fanged 有毒牙的蝰蛇
11 mandate 指令
12 sweep my way 为我扫清道路 / 做好铺垫
13 marshal me to knavery 引导我走进陷阱
14 Hoist with his own petar 被自己埋的炸药炸飞
15 an't = and it
16 delve 下挖
17 crafts 阴谋
18 set me packing 给我上路
19 lug the guts 把这堆肉拖走

HAMLET
Not this by no means that I bid you do:
Let the bloat[1] king tempt you again to bed,
Pinch wanton on[2] your cheek, call you his mouse,
And let him for a pair of reechy[3] kisses,
Or paddling in your neck with his damned fingers,
Make you to ravel[4] all this matter out,
That I essentially am not in madness,
But mad in craft[5]. 'Twere good you let him know,
For who that's but a queen, fair, sober, wise,
Would from a paddock[6], from a bat, a gib[6],
Such dear concernings[7] hide? Who would do so?
No, in despite of sense and secrecy,
Unpeg the basket on the house's top[8],
Let the birds fly, and like the famous ape,
To try conclusions[9], in the basket creep
And break your own neck down.

GERTRUDE
Be thou assured, if words be made of breath,
And breath of life, I have no life to breathe
What thou hast said to me.

HAMLET
I must to England, you know that?

GERTRUDE
Alack,
I had forgot. 'Tis so concluded on.

HAMLET
[There's letters sealed, and my two schoolfellows,
Whom I will trust as I will adders fanged[10],
They bear the mandate[11]. They must sweep my way[12]
And marshal me to knavery[13]. Let it work,
For 'tis the sport to have the engineer
Hoist with his own petar[14], an't[15] shall go hard
But I will delve[16] one yard below their mines
And blow them at the moon. Oh 'tis most sweet
When in one line two crafts[17] directly meet.]
This man shall set me packing[18].
I'll lug the guts[19] into the neighbour room.
Mother, good night. Indeed, this counsellor
Is now most still, most secret, and most grave,
Who was in life a foolish prating knave.
Come sir, to draw toward an end with you.
Good night mother.

Exit Hamlet tugging in Polonius; [*Gertrude remains*]

Looking back at Act 3 第3幕回顾

Activities for groups or individuals

1 Hamlet: speech, action and response

Hamlet appears in each of the four scenes in Act 3. To further your understanding of his relationships with other characters, copy the table below onto a large sheet of paper and then fill it in.

Scene	Hamlet speaks to or about	A typical line or lines	Hamlet's mood and intention
1	Ophelia		
2	The players		
	Horatio		
	Claudius		
	Polonius		
	Gertrude		
	Ophelia		
	Rosencrantz and Guildenstern		
3	Claudius		
4	Gertrude		

2 Developing themes

Throughout the play so far, you have been encouraged to identify themes and map them in relation to each other.

a Review your work to date, and update it to take into account the major themes to have emerged in Act 3: the mother–son relationship; the relationship between appearance and reality as manifested in the play-within-a-play; the 'idea of the play'; Hamlet's madness; attitudes towards sex and their relation to death and honour; and any others that you might identify.

b Do you think that the emphasis of Act 3 has been primarily on the personal or the public?

3 Staging a shortened version of Act 3

Divide into four groups. Each group works out a shortened version of one scene in Act 3 – two or three minutes per scene (Scene 2 is the longest, so you might want to give it a little more time). Present the shortened scenes to the rest of the class in sequence. You can present the scenes in any one of four ways:

- as a mime
- as an edited version of the original Shakespearean language
- in modern English
- in the language or dialect of your choice.

When all four scenes have been shown, discuss as a whole class what has been lost, and what gained, in your compressed version of the act.

4 Hamlet as playwright

Hamlet asks the First Player (Act 2 Scene 2, lines 493–4) to 'study a speech of some dozen or sixteen lines' he would write specially for *The Murder of Gonzago*. No one knows for certain if those lines were actually spoken in Scene 2.

- Try to identify (giving reasons) which lines were those written by Hamlet. If you think none of the lines were his, write a dozen lines that you think he would have put in.

5 The plot thickens …

… but does it advance? Look back at the plot of the play so far, and write 100-word written summaries of each act. How does Act 3 move the story forward? If you haven't read the whole play, predict three possible ways in which the story might develop from this point onwards. Extend one of these into a longer written piece: an alternative ending to *Hamlet*, in play or prose form.

Find lines from Act 3 Scene 4 that could make suitable captions for these pictures of Hamlet and Gertrude. In pairs or small groups, discuss what you think the director of each production might have had in mind about the mother-son relationship. Which production comes closest to your own imagined version, and why?

Gertrude tells Claudius that Hamlet has killed Polonius. Claudius fears that he himself might have been the victim and that he will be blamed for Polonius's death. He lies about his love for Hamlet.

剧情简介：葛楚德告诉克劳迭哈慕雷杀了珀娄涅。克劳迭害怕哈慕雷原本是冲着自己来的，人们会把珀娄涅的死归罪到他头上。他谎称自己疼爱哈慕雷。

Stagecraft 导演技巧

Director's decisions

At the end of Act 3 the stage direction '*Gertrude remains*' is in square brackets because it does not appear in one of the early editions of the play (see p. 268).

a As director, advise Gertrude whether she should remain on stage until the arrival of Claudius, Rosencrantz and Guildenstern, or whether she should exit and re-enter with Claudius. Which is the more dramatically convincing?

b Decide if you would cut line 4 opposite, 'Bestow this place on us a little while' – why bring on Rosencrantz and Guildenstern only to dismiss them? You can discuss this and/or record your notes in your Director's Journal.

1 A chorus of disapproval (whole class)

This short scene is the only time that Claudius and Gertrude are alone together. Rather than take the roles of Rosencrantz and Guildenstern, who are complicit in the surveillance of Hamlet and unreliable in terms of speaking the truth, set up the following:

- Claudius and Gertrude speak the lines in the script opposite. As they rehearse for this reading, they can decide what state Gertrude is in and how she will speak her lines, and how self-interested Claudius is.
- The rest of the class, in groups, prepares accusations to put to Claudius and Gertrude at lines 5, 12 and 23. These challenges are prepared on the basis of the play so far, and might include: reflections of Claudius's and Gertrude's conscience; genuine accusations that they do not see or speak the truth; comments and questions on their own relationship as king and queen, and as lovers.
- To frame the performance, Claudius and Gertrude stand or sit at the centre of a circle. The rest of the class surrounds them and makes the challenges and comments.
- Afterwards, Claudius and Gertrude can speak in role describing how it felt to be challenged, and whether they wish to defend their speeches and actions. Is the rest of the class satisfied with the two characters' answers?

1 matter 隐情
2 profound heaves 长叹
3 translate 解释
4 Bestow this place on us 将此处让给我们
5 contend 相争
6 lawless fit 控制不住的癫狂
7 brainish apprehension 胡思乱想
8 laid to us 怪罪到朕身上
9 providence 远见
10 kept short, restrained 严加管束（short指把狗带收短）
11 out of haunt 避开公共场所
12 fit 妥当
13 divulging 泄露
14 pith 精髓
15 apart = away
16 ore … pure 夹杂在贱金属矿中的贵金属（尤其黄金）

Act 4 Scene 1

Gertrude's private room

Enter CLAUDIUS *with* ROSENCRANTZ *and* GUILDENSTERN

CLAUDIUS There's matter[1] in these sighs, these profound heaves[2].
You must translate[3], 'tis fit we understand them.
Where is your son?

GERTRUDE [Bestow this place on us[4] a little while.]
[*Exeunt Rosencrantz and Guildenstern*]
Ah mine own lord, what have I seen tonight!

CLAUDIUS What, Gertrude? How does Hamlet?

GERTRUDE Mad as the sea and wind, when both contend[5]
Which is the mightier. In his lawless fit[6],
Behind the arras hearing something stir,
Whips out his rapier, cries 'A rat, a rat!',
And in this brainish apprehension[7] kills
The unseen good old man.

CLAUDIUS Oh heavy deed!
It had been so with us had we been there.
His liberty is full of threats to all,
To you yourself, to us, to everyone.
Alas, how shall this bloody deed be answered?
It will be laid to us[8], whose providence[9]
Should have kept short, restrained[10], and out of haunt[11],
This mad young man. But so much was our love,
We would not understand what was most fit[12],
But like the owner of a foul disease,
To keep it from divulging[13], let it feed
Even on the pith[14] of life. Where is he gone?

GERTRUDE To draw apart[15] the body he hath killed,
O'er whom his very madness, like some ore
Among a mineral of metals base,
Shows itself pure[16]; a weeps for what is done.

Claudius decides to send Hamlet away from Denmark. He orders Rosencrantz and Guildenstern to join with others to find Polonius's body and take it to the chapel. He hopes he can avoid slanderous accusations.

剧情简介：克劳迭决定把哈慕雷送出丹麦。他命柔森克阮茨和吉尔顿斯登跟其他人同去寻找珀娄涅的遗体，然后送到教堂。他希望自己能避免人们的诋毁中伤。

Write about it 写作练习

Character and relationships

Neither Gertrude nor Claudius offers comforting words to the other in Scene 1. Lines 28–45 afford dramatic opportunities for actors to express character and relationships.

Write a paragraph on each of the following, saying how you would use each to give the audience insight into character and relationships:

- Claudius three times gives an order to Gertrude: 'come away', 'Come', 'come away'. How might she respond each time?
- Gertrude says nothing during Claudius's final speech. What is she doing throughout?
- Claudius makes a decision to exile Hamlet, but to whom might he speak lines 29–32?
- In lines 41–4, Claudius seems concerned that slanders and rumours must not damage his reputation. He proposes to brief his 'wisest friends' to prevent it happening. What does that suggest about his character?

1 Ambiguous lines (in pairs)

Lines 40–4 present an interesting problem for a director. The incomplete line 40 (thought to be lost) and the bracketed lines 41–4 (thought to be a deletion by Shakespeare) leave a decision for every director (see p. 268). The incomplete line is the lesser of the problems. The meaning is clear without any further text, from 'Come Gertrude' to 'And what's untimely done'. But what about the bracketed lines?

a Explore the meaning of the bracketed lines by reading them through and then drawing what you think is being described.

b Read the passage from 'Come Gertrude' to the end of the scene without the excised passage. Then read it again with the passage left in.

c Discuss with your partner, and then in the class a whole, what is lost and gained through the inclusion or exclusion of the lines.

d Record in your Director's Journal how you would direct the last twelve lines of the scene.

1 countenance 面对；接受
2 join … aid 你们找些帮手
3 speak fair 好言哄劝
4 wisest friends 最有智慧的朋友（克劳迭的智囊）
5 what's untimely done 发生了什么意外
6 o'er the world's diameter 传遍世界
7 As … blank 像大炮对准靶子
8 miss our name 不伤害朕的名声
9 woundless 刀枪不入
10 Compounded it with dust 将它送归泥土
11 kin 同宗

CLAUDIUS Oh Gertrude, come away!
The sun no sooner shall the mountains touch
But we will ship him hence, and this vile deed
We must with all our majesty and skill
Both countenance[1] and excuse. Ho, Guildenstern!

Enter Rosencrantz and Guildenstern

Friends both, go join you with some further aid[2].
Hamlet in madness hath Polonius slain,
And from his mother's closet hath he dragged him.
Go seek him out, speak fair[3], and bring the body
Into the chapel. I pray you haste in this.

Exeunt Rosencrantz and Guildenstern

Come Gertrude, we'll call up our wisest friends[4]
And let them know both what we mean to do
And what's untimely done[5]. . . . . . .
[Whose whisper o'er the world's diameter[6],
As level as the cannon to his blank[7],
Transports his poisoned shot, may miss our name[8]
And hit the woundless[9] air.] Oh come away,
My soul is full of discord and dismay.

Exeunt

Act 4 Scene 2

A corridor in the castle

Enter HAMLET

HAMLET Safely stowed.

GENTLEMEN (*Within*) Hamlet! Lord Hamlet!

HAMLET But soft, what noise? Who calls on Hamlet? Oh here they come.

Enter ROSENCRANTZ *and* GUILDENSTERN

ROSENCRANTZ What have you done my lord with the dead body?

HAMLET Compounded it with dust[10] whereto 'tis kin[11].

Hamlet's replies bewilder Rosencrantz and Guildenstern. He does not reveal where Polonius's body is hidden. Claudius feels he cannot punish Hamlet severely because the prince is popular in Denmark.

剧情简介：哈慕雷的回话令柔森克阮茨和吉尔顿斯登摸不着头脑。他不透露自己把珀娄涅藏在何处。克劳迭觉得自己不可严厉处罚哈慕雷，因为这位王子很受丹麦百姓拥戴。

1 Act it out – Hamlet's evasiveness (in threes)

The very short Scene 2 offers excellent opportunities for acting. Hamlet has been presented in many different ways (washing a bloodstained shirt, waking from sleep and so on), and his mocking language invites the actor to all kinds of stage business.

Take parts and act the scene to maximise dramatic effect. It will help your performance if you think about the different strategies Hamlet uses in lines 9–27 to avoid telling Rosencrantz and Guildenstern where Polonius's body is hidden:

- He insults Rosencrantz with the 'sponge' and 'ape' comparisons.
- He brands Rosencrantz as too dull to recognise satire.
- He speaks an enigmatic riddle, 'The body is with the king …'.
- 'Hide fox, and all after!' In some productions, Hamlet runs away as he speaks line 27, chased by the two courtiers. But consider other possibilities and work out how the three characters leave the stage. Discuss how the hunting image might be applicable to the play as a whole.

1 **be demanded of a sponge** 被一块海绵问话

2 **replication** 回答

3 **countenance** 恩宠

4 **authorities** 君威

5 **like … jaw** 像猿猴把食物存在腮帮子里

6 **gleaned** 捡拾，收罗

7 **knavish** 奸诈

8 **Hide fox** 藏狐狸（一种游戏）

9 **put … him** 对他施以严刑峻法

10 **distracted multitude** 无主见的老百姓

11 **like … eyes** 不喜欢理性判断，仅喜欢眼睛所见

Characters 人物分析

Hamlet's mercurial (变幻莫测) nature

We have seen different aspects of Hamlet's character so far in the play: his impulsiveness, his procrastination, his melancholy, his gravity.

a What further aspect is reflected in the lines opposite, as Hamlet mocks Rosencrantz and Guildenstern and refuses to reveal where the body is? Remember that, according to the time in the play, he has just killed a man.

b Using your own new terms to describe his state of mind, build up a longer list to explore the different sides to Hamlet's character.

c Putting together all the aspects of his character, write a psychiatrist's or counsellor's report on Hamlet.

ROSENCRANTZ Tell us where 'tis, that we may take it thence and bear it to the chapel.

HAMLET Do not believe it.

ROSENCRANTZ Believe what?

HAMLET That I can keep your counsel and not mine own. Besides, to be demanded of a sponge[1], what replication[2] should be made by the son of a king?

ROSENCRANTZ Take you me for a sponge my lord?

HAMLET Ay sir, that soaks up the king's countenance[3], his rewards, his authorities[4]. But such officers do the king best service in the end: he keeps them like an ape in the corner of his jaw[5], first mouthed to be last swallowed. When he needs what you have gleaned[6], it is but squeezing you, and, sponge, you shall be dry again.

ROSENCRANTZ I understand you not my lord.

HAMLET I am glad of it, a knavish[7] speech sleeps in a foolish ear.

ROSENCRANTZ My lord, you must tell us where the body is, and go with us to the king.

HAMLET The body is with the king, but the king is not with the body. The king is a thing –

GUILDENSTERN A thing my lord?

HAMLET Of nothing. Bring me to him. Hide fox[8], and all after!

Exeunt

Act 4 Scene 3

A state room

Enter CLAUDIUS, *and two or three* ATTENDANTS

CLAUDIUS
I have sent to seek him, and to find the body.
How dangerous is it that this man goes loose,
Yet must not we put the strong law on him[9];
He's loved of the distracted multitude[10],
Who like not in their judgement, but their eyes[11];

Claudius reflects that he must use desperate methods. Hamlet is brought in. He taunts Claudius with images of the corruption of dead bodies, then reveals where Polonius's body is hidden.

剧情简介：克劳迭认定他必须使用铤而走险的招数。哈慕雷被带了进来，他用死尸的腐烂做比喻，讽刺克劳迭， 然后说出珀娄涅的尸体藏在何处。

1 'through the guts of a beggar' (in pairs)

In taunting Claudius, Hamlet stresses corruption ('worms') and the levelling nature of death: a king may go 'a progress' (a royal journey) through the guts of a beggar. Hamlet also puns on the Diet ('convocation') of Worms (a town in Germany), where in 1521 the Protestant Martin Luther defended his anti-papal (反教皇) views. The worms are 'politic' because they infiltrate (渗入) the body in the same way that Polonius had insinuated his way into state affairs and Hamlet's privacy.

- Take parts and speak lines 16–49. Hamlet should be mockingly ironic and Claudius should struggle to control his anger.

▼ Does this representation of Hamlet align with the reading of the lines suggested in Activity 1 above?

1 th'offender's scourge is weighed 权衡的是对案犯的惩罚

2 bear all smooth and even 一切都办得顺当又公道

3 must seem / Deliberate pause 一定会显出是故意安排的

4 Diseases … relieved = Diseases grown desperate are relieved by desperate appliance 已到最后关头的病要用铤而走险的药来治

5 Without = Outside

6 pleasure 旨意，吩咐

7 convocation 聚集

8 variable service 不同菜品

9 go a progress 出行；巡幸

10 i'th'other place 去另外那个地方（即地狱）

11 nose 嗅到（不到一个月死尸就会腐烂发臭）

And where 'tis so, th'offender's scourge is weighed[1],
But never the offence. To bear all smooth and even[2],
This sudden sending him away must seem
Deliberate pause[3]. Diseases desperate grown
By desperate appliance are relieved[4],
Or not at all.

Enter ROSENCRANTZ

How now, what hath befallen?

ROSENCRANTZ Where the dead body is bestowed, my lord,
We cannot get from him.

CLAUDIUS But where is he?

ROSENCRANTZ Without[5], my lord, guarded, to know your pleasure[6].

CLAUDIUS Bring him before us.

ROSENCRANTZ Ho! bring in my lord.

Enter HAMLET *and* GUILDENSTERN

CLAUDIUS Now Hamlet, where's Polonius?

HAMLET At supper.

CLAUDIUS At supper? Where?

HAMLET Not where he eats, but where a is eaten. A certain convocation[7] of politic worms are e'en at him. Your worm is your only emperor for diet: we fat all creatures else to fat us, and we fat ourselves for maggots. Your fat king and your lean beggar is but variable service[8], two dishes, but to one table; that's the end.

CLAUDIUS Alas, alas.

HAMLET A man may fish with the worm that hath eat of a king, and eat of the fish that hath fed of that worm.

CLAUDIUS What dost thou mean by this?

HAMLET Nothing but to show you how a king may go a progress[9] through the guts of a beggar.

CLAUDIUS Where is Polonius?

HAMLET In heaven, send thither to see. If your messenger find him not there, seek him i'th'other place[10] yourself. But if indeed you find him not within this month, you shall nose[11] him as you go up the stairs into the lobby.

CLAUDIUS Go seek him there.

HAMLET A will stay till you come.

[*Exeunt Attendants*]

Claudius tells Hamlet a ship and attendants wait to take him to England. Hamlet bids Claudius an ironic farewell. Claudius reveals he has written letters ordering Hamlet's immediate execution in England.

剧情简介：克劳迭告诉哈慕雷，已备好一艘船和一行随从送他去英格兰。哈慕雷用反讽的口吻跟克劳迭告别。克劳迭透露说他已修书一封，命人一到英格兰便将哈慕雷处决。

1 Two crucial moments (in pairs)

a **Hamlet's suspicions** Who is the 'cherub'? At line 44, Claudius replies to Hamlet's positive acceptance of exile to England with: 'So is it if thou knew'st our purposes.' The words have sinister implications: Claudius is planning to have Hamlet killed. Hamlet responds: 'I see a cherub that sees them' (line 45). At whom (or what) does Hamlet look when he says 'cherub', and why does he use that word? Discuss reasons for your decisions, and say whether you think Hamlet suspects that Claudius intends to have him killed.

b **Hamlet's obsession** 'man and wife is one flesh'. Throughout the play, Hamlet has been obsessed by his mother's sexuality. His lines 48–9 reveal that fixation. But how does he speak the lines (with loathing, humour, calm logic, or with some other feeling or combination of feelings)? Advise the actor, giving reasons.

2 'Do it England'

The first performances of *Hamlet* would have been in London, so the resonance of the passage about England would have had a special significance for the English audience. England (or possibly the King of England) would have been seen at the time as an ally of Denmark, and a country that owes Claudius a favour.

a Divide the class into two groups: those who favour the death of Hamlet, and those who do not. Have Claudius stand in the middle of the two groups and deliver his lines. They consist of three sentences. At the end of each sentence, each group expresses its thoughts about what Claudius is saying. This can be done chorally, and/or with individual voices.

b Afterwards, sit together and reflect: how did Claudius feel about the response of the choral groups? And how did they, in turn feel about his resolution to kill Hamlet?

c As choruses again, change your allegiance to 'England' and 'Denmark', or two countries you know that are both closely allied but potentially competitive. How does this shift affect your understanding of what the London audience might have felt?

1 do tender 确实重视
2 With fiery quickness 火速
3 bark 船
4 at help 助力；顺风
5 Th'associates tend 随从在候着了
6 bent 就绪
7 cherub 小天使
8 one flesh 一体（哈慕雷在引用《旧约•创世纪》里的这句话为自己辩解：Therefore shall a man leave his father and his mother, and shall cleave unto his wife: and they shall be one flesh.）
9 at foot 寸步不离
10 tempt 鼓励
11 else leans on 否则会关系到
12 England … aught 英格兰王，你如果把我对你的友爱看得一钱不值
13 cicatrice 伤疤
14 Danish sword 与丹麦的交锋
15 free … us 自愿向朕表示臣服
16 mayst … process 不得将朕的谕旨晾在一边
17 imports at full 详细载明
18 congruing to that effect 表达这一意思
19 hectic 热病
20 haps 命运

CLAUDIUS Hamlet, this deed, for thine especial safety,
Which we do tender[1], as we dearly grieve
For that which thou hast done, must send thee hence
With fiery quickness[2]. Therefore prepare thyself.
The bark[3] is ready and the wind at help[4],
Th'associates tend[5], and everything is bent[6]
For England.

HAMLET For England?

CLAUDIUS Ay Hamlet.

HAMLET Good.

CLAUDIUS So is it if thou knew'st our purposes.

HAMLET I see a cherub[7] that sees them. But come, for England! Farewell dear mother.

CLAUDIUS Thy loving father, Hamlet.

HAMLET My mother. Father and mother is man and wife, man and wife is one flesh[8], and so, my mother. Come, for England. *Exit*

CLAUDIUS Follow him at foot[9], tempt[10] him with speed aboard.
Delay it not, I'll have him hence tonight.
Away, for everything is sealed and done
That else leans on[11] th'affair. Pray you make haste.
[*Exeunt Rosencrantz and Guildenstern*]
And England, if my love thou hold'st at aught[12],
As my great power thereof may give thee sense,
Since yet thy cicatrice[13] looks raw and red
After the Danish sword[14], and thy free awe
Pays homage to us[15] – thou mayst not coldly set
Our sovereign process[16], which imports at full[17],
By letters congruing to that effect[18],
The present death of Hamlet. Do it England,
For like the hectic[19] in my blood he rages,
And thou must cure me. Till I know 'tis done,
Howe'er my haps[20], my joys were ne'er begun. *Exit*

Fortinbras sends a captain to ask Claudius for permission to pass through Danish territory. The captain tells Hamlet the army will fight for a tiny, unprofitable part of Poland. Hamlet reflects on a sick society.

剧情简介：福庭布拉派一名军官去向克劳迭申请让军队过境丹麦。这位军官告诉哈慕雷他们要去攻打波兰一个没有价值的小地方。哈慕雷思考这是一个怎样的病态社会。

Themes 主题分析

Sickness and corruption

The use of the word 'rank', and the metaphor of 'th'impostume … / That inward breaks, and shows no cause without / Why the man dies' raises again the imagery and theme of sickness and corruption.

a Look back through the play and try to identify some of the images and themes of sickness and corruption (for example, see Act 1 Scene 5, lines 82–3). Hamlet's own melancholy is closely associated with the health and well-being of the state of Denmark: his sickness reflects that of the country, and vice-versa. The purging of this sickness is part of the action of the play, and reveals much about Hamlet as a character: his inward melancholy and imbalance, his sense that 'the time is out of joint'.

b Yet another theme that is evident here is the contrast between action and thought/reflection. How does it relate to the theme of sickness and corruption? Fortinbras represents to Hamlet the epitome (典范) of action – even over a seemingly pointless piece of land in Poland. Look at the two parts of this scene, and perform them to mark the change of mood and resolution in Hamlet.

▼ **Fortinbras and his army in the Russian film director Kozintsev's imaginative re-creation of Scene 4. What is Fortinbras's function in the play as a whole?**

1 Craves the conveyance 请求通过
2 You know the rendezvous 您知道会见地点
3 would aught with us 想与本王子面谈
4 in his eye 当他的面
5 softly 悄悄
6 powers 军队
7 How purposed 有何目的
8 main = mainland
9 addition 夸大
10 farm it 租作农场
11 the Pole 波兰人
12 ranker rate 比这高的价钱
13 sold in fee 整个卖掉
14 garrisoned 严阵以待
15 Will … straw 都敌不过这件麦秆一样大的事
16 impostume 脓肿
17 God buy you = God be with you

Act 4 Scene 4

The sea coast near Elsinore

Enter FORTINBRAS *with his* army

FORTINBRAS Go captain, from me greet the Danish king.
Tell him that by his licence, Fortinbras
Craves the conveyance[1] of a promised march
Over his kingdom. You know the rendezvous[2].
If that his majesty would aught with us[3],
We shall express our duty in his eye[4],
And let him know so.

CAPTAIN I will do't, my lord.

FORTINBRAS Go softly[5] on.

[*Exit Fortinbras, with the army*]

[*Enter* HAMLET, ROSENCRANTZ, *etc.*

HAMLET Good sir, whose powers[6] are these?

CAPTAIN They are of Norway sir.

HAMLET How purposed[7] sir I pray you?

CAPTAIN Against some part of Poland.

HAMLET Who commands them sir?

CAPTAIN The nephew to old Norway, Fortinbras.

HAMLET Goes it against the main[8] of Poland sir,
Or for some frontier?

CAPTAIN Truly to speak, and with no addition[9],
We go to gain a little patch of ground
That hath in it no profit but the name.
To pay five ducats, five, I would not farm it[10],
Nor will it yield to Norway or the Pole[11]
A ranker rate[12], should it be sold in fee[13].

HAMLET Why then the Polack never will defend it.

CAPTAIN Yes, it is already garrisoned[14].

HAMLET Two thousand souls and twenty thousand ducats
Will not debate the question of this straw[15].
This is th'impostume[16] of much wealth and peace,
That inward breaks, and shows no cause without
Why the man dies. I humbly thank you sir.

CAPTAIN God buy you[17] sir. [*Exit*]

Hamlet criticises his delay in revenging his father's death. Is it forgetfulness or too much thought that stops him? Prompted by his encounter with Fortinbras's army, he resolves to speed to his revenge.

剧情简介：哈慕雷批评自己迟迟不为父亲的死复仇。拖他后腿的是淡忘还是多虑？偶遇福庭布拉的军队对他起到敦促的作用，他决定加快复仇的步伐。

1 Hamlet is spurred on to revenge (in pairs)

The soliloquy opposite marks a turning point for Hamlet: between inaction and reflection on the one hand (putting aside the impulsive killing of Polonius), and the carrying out of his revenge mission on the other. Sometimes the soliloquy is cut in performance because it does not appear in the First Folio (第一对开本) (see p. 268). Although Hamlet finally decides on revenge, he deludes himself when in line 45 he says he has 'cause, and will, and strength, and means' to do it: he is a prisoner under guard being escorted to exile. Scene 6 will reveal that another chance encounter (this time with pirates) frees him to find the strength and means for revenge.

a First, divide the soliloquy into sections. You might feel that it splits into three parts or more, according to your interpretation of the meaning and the state of Hamlet's resolve.

b Read the soliloquy, taking turns to read each of the sections to each other. Does your interpretation fit the structure and meaning of the speech? Does it work well?

c Now perform some of these interpretations to the class as a whole. What differences did pairs see in terms of the sections and structure?

d Explore different ways of speaking the soliloquy: individually; echoing words and phrases you think especially important; speaking short sections in turn as a kind of anxious 'conversation'; or as if you are trying to persuade someone of the argument you are developing. You might also decide that some parts of the soliloquy are best performed chorally.

e After your explorations, write notes in your Director's Journal on how the soliloquy might be delivered on stage.

2 Hamlet's soliloquies

In preparation for work later in your study of the play, look back at the previous soliloquies by Hamlet.

a Draw up a table to indicate the key characteristics of each of these soliloquies, and to consider the extent to which each marks a turning point in the play so far. Column headings such as 'Quotation', 'Language/theatrical device', 'Effect', and 'Significance' (in the play as a whole or in Hamlet's development) will help you organise your ideas.

1 inform against 指责
2 spur 催促（spur的本义是"马刺"，这里用作动词，表示"催马"）
3 dull 慢吞吞
4 good and market 优点和价值
5 large discourse 强大的思维
6 fust 退化
7 Bestial oblivion 畜生一样的忘性
8 craven scruple 瞻前顾后
9 quartered 一分为四
10 gross as earth 像大地一样分明
11 mass and charge 规模和花费
12 Makes … event 朝着看不见的未来做鬼脸
13 death … egg-shell = dare death and danger even for an egg-shell 甚至为了一个鸡蛋壳而胆敢挑战死亡和危险
14 Rightly to be great = To be great correctly 做伟大人物的正确途径
15 stir without great argument 没有伟大理由就轻举妄动
16 greatly … straw 在一根麦秆上找到大吵一架的理由
17 stained 玷污；失节
18 for … fame 为了一场虚幻和浮名
19 Whereon … cause 地盘不够打这场仗的人站的
20 continent 棺材坑

ROSENCRANTZ Will't please you go my lord?
HAMLET I'll be with you straight; go a little before.

[*Exeunt all but Hamlet*]

How all occasions do inform against[1] me,
And spur[2] my dull[3] revenge! What is a man
If his chief good and market[4] of his time
Be but to sleep and feed? A beast, no more.
Sure he that made us with such large discourse[5],
Looking before and after, gave us not
That capability and god-like reason
To fust[6] in us unused. Now whether it be
Bestial oblivion[7], or some craven scruple[8]
Of thinking too precisely on th'event –
A thought which quartered[9] hath but one part wisdom
And ever three parts coward – I do not know
Why yet I live to say this thing's to do,
Sith I have cause, and will, and strength, and means
To do't. Examples gross as earth[10] exhort me.
Witness this army of such mass and charge[11],
Led by a delicate and tender prince,
Whose spirit with divine ambition puffed
Makes mouths at the invisible event[12],
Exposing what is mortal and unsure
To all that fortune, death and danger dare,
Even for an egg-shell[13]. Rightly to be great[14]
Is not to stir without great argument[15],
But greatly to find quarrel in a straw[16]
When honour's at the stake. How stand I then,
That have a father killed, a mother stained[17],
Excitements of my reason and my blood,
And let all sleep, while to my shame I see
The imminent death of twenty thousand men,
That for a fantasy and trick of fame[18]
Go to their graves like beds, fight for a plot
Whereon the numbers cannot try the cause[19],
Which is not tomb enough and continent[20]
To hide the slain. Oh from this time forth,
My thoughts be bloody or be nothing worth. *Exit*]

Gertrude refuses to see Ophelia, but is told that Ophelia is mad and needs pity. Gertrude agrees to admit Ophelia, but expresses guilt and misgivings about the future.

剧情简介：葛楚德不愿见奥菲丽叶，却被告知奥菲丽叶疯了，需要得到怜悯。葛楚德同意见奥菲丽叶，却表示了她的愧疚和对未来的忧虑。

Themes 主题分析

More sickness and corruption

See the previous reference to sickness and corruption on page 166. While it cannot be said that Ophelia is corrupt, she is certainly corrupted – and she appears to be sick. Link your exploration of the imagery and theme of sickness to Ophelia's state in this scene.

1 Does Gertrude share Claudius's secret? (in pairs)

Gertrude's lines 17–20 display a guilty conscience. She speaks of her 'sick soul', and says that guilty people give themselves away because they cannot hide their fear of being found out. Some critics argue that these lines show she shares, or suspects, Claudius's secret, and is complicit in her first husband's murder. What is your view?

a Look back at Gertrude's appearances (Act 1 Scene 2; Act 2 Scene 2; Act 3 Scenes 1, 2 and 4; Act 4 Scene 1). One person looks for evidence to support the view that Gertrude does not know that Claudius killed King Hamlet. The other person tries to find evidence that Gertrude *does* know about Claudius's crime.

b Present your conflicting arguments as powerfully as possible in one of the following forms: question-and-answer (spoken or written); an essay; a scene in a legal court (like a disciplinary hearing or public hearing).

Stagecraft 导演技巧

Ophelia enters – '*playing on a lute*'?

In the First Quarto (第一四开本) (see p. 268) the stage direction at line 20 is '*Enter Ophelia playing on a lute, and her hair down singing*'. In Shakespeare's time it was customary for madness in women to be marked by a long wig of loose hair.

a How would you stage Ophelia's entrance? The images on pages 172 and 180 might help you decide.

b What signs of madness in women might be used in a modern production? Give reasons for your answer.

1 importunate 缠人
2 distract 精神失常
3 What would she have? 她想干什么？
4 hems 口中说着"哼，哼"
5 Spurns enviously at straws 脚恨恨地踢着地上的麦秆
6 unshapèd use 前言不搭后语
7 collection 缓过神来
8 yawn at 目瞪口呆
9 botch … thoughts 把词语拼凑在一起，按照自己的想法理解
10 much unhappily 很大程度是误解了
11 conjectures 猜测
12 ill-breeding 不怀好意
13 toy 小事
14 prologue 引子
15 amiss 岔子
16 So … itself = Guilt is so full of artless jealousy that it spills itself

Act 4 Scene 5

The Great Hall of Elsinore Castle

Enter HORATIO, GERTRUDE *and a* GENTLEMAN

GERTRUDE I will not speak with her.

GENTLEMAN She is importunate[1], indeed distract[2];
Her mood will needs be pitied.

GERTRUDE What would she have?[3]

GENTLEMAN She speaks much of her father, says she hears
There's tricks i'th'world, and hems[4], and beats her heart,
Spurns enviously at straws[5], speaks things in doubt
That carry but half sense. Her speech is nothing,
Yet the unshapèd use[6] of it doth move
The hearers to collection[7]. They yawn at[8] it,
And botch the words up fit to their own thoughts[9],
Which, as her winks and nods and gestures yield them,
Indeed would make one think there might be thought,
Though nothing sure, yet much unhappily[10].

HORATIO 'Twere good she were spoken with, for she may strew
Dangerous conjectures[11] in ill-breeding[12] minds.

GERTRUDE Let her come in.

[*Exit Gentleman*]

(*Aside*) To my sick soul, as sin's true nature is,
Each toy[13] seems prologue[14] to some great amiss[15].
So full of artless jealousy is guilt,
It spills itself[16] in fearing to be spilt.

Enter OPHELIA *distracted*

OPHELIA Where is the beauteous majesty of Denmark?

Ophelia's first song recalls the death of her father. She replies enigmatically to Claudius, declares that the future is uncertain, then sings a song about the loss of virginity.

剧情简介：奥菲丽叶第一首歌追忆父亲的死。她回复克劳迭的话像谜语一样令人费解，又说未来不确定，然后又唱起一首关于失去贞操的歌。

▼ Ophelia's mental and emotional derangement has been acted in many ways: dreamily trance-like, frantically angry, sexually obsessed, distanced. This picture shows how Ophelia appeared in a 2003 Birmingham Repertory Theatre/Edinburgh International Festival co-production. How closely does she match your idea of Ophelia driven into madness?

1 cockle hat 鸟蛤帽（朝圣者戴的鸟蛤壳形状的帽子）

2 sandal shoon 凉鞋（shoon是古老歌谣里shoe的复数形式。古代游吟诗人在其吟诵的歌谣里，常把恋人比喻成朝圣者。这种比喻在莎士比亚时代的诗剧里也很常见，如柔密欧与茱丽叶一见钟情时说的话。而中世纪朝圣者的典型装备是鸟蛤帽、木杖和凉鞋。）

3 what imports this song? 这首歌什么意思？

4 shrowd 裹尸布

5 Larded 装饰着

6 good dild you = God yield you 上帝奖赏您

7 owl 猫头鹰

8 baker's daughter 面包师的女儿（有一个民间故事：耶稣向一个面包师的女儿乞讨面包，遭到她的吝啬对待，结果她被变成了一只猫头鹰）

9 Conceit 胡思乱想

10 betime 早早

11 donned 穿上

12 dupped 打开

13 Let … more = He let in the maid, who never came out of his chamber and yet remained a maid （这里maid既有“女孩”的意思，又有“处女”的意思）

GERTRUDE How now Ophelia?

OPHELIA *She sings*

How should I your true love know
From another one?
By his cockle hat[1] and staff
And his sandal shoon[2].

GERTRUDE Alas sweet lady, what imports this song?[3]

OPHELIA Say you? Nay, pray you mark.

He is dead and gone lady, *Song*
He is dead and gone;
At his head a grass-green turf,
At his heels a stone.

Oho!

GERTRUDE Nay but Ophelia –

OPHELIA Pray you mark.

White his shrowd[4] as the mountain snow – *Song*

Enter CLAUDIUS

GERTRUDE Alas, look here my lord.

OPHELIA Larded[5] all with sweet flowers,
Which bewept to the grave did not go
With true-love showers.

CLAUDIUS How do you, pretty lady?

OPHELIA Well good dild you[6]. They say the owl[7] was a baker's daughter[8]. Lord, we know what we are, but know not what we may be. God be at your table.

CLAUDIUS Conceit[9] upon her father.

OPHELIA Pray let's have no words of this, but when they ask you what it means, say you this –

Tomorrow is Saint Valentine's day, *Song*
All in the morning betime[10],
And I a maid at your window,
To be your Valentine.
Then up he rose and donned[11] his clothes
And dupped[12] the chamber door;
Let in the maid that out a maid
Never departed more[13].

CLAUDIUS Pretty Ophelia!

Ophelia sings of betrayed love. She talks distractedly. Claudius reflects that sorrows never come alone: Polonius killed, the citizens restless, Ophelia mad and Laertes a prey to rumour among the people.

剧情简介：奥菲丽叶唱着被辜负的爱，疯疯癫癫地说着话。克劳迭心里想，真是祸不单行：珀娄涅被杀，民心骚动，奥菲丽叶发疯，雷厄提被小道消息包围。

1 Act out Ophelia's troubled state (in threes)

Ophelia's song tells of young men's sexual appetite, and how they refuse to marry women with whom they have slept. The song has been interpreted both as Ophelia's seduction by Hamlet, and as Gertrude's seduction by Claudius. Ophelia's songs, her sorrow for her father, her threat that 'My brother shall know of it' and her strange farewell – 'Good night ladies …' – both enthrall and disturb audiences in the theatre.

- To experience the emotional and dramatic power of Ophelia's first 'mad' appearance, take parts as Gertrude, Claudius and Ophelia, and act out lines 21–72.

Characters 人物分析

Ophelia's attitude to sex

Shakespeare provides no evidence that Hamlet and Ophelia have had sex together, although both his and her obsession with sexual matters suggests a preoccupation with the subject. We have already identified that Hamlet associates sex with death, corruption, his mother's infidelity and licentiousness (放荡). But what about Ophelia?

a Look back at Ophelia's appearances before this moment, especially in Act 1 Scene 3 and Act 3 Scene 2, and gauge the degree to which she was 'innocent' of sex. Look at her speeches in the present scene, where 'madness' is associated with an obsessiveness about sex.

b Can you characterise the different approach to this theme of love, identity and sexuality between Hamlet and Ophelia? Ophelia is depicted as a victim for much of the play, and subject to the directions of her father, brother and lover. Is this a fair reflection of your view of her, or would you see her as stronger and more independent than this 'victim' theory allows?

c If you wish to make notes at this stage, you could do so in the form of character notes (building up toward a more considered view and piece of writing later) or in the form of a letter from a courtier who has observed Ophelia's behaviour.

1 By Gis = By Jesus 向耶稣发誓
2 By Cock = By God 向上帝发誓（不过公鸡也是cock）
3 tumbled 碾压（指与之上床）
4 And = If
5 single spies 单个探子
6 author 造成……的人
7 just remove 合理地除掉
8 muddied 鼎沸
9 greenly 傻乎乎
10 In hugger-mugger 偷偷摸摸
11 inter 埋葬
12 as much containing 同样要紧
13 Feeds … clouds 整日琢磨如何破解自己的疑惑，心神不定
14 buzzers 散布谣言者
15 infect his ear 毒害他的耳朵
16 necessity 必然
17 of matter beggared 查无实证
18 Will … ear 不可避免会逢人就指控朕（In ear and ear可以解读为“在一个又一个人的耳朵里”）
19 murdering piece 连环炮
20 superfluous death 杀死好几回

OPHELIA Indeed la! Without an oath I'll make an end on't.

By Gis[1] and by Saint Charity,
Alack and fie for shame,
Young men will do't if they come to't –
By Cock[2], they are to blame.
Quoth she, 'Before you tumbled[3] me,
You promised me to wed.'
He answers –
So would I ha' done, by yonder sun,
And[4] thou hadst not come to my bed.

CLAUDIUS How long hath she been thus?

OPHELIA I hope all will be well. We must be patient, but I cannot choose but weep to think they would lay him i'th' cold ground. My brother shall know of it, and so I thank you for your good counsel. Come, my coach. Good night ladies, good night sweet ladies, good night, good night. *Exit*

CLAUDIUS Follow her close, give her good watch I pray you.

[*Exit Horatio*]

Oh this is the poison of deep grief, it springs
All from her father's death, [and now behold –]
Oh Gertrude, Gertrude,
When sorrows come, they come not single spies[5],
But in battalions. First, her father slain;
Next, your son gone, and he most violent author[6]
Of his own just remove[7]; the people muddied[8],
Thick and unwholesome in their thoughts and whispers
For good Polonius' death – and we have done but greenly[9]
In hugger-mugger[10] to inter[11] him; poor Ophelia
Divided from herself and her fair judgement,
Without the which we are pictures, or mere beasts;
Last, and as much containing[12] as all these,
Her brother is in secret come from France,
Feeds on his wonder, keeps himself in clouds[13],
And wants not buzzers[14] to infect his ear[15]
With pestilent speeches of his father's death,
Wherein necessity[16], of matter beggared[17],
Will nothing stick our person to arraign
In ear and ear[18]. O my dear Gertrude, this,
Like to a murdering piece[19], in many places
Gives me superfluous death[20].

A Messenger tells Claudius that Laertes and an angry mob are coming, and that some of the rioters shout that Laertes should be king. Laertes bursts in and demands to know what happened to his father.

剧情简介：一个信使禀告克劳迭说雷厄提带着一伙怒气冲冲的暴民就要来了，暴徒中有人大喊雷厄提应该当王。雷厄提突然冲了进来，质问他父亲是怎么死的。

1 A political crisis (in pairs)

After so much attention to 'family matters' in the play, politics makes a full-blooded return. Laertes, leading a 'rabble' of citizens, has swept aside Claudius's bodyguards. The citizens wish to overthrow Claudius's regime and place Laertes on the throne. The Messenger gives a graphic account of the insurrection (暴动), comparing the violent approach of the citizens to the ocean's tide rushing over the shore.

a Take turns to speak the Messenger's lines 98–108. Bring out the urgency (and fear?) he feels as he sees the potential collapse of Claudius's regime.

b Talk together about how you would stage the episode between lines 110 and 116, in which the ordinary people of Denmark are briefly glimpsed and heard.

c Discuss what might have prompted the people to support Laertes for the kingship, and to overthrow Claudius.

Characters 人物分析

Laertes's return

Laertes has returned from France on the news of his father's death. He has acted swiftly and with some degree of reason, though he seems impelled by motives of revenge. Laertes provides another model for Hamlet, after the prince's recent encounter with Fortinbras.

a Look particularly at lines 118–21, where Polonius's death has been converted in Laertes's mind to an act that has made him a 'bastard', as if he were not born of a true marriage between Polonius and Laertes's mother (whom we do not see in the play). Why is there reference to a 'harlot', and how might a director ask an actor to play these lines? For example, branding the harlot 'Even here' could be interpreted as a reference to Gertrude. Is Gertrude his mother, or is he making a more general point?

b Although it is unlikely you will write a full character study of Laertes himself, his similarities and differences in relation to Hamlet are worth recording as you move through the play. Indeed, Laertes and Fortinbras act as foils to Hamlet. In what ways do each of them, and their actions, shed light on Hamlet himself? Conversely, what does Hamlet's presence suggest about them?

1 Attend! 来人！
2 Swissers 禁卫军（瑞士人是雇佣军，尤其是皇家侍卫的著名来源）
3 overpeering of his list 冲上海岸
4 Eats 吞没
5 flats 低地
6 impitious haste 无情的速度
7 in a riotous head 率领一伙暴乱者
8 The rabble 这伙暴民
9 Antiquity forgot, custom not known = With ancient tradition forgotten and current customs not known 忘了古老的传统，也不知道当下的风俗
10 ratifiers … word 佐证和支持每句话的事物（这里指上一行里说的传统和风俗）
11 cheerfully … cry = cry on the false trail cheerfully 冲着错误的踪迹狂吠
12 counter 跟反了（猎狗朝猎物踪迹的相反方向追踪）
13 That … calm 有一滴不沸腾的血
14 cuckold 王八（被妻子戴了绿帽子的人）
15 brands the harlot 烙上婊子的烙印
16 Even … brow 就在贞洁而没有被玷污的眉宇之间

A noise within

GERTRUDE Alack, what noise is this?

CLAUDIUS Attend![1] Where are my Swissers[2]? Let them guard the door.

Enter a MESSENGER

What is the matter?

MESSENGER Save yourself my lord.
The ocean, overpeering of his list[3],
Eats[4] not the flats[5] with more impitious haste[6]
Than young Laertes in a riotous head[7]
O'erbears your officers. The rabble[8] call him lord,
And, as the world were now but to begin,
Antiquity forgot, custom not known[9],
The ratifiers and props of every word[10],
They cry 'Choose we! Laertes shall be king.'
Caps, hands and tongues applaud it to the clouds,
'Laertes shall be king, Laertes king!'

GERTRUDE How cheerfully on the false trail they cry[11]!
Oh this is counter[12], you false Danish dogs!

A noise within

CLAUDIUS The doors are broke.

Enter LAERTES *with others*

LAERTES Where is this king? – Sirs, stand you all without.

ALL No, let's come in.

LAERTES I pray you give me leave.

ALL We will, we will.

LAERTES I thank you. Keep the door.

[*Exeunt followers*]

O thou vile king,
Give me my father.

GERTRUDE Calmly, good Laertes.

LAERTES That drop of blood that's calm[13] proclaims me bastard,
Cries cuckold[14] to my father, brands the harlot[15]
Even here, between the chaste unsmirchèd brow[16]
Of my true mother.

Claudius is unafraid to face the wrath of Laertes. Claudius claims to be protected by the divine aura of kingship. He urges Laertes to distinguish between friends and foes, and says he is innocent of Polonius's death.

剧情简介：面对愤怒的雷厄提，克劳迭并不害怕，自称有君王光环的保护。他极力劝说雷厄提分清楚敌友，声称自己与珀娄涅的死无关。

1 Claudius the hypocrite (in threes)

Claudius is unperturbed by Laertes's anger. He asserts that God prevents a monarch coming to harm ('There's such divinity doth hedge a king'). Claudius sounds completely confident, but his words betray his utter hypocrisy: God did not protect old Hamlet from being murdered by his own brother.

- Take parts and speak all the lines in the script opposite. Bring out Claudius's devious self-assurance, Gertrude's protectiveness and Laertes's enraged desire for revenge.

Write about it 写作练习

Claudius the manipulator

Claudius continues to scheme. He is engineering Hamlet's removal to England, and planning Hamlet's death there. But perhaps it is also occurring to him that Laertes might wish to kill Hamlet himself. Claudius's skill in manoeuvring others to his will is evident; yet, at the same time, do you think he is stupid and incompetent in trying to cover his own malevolent (恶毒) acts?

a Design a diagram or set of notes in which Claudius is at the centre, with the other characters around him. Indicate, in a few words, how hypocritical he is to all the characters linked to him.

b If hypocrisy is one of Claudius's defining characteristics, what are the other aspects of his character? Write a paragraph or two to capture the complexity of his character as revealed so far in the play. Include quotations.

2 Four revengers

Laertes swears to avenge his father's death. He becomes the fourth revenger in the play. The others are Hamlet (revenge for his father's death); Fortinbras (campaigns to win back his father's lost land); and Pyrrhus (slaughters Priam to avenge his own father's death).

In lines 130–6 Laertes uses the exaggerated language of the traditional hero of revenge tragedy.

a Speak the lines as bombastically as you can. Then identify lines earlier in the play where Hamlet's language is similar in tone to Laertes's.

b Which of the four has the greatest motive and justification for revenge?

1 fear our person 担心朕的人身安全

2 hedge 护佑

3 Acts little of his will 做不了什么它想做的事（his = its）

4 incensed 怒气冲冲

5 demand his fill 索取他应得的那一份（即让他问个够）

6 be juggled with 被耍弄

7 vows 效忠誓言

8 I dare damnation 我下地狱也在所不惜

9 both … negligence 生和死这两个世界我都不在乎

10 throughly = thoroughly

11 stay = stop

12 And … well 至于我的钱财，我会好好筹划

13 go far with little 一点点钱也会支撑很久

14 soopstake 赌注包揽（类似"一竿子打翻一船人"）

15 draw 召集

16 pelican 鹈鹕（一种大型水禽，俗称塘鹅；到了繁殖季节，其喙、喉囊和面部皮肤的颜色会变得鲜红；当时人们误认为这是母鸟用喙戳破自己的胸脯，以血哺育幼鸟）

17 Repast 喂养

18 most sensibly in grief 痛心至极

19 It … eye 这一点对您的判断力来说将显得直截了当，就像白天所见对您的眼睛来说那样（level在这里的意思是straightforward；在其他版本里pierce作'pear，即appear的缩略形式）

CLAUDIUS What is the cause, Laertes,
That thy rebellion looks so giant-like? –
Let him go, Gertrude, do not fear our person[1].
There's such divinity doth hedge[2] a king
That treason can but peep to what it would,
Acts little of his will[3]. – Tell me Laertes,
Why thou art thus incensed[4]. – Let him go Gertrude. –
Speak man.

LAERTES Where is my father?

CLAUDIUS Dead.

GERTRUDE But not by him.

CLAUDIUS Let him demand his fill[5].

LAERTES How came he dead? I'll not be juggled with[6].
To hell allegiance, vows[7] to the blackest devil,
Conscience and grace to the profoundest pit!
I dare damnation[8]. To this point I stand,
That both the worlds I give to negligence[9],
Let come what comes, only I'll be revenged
Most throughly[10] for my father.

CLAUDIUS Who shall stay you[11]?

LAERTES My will, not all the world.
And for my means, I'll husband them so well[12],
They shall go far with little[13].

CLAUDIUS Good Laertes,
If you desire to know the certainty
Of your dear father, is't writ in your revenge
That, soopstake[14], you will draw[15] both friend and foe,
Winner and loser?

LAERTES None but his enemies.

CLAUDIUS Will you know them then?

LAERTES To his good friends thus wide I'll ope my arms,
And like the kind life-rendering pelican[16],
Repast[17] them with my blood.

CLAUDIUS Why now you speak
Like a good child and a true gentleman.
That I am guiltless of your father's death,
And am most sensibly in grief[18] for it,
It shall as level to your judgement pierce
As day does to your eye[19].

Laertes is appalled by Ophelia's madness. It moves him even more strongly to revenge. Ophelia sings again of death. She distributes flowers and herbs.

剧情简介：看到奥菲丽叶疯了，雷厄提感到震惊，这使他的报仇之心更加强烈。奥菲丽叶又唱起关于死亡的歌来，并分发花和香草。

1 sense and virtue 感知功能（视觉）
2 paid with weight 加倍偿还
3 our scale turn the beam 天平朝我们倾斜
4 fine 精细
5 instance 部分；样品
6 bier 灵柩
7 Hey … nonny （歌曲里没有意义的衬词）
8 a-down （一首著名歌曲里的和词）
9 how the wheel becomes it 命运之轮如何转
10 steward 管家
11 nothing 胡话
12 matter 清醒的话
13 pansies 大花三色堇
14 thoughts 忧伤
15 A document 一堂课
16 columbines 耧斗菜（有毒）
17 a made a good end 他得了善终（a = he）
18 favour 楚楚动人

1 Ophelia trapped

The photograph above is from a 2011 production of *Hamlet*. It shows Ophelia trapped in a net, mad and unable to relate to the social situation in which she finds herself. Although entrapment is not a major image or theme in the play, the notion of general confinement is – and it is not just Ophelia who is confined.

- Discuss how appropriate you think the depiction of Ophelia is in the photograph, and in what other ways you could imagine presenting her in this scene.

2 'There's rosemary' (in pairs)

There is a symbolic significance in the herbs and flowers that Ophelia mentions, which include: fennel (茴香) (flattery), columbines (ingratitude and infidelity), rue (芸香) (sorrow), daisy (雏菊) (springtime, love) and violets (紫罗兰) (sweetness).

a Which flowers does Ophelia give to whom, and why?

b What is the dramatic effect of giving these gifts?

A noise within: 'Let her come in'

LAERTES How now, what noise is that?

Enter OPHELIA

O heat dry up my brains, tears seven times salt
Burn out the sense and virtue[1] of mine eye!
By heaven, thy madness shall be paid with weight[2]
Till our scale turn the beam[3]. O rose of May,
Dear maid, kind sister, sweet Ophelia –
O heavens, is't possible a young maid's wits
Should be as mortal as an old man's life?
Nature is fine[4] in love, and where 'tis fine,
It sends some precious instance[5] of itself
After the thing it loves.

OPHELIA *Song*
They bore him bare-faced on the bier[6]
Hey non nonny, nonny, hey nonny[7],
And in his grave rained many a tear –
Fare you well my dove.

LAERTES Hadst thou thy wits, and didst persuade revenge,
It could not move thus.

OPHELIA You must sing a-down[8] a-down, and you call him a-down-a. Oh how the wheel becomes it[9]. It is the false steward[10] that stole his master's daughter.

LAERTES This nothing's[11] more than matter[12].

OPHELIA There's rosemary, that's for remembrance – pray you, love, remember – and there is pansies[13], that's for thoughts[14].

LAERTES A document[15] in madness, thoughts and remembrance fitted.

OPHELIA There's fennel for you, and columbines[16]. There's rue for you, and here's some for me; we may call it herb of grace a Sundays. Oh you must wear your rue with a difference. There's a daisy. I would give you some violets, but they withered all when my father died. They say a made a good end[17].

[*Sings*]

For bonny sweet Robin is all my joy.

LAERTES Thought and affliction, passion, hell itself,
She turns to favour[18] and to prettiness.

Ophelia again sings about her father's death. Claudius sympathises with Laertes's grief, and makes an offer: if Claudius proves to blame, Laertes can be king. If not, Claudius will help Laertes find justice and revenge.

剧情简介：奥菲丽叶又唱起关于父亲之死的歌。克劳迭同情悲痛的雷厄提，向他提议：如果自己最后证明有罪，就让雷厄提当国王；如果自己无罪，他会帮雷厄提主持正义，报仇雪恨。

1 Songs in Shakespeare (in small groups)

Ophelia's songs are typical of many that appear in Shakespeare's plays. Most of them conform to a simple rhyming pattern, and they are often performed live on stage with lute or guitar accompaniment to suit the production style and the director's conception of the play.

a Research other songs in Shakespeare, and work out which types of characters sing these songs, and why.

b Find some recordings of songs in Shakespeare, and listen to them (there are four songs in this scene alone). Work in small groups to research and interpret the songs, then present them to the rest of the class.

2 The end of Ophelia

This is the last time we see Ophelia alive in the play. In Scene 7, we hear from Gertrude that she has drowned, either through suicide or accident.

- In the light of this information, how would you design Ophelia's exit from the stage at line 195?

3 Claudius seizes his opportunity (in pairs)

Claudius has been trying to control and direct Laertes's anger. Now, the entrance of Ophelia and her effect on Laertes give the king an opportunity to exploit the situation to his own advantage.

a Take parts and read lines 196–214 several times. Make Claudius as persuasive as you can, and consider Laertes's confused feelings as he watches his sister's bizarre behaviour. Express his anger about his father being buried without ceremony. Also, think about whether you should leave a long pause before Laertes says 'Let this be so' in line 207.

b Talk together about how Claudius manages to turn Laertes's passion for revenge to his own ends.

1 All flaxen was his poll 他满头白发（poll：头）

2 God-a-mercy = God have mercy 上帝宽恕

3 commune with 分享

4 Go but apart 借一步说话

5 of whom = of whichever

6 by collateral hand 通过指使他人

7 touched 卷入其中

8 lend 给

9 jointly labour 合力

10 means 方式

11 No trophy, sword, nor hatchment 没有奖杯、剑，也没有盾徽 / 族徽

12 ostentation 丧葬仪式

13 where … fall 愿巨大的斧钺落在罪人头上

OPHELIA And will a not come again? *Song*
And will a not come again?
No, no, he is dead,
Go to thy death-bed,
He never will come again.
His beard was as white as snow,
All flaxen was his poll[1],
He is gone, he is gone,
And we cast away moan,
God-a-mercy[2] on his soul.
And of all Christian souls, I pray God. God buy you. *Exit*

LAERTES Do you see this, O God?

CLAUDIUS Laertes, I must commune with[3] your grief,
Or you deny me right. Go but apart[4],
Make choice of whom[5] your wisest friends you will,
And they shall hear and judge 'twixt you and me.
If by direct or by collateral hand[6]
They find us touched[7], we will our kingdom give,
Our crown, our life, and all that we call ours,
To you in satisfaction. But if not,
Be you content to lend[8] your patience to us,
And we shall jointly labour[9] with your soul
To give it due content.

LAERTES Let this be so.
His means[10] of death, his obscure funeral,
No trophy, sword, nor hatchment[11] o'er his bones,
No noble rite, nor formal ostentation[12],
Cry to be heard, as 'twere from heaven to earth,
That I must call't in question.

CLAUDIUS So you shall.
And where th'offence is, let the great axe fall[13].
I pray you go with me.

Exeunt

Hamlet's letter reveals that he has been captured in a sea battle. By doing a deal with the pirates, he has returned to Denmark. He has sent letters to the king, and urgently wishes to meet Horatio.

剧情简介：哈慕雷的来信中说他在一场海战中被俘。他跟海盗做了个交易，回到了丹麦。他已给国王送信，并迫切想见何瑞修。

1 Hamlet and the pirates (in groups of four or more)

One production solved the problem of why Horatio reads the letter aloud by having the sailor hold the letter up in front of him. Horatio gently turned the letter the right way up (showing that the sailors cannot read). He began to read it silently. The sailors then threatened him, obviously wanting to know how the letter affected them, having done a deal with Hamlet. So Horatio was forced to read it aloud.

a **Act it out** Occasionally, a production has acted out the letter's contents at the back of the stage, as Horatio reads the action. Follow that example. As one person speaks as Horatio, the others enact what is described in lines 13–18.

b **Improvise** (即兴表演) Imagine the scene where Hamlet has boarded the pirate ship. The pirates would be puzzled to find out who Hamlet was, where he was going and why he needed to return to Denmark. Some of them may wish to kill him. Others see him as a valuable prisoner whom they can exchange for a large ransom. Improvise the scene where Hamlet persuades the pirates to spare him and to help him return to Denmark. Start with his being threatened by them. What deal might he strike with the pirates?

c **Write a movie script** Work in pairs. You are the joint directors of a movie of *Hamlet*. Movies have different opportunities from stage productions: settings can be changed instantly, a character's thoughts can be presented visually, 'realistic' settings can be used. Work out how you will film Scene 6. For example, Horatio's reading might be done as a voice-over, while the movie shows the action described. Your task is to rewrite Scene 6 as a movie script.

Language in the play 剧中语言

Letter style as opposed to blank verse

The difference between prose and verse style is always significant in Shakespeare.

- Translate the letter into blank verse; then take one section of the verse part of the play (for example, the beginning of the following scene) and translate it into prose.
- What difference does it make, and why do you think Shakespeare uses such variation?

1 and = if
2 overlooked 读完
3 give … to 让这些人有办法见到
4 of very warlike appointment 武装齐备
5 put on a compelled valour 只得拼尽所有胆气
6 grapple 打斗，格斗
7 thieves of mercy 仁慈的强盗
8 repair thou 你赶来
9 for … matter 与信中的事相比
10 give you way 引见你们

Act 4 Scene 6

A room in the castle

Enter HORATIO *with an* ATTENDANT

HORATIO What are they that would speak with me?

ATTENDANT Seafaring men sir, they say they have letters for you.

HORATIO Let them come in.

[*Exit Attendant*]

I do not know from what part of the world
I should be greeted, if not from Lord Hamlet.

Enter SAILORS

I SAILOR God bless you sir.

HORATIO Let him bless thee too.

I SAILOR A shall sir, and[1] please him. There's a letter for you sir, it came from th'ambassador that was bound for England, if your name be Horatio, as I am let to know it is.

HORATIO (*Reads the letter*) 'Horatio, when thou shalt have overlooked[2] this, give these fellows some means to[3] the king; they have letters for him. Ere we were two days old at sea, a pirate of very warlike appointment[4] gave us chase. Finding ourselves too slow of sail, we put on a compelled valour[5], and in the grapple[6] I boarded them. On the instant they got clear of our ship, so I alone became their prisoner. They have dealt with me like thieves of mercy[7], but they knew what they did: I am to do a good turn for them. Let the king have the letters I have sent, and repair thou[8] to me with as much speed as thou wouldest fly death. I have words to speak in thine ear will make thee dumb, yet are they much too light for the bore of the matter[9]. These good fellows will bring thee where I am. Rosencrantz and Guildenstern hold their course for England. Of them I have much to tell thee. Farewell.

He that thou knowest thine,
Hamlet.'

Come, I will give you way[10] for these your letters,
And do't the speedier that you may direct me
To him from whom you brought them.

Exeunt

Claudius claims that Hamlet not only killed Polonius, but was intent on killing him, too. He explains that he did not punish Hamlet for two reasons: love of Gertrude, and Hamlet's popularity with the people.

剧情简介：克劳迭称哈慕雷不仅杀了珀娄涅，还意图杀死他。他解释说他没有惩罚哈慕雷有两个原因：一是因为他爱葛楚德，二是哈慕雷很受人民拥戴。

1 Why doesn't he mention Hamlet's madness?

The previous 'letter' scene has given Claudius time to tell Laertes how Polonius was killed. Now he gives two reasons why he took no action against Hamlet (lines 9–24). He does not mention Hamlet's madness.

- Suggest a reason for Claudius's omission. Relate your answer to the image below.

▼ This image of Laertes from a 2008 production shows him as resolute, noble and flanked by (两侧有) guards. Imagine, as the Messenger reported in Act 4 Scene 5, lines 106–8, that 'Laertes shall be king'. What kind of king would he make? Does he have the right qualities?

1 my acquittance seal = seal my acquittance 判定我无罪
2 with a knowing ear 心明眼亮
3 feats 所作所为
4 capital 够判死刑
5 mainly 极大
6 unsinewed 站不住脚
7 My virtue or my plague 我的长处或短处
8 conjunctive 密切相连
9 sphere 运行轨道
10 but by her 离了她 / 除非在她身边
11 count 关系重大
12 general gender 一般百姓
13 spring 泉水（含钙多的泉水能把木头钙化为石头）
14 gyves 镣铐
15 Too slightly timbered 箭杆太轻巧
16 loud 强劲
17 driven into desperate terms 被逼疯
18 Stood … perfections 她的完美足以击败各个年龄的女子

Act 4 Scene 7

A state room in the castle

Enter CLAUDIUS *and* LAERTES

CLAUDIUS Now must your conscience my acquittance seal[1],
And you must put me in your heart for friend,
Sith you have heard, and with a knowing ear[2],
That he which hath your noble father slain
Pursued my life.

LAERTES It well appears. But tell me
Why you proceeded not against these feats[3],
So crimeful and so capital[4] in nature,
As by your safety, wisdom, all things else,
You mainly[5] were stirred up.

CLAUDIUS Oh for two special reasons,
Which may to you perhaps seem much unsinewed[6],
But yet to me they're strong. The queen his mother
Lives almost by his looks, and for myself,
My virtue or my plague[7], be it either which,
She's so conjunctive[8] to my life and soul,
That as the star moves not but in his sphere[9],
I could not but by her[10]. The other motive,
Why to a public count[11] I might not go,
Is the great love the general gender[12] bear him,
Who, dipping all his faults in their affection,
Work like the spring[13] that turneth wood to stone,
Convert his gyves[14] to graces, so that my arrows,
Too slightly timbered[15] for so loud[16] a wind,
Would have reverted to my bow again,
And not where I had aimed them.

LAERTES And so have I a noble father lost,
A sister driven into desperate terms[17],
Whose worth, if praises may go back again,
Stood challenger on mount of all the age
For her perfections[18]. But my revenge will come.

Claudius assures Laertes that he will not let Hamlet's actions go unpunished. A Messenger brings letters from Hamlet, telling of his return to Denmark. Laertes welcomes the chance to be revenged on Hamlet.

剧情简介：克劳迭向雷厄提保证他不会让哈慕雷的所作所为逃脱惩罚。信使带来了哈慕雷的信，禀报哈慕雷回到丹麦了。雷厄提欢迎向哈慕雷复仇的机会。

1 Claudius's pleasure is abruptly ended (in pairs)

Claudius makes it clear that he intends to punish Hamlet. He uses an image familiar to Elizabethans: don't let anyone think they can pull my beard and get away with it (lines 32–3). Indeed, at this moment Claudius thinks that on his orders Hamlet will shortly be executed in England. Very soon, he hopes to tell Laertes of Hamlet's death. The letter from Hamlet denies him that pleasure.

a **Reading between the lines** Imagine you are Hamlet writing his letter (lines 43–6) to Claudius. One person reads up to a punctuation mark, then pauses. In each pause, the other person speaks Hamlet's thoughts on what he has just written.

b **Naked** Claudius is puzzled by Hamlet describing himself as 'set naked on your kingdom'. This probably doesn't mean that Hamlet is literally without clothes – but what can it mean? Suggest several explanations for the word that seem to you to be appropriate to the play.

c **Laertes's reaction?** Laertes seems 'lost in it' (line 53). Can you explain why?

Stagecraft 导演技巧

The arrival of the letter

Letters in movies and on stage have the effect of interrupting the action and bringing a different dimension in time as well as character on to the stage or into the foreground. In films, the reading of a letter is often carried out in voice-over, as if it is the inner thoughts of the character reading it, or of a character off stage.

a Which of the following would you advise a director to use, and why? Remember, you do not have to follow the stage directions – they are almost certainly not Shakespeare's.

- The letter read out by Claudius on stage
- Hamlet's disembodied voice.

b What would happen to the letter after it was read? You might like to record your notes in your Director's Journal.

1 flat 迟钝
2 pastime 消遣，乐子
3 we love ourself 朕也要顾及自己
4 abuse 恶作剧
5 no such thing 没这回事
6 hand 手书
7 character 字迹
8 devise me 解读（me无实际意义）
9 warms 抚慰
10 very = real
11 live … teeth 有机会当面指着他的鼻子说
12 ruled by me 听我指挥
13 o'errule me to a peace 压制我让我作罢

CLAUDIUS Break not your sleeps for that. You must not think
That we are made of stuff so flat[1] and dull
That we can let our beard be shook with danger
And think it pastime[2]. You shortly shall hear more.
I loved your father, and we love ourself[3],
And that I hope will teach you to imagine –

Enter a MESSENGER *with letters*

How now? What news?

MESSENGER Letters my lord from Hamlet.
This to your majesty, this to the queen.

CLAUDIUS From Hamlet? Who brought them?

MESSENGER Sailors my lord they say, I saw them not;
They were given me by Claudio – he received them
Of him that brought them.

CLAUDIUS Laertes, you shall hear them. –
Leave us.

Exit Messenger

[*Reads*] 'High and mighty, you shall know I am set naked on your kingdom. Tomorrow shall I beg leave to see your kingly eyes, when I shall, first asking your pardon thereunto, recount th'occasion of my sudden and more strange return.

Hamlet.'

What should this mean? Are all the rest come back?
Or is it some abuse[4], and no such thing[5]?

LAERTES Know you the hand[6]?

CLAUDIUS 'Tis Hamlet's character[7]. Naked?
And in a postscript here he says alone.
Can you devise me[8]?

LAERTES I'm lost in it my lord. But let him come –
It warms[9] the very[10] sickness in my heart
That I shall live and tell him to his teeth[11]
'Thus didest thou!'

CLAUDIUS If it be so, Laertes –
As how should it be so? – how otherwise? –
Will you be ruled by me[12]?

LAERTES Ay my lord,
So you will not o'errule me to a peace[13].

Claudius begins to hatch a new plot to kill Hamlet. He says that Hamlet envies Laertes, but delays naming the reason for that envy. Instead, Claudius talks of Lamord, an accomplished French soldier.

剧情简介：克劳迭开始酝酿杀死哈慕雷的新计策。他说哈慕雷妒忌雷厄提，却迟迟不说为何妒忌，反而说起了拉默德，一位武艺高强的法国士兵。

1 The temptation scene (in pairs)

Claudius realises that his plan to have Hamlet killed in England has failed. Now he sees he can use Laertes's desire for revenge to achieve his aim. Claudius's plot against Hamlet will 'work him / To an exploit … Under the which he shall not choose but fall' (lines 62–4).

Claudius does not immediately tell Laertes of his plan. Instead he talks of 'a quality' of Laertes. When Laertes asks him what that quality is (line 75), Claudius again does not reply directly, but calls the unnamed quality 'A very riband in the cap of youth' (mere ribbon, a decoration on a cap). Yet this quality is 'needful' (or necessary), because it suits youth in the same way that 'health and graveness' suit older people. Claudius then talks about a Frenchman, Lamord.

- Lines 60–161 are often called the 'temptation' scene because Claudius tempts Laertes into a murderous plot. To gain a sense of the conspiracy, sit closely together and quietly speak the lines to each other.

Characters 人物分析

Further sides to Claudius

In addition to using sophisticated persuasive techniques to motivate Laertes to revenge, Claudius reveals other dimensions to his own character: his enthusiasm for Lamord (which sounds like *la mort* – French for 'death') and his horse-riding skills; his knowledge of Hamlet; and his understanding of Laertes's psychology.

a Do you think Shakespeare is painting the picture of a complex man and king, who is not purely evil but is partially repentant, and also full of earthly enthusiasm and delight – and a good tactician and diplomat? Or are we to read this later episode completely cynically, as the clever operations of a Machiavellian (cunning and opportunist) villain? Discuss this in pairs or small groups, and then report to the class with supporting evidence (look particularly at Act 1 Scene 2, Act 2 Scene 2, Act 3 Scene 1 and Act 3 Scene 3).

b Capture your discussion in the form of an initial character study of Claudius. At this stage, you might write a number of paragraphs on the various sides to his character – and what are, in your view, his prevailing characteristics.

1 checking at 中断
2 exploit （下）套，（设）局
3 ripe in my device 谋划成熟
4 shall uncharge the practice 将不控诉此事
5 The rather 最好是
6 I might be the organ 由我来动手（organ：工具）
7 falls right 再好不过了
8 parts 特长
9 Of the unworthiest siege 最不值钱
10 very riband = mere ribbon 不过是一条绶带
11 becomes 适合，符合
12 weeds 粗麻布衣
13 served against 跟……打过仗 / 交过手
14 can well 精通
15 gallant 勇士；时尚男子
16 incorpsed 合为一体
17 demi-natured / With the brave beast 与这匹漂亮的牲畜合二为一，成为半神
18 So … did 他的功夫远超我的想象，我的语言能力和技巧都形容不来（forgery：编造）
19 brooch （王冠上的）宝石

CLAUDIUS To thine own peace. If he be now returned,
As checking at[1] his voyage, and that he means
No more to undertake it, I will work him
To an exploit[2], now ripe in my device[3],
Under the which he shall not choose but fall,
And for his death no wind of blame shall breathe,
But even his mother shall uncharge the practice[4]
And call it accident.

[LAERTES My lord, I will be ruled,
The rather[5] if you could devise it so
That I might be the organ[6].

CLAUDIUS It falls right[7].
You have been talked of since your travel much,
And that in Hamlet's hearing, for a quality
Wherein they say you shine. Your sum of parts[8]
Did not together pluck such envy from him
As did that one, and that in my regard
Of the unworthiest siege[9].

LAERTES What part is that my lord?

CLAUDIUS A very riband[10] in the cap of youth,
Yet needful too, for youth no less becomes[11]
The light and careless livery that it wears
Than settled age his sables and his weeds[12]
Importing health and graveness.] Two months since
Here was a gentleman of Normandy.
I've seen myself, and served against[13], the French,
And they can well[14] on horseback, but this gallant[15]
Had witchcraft in't. He grew unto his seat,
And to such wondrous doing brought his horse
As had he been incorpsed[16] and demi-natured
With the brave beast[17]. So far he topped my thought,
That I in forgery of shapes and tricks
Come short of what he did[18].

LAERTES A Norman was't?

CLAUDIUS A Norman.

LAERTES Upon my life Lamord.

CLAUDIUS The very same.

LAERTES I know him well, he is the brooch[19] indeed
And gem of all the nation.

Claudius relates Lamord's praise of Laertes's swordsmanship. Laertes asks what the point of Claudius's words is. Claudius talks of how love fades with time. His words prompt Laertes to seek bloody revenge.

剧情简介：克劳迭将拉默德的称赞和雷厄提的剑术放在一起说。雷厄提问克劳迭他的话是什么意思。克劳迭说爱会随着时间而淡化。他的话敦促雷厄提血腥复仇。

1 Intensifying Laertes's fury (in pairs)

Claudius's two long speeches opposite are intended to work on Laertes's already-inflamed emotions. The first speech reports that Lamord and the best swordsmen in France thought that Laertes was a superior swordsman, outclassing them all. In his long second speech, Claudius reflects on how time kills love, goodness dies of its own excess, and intentions fade away if not quickly carried out. Only when Claudius asks a direct question, 'Laertes, was your father dear to you?' (line 106), does he seem to address what is uppermost in Laertes's thoughts and feelings.

Claudius is deliberately spinning out his story to increase Laertes's resentment against Hamlet: first, by saying that Hamlet envies Laertes's swordsmanship, and wishes to duel with him; second, by implying that Laertes's desire for revenge will fade over time, like love. Claudius wants to work Laertes up into a fury so that he will quickly seize any opportunity to be revenged on Hamlet.

a Experiment with different ways of speaking Claudius's lines opposite. For example, try Claudius always maintaining eye contact with Laertes. Then have Claudius mainly avoiding eye contact, and in his second long speech drifting off into an internal meditation about how love fades with time. Find the style you think is most appropriate.

b Lines 99–101 and 113–22 are in square brackets. They did not appear in the First Folio version of the play (see p. 268). Imagine you are about to put on the play. Will you include these lines or cut them? One of you argues for cutting the lines, the other against. The person arguing to include them might stress how the second bracketed passage echoes the theme of delay. Many of Shakespeare's plays have a long and discursive Act 4, in which key characters deliberate about the action to follow in Act 5. *Macbeth* is a good example of this.

c Laertes's replies are short – indeed curt. Is he a man of action, or simply one who finds it difficult to listen to long passages of persuasive language? Or is there something else on his mind? In your pairs, one of you speaks Laertes's thoughts in response to Claudius's rhetoric, thus elaborating the short responses that he gives in the script. From what you know of Laertes's character in the earlier part of the play, what types of inner responses are most appropriate here?

1 **made confession** 坦言
2 **For … defence** 说到您高超的防守剑法和剑术
3 **escrimers** 击剑大师
4 **envenom** 加抹毒药
5 **play** 比试
6 **begun by time** 起始于某一时间点
7 **in passages of proof** 经验证明
8 **qualifies** 减少，减弱
9 **wick … abate** 让火苗减弱的灯芯或灯捻
10 **a like goodness still** 一种同样好的状态
11 **plurisy** 胸膜炎（被认为是由体液过剩导致）；过量
12 **spendthrift** 节俭，手紧
13 **to … th'ulcer** 直击痈疮病灶

CLAUDIUS He made confession[1] of you,
And gave you such a masterly report
For art and exercise in your defence[2],
And for your rapier most especial,
That he cried out 'twould be a sight indeed
If one could match you. [Th'escrimers[3] of their nation
He swore had neither motion, guard, nor eye,
If you opposed them.] Sir, this report of his
Did Hamlet so envenom[4] with his envy
That he could nothing do but wish and beg
Your sudden coming o'er to play[5] with you.
Now out of this –

LAERTES What out of this, my lord?

CLAUDIUS Laertes, was your father dear to you?
Or are you like the painting of a sorrow,
A face without a heart?

LAERTES Why ask you this?

CLAUDIUS Not that I think you did not love your father,
But that I know love is begun by time[6],
And that I see, in passages of proof[7],
Time qualifies[8] the spark and fire of it.
[There lives within the very flame of love
A kind of wick or snuff that will abate[9] it,
And nothing is at a like goodness still[10],
For goodness, growing to a plurisy[11],
Dies in his own too much. That we would do,
We should do when we would, for this 'would' changes,
And hath abatements and delays as many
As there are tongues, are hands, are accidents;
And then this 'should' is like a spendthrift[12] sigh,
That hurts by easing. But to the quick of th'ulcer[13] –]
Hamlet comes back; what would you undertake
To show yourself in deed your father's son
More than in words?

LAERTES To cut his throat i'th'church.

Claudius plans a duel in which one of the swords will not be blunted. Laertes offers to poison the sharpened foil. To make Hamlet's death certain, Claudius proposes to poison Hamlet's drink.

剧情简介：克劳迭策划一场决斗，让其中一把剑为开刃剑。雷厄提提出在尖锐的剑上涂毒，让哈慕雷难逃一死，克劳迭则提出在哈慕雷的酒中下毒。

Characters 人物分析

Insights into character (in pairs)

After careful preparation, Claudius has raised Laertes's hatred of Hamlet to fever pitch. Laertes now plots with Claudius a devious and seemingly foolproof way to murder Hamlet. The two men build upon each other's wickedness in devising ways of ensuring Hamlet's death in a duel. The plot to kill Hamlet involves a duelling sword, sharp ('unbated') and poisoned. With it, Laertes will strike Hamlet in a deceitful thrust ('pass of practice'). A poisoned drink will kill Hamlet if Laertes fails to kill him with his sword.

Take parts and read the script opposite. Then talk together to discover how far you agree with the following statements:

- It is surprising that Laertes has brought a poison ('unction') with him.
- Hamlet is accurately described by Claudius as 'remiss, / Most generous, and free from all contriving' ('remiss' = unsuspecting, 'contriving' = deviousness [算计]).
- Claudius has all the details of his plot already in his mind, and only pretends to think up the 'back or second' (the poisoned cup).

1 Another turning point

Act 4 in Shakespeare's plays often marks a turning point. We have already seen that Hamlet is now more focused on revenge in the wake of seeing Fortinbras's army march to fight for a small patch of ground in Poland. Laertes is resolved, and plots with Claudius the downfall and death of Hamlet. In tragedy, the spring (弹簧) has been tightened and now unwinds towards its conclusion.

a See if you can identify the exact line at which the turn takes place for Hamlet and for Laertes.

b At the same time, the movement toward resolution is a slow one. This scene, in particular, unfolds at a sedate (沉静) and reflective pace. If you were forced to cut part of it, which sections or lines would you eliminate? Make your decisions, then compare notes and discuss in the class as a whole.

1 sanctuarize 庇护
2 keep close 好好藏起来
3 put on those 安排那些
4 wager 下注，押注
5 remiss 不留心，马大哈
6 peruse the foils 细查那些剑
7 shuffling 搅乱，打乱
8 pass of practice 蓄意一击
9 Requite 报复
10 unction of mountebank 江湖郎中的膏药
11 cataplasm 药膏
12 simples 草药
13 virtue 功效
14 withal = with it
15 shape 谋划
16 drift 用意，居心
17 back or second 补救方案
18 blast in proof 证实失败（blast 意思是“爆炸”，引申为“行动失败”）
19 preferred him / A chalice 给他端来一杯
20 for the nonce 这一次

CLAUDIUS No place indeed should murder sanctuarize[1];
Revenge should have no bounds. But, good Laertes,
Will you do this, keep close[2] within your chamber;
Hamlet, returned, shall know you are come home;
We'll put on those[3] shall praise your excellence,
And set a double varnish on the fame
The Frenchman gave you; bring you in fine together,
And wager[4] on your heads. He being remiss[5],
Most generous, and free from all contriving,
Will not peruse the foils[6], so that with ease,
Or with a little shuffling[7], you may choose
A sword unbated, and in a pass of practice[8]
Requite[9] him for your father.

LAERTES I will do't,
And for that purpose I'll anoint my sword.
I bought an unction of a mountebank[10],
So mortal that but dip a knife in it,
Where it draws blood no cataplasm[11] so rare,
Collected from all simples[12] that have virtue[13]
Under the moon, can save the thing from death
That is but scratched withal[14]. I'll touch my point
With this contagion, that if I gall him slightly,
It may be death.

CLAUDIUS Let's further think of this,
Weigh what convenience both of time and means
May fit us to our shape[15]. If this should fail,
And that our drift[16] look through our bad performance,
'Twere better not assayed. Therefore this project
Should have a back or second[17], that might hold
If this did blast in proof[18]. Soft, let me see.
We'll make a solemn wager on your cunnings –
I ha't!
When in your motion you are hot and dry,
As make your bouts more violent to that end,
And that he calls for drink, I'll have preferred him
A chalice[19] for the nonce[20], whereon but sipping,
If he by chance escape your venomed stuck,
Our purpose may hold there. But stay, what noise?

Enter GERTRUDE

How, sweet queen!

Gertrude tells how Ophelia drowned: she fell from a willow as she tried to hang flowers on it, and was pulled under by her clothes. Laertes unsuccessfully fights back tears. Claudius lies about calming Laertes.

剧情简介：葛楚德讲了奥菲丽叶溺死的情形：她往一棵柳树上挂花时从树上掉了下来，被身上的衣服拖到了水下。雷厄提忍了又忍还是掉下泪来。克劳迭撒谎说他安抚了雷厄提。

▲ *Ophelia* by the Victorian painter Sir John Everett Millais.

1 'There is a willow grows askant a brook'

(in small groups)

Lines 166–83 are much admired for their imaginative and poetic quality. The images of nature reflect Shakespeare's use of flowers in the play. Ophelia's innocence and chanting of 'old lauds' (religious hymns) contrast with Laertes's fall from grace. But Laertes, moments ago a pitiless revenger, is moved to tears.

a Explore different ways of speaking the lines: individually, chorally, echoing, and/or sharing them between you.

b Discuss together: does Gertrude know all the details of Ophelia's death?

Stagecraft 导演技巧

Claudius and Gertrude (in threes)

Claudius lies to his wife, saying he has attempted to calm Laertes. Will she obey his two commands to 'follow'?

a Decide how the three characters will exit, starting with Laertes at line 191 and taking in Claudius's line 'Let's follow, Gertrude'.

b Perform the end of the scene together, indicating through your actions your interpretation of the three characters at this point.

1 grows askant a brook 斜伸到一条小溪上方

2 hoar 苍白

3 garlands 花环

4 crow-flowers = water crowfoot 毛茛花（生长在水边的一种草本植物，花多为黄色）

5 nettles 荨麻花

6 long purples 雄红门兰花（学名是*orchis mascula*，花多为紫色；*orchis*和*mascula*的词源义分别是“睾丸”和“雄性”，前者得名自这种花的双球状根）

7 liberal ... name 什么话都说的羊倌给了它一个更粗俗的名字

8 cold ... them 贞洁的少女称之为“死人手指”

9 pendant boughs 下伸的大树枝

10 cronet 花环

11 envious sliver 不怀好意的枝丫

12 bore her up 把她托起来

13 lauds 颂歌

14 incapable of 意识不到

15 native ... element 天生就适应水

16 with their drink 吸足了水

17 lay 歌声

18 trick 自然习惯

19 The woman will be out （我的）女人气就会消失

20 douts 浇熄

GERTRUDE One woe doth tread upon another's heel,
So fast they follow. Your sister's drowned, Laertes.

LAERTES Drowned! Oh where?

GERTRUDE There is a willow grows askant a brook[1],
That shows his hoar[2] leaves in the glassy stream.
Therewith fantastic garlands[3] did she make,
Of crow-flowers[4], nettles[5], daisies, and long purples[6],
That liberal shepherds give a grosser name[7],
But our cold maids do dead men's fingers call them[8].
There on the pendant boughs[9] her cronet[10] weeds
Clamb'ring to hang, an envious sliver[11] broke,
When down her weedy trophies and herself
Fell in the weeping brook. Her clothes spread wide,
And mermaid-like awhile they bore her up[12],
Which time she chanted snatches of old lauds[13]
As one incapable of[14] her own distress,
Or like a creature native and indued
Unto that element[15]. But long it could not be
Till that her garments, heavy with their drink[16],
Pulled the poor wretch from her melodious lay[17]
To muddy death.

LAERTES Alas, then she is drowned?

GERTRUDE Drowned, drowned.

LAERTES Too much of water hast thou, poor Ophelia,
And therefore I forbid my tears. But yet
It is our trick[18]; nature her custom holds,
Let shame say what it will. When these are gone,
The woman will be out[19]. Adieu my lord,
I have a speech of fire that fain would blaze,
But that this folly douts[20] it. *Exit*

CLAUDIUS Let's follow, Gertrude.
How much I had to do to calm his rage!
Now fear I this will give it start again.
Therefore let's follow.

Exeunt

Looking back at Act 4 第4幕回顾

Activities for groups or individuals

1 Appearance versus reality

All Shakespeare's plays in some way explore the theme of reality versus appearance. To complicate matters, it is not always a case of appearance versus reality, but rather that appearance and reality are indistinguishable at times.

- Identify an example in each scene of Act 4 where things are not as they seem. Present your examples (in the form of references, quotations and events) in an assignment on 'Reality and appearance in Act 4 of *Hamlet*'. You may wish to revisit your work on themes in the earlier acts. Is the issue of appearance and reality the dominant theme in *Hamlet*, or do other themes vie for centrality? More generally, show how a theme is developed through the use of imagery, action and ideas. Use quotations to back up your perceptions.

2 Political matters, family matters: a citizen's view

Act 4 offers reminders of the play's political context. The audience learn in Scene 3 that England, recently defeated by Claudius, is now Denmark's client state. In Scene 4, Hamlet encounters the Norwegian army marching against Poland. In Scene 7, Claudius reveals he has fought against the French. Insurrection briefly threatens Claudius's rule when in Scene 5 the citizens of Denmark ('the rabble') sweep aside the palace guards and call for Laertes to be king.

- Imagine that you are a lifelong Danish citizen, who has served in Denmark's army, heard gossip about court happenings, and seen Laertes's return. Either write your account of what you know, or join a group of other 'citizens' and improvise a discussion about events in Act 4.

3 Honour and revenge

Revenge is both a theme and a plot device in *Hamlet*. It is an idea that pervades the play, resurfacing especially towards the end of the play as the revenge theme begins to drive the plot again. But in Act 4, Hamlet, Fortinbras and Laertes are all concerned with 'honour' and 'manhood' as well as 'revenge'.

a Draw a table to compare their different perspectives (see also the activity on p. 176).

b One of the distinctive features of *Hamlet* is that it is a revenge play with a difference – indeed, with a range of dimensions. Can you characterise what these are?

4 Turning points

During Act 4, both Laertes and Hamlet experience turning points in their trajectories as characters: Hamlet is galvanised (激励) into action by witnessing Fortinbras's resolve; and Laertes is spurred to revenge through the machinations of Claudius and his own father's death. The parallels and connections between the two characters are plain to see (both revenge the death of a father).

- Make a comparison, in terms of turning points, with another Shakespeare play that you know well. One example is *Macbeth*, in which Malcolm and Macduff engage in a relatively lengthy deliberation that moves Macduff to take his revenge on Macbeth. Both in *Hamlet* and in *Macbeth*, the turn is a slow one, aided by deliberation, persuasion and a re-orientation on the part of the 'avenger'. At the same time, the action is quickening on a number of fronts via other characters. Write up your comparisons in the form of a short essay. You might find it helpful to map the acts in parallel on a wall – see 'Writing about Shakespeare' on pages 278–9 for more ideas on this.

Throughout the play, Ophelia is dominated by her father, her lover and her brother. Her father makes her reveal her secrets (Act 1) and uses her so that he can spy on Hamlet (Act 2). Hamlet denies he loves her and subjects her to a cruel tongue-lashing (Act 3). Her brother counsels her against Hamlet (Act 1) and is driven to tears by her madness (Act 4). Use the pictures on this page as the basis for an extended essay analysing Ophelia's character and her relationship with the men in the play. You need not necessarily agree that she is dominated by Polonius, Hamlet and Laertes.

Two gravediggers discuss Ophelia's death. They think she committed suicide, but is being allowed a Christian burial because of her high rank.

剧情简介：两个掘墓人谈论奥菲丽叶的死。他们认为她尽管是自杀，还能享受基督教葬礼，是因为她身世显赫。

1 Two gravediggers – alternative perspectives

(in pairs)

After the sombre atmosphere of the previous scene, the mood of the play switches abruptly to comedy – in a graveyard. But Shakespeare is not simply providing comic relief. He is doing here what he does so often: using comedy and ordinary people to provide alternative perspectives on major issues and themes.

a To gain a first impression of the humour, take parts as the two gravediggers (Clown and Other) and read lines 1–50. Afterwards, work out how you would set this scene, and decide how the gravediggers are dressed (see p. 202).

b Invent stage business (actions) to accompany lines 13–17 as the Clown makes clear his meaning.

Write about it 写作练习

Comic relief

There has not been much comedy in the play so far, apart from Hamlet poking fun at Polonius, Rosencrantz and Guildenstern – and that has been very much as part of the core action, with the main characters and their associates. On the contrary, *Hamlet* seems a dark play with a complex central character. Its unrelenting darkness and prison-like feel ('Denmark's a prison') is reinforced by the fact that most of the action (with the exception of Act 4 Scene 4) takes place in the castle. The comic relief offered by the present scene comes late in the play.

Compare this scene with one other such scene of comic relief, for example the Porter's scene immediately after Duncan's murder in *Macbeth* (Act 2 Scene 3).

- Why do the comic scenes occur where they do?
- Is their function the same or different in each tragedy?
- Do they reinforce or distract from the themes of the plays?

1 wilfully 故意
2 straight = straight away 赶紧
3 crowner has sat on her 验尸官已经验明了她的死因
4 *se offendendo* = self-defence
5 Argal = Ergo 因此
6 goodman delver 掘墓家主（goodman是人们对乡绅的尊称）
7 will he, nill he 无论他愿意不愿意
8 quest law 验尸法（quest = inquest）
9 countenance 准许
10 even-Christen 普通基督徒
11 hold up Adam's profession 维持亚当的职业（亚当生活在伊甸园，其职业是园丁，后面说到亚当挖地，这就是在干园丁的活儿）
12 A … arms = He was the first gentleman that ever bore arms 他是第一个有族徽的绅士（bore arms在这里是双关语，也可以表示"长着胳膊"；下面说亚当挖地，没有胳膊当然无法挖地）
13 heathen 异教徒
14 the scripture 《圣经》
15 confess thyself （这是一句俗语的前半句，后半句是and behanged）

Act 5 Scene 1

A graveyard near the castle

Enter TWO CLOWNS *(gravediggers)*

CLOWN Is she to be buried in Christian burial, when she wilfully[1] seeks her own salvation?

OTHER I tell thee she is, therefore make her grave straight[2]. The crowner hath sat on her[3], and finds it Christian burial.

CLOWN How can that be, unless she drowned herself in her own defence?

OTHER Why, 'tis found so.

CLOWN It must be *se offendendo*[4], it cannot be else. For here lies the point: if I drown myself wittingly, it argues an act, and an act hath three branches – it is to act, to do, to perform. Argal[5], she drowned herself wittingly.

OTHER Nay, but hear you goodman delver[6] –

CLOWN Give me leave. Here lies the water – good. Here stands the man – good. If the man go to this water and drown himself, it is will he, nill he[7], he goes – mark you that. But if the water come to him, and drown him, he drowns not himself. Argal, he that is not guilty of his own death shortens not his own life.

OTHER But is this law?

CLOWN Ay marry is't, crowner's quest law[8].

OTHER Will you ha' the truth on't? If this had not been a gentlewoman, she should have been buried out o' Christian burial.

CLOWN Why, there thou sayst – and the more pity that great folk should have countenance[9] in this world to drown or hang themselves more than their even-Christen[10]. Come, my spade; there is no ancient gentlemen but gardeners, ditchers, and gravemakers; they hold up Adam's profession[11].

OTHER Was he a gentleman?

CLOWN A was the first that ever bore arms[12].

OTHER Why, he had none.

CLOWN What, art a heathen[13]? How dost thou understand the scripture[14]? The scripture says Adam digged. Could he dig without arms? I'll put another question to thee. If thou answerest me not to the purpose, confess thyself[15] –

The gravedigger's question puzzles his mate; the answer praises gravediggers. The gravedigger sings about becoming old. Hamlet speculates on whose skull has been thrown out of the grave.

剧情简介：掘墓人甲的问题把他的同伴搞糊涂了。他的答案赞扬了掘墓人。掘墓人甲唱起一首关于人变老的歌。哈慕雷仔细辨认他们从坟墓里扔出的是谁的头骨。

▼ How can death be considered humorous? Why is this? Use this image to debate the idea. How does your answer fit with Hamlet's approach, and with themes in the play?

1 'the hand of little employment hath the daintier sense'

Do you think lines 58–9 mean that people who don't work have finer feelings than those who do? Or that the less often you do something, the more emotional impact it's likely to have on you? Or is Hamlet echoing the Player King's sentiments that custom deadens the senses (as the previous line suggests: 'property of easiness' = a job that causes him no worry)?

2 Hamlet's return to action

We have not seen Hamlet for a while. He has returned from the journey to England, as we learnt via the letter to Horatio in Act 4 Scene 6. Has he been met by Horatio, and is he now walking 'near the castle' (the given setting for Act 5 Scene 1) on his way back?

- Write a note in your Director's Journal on how you would ask Hamlet to play this re-entry. Fired up and ready for revenge, as appeared the case at the end of Act 4 Scene 4; or calm and purposeful, in a new state of 'readiness'? Or neither of these? How would you account for the change in mood and purpose?

1 shipwright 造船工
2 frame 绞架
3 unyoke 给你卸套（让你歇工）
4 Mass = By the Mass 以弥撒起誓
5 Cudgel thy brains 烧你的脑子；绞尽脑汁
6 dull ass 蠢驴（可能是个双关）
7 mend his pace 加快脚步
8 Yaughan （酒馆名字）
9 stoup of liquor 大杯啤酒
10 behove 取乐
11 hath the daintier sense 触觉更敏感
12 clawed me in his clutch 一把把我抓在他手心
13 intil = into
14 jowls 丢
15 Cain 该隐（据说该隐用驴的下颌骨打死了弟弟亚伯）
16 o'erreaches 骑在……头上
17 circumvent 智胜；瞒过

OTHER Go to!

CLOWN What is he that builds stronger than either the mason, the shipwright[1], or the carpenter?

OTHER The gallows-maker, for that frame[2] outlives a thousand tenants.

CLOWN I like thy wit well in good faith. The gallows does well, but how does it well? It does well to those that do ill. Now, thou dost ill to say the gallows is built stronger than the church; argal, the gallows may do well to thee. To't again, come.

OTHER Who builds stronger than a mason, a shipwright, or a carpenter?

CLOWN Ay, tell me that, and unyoke[3].

OTHER Marry, now I can tell.

CLOWN To't.

OTHER Mass[4], I cannot tell.

Enter HAMLET *and* HORATIO *afar off*

CLOWN Cudgel thy brains[5] no more about it, for your dull ass[6] will not mend his pace[7] with beating; and when you are asked this question next, say a grave-maker. The houses he makes lasts till doomsday. Go, get thee to Yaughan[8], fetch me a stoup of liquor[9].

[*Exit Second Clown*]

In youth when I did love, did love, *Song*
Methought it was very sweet
To contract-o the time for-a my behove[10],
Oh methought there-a was nothing-a meet.

HAMLET Has this fellow no feeling of his business? A sings in grave-making.

HORATIO Custom hath made it in him a property of easiness.

HAMLET 'Tis e'en so, the hand of little employment hath the daintier sense[11].

CLOWN But age with his stealing steps *Song*
Hath clawed me in his clutch[12],
And hath shipped me intil[13] the land,
As if I had never been such.

[*Throws up a skull*]

HAMLET That skull had a tongue in it, and could sing once. How the knave jowls[14] it to th' ground, as if 'twere Cain's[15] jawbone, that did the first murder. This might be the pate of a politician which this ass now o'erreaches[16], one that would circumvent[17] God, might it not?

HORATIO It might my lord.

The two skulls thrown out by the gravedigger provoke Hamlet to muse on mortality. He reflects that, in spite of all a lawyer's legal documents entitling him to land, death is the only end.

剧情简介：掘墓人丢出来的两个头骨引发哈慕雷对死亡的沉思。他心想，一位律师就算有地契又如何，死亡才是唯一的结局。

Themes 主题分析

Land and its relationship to death (in small groups)

Hamlet's extended reflection on lawyers, their arcane (晦涩难懂) diction and their preoccupation with laws and cases that deal with land and property, introduces a new dimension in the play: the relationship between land and death.

Each group should discuss one of the following propositions and then present their comments and conclusions to the whole class, who can contribute further points.

a Hamlet is satirical about the law and lawyers (as were many Elizabethan and Jacobean playwrights, including Shakespere) because they make money from common law disputes, and their language is always impenetrable. You might bring in a present-day statute or legal document to see if anything has changed.

b Land is the earth, which all buried people return to in death. But land is fought over – remember Fortinbras and his army, heading south through Denmark to fight over a patch of land in Poland – because territory is precious. Hamlet and Laertes will soon grapple on the ground over Ophelia's body. Therefore death is tied up not only with Hamlet's reflection on mankind in general, but also with his position as prince of Denmark and as a lover.

c Death is a great leveller. For all the qualities of spirit, soul, heart and mind that have been explored in the play so far, everyone – from a king or queen to a gravedigger – ends up dead. Track Hamlet's preoccupation with death throughout the play, and discuss why he is so fascinated by the work of the gravediggers and their humour. What is his mood in this scene?

d There is a great deal of **dramatic irony** (戏剧反讽) here, which means that the audience knows something that the characters do not. Neither Hamlet nor Horatio seems aware that Ophelia is dead and is about to be buried. Indeed, the gravediggers were talking about her death at the start of the scene. What else does Hamlet not know that is conspiring toward his own death?

e Sex and death: why are these so closely associated in Hamlet's consciousness? See line 77 where he talks about 'breeding'. Is he driven by an excessive puritan morality that sees the body, and physical pleasures, as sinful? Could his education at the Protestant, Lutheran Wittenburg University be influential in this regard? In terms of religion, where does Hamlet stand?

1 Good morrow = Good morning
2 my Lady Worm's 蛆虫女士的
3 chopless 没下颌骨
4 mazard 脑瓜
5 revolution 命运轮转
6 breeding 教养
7 loggets 木棍游戏（参加者比赛朝一个木桩丢木棍）
8 For and = And moreover
9 shrowding sheet 裹尸布
10 quiddities/quillets 抠字眼儿
11 tenures （租地或雇佣）契约
12 sconce 脑壳
13 battery 殴打
14 statutes 法律文书
15 recognizances 债权书
16 fines 地契
17 vouchers 双保人
18 recoveries （财产）回归文书
19 fines … recoveries 地契中的终极地契和回归文书中的终极回归（fine在中代英语里写作fin，与法文*finis*同源，都表示“最后；终点”）
20 fine pate 漂亮脑瓜
21 fine dirt 好土（fine可以用来表示沙土的细腻）
22 length … indentures 一式两份契约约定的事项
23 conveyances 财产转移证书
24 parchment 羊皮纸
25 They … that 从这当中求取保险者与牛羊有何不同
26 sirrah 伙计（上等人对下等人的称呼）

HAMLET Or of a courtier, which could say 'Good morrow[1] sweet lord, how dost thou sweet lord?' This might be my Lord Such-a-one, that praised my Lord Such-a-one's horse when a meant to beg it, might it not?

HORATIO Ay my lord.

HAMLET Why, e'en so, and now my Lady Worm's[2], chopless[3], and knocked about the mazard[4] with a sexton's spade. Here's fine revolution[5], and we had the trick to see't. Did these bones cost no more the breeding[6] but to play at loggets[7] with 'em? Mine ache to think on't.

CLOWN A pickaxe and a spade, a spade, *Song*
For and[8] a shrowding sheet[9],
Oh a pit of clay for to be made,
For such a guest is meet.
[*Throws up another skull*]

HAMLET There's another. Why may not that be the skull of a lawyer? Where be his quiddities[10] now, his quillets[10], his cases, his tenures[11], and his tricks? Why does he suffer this rude knave now to knock him about the sconce[12] with a dirty shovel, and will not tell him of his action of battery[13]? Hum, this fellow might be in's time a great buyer of land, with his statutes[14], his recognizances[15], his fines[16], his double vouchers[17], his recoveries[18]. Is this the fine of his fines and the recovery of his recoveries[19], to have his fine pate[20] full of fine dirt[21]? Will his vouchers vouch him no more of his purchases, and double ones too, than the length and breadth of a pair of indentures[22]? The very conveyances[23] of his lands will scarcely lie in this box, and must th'inheritor himself have no more, ha?

HORATIO Not a jot more my lord.

HAMLET Is not parchment[24] made of sheepskins?

HORATIO Ay my lord, and of calves' skins too.

HAMLET They are sheep and calves which seek out assurance in that[25]. I will speak to this fellow. Whose grave's this sirrah[26]?

CLOWN Mine sir.

(*Sings*)
Oh a pit of clay for to be made
For such a guest is meet.

HAMLET I think it be thine indeed, for thou liest in't.

CLOWN You lie out on't sir, and therefore 'tis not yours. For my part, I do not lie in't, yet it is mine.

The gravedigger's punning and playing with language prompt Hamlet to reflect on the way peasants imitate courtiers. The gravedigger's remarks reveal that Hamlet is about thirty years old.

剧情简介： 掘墓人的双关语和文字游戏让哈慕雷思考起农民对朝臣的模仿。掘墓人的话透露出哈慕雷大概30岁。

Language in the play 剧中语言

Quick-fire dialogue? (in pairs)

The dialogue opposite between Hamlet and the Clown is full of innuendo, wit and humour. Notice that almost all Hamlet's speeches are in the form of questions. Try reading aloud this dialogue in different ways:

- with Hamlet responding quickly, and the gravedigger responding more slowly
- the other way round
- with both of them exchanging utterances at speed
- with some variation throughout the exchange.

Which works best, and why?

1 How old is Hamlet?

Identify the two lines spoken by the Clown that suggest Hamlet is about thirty. Then think about whether you imagine Hamlet as thirty, or older or younger. In what senses might he seem adolescent? How old do you imagine Gertrude to be? Claudius? Horatio? (See also p. 271.)

2 Social class (in pairs)

In lines 117 – 18, Hamlet says that 'the toe of a peasant comes so near the heel of a courtier'. Earlier in the play, he had expressed the view that 'The time is out of joint'. Does the death of King Hamlet so upset the state of Denmark and of Hamlet's state of mind that social order is turned upside down? Discuss these points with your partner:

- Does social class play a part in Hamlet's attitude towards a) Horatio, b) Ophelia, c) Polonius and d) Rosencrantz and Guildenstern?
- Does Hamlet's status as a prince help or hinder him in relations with other characters in the play? Remember that Hamlet, as a prince, is loved by the people.
- Where would you place Hamlet on a spectrum of political views: as a conservative, a liberal or a socialist? (You may wish to change those categories according to the political system in which you live – they do not mean the same across the world!)

1 **quick** 活着的
2 **absolute** 十足
3 **by the card** 照本宣科（这是航海术语，本义是“根据海图航行”；card = chart）
4 **equivocation** 含糊
5 **picked** 讲究
6 **galls his kibe** 磨到他脚后跟上的冻疮
7 **pocky corses** 满是红疹的尸体（这是墓主人生前染上梅毒的症状；corses = corpses）
8 **laying in** 下葬
9 **tanner** 制革匠

HAMLET Thou dost lie in't, to be in't and say 'tis thine. 'Tis for the dead, not for the quick[1], therefore thou liest.

CLOWN 'Tis a quick lie sir, 'twill away again from me to you.

HAMLET What man dost thou dig it for?

CLOWN For no man sir.

HAMLET What woman then?

CLOWN For none neither.

HAMLET Who is to be buried in't?

CLOWN One that was a woman sir, but rest her soul she's dead.

HAMLET How absolute[2] the knave is! We must speak by the card[3], or equivocation[4] will undo us. By the lord, Horatio, this three years I have took note of it: the age is grown so picked[5], that the toe of the peasant comes so near the heel of the courtier, he galls his kibe[6]. How long hast thou been grave-maker?

CLOWN Of all the days i'th'year, I came to't that day that our last King Hamlet o'ercame Fortinbras.

HAMLET How long is that since?

CLOWN Cannot you tell that? Every fool can tell that. It was the very day that young Hamlet was born, he that is mad and sent into England.

HAMLET Ay marry, why was he sent into England?

CLOWN Why, because a was mad. A shall recover his wits there, or if a do not, 'tis no great matter there.

HAMLET Why?

CLOWN 'Twill not be seen in him there. There the men are as mad as he.

HAMLET How came he mad?

CLOWN Very strangely they say.

HAMLET How, strangely?

CLOWN Faith, e'en with losing his wits.

HAMLET Upon what ground?

CLOWN Why, here in Denmark. I have been sexton here man and boy thirty years.

HAMLET How long will a man lie i'th'earth ere he rot?

CLOWN Faith, if a be not rotten before a die, as we have many pocky corses[7] nowadays that will scarce hold the laying in[8], a will last you some eight year, or nine year. A tanner[9] will last you nine year.

HAMLET Why he more than another?

Hamlet expresses disgust at the thought that Yorick, once so full of tricks and laughter, is now merely a skull. The physical corruption brings his mother (or women in general) bitterly to his mind.

剧情简介：哈慕雷表示恶心，因为他想起曾经一肚子鬼点子而又笑声不断的约瑞如今仅剩一个头骨。人体的腐败令他想起母亲（或者所有女人），一阵难受。

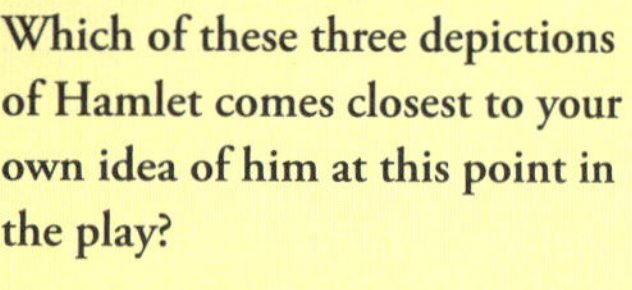

Which of these three depictions of Hamlet comes closest to your own idea of him at this point in the play?

1 hide 皮
2 whoreson 小贱人（对关系极好的人的戏谑称呼）
3 lien = lain
4 pestilence 瘟疫
5 flagon 大酒瓶
6 jester 俳优（中世纪欧洲宫廷或贵族家中讲笑话供人取乐的小丑，也称作fool）
7 fancy 想象
8 My gorge rises 我的胃直往上翻
9 gibes 俏皮话
10 gambols 胡闹
11 were … roar 以前常常笑翻一桌子人
12 chop-fallen 耷拉个脸
13 favour 模样
14 Alexander 亚历山大大帝（前356—前323年，马其顿王国国王）
15 base uses 低贱的用处
16 bunghole 桶眼
17 too curiously 太细

CLOWN Why sir, his hide[1] is so tanned with his trade, that a will keep out water a great while, and your water is a sore decayer of your whoreson[2] dead body. Here's a skull now: this skull hath lien[3] you i'th'earth three and twenty years.

HAMLET Whose was it?

CLOWN A whoreson mad fellow's it was. Whose do you think it was?

HAMLET Nay I know not.

CLOWN A pestilence[4] on him for a mad rogue, a poured a flagon[5] of Rhenish on my head once. This same skull sir, was Yorick's skull, the king's jester[6].

HAMLET This?

CLOWN E'en that.

HAMLET Let me see. [*Takes the skull.*] Alas poor Yorick! I knew him Horatio, a fellow of infinite jest, of most excellent fancy[7], he hath borne me on his back a thousand times – and now how abhorred in my imagination it is! My gorge rises[8] at it. Here hung those lips that I have kissed I know not how oft. Where be your gibes[9] now? your gambols[10], your songs, your flashes of merriment that were wont to set the table on a roar[11]? Not one now, to mock your own grinning? Quite chop-fallen[12]? Now get you to my lady's chamber, and tell her, let her paint an inch thick, to this favour[13] she must come. Make her laugh at that. – Prithee Horatio, tell me one thing.

HORATIO What's that my lord?

HAMLET Dost thou think Alexander[14] looked o' this fashion i'th'earth?

HORATIO E'en so.

HAMLET And smelt so? Pah! [*Puts down the skull*]

HORATIO E'en so my lord.

HAMLET To what base uses[15] we may return, Horatio! Why may not imagination trace the noble dust of Alexander, till a find it stopping a bunghole[16]?

HORATIO 'Twere to consider too curiously[17] to consider so.

Hamlet reasons that death transforms great kings into trivial objects. A Priest tells Laertes that Claudius's command has granted Ophelia a Christian funeral. As a suicide, the Church would deny her burial.

剧情简介：哈慕雷思考着死亡将伟大帝王化成微不足道的东西。神父告诉雷厄提，克劳迭准许给奥菲丽叶举行基督教葬礼。原本教堂是要拒绝她这个自杀者的。

1 Laertes (in threes)

The last time we saw Laertes, he was in tears at the news of Ophelia's death and suppressing an immediate urge to avenge his sister's death. Now he follows her coffin to her burial. It is not so much the Priest's views on the kind of burial she is allowed, but Laertes's persistent questioning, that is dramatically significant here.

a Take lines 190–209 and prepare Laertes's background thoughts behind each of the questions he asks. You might write these in prose or verse as asides, or simply as his thoughts. Aim for ten or so lines, which you can act out, to represent his background thinking for each question.

b Then perform the dialogue, complete with thoughts expressed aloud by the third person. Which way will the third person face? Will the third person be less or more incensed than Laertes? Will the dialogue increase in intensity – and if so, how will lines 205–9 be delivered?

2 'Her death was doubtful'

It looks as though the Priest has found a compromise: 'virgin crants' and 'maiden strewments' are to be thrown in the grave, instead of the customary stones and broken fragments of a suicide burial.

a What evidence can you find in the script that Ophelia did commit suicide?

b As a class, debate contemporary attitudes toward suicide, as well as religious beliefs and taboos about it.

1 loam 沃土，肥土
2 flaw 寒风
3 Aside 站一边儿
4 maimèd rites 简薄 / 不完整的葬礼
5 Fordo 糟践
6 of some estate 有些地位的
7 Couch 躲起来
8 *Retiring* 退至幕后
9 obsequies 葬礼仪式
10 warranty 许可
11 ground unsanctified 没有被神圣化的地方
12 last trumpet 最后审判日的号角
13 Shards 瓦片
14 crants 花圈
15 strewments 撒花
16 profane 亵渎
17 sage requiem 安魂曲

HAMLET No faith, not a jot, but to follow him thither with modesty enough, and likelihood to lead it, as thus: Alexander died, Alexander was buried, Alexander returneth to dust, the dust is earth, of earth we make loam[1], and why of that loam whereto he was converted might they not stop a beer-barrel?

Imperious Caesar, dead and turned to clay,
Might stop a hole, to keep the wind away.
Oh that that earth which kept the world in awe
Should patch a wall t'expel the winter's flaw[2]!

But soft, but soft! Aside[3] – here comes the king,
The queen, the courtiers.

Enter CLAUDIUS, GERTRUDE, LAERTES, *and a coffin*, [*with* PRIEST] *and* LORDS *attendant*

Who is this they follow?
And with such maimèd rites[4]? This doth betoken
The corse they follow did with desperate hand
Fordo[5] it own life. 'Twas of some estate[6].
Couch[7] we awhile and mark. [*Retiring*[8] *with Horatio*]

LAERTES What ceremony else?

HAMLET That is Laertes, a very noble youth. Mark.

LAERTES What ceremony else?

PRIEST Her obsequies[9] have been as far enlarged
As we have warranty[10]. Her death was doubtful,
And but that great command o'ersways the order,
She should in ground unsanctified[11] have lodged
Till the last trumpet[12]. For charitable prayers,
Shards[13], flints, and pebbles should be thrown on her.
Yet here she is allowed her virgin crants[14],
Her maiden strewments[15], and the bringing home
Of bell and burial.

LAERTES Must there no more be done?

PRIEST No more be done.
We should profane[16] the service of the dead
To sing sage requiem[17] and such rest to her
As to peace-parted souls.

Laertes insults the Priest. Gertrude mourns Ophelia. Laertes curses Hamlet and leaps into the grave. Hamlet comes forward, and Laertes tries to strangle him. The attendants stop the fight.

剧情简介：雷厄提骂神父。葛楚德为奥菲丽叶哀悼。雷厄提诅咒哈慕雷，并跳入奥菲丽叶的墓穴。哈慕雷上前去，雷厄提要掐死他。仆从们阻止了这场打斗。

1 Gertrude's wish (in pairs)

Talk together about how lines 210–13 add to your knowledge of Gertrude. Begin by telling each other whether her wish for Hamlet and Ophelia to marry came as a surprise to you. Do you think her words are genuine?

Stagecraft 导演技巧

Where do they fight – in or out of the grave?

In some productions, Hamlet leaps into the grave and Laertes struggles with him there. The directors of these productions argue that the fight in the grave is dramatically symbolic. Other directors feel strongly that Laertes should climb out of the grave to attack Hamlet.

- What is your view? Draw up a list of the advantages and disadvantages of each practice. Use the list to reach a conclusion about your own preferences.

Language in the play 剧中语言

A heightened state (in pairs)

Although we know that Claudius has persuaded Laertes to fight with Hamlet in a duel with a poisoned sword and chalice, the chance opportunity to fight comes earlier as they encounter each other over (and/or in) Ophelia's grave. Consider the language in this encounter.

a Look at each of the six sentences Laertes speaks in the script opposite. For each, write two words expressing the emotional tone of the sentence (the first might be 'tender, loving').

b 'This is I, / Hamlet the Dane.' Hamlet seems to be claiming the throne: 'the Dane' usually means 'King of Denmark'. Suggest how he speaks the first half of line 225 and how each main character (Claudius, Gertrude, Laertes, Horatio) should react.

c In lines 213–25, both Laertes and Hamlet use the hyperbolic (exaggerated) language of the traditional hero of revenge tragedy. Take parts and read the lines aloud, emphasising this heroic style of language.

1 churlish 无知；傲慢
2 ministering 照拂苍生的灵魂
3 liest howling 在地狱哭号
4 decked = decorated
5 thy most ingenious sense 你无人可比的聪慧
6 Pelion 佩琉山（又译作“皮立翁山”，位于希腊中东部色萨利［Thessaly］的一座山，得名自希腊神话中的宙斯之孙、阿喀琉斯之父、色萨利国王佩琉［Pelius］）
7 Olympus 奥林珀斯山（又译作“奥林匹斯山”，位于希腊北部的一座山，在希腊神话中是众神所居之所）
8 Bears such an emphasis 值得这样重视
9 Conjures the wandering stars 感召漫游的群星
10 wonder-wounded 惊愕
11 splenitive 脾气暴
12 asunder 分开
13 theme 事情
14 wag 眨

LAERTES Lay her i'th'earth,
And from her fair and unpolluted flesh
May violets spring. I tell thee, churlish[1] priest,
A ministering[2] angel shall my sister be
When thou liest howling[3].

HAMLET What, the fair Ophelia!

GERTRUDE Sweets to the sweet, farewell. [*Scattering flowers*]
I hoped thou shouldst have been my Hamlet's wife.
I thought thy bride-bed to have decked[4], sweet maid,
And not t'have strewed thy grave.

LAERTES Oh treble woe
Fall ten times treble on that cursèd head
Whose wicked deed thy most ingenious sense[5]
Deprived thee of. Hold off the earth awhile
Till I have caught her once more in mine arms.
Leaps in the grave
Now pile your dust upon the quick and dead
Till of this flat a mountain you have made
T'o'ertop old Pelion[6] or the skyish head
Of blue Olympus[7].

HAMLET [*Advancing*] What is he whose grief
Bears such an emphasis[8]? whose phrase of sorrow
Conjures the wandering stars[9], and makes them stand
Like wonder-wounded[10] hearers? This is I,
Hamlet the Dane.
[*Laertes climbs out of the grave*]

LAERTES The devil take thy soul. [*Grappling with him*]

HAMLET Thou pray'st not well.
I prithee take thy fingers from my throat,
For though I am not splenitive[11] and rash,
Yet have I in me something dangerous
Which let thy wisdom fear. Hold off thy hand.

CLAUDIUS Pluck them asunder[12].

GERTRUDE Hamlet, Hamlet!

ALL Gentlemen!

HORATIO Good my lord, be quiet.
[*The Attendants part them*].

HAMLET Why, I will fight with him upon this theme[13]
Until my eyelids will no longer wag[14].

Hamlet rants that his love for Ophelia was infinitely greater than Laertes's, and that he can match any action, however improbable. He leaves with an enigmatic remark. Claudius takes control.

剧情简介：哈慕雷大声说他对奥菲丽叶的爱要无限大于雷厄提对她的爱，不管多不可能的事，他都可以跟雷厄提比。他丢下一句令人不解的话后离去。克劳迭掌控局面。

1 'I'll rant (怒吼，咆哮) as well as thou' (in pairs)

On page 212, you were invited to speak in the exaggerated style of the traditional revenger. Hamlet continues in that bombastic manner. In lines 236–51, he rants furiously against Laertes's love for his sister.

a Speak the lines to each other several times in an over-the-top way, using gestures.

b Talk together about Hamlet's motivation for using such extravagant language. Is it to convince Claudius he is mad? Discuss what Hamlet's final lines 258–9 might mean (no one can be totally sure).

c Why does Hamlet exit early, and how? See the 'Stagecraft' box below for more exploration of the exits from the stage.

2 What is Claudius actually thinking? (in pairs)

Events may be overtaking Claudius's plans. One person speaks Claudius's five sentences in lines 260–6. After each sentence, the other person voices what Claudius has in mind (and notice he says 'your son', not 'our son' or 'my son' as earlier).

Stagecraft 导演技巧

'*Exeunt*' – everyone leaves the stage (in small groups)

The action has suddenly accelerated, after a period at the beginning of this scene that was more reflective, humorous and appeared to bring some light relief. Given that much of the play has proceeded slowly, driven by Hamlet's procrastination and reflection, the scene is now set for a tumultuous (喧嚣的；动荡的) descent to the end of the play.

a Invent a piece of business (an action) for each character as they exit. Perhaps some actions take place over Ophelia's grave. Each character's wordless action expresses their feelings about what has happened in the scene. Don't forget the Clown (gravedigger) and the Priest.

b If you have not yet read to the end of the play, make predictions about what fate and the plot will bring to each of Claudius, Gertrude, Hamlet, Laertes and Horatio.

1 **forbear him** 别跟他计较
2 **Woo't** = Would you
3 **eisel** 醋
4 **eat a crocodile** 吃鳄鱼（鳄鱼会假流泪）
5 **outface** 让我没脸
6 **prate** 吹，吹嘘
7 **our … zone** 我俩头上的封土堆增高到被大火球（指太阳）烧焦其脑壳（Singeing：烧焦）
8 **Make Ossa like a wart** 让奥萨山变得跟疣子一般大小（奥萨山位于佩琉山和奥林珀斯山之间）
9 **golden couplets are disclosed** 那对儿金黄色的幼雏破壳（刚破壳的幼鸽绒毛是金黄色的）
10 **sit drooping** 乖乖地孵蛋（即不再闹了）
11 **The cat … day** 猫会喵喵叫，狗会撒欢儿跳（这是一句成语，意思是“一个人总会有出头之日”）
12 **the present push** 立即行动
13 **living** 不易朽坏（在雷厄提听来会以为是有人要祭出性命）

GERTRUDE O my son, what theme?
HAMLET I loved Ophelia; forty thousand brothers
Could not with all their quantity of love
Make up my sum. What wilt thou do for her?
CLAUDIUS Oh he is mad Laertes.
GERTRUDE For love of God forbear him[1].
HAMLET 'Swounds, show me what thou't do.
Woo't[2] weep, woo't fight, woo't fast, woo't tear thyself?
Woo't drink up eisel[3], eat a crocodile[4]?
I'll do't. Dost thou come here to whine,
To outface[5] me with leaping in her grave?
Be buried quick with her, and so will I.
And if thou prate[6] of mountains, let them throw
Millions of acres on us, till our ground,
Singeing his pate against the burning zone[7],
Make Ossa like a wart[8]. Nay, and thou'lt mouth,
I'll rant as well as thou.
GERTRUDE This is mere madness,
And thus awhile the fit will work on him;
Anon, as patient as the female dove
When that her golden couplets are disclosed[9],
His silence will sit drooping[10].
HAMLET Hear you sir,
What is the reason that you use me thus?
I loved you ever – but it is no matter.
Let Hercules himself do what he may,
The cat will mew, and dog will have his day[11]. *Exit*
CLAUDIUS I pray thee good Horatio wait upon him.
Exit Horatio
(*To Laertes*) Strengthen your patience in our last night's speech;
We'll put the matter to the present push[12]. –
Good Gertrude, set some watch over your son. –
This grave shall have a living[13] monument.
An hour of quiet shortly shall we see,
Till then in patience our proceeding be.
Exeunt

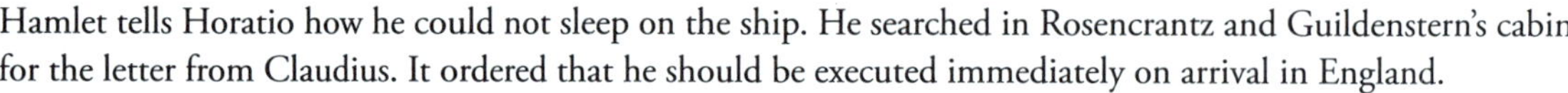

Hamlet tells Horatio how he could not sleep on the ship. He searched in Rosencrantz and Guildenstern's cabin for the letter from Claudius. It ordered that he should be executed immediately on arrival in England.

剧情简介：哈慕雷告诉何瑞修他在船上如何无法入眠。他在柔森克阮茨和吉尔顿斯登的船舱里搜寻克劳迭的手信。信上下令等哈慕雷一到英格兰就处死他。

1 Hamlet's story (in pairs)

It can be considered strange that Hamlet's retelling of his experience on the ship to England comes after the events of the previous scene. But, as the 'Themes' box below asks, perhaps there is a significant development in the depiction of Hamlet's character at this point – and it could be that Ophelia's burial and the contemplation of death has focused his mind.

Retell the story, so that you are clear about what happened en route to England from Denmark, in one of a number of ways:

- as a told tale, in role as Hamlet
- as a storyboard for a filmic sequence
- in a dialogue between the prosecuting lawyer and Hamlet in a court of law
- as if Horatio were retelling it to Marcellus and Barnardo afterwards
- in mime.

Themes 主题分析

'There's a divinity that shapes our ends'

'Divinity' is the will of God, a type of Christian plan that determines people's lives. Hamlet says that important matters are decided by a divine force, however much humans try to plan their lives: an individual has little power over what they will become.

With lines 10–11 in mind, write a paragraph on each of the following:

- Is Hamlet's fate in the play shaped by a 'divinity' or by other factors (his character, chance, other people's actions and so on)?
- Do you believe 'There's a divinity that shapes our ends, / Rough-hew them how we will'? (However you plan and act, what will happen to you is not in your power to determine.)
- How do these two lines signify a development in Hamlet's character? And how do they relate to previous soliloquies?
- How does this world view compare with Horatio's? Is Horatio's reply ('That is most certain') one of deferential agreement, or a real meeting of minds and ideologies between him and Hamlet? Find evidence to prove your case.

1 mutines in the bilboes 戴足枷的叛贼

2 indiscretion 直觉

3 pall 失败

4 learn = teach

5 Rough-hew 修整；打造

6 Fingered their packet 摸到他们的包袱

7 Larded 附着

8 Importing 涉及，关系

9 bugs and goblins 地精妖怪（bug = bugbear）

10 supervise 阅读

11 no leisure bated 不要耽搁

Act 5 Scene 2

The Great Hall of Elsinore Castle

Enter HAMLET *and* HORATIO

HAMLET So much for this sir, now shall you see the other.
You do remember all the circumstance?
HORATIO Remember it my lord!
HAMLET Sir, in my heart there was a kind of fighting
That would not let me sleep. Methought I lay
Worse than the mutines in the bilboes[1]. Rashly,
And praised be rashness for it – let us know,
Our indiscretion[2] sometime serves us well
When our deep plots do pall[3], and that should learn[4] us
There's a divinity that shapes our ends,
Rough-hew[5] them how we will –
HORATIO That is most certain.
HAMLET Up from my cabin,
My sea-gown scarfed about me, in the dark
Groped I to find out them, had my desire,
Fingered their packet[6], and in fine withdrew
To mine own room again, making so bold,
My fears forgetting manners, to unseal
Their grand commission; where I found, Horatio –
O royal knavery! – an exact command,
Larded[7] with many several sorts of reasons,
Importing[8] Denmark's health, and England's too,
With ho! such bugs and goblins[9] in my life,
That on the supervise[10], no leisure bated[11],
No, not to stay the grinding of the axe,
My head should be struck off.
HORATIO Is't possible?
HAMLET Here's the commission, read it at more leisure.
But wilt thou hear now how I did proceed?
HORATIO I beseech you.

Hamlet tells how he wrote a substitute letter commanding the execution of Rosencrantz and Guildenstern. He feels no remorse for their death, dismissing them as mere instruments of Claudius.

剧情简介：哈慕雷讲述他如何写信调包原来那封信，在信里他命令处死柔森克阮茨和吉尔顿斯登。他不为二人的死感到悲痛，将他二人视为克劳迭的工具。

1 Activities on Hamlet's story (in small groups)

In the script opposite, Hamlet describes the letter from Claudius to the king of England, asking the latter to execute Rosencrantz and Guildenstern.

a Write the letter 'fair' (neatly), using lines 31–47 as a guide. Seal it with wax and the imprint of a ring, or design your own seal.

b Hamlet sends Rosencrantz and Guildenstern to their death without a qualm of conscience (line 58). Talk together about whether the two courtiers deserve their fate. What does the decision and his lack of remorse suggest about Hamlet's character?

c Tom Stoppard's play *Rosencrantz and Guildenstern Are Dead* acts out lines 4–55, in which Hamlet describes the theft, the forging, his escape, and how Rosencrantz and Guildenstern sail on to England and death. The 1990 Zeffirelli movie also shows the sequence (and the beheading of the two courtiers in England). Write and/or enact the scene that awaits Rosencrantz and Guildenstern in England.

Themes 主题分析

'mighty opposites'

So far in the play, we have identified a number of interlocking themes that have arisen from the action and speeches.

a Refer back to your notes on these themes, and now see if you can cast them as opposites – for example 'love and its relationship with death', 'the personal and the public', 'kingship and ignominy (耻辱)'; and 'action and inaction'. What others are there?

b Does 'oppositional thinking' like this help clarify your thoughts – or does it limit them? Do all themes have to be expressed in conflicting opposites?

c Does Hamlet mean in lines 60–2 that it was dangerous for Rosencrantz and Guildenstern to come between his plans and those of Claudius (as represented by Laertes in the forthcoming duel)? Is he being prescient (seeing what is to come) and/or just making a larger and more general point?

1 benetted round with 被……团团围住
2 Or = Ere = Before
3 make a prologue 说开场白
4 statists 政客
5 yeoman 仆从
6 conjuration 请求
7 tributary 附庸国
8 the palm 棕榈树枝（象征和平）
9 comma 停顿
10 as-es （as的复数）
11 debatement 考虑到……的工具
12 shriving time 死前忏悔时间
13 ordinant 旨意
14 signet 印戒（小图章）
15 Subscribed it 在它上面签字
16 gave't th'impression 盖上蜡封
17 was sequent 接下来
18 insinuation 搅和进来
19 the baser nature 社会下层之人
20 pass and fell incensèd points 刀剑的无情突刺

HAMLET Being thus benetted round with[1] villainies,
Or[2] I could make a prologue[3] to my brains,
They had begun the play. I sat me down,
Devised a new commission, wrote it fair.
I once did hold it, as our statists[4] do,
A baseness to write fair, and laboured much
How to forget that learning; but sir, now
It did me yeoman's[5] service. Wilt thou know
Th'effect of what I wrote?

HORATIO Ay good my lord.

HAMLET An earnest conjuration[6] from the king,
As England was his faithful tributary[7],
As love between them like the palm[8] might flourish,
As peace should still her wheaten garland wear,
And stand a comma[9] 'tween their amities,
And many suchlike as-es[10] of great charge,
That on the view and knowing of these contents,
Without debatement[11] further, more, or less,
He should those bearers put to sudden death,
Not shriving time[12] allowed.

HORATIO How was this sealed?

HAMLET Why, even in that was heaven ordinant[13].
I had my father's signet[14] in my purse,
Which was the model of that Danish seal;
Folded the writ up in the form of th'other,
Subscribed it[15], gave't th'impression[16], placed it safely,
The changeling never known. Now, the next day
Was our sea-fight, and what to this was sequent[17]
Thou know'st already.

HORATIO So Guildenstern and Rosencrantz go to't.

HAMLET Why man, they did make love to this employment.
They are not near my conscience. Their defeat
Does by their own insinuation[18] grow.
'Tis dangerous when the baser nature[19] comes
Between the pass and fell incensèd points[20]
Of mighty opposites.

HORATIO Why, what a king is this!

Hamlet argues that he is well justified in killing Claudius. He regrets his behaviour towards Laertes, seeing him as a fellow revenger. Hamlet comments dismissively on Osric, and mocks him. Osric tells of a wager.

剧情简介：哈慕雷说他有足够正当的理由杀掉克劳迭。看到雷厄提跟自己一样身负家仇，他很后悔那样对待雷厄提。哈慕雷很不屑地评论奥斯睿并嘲笑他。奥斯睿描述了一个赌局。

Write about it 写作练习

Four reasons for revenge

Hamlet lists four reasons for revenge in lines 63–6: Claudius has killed his father ('my king'), slept with his mother, pushed in front of Hamlet's own claim to the throne ('Popped in between th'election and my hopes'), and plotted Hamlet's death.

- Write the four reasons in order of their importance to Hamlet. Add a paragraph explaining why you have chosen that order.

Language in the play 剧中语言

Explanatory versus dramatic language (in pairs)

In the script opposite, Hamlet acknowledges that he has only a short time to kill Claudius. But he thinks the advantage is briefly with him because Claudius has not yet learned the news from England. Hamlet expresses regret that he overreacted to Laertes's grief, and recognises that they have a similar motive for revenge. He wishes to make peace with Laertes, and says Laertes's exaggerated grief caused his own outburst.

a Match each sentence in the paragraph above with the appropriate lines in the script, then talk together about the ways in which Shakespeare's language is so much more dramatic and suited to performance than the bare description given above.

b The explanatory prose is in the third person, as past 'reported' speech; Hamlet speaks from his own experience, in the first person. Try rewriting the passage in first-person explanatory prose to gauge the further difference that dramatic verse makes.

1 Osric: character or caricature (漫画人物)?

A character might have many sides, but a caricature is usually two-dimensional, emphasising one trait.

- What is your impression of Osric so far? What dramatic function do you think he will serve?

1 Does … me 你难道不认为我现在必须
2 angle 钓钩
3 cozenage 欺瞒，哄骗
4 quit him 杀了他
5 canker of our nature 人性的溃烂
6 The interim's mine 中场休息交给我
7 to say 'one' 说个"一"（那么短的时间）
8 the image of my cause 我复仇事业的样子
9 portraiture 影子
10 court his favours 与他修好
11 bravery 浮夸
12 crib … mess 食槽就能搬到国王的宴会桌上
13 chough 老鸹
14 spacious 广袤
15 bonnet 帽子
16 his = its
17 sultry 闷热

HAMLET Does it not, think thee, stand me[1] now upon –
He that hath killed my king, and whored my mother,
Popped in between th'election and my hopes,
Thrown out his angle[2] for my proper life,
And with such cozenage[3] – is't not perfect conscience
To quit him[4] with this arm? And is't not to be damned
To let this canker of our nature[5] come
In further evil?

HORATIO It must be shortly known to him from England
What is the issue of the business there.

HAMLET It will be short. The interim's mine[6],
And a man's life's no more than to say 'one'[7].
But I am very sorry, good Horatio,
That to Laertes I forgot myself,
For by the image of my cause[8], I see
The portraiture[9] of his. I'll court his favours[10].
But sure the bravery[11] of his grief did put me
Into a towering passion.

HORATIO Peace, who comes here?

Enter young OSRIC

OSRIC Your lordship is right welcome back to Denmark.

HAMLET I humbly thank you sir. – Dost know this water-fly?

HORATIO No my good lord.

HAMLET Thy state is the more gracious, for 'tis a vice to know him. He hath much land and fertile; let a beast be lord of beasts, and his crib shall stand at the king's mess[12]. 'Tis a chough[13], but as I say, spacious[14] in the possession of dirt.

OSRIC Sweet lord, if your lordship were at leisure, I should impart a thing to you from his majesty.

HAMLET I will receive it sir with all diligence of spirit. Put your bonnet[15] to his[16] right use, 'tis for the head.

OSRIC I thank your lordship, it is very hot.

HAMLET No believe me, 'tis very cold, the wind is northerly.

OSRIC It is indifferent cold my lord, indeed.

HAMLET But yet methinks it is very sultry[17] and hot for my complexion.

OSRIC Exceedingly my lord, it is very sultry, as 'twere – I cannot tell how. But my lord, his majesty bade me signify to you that a has laid a great wager on your head. Sir, this is the matter –

Osric praises Laertes as an outstanding model of a gentleman. He uses such affected language that Hamlet makes fun of him by responding in a style that is even more elaborate and obscure.

剧情简介：奥斯睿夸赞雷厄提是绅士中的杰出典范。他的言语十分做作，哈慕雷便用风格更加浮夸和晦涩的回应来取笑他。

▼ How does this image compare to your own vision of Osric? How would you clothe him for a modern-dress production?

1 excellent differences 卓越品质
2 soft society 温文尔雅
3 the card or calendar 榜样，楷模
4 continent 汇集（字面义为“容器”）
5 his … you = your definement of him suffers no perdition 您对他的描述既没有任何遗漏（从这句话开始的这段台词大概是所有莎剧中难点最密集而且最难懂的一段。definement和definition的词干都是define。）
6 divide him inventorially 像商店盘点那样对他条分缕析（inventory的意思是“存货”）
7 dozy th'arithmetic of memory 令记忆晕头转向，不会算数（dozy = make dizzy）
8 and yet but yaw neither 又不忽左忽右（yaw的意思是“船航行时一会儿左拐，一会儿右拐”；neither与此段第一个语句里的no相互关联）
9 in … sail 考虑到他生前一帆风顺
10 in the verity of extolment 在对他的实实在在的颂扬中
11 take … article 认为他是一个具有伟大德行的魂灵
12 his … rareness 他的禀赋实在珍贵又稀有（infusion：融入体内的素质）
13 make true diction of him 要想真实地描述他
14 his semblable is his mirror 与他相像的只有他自己的镜像
15 who … umbrage 此外还有谁可以与他并驾齐驱？他的影子
16 infallibly 无可挑剔；无可反驳
17 concernancy 关系，相关性
18 Why … breath? 我们为何要用远不如他成熟的话来谈论他呢？
19 to't = fall to it 着手做此事（此处何瑞修在跟哈慕雷悄悄说话）
20 What imports the nomination 提……的意义是什么
21 golden words are spent 金句用光了（这里说的是奥斯睿）
22 approve 表扬
23 for his weapon 因其武器（卓尔不群）
24 imputation laid on him 他身上的名声
25 meed 优秀品质
26 unfellowed 无人可及

1 Mocking Osric – without drawing breath

Hamlet obviously detests Osric's affected manner and language. In lines 106–12, Hamlet makes up words ('definement' = definition, 'inventorially' = as an inventory/list), uses pompous phrases ('the verity of extolment' = the truth of praising), and mocks Osric's praise of Laertes.

- These lines can be spoken at high speed, emphasising the flamboyant nature of the speech. Try it yourself!

I beseech you remember.

[*Hamlet moves him to put on his hat*]

OSRIC Nay good my lord, for my ease in good faith. Sir, [here is newly come to court Laertes; believe me an absolute gentleman, full of most excellent differences[1], of very soft society[2] and great showing. Indeed, to speak feelingly of him, he is the card or calendar[3] of gentry, for you shall find in him the continent[4] of what part a gentleman would see.

HAMLET Sir, his definement suffers no perdition in you[5], though I know to divide him inventorially[6] would dozy th'arithmetic of memory[7], and yet but yaw neither[8] in respect of his quick sail[9]. But in the verity of extolment[10], I take him to be a soul of great article[11], and his infusion of such dearth and rareness[12] as, to make true diction of him[13], his semblable is his mirror[14], and who else would trace him, his umbrage[15], nothing more.

OSRIC Your lordship speaks most infallibly[16] of him.

HAMLET The concernancy[17], sir? Why do we wrap the gentleman in our more rawer breath?[18]

OSRIC Sir?

HORATIO Is't not possible to understand in another tongue? You will to't[19] sir, really.

HAMLET What imports the nomination[20] of this gentleman?

OSRIC Of Laertes?

HORATIO His purse is empty already, all's golden words are spent[21].

HAMLET Of him sir.

OSRIC I know you are not ignorant –

HAMLET I would you did sir, yet in faith if you did, it would not much approve[22] me. Well sir?]

OSRIC You are not ignorant of what excellence Laertes is.

[HAMLET I dare not confess that, lest I should compare with him in excellence, but to know a man well were to know himself.

OSRIC I mean sir for his weapon[23]; but in the imputation laid on him[24] by them, in his meed[25] he's unfellowed[26].]

HAMLET What's his weapon?

OSRIC Rapier and dagger.

HAMLET That's two of his weapons, but well.

Osric tells of Claudius's wager: in a twelve-bout duel between Hamlet and Laertes, Laertes will not win three more bouts than Hamlet. Osric leaves, and Hamlet and Horatio exchange amused comments about him.

剧情简介： 奥斯睿说到克劳迭押的注：哈慕雷和雷厄提决斗，12回合之中雷厄提赢哈慕雷的次数多不过3回 。奥斯睿离开，哈慕雷和何瑞修互相说一些打趣奥斯睿的话。

1 'How if I answer no?'

In this exchange of wit and engagement with Osric's frothy (华而不实) verbiage (冗词), there is a line that stands out as potentially of a different tone: 'How if I answer no? (line 151)

a Experiment with different ways of speaking this line. For example, try it as if Hamlet does not want to fight the duel, or as if he doesn't care what happens, or with defiance. Try leaving a long pause between 'answer' and 'no' to experience the dramatic effect it makes.

b Decide which style of speaking you think is most appropriate, and write notes advising an actor on your preferred style of delivery.

Characters 人物分析

Osric's character – and is he in on the plot?

Horatio sees Osric as a precocious (very forward) juvenile: 'This lapwing runs away with the shell on his head.' A lapwing chick leaves its nest very shortly after hatching, often with parts of its shell still sticking to its head.

Hamlet suggests that no one else is likely to praise Osric ('there are no tongues else for's turn') so he does well 'to commend it [his duty] himself'. He compares Osric to a baby that 'did comply with his dug' (made a deal with his mother's breast). Hamlet goes on to say that Osric is typical of the flock ('bevy') of frothy, superficial people fashionable in these frivolous ('drossy') times. They burst like bubbles when they face some real test. The 'fanned and winnowed opinions' are the lightweight opinions that people like Osric simply ignore.

a List Osric's character traits, finding lines to support your ideas. Try to think of someone in public life today who is like Osric.

b Imagine Osric knows of Claudius's murderous plan. How would that affect his performance? How likely is it that he knows?

c Write a short character (or caricature) study of Osric: drawing on evidence from the script will be good practice for a longer study of one of the major characters later. Are there any reasons an audience might feel sympathy for Osric?

1 **Barbary horses** 巴巴利马（名贵的阿拉伯马种）
2 **impawned** 押注
3 **poniards … so** 三棱刺剑连同其附件，如佩剑腰带、剑挂，等等
4 **Three … fancy** 其中三套剑挂，说真的，让人爱不释手（carriage指将剑挂在腰带上的皮装置）
5 **responsive to the hilts** 与剑柄非常匹配
6 **of very liberal conceit** 设计别出心裁
7 **edified by the margent** 查看边上的注释（margent = margin）
8 **germane to the matter** 贴近主题
9 **carry … sides** 腰间佩的是一把火枪
10 **on** = go on 继续说
11 **in … hits** 在您和雷厄提的12个回合里雷厄提超过您的比分不超过3分
12 **vouchsafe the answer** 接受挑战
13 **trial** 决斗
14 **breathing time** 锻炼时间
15 **redeliver you e'en so** 就这样传您的话
16 **after … will** 您说得怎样天花乱坠都行
17 **commend my duty** 甘愿效劳
18 **no … turn** 没有比他更能说会道的人了
19 **lapwing … head** 刚孵出来的小凤头鸡顶着蛋壳就跑了
20 **comply … it** 小时候吃奶前一定先向乳头行礼
21 **same bevy** 同类
22 **drossy age dotes on** 这一垃圾时代宠爱
23 **tune of the time** 这一时代的腔调
24 **habit of encounter** 人际交往的行头（habit的意思是"外衣"）
25 **yesty collection** 浮沫沉渣（yesty = yeasty，派生自yeast［酵母］，指做果酒时果浆发酵后果汁与果皮渣分离，后者浮在果汁之上，成为没有什么价值、只能用来喂猪的酒糟）
26 **fanned and winnowed** 经过千扬万簸的
27 **and do but** 只要

OSRIC The king sir hath wagered with him six Barbary horses[1], against the which he has impawned[2], as I take it, six French rapiers and poniards, with their assigns, as girdle, hangers, and so[3]. Three of the carriages in faith are very dear to fancy[4], very responsive to the hilts[5], most delicate carriages, and of very liberal conceit[6].

HAMLET What call you the carriages?

HORATIO I knew you must be edified by the margent[7] ere you had done.

OSRIC The carriages sir are the hangers.

HAMLET The phrase would be more germane to the matter[8] if we could carry a cannon by our sides[9]; I would it might be hangers till then. But on[10], six Barbary horses against six French swords, their assigns, and three liberal-conceited carriages – that's the French bet against the Danish. Why is this impawned, as you call it?

OSRIC The king sir, hath laid sir, that in a dozen passes between yourself and him, he shall not exceed you three hits[11]. He hath laid on twelve for nine. And it would come to immediate trial, if your lordship would vouchsafe the answer[12].

HAMLET How if I answer no?

OSRIC I mean my lord, the opposition of your person in trial[13].

HAMLET Sir, I will walk here in the hall. If it please his majesty, it is the breathing time[14] of day with me. Let the foils be brought, the gentleman willing, and the king hold his purpose, I will win for him and I can. If not, I will gain nothing but my shame and the odd hits.

OSRIC Shall I redeliver you e'en so[15]?

HAMLET To this effect sir, after what flourish your nature will[16].

OSRIC I commend my duty[17] to your lordship.

HAMLET Yours, yours.

[*Exit Osric*]

He does well to commend it himself, there are no tongues else for's turn[18].

HORATIO This lapwing runs away with the shell on his head[19].

HAMLET A did comply with his dug before a sucked it[20]. Thus has he, and many more of the same bevy[21] that I know the drossy age dotes on[22], only got the tune of the time[23] and outward habit of encounter[24], a kind of yesty collection[25], which carries them through and through the most fanned and winnowed[26] opinions; and do but[27] blow them to their trial, the bubbles are out.

[*Enter a* LORD

A lord asks if Hamlet will duel with Laertes now or later. Hamlet is ready. Horatio warns that he will lose, but Hamlet feels the time is ripe. He asks Laertes to pardon him.

剧情简介：一位贵族问哈慕雷是现在就开始决斗还是稍后开始。哈慕雷准备好了。何瑞修警告哈慕雷说他会被打败，可哈慕雷觉得时机已成熟。他请雷厄提原谅他。

Characters 人物分析

From 'To be, or not to be' to 'Let be' (in pairs)

Hamlet has been on a long emotional journey from the anxiety of 'To be, or not to be' to the simple acceptance of 'Let be'. He does not think he will lose the duel, but feels foreboding ('how ill all's here about my heart'). However, he is resolute, and sees 'special providence in the fall of a sparrow' (an image from St Matthew's Gospel, suggesting the seemingly insignificant nature of the small bird).

Hamlet seems ready to accept whatever fate has in store for him. Whether death comes sooner or later, it will come. What matters is the frame of mind to meet death: 'the readiness is all'. Since no one really knows the meaning of life or what he will miss by dying young, what does it matter to die early ('betimes')?

a Talk together about how Hamlet's mood at this point contrasts with that earlier in the play.

b Experiment with ways of speaking the lines. How might Hamlet vary his tone from thought to thought?

c After the first two sentences, Hamlet uses almost only monosyllables ('If it be now … Let be.'). Speak the lines, making each monosyllable sharp and clear. Discuss the dramatic effect of such simple words.

d 'The readiness is all'. In reflecting on life, death and whether fate plays a part or not in one's existence, Hamlet seems to have come to a state in which he is ready for death, and for life. His balanced, focused, calm position stands between the two, making him (in some eyes) a great tragic figure. Discuss what you think 'the readiness is all' means, and whether you agree with the statement that Hamlet is achieving greatness.

e 'I am punished / With a sore distraction'. How seriously do we take Hamlet's gracious confession to Claudius? Has Hamlet really been punished, and have his actions during the play been the result of a form of melancholy that has caused him distraction and delay? Or is he purposely overstating this to Claudius, keeping up the pretence of madness while engineering a moment to kill him?

1 commended him to you 向您致意
2 attend 等候
3 If his fitness speaks 如果他时间方便
4 In happy time 正是时候
5 gentle entertainment 和气对待
6 at the odds 在赌的数上（即9个回合）
7 gaingiving 疑虑
8 forestall their repair hither 预防他们退到这里
9 Not a whit 一点儿也没有
10 augury 预兆
11 Let be 算了吧
12 This presence 在场的各位
13 sore distraction 严重的精神问题
14 exception 仇怨

LORD My lord, his majesty commended him to you[1] by young Osric, who brings back to him that you attend[2] him in the hall. He sends to know if your pleasure hold to play with Laertes, or that you will take longer time.

HAMLET I am constant to my purposes, they follow the king's pleasure. If his fitness speaks[3], mine is ready; now or whensoever, provided I be so able as now.

LORD The king and queen, and all, are coming down.

HAMLET In happy time[4].

LORD The queen desires you to use some gentle entertainment[5] to Laertes, before you fall to play.

HAMLET She well instructs me.]

[*Exit Lord*]

HORATIO You will lose, my lord.

HAMLET I do not think so. Since he went into France, I have been in continual practice; I shall win at the odds[6]. But thou wouldst not think how ill all's here about my heart – but it is no matter.

HORATIO Nay good my lord –

HAMLET It is but foolery, but it is such a kind of gaingiving[7] as would perhaps trouble a woman.

HORATIO If your mind dislike anything, obey it. I will forestall their repair hither[8], and say you are not fit.

HAMLET Not a whit[9], we defy augury[10]. There is special providence in the fall of a sparrow. If it be now, 'tis not to come; if it be not to come, it will be now; if it be not now, yet it will come – the readiness is all. Since no man of aught he leaves knows, what is't to leave betimes? Let be[11].

A table prepared, with flagons of wine on it. Trumpets, Drums and Officers with cushions. Enter CLAUDIUS, GERTRUDE, LAERTES *and* LORDS, *with other Attendants with foils, daggers and gauntlets*

CLAUDIUS Come Hamlet, come and take this hand from me.
[*Hamlet takes Laertes by the hand*]

HAMLET Give me your pardon sir, I've done you wrong;
But pardon't as you are a gentleman.
This presence[12] knows,
And you must needs have heard, how I am punished
With a sore distraction[13]. What I have done,
That might your nature, honour and exception[14]
Roughly awake, I here proclaim was madness.

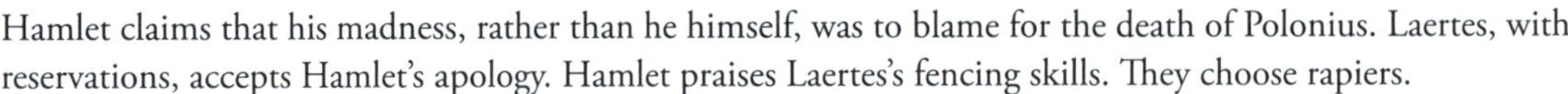

Hamlet claims that his madness, rather than he himself, was to blame for the death of Polonius. Laertes, with reservations, accepts Hamlet's apology. Hamlet praises Laertes's fencing skills. They choose rapiers.

剧情简介：哈慕雷说杀死珀娄涅的罪魁祸首不是他，而是他的疯病。雷厄提有所保留地接受了哈慕雷的道歉。哈慕雷夸赞雷厄提的剑术。他们挑选决斗用剑。

1 True or false? Laertes's reply (in pairs)

Laertes intends, secretly and treacherously, to kill Hamlet. In lines 216–24, he says he is satisfied as far as natural feelings go ('in nature'), but he must obey a higher moral code (that of vengeance, his 'terms of honour') to keep his reputation pure ('name ungored'). He promises not to wrong Hamlet's love.

- One person reads lines 216–24, pausing at each punctuation mark. In each pause the other person, as Laertes, says either 'true' or 'false', and explains what his secret thoughts really are at that moment.

Stagecraft 导演技巧

The choosing of foils – how is it performed?

The choosing of the foils is an important dramatic moment, as notwithstanding the skill or luck of each contestant, life or death hangs upon the choice.

- Write notes in your Director's Journal for actors performing lines 226–38. Your aim is to make the choosing of the foils as dramatically effective as possible. Remember: Laertes knows one has an unblunted blade, so how does he ensure he gets the right rapier?

2 Resorting to honour

There is a strong emphasis on honour and making peace with each other before the duel. We know that Laertes, despite his protestations of honour, is in league with Claudius; but Hamlet acts, for the moment, according to the highest principles of honour and selflessness.

Despite there being 'special providence in the fall of a sparrow', there is the potential downfall of a major heroic figure here. Hamlet's 'readiness' in Act 5 has been noticeable – part of the tragic trajectory (轨迹) in this play (it is not the same in all) is for Hamlet to reach a peak of dignity and honour just before the fall from greatness, or just before death.

- Draw a graph, act by act, to show Hamlet's trajectory as a tragic hero. You can annotate it with quotations and comments. Compare your graph and annotations with someone else's in the class, and see if you both agree on the line of the graph. What is its high point? And where are its lows? Discuss and debate any variations between your graphs.

1 faction 一方

2 disclaiming from a purposed evil 否认我有意作恶

3 I … brother 我把箭射到房子那边却误伤自己兄弟

4 by … honour 从某位德高望重的大人物那里

5 I … peace 我得到一种判断以及和好的先兆

6 Stick fiery off （光芒）四射

7 bettered 进益

8 all a length 一样长

Was't Hamlet wronged Laertes? Never Hamlet.
If Hamlet from himself be tane away,
And when he's not himself does wrong Laertes,
Then Hamlet does it not, Hamlet denies it.
Who does it then? His madness. If't be so,
Hamlet is of the faction[1] that is wronged,
His madness is poor Hamlet's enemy.
Sir, in this audience,
Let my disclaiming from a purposed evil[2]
Free me so far in your most generous thoughts,
That I have shot my arrow o'er the house
And hurt my brother[3].

LAERTES I am satisfied in nature,
Whose motive in this case should stir me most
To my revenge; but in my terms of honour
I stand aloof, and will no reconcilement
Till by some elder masters of known honour[4]
I have a voice and precedent of peace[5]
To keep my name ungored. But till that time
I do receive your offered love like love,
And will not wrong it.

HAMLET I embrace it freely,
And will this brother's wager frankly play.
Give us the foils, come on.

LAERTES Come, one for me.

HAMLET I'll be your foil Laertes. In mine ignorance
Your skill shall like a star i'th'darkest night
Stick fiery off[6] indeed.

LAERTES You mock me sir.

HAMLET No, by this hand.

CLAUDIUS Give them the foils, young Osric. Cousin Hamlet,
You know the wager?

HAMLET Very well my lord.
Your grace has laid the odds a'th'weaker side.

CLAUDIUS I do not fear it, I have seen you both.
But since he is bettered[7], we have therefore odds.

LAERTES This is too heavy, let me see another.

HAMLET This likes me well. These foils have all a length[8]?

Claudius orders wine and celebrations if Hamlet is successful. He will drink a toast if Hamlet wins, and put a pearl in the wine. Hamlet makes two hits. Claudius offers the poisoned cup, but Hamlet declines to drink.

剧情简介：克劳迭命人上酒，下令说如果哈慕雷击中就庆祝。如果哈慕雷赢了，他就举杯祝酒，并放一颗珍珠在酒里。哈慕雷赢了两个回合。克劳迭端来那杯毒酒，可哈慕雷没有喝。

1 The poisoned cup

Imagine you are directing a rehearsal of the play. You are asked two questions by the actors:

- Is Hamlet suspicious about the drink at line 260?
- How should Claudius say 'Gertrude, do not drink!' at line 268?

Invent your replies, and write them down as notes for the actors.

▼ **Identify which is Hamlet and which is Laertes in this production photograph.**

1 stoups 酒罐
2 quit 扳回（一个回合）
3 their ordnance fire = fire their ordnance 放礼炮
4 an union 一颗珍珠
5 kettle = kettle drum 定音鼓
6 bear a wary eye 眼睛要瞪大
7 palpable 明显
8 Stay 等一等
9 fat 虚胖
10 scant of breath 喘不过气来
11 carouses 痛饮

OSRIC Ay my good lord.

Prepare to play

CLAUDIUS Set me the stoups[1] of wine upon that table.
If Hamlet give the first or second hit,
Or quit[2] in answer of the third exchange,
Let all the battlements their ordnance fire[3].
The king shall drink to Hamlet's better breath,
And in the cup an union[4] shall he throw
Richer than that which four successive kings
In Denmark's crown have worn. Give me the cups,
And let the kettle[5] to the trumpet speak,
The trumpet to the cannoneer without,
The cannons to the heavens, the heaven to earth,
'Now the king drinks to Hamlet!' Come, begin,
And you the judges bear a wary eye[6].

Trumpets the while

HAMLET Come on sir.
LAERTES Come my lord.

They play

HAMLET One.
LAERTES No.
HAMLET Judgement.
OSRIC A hit, a very palpable[7] hit.
LAERTES Well, again.
CLAUDIUS Stay[8], give me drink. Hamlet, this pearl is thine.
Here's to thy health.

Drum, trumpets sound, and shot goes off

Give him the cup.
HAMLET I'll play this bout first, set it by awhile.
Come.

[*They play*]

Another hit. What say you?
LAERTES A touch, a touch, I do confess't.
CLAUDIUS Our son shall win.
GERTRUDE He's fat[9] and scant of breath[10].
Here Hamlet, take my napkin, rub thy brows.
The queen carouses[11] to thy fortune, Hamlet.
HAMLET Good madam.
CLAUDIUS Gertrude, do not drink!

Gertrude drinks from the poisoned cup. Laertes wounds Hamlet. In a scuffle, they exchange rapiers and Hamlet wounds Laertes. The queen falls and dies. Laertes reveals the treacherous plot.

剧情简介：葛楚德喝了那杯毒酒。雷厄提击伤哈慕雷。打斗中二人互换了手中的剑，哈慕雷又击伤了雷厄提。王后倒地而亡。雷厄提揭露了这场奸诈的阴谋。

Stagecraft 导演技巧

Staging the duel (in small groups)

The duel and its bloody outcome last only around sixty lines. But Shakespeare provides opportunities to create thrilling stage action. In many productions Laertes wounds Hamlet deceitfully at line 280, a moment that Hamlet thinks is an interval in the fight.

a Act out a non-contact but dramatic fight scene, weaving the words of the script into the action.

b Are you sure that Laertes acts dishonourably? To make your decision clear to an audience, work out how you would stage: the wounding of Hamlet by Laertes; the scuffle that follows; the exchange of rapiers; and the wounding of Laertes.

1 The death of Gertrude: accident or suicide? (in pairs)

The queen dies by drinking from the poisoned cup that Claudius intended for her son. Every actor playing Gertrude thinks hard about whether she knows the cup is poisoned and therefore whether her death is an accident or suicide (see line 269). If the actor decides that Gertrude suspects the cup is poisoned, to be theatrically convincing she should be seen distancing herself from Claudius in earlier scenes (she may point to Claudius as she speaks her final words).

- One partner argues for Gertrude committing suicide. The other argues for Gertrude not knowing the drink is poisoned. How could 'I will, my lord' be said in different ways to show either her ignorance or her knowledge? How do these different interpretations affect our empathy towards Gertrude? Look at her words carefully to determine your answers.

Themes 主题分析

Does divinity shape their ends? (in small groups)

The tragic end to this play is unfolding via a treacherous plot by Claudius to kill Hamlet. Unwittingly, or perhaps deliberately on Claudius's part, Laertes and Gertrude (and he) will die too.

- On page 216, you wrote about the extent to which divine force controls the characters in *Hamlet*. Read through this answer, and make notes on whether or not you still agree with what you wrote.

1 do but dally 不过打着玩儿
2 make a wanton of me 拿我当惯坏的小孩子哄
3 incensed （打）恼了
4 as … springe 一只笨鸟掉进自己下的套里
5 sounds 晕倒
6 Unbated and envenomed 开了刃，且涂了毒

GERTRUDE I will my lord, I pray you pardon me.

[Drinks]

CLAUDIUS *[Aside]* It is the poisoned cup. It is too late.

HAMLET I dare not drink yet madam, by and by.

GERTRUDE Come, let me wipe thy face.

LAERTES My lord, I'll hit him now.

CLAUDIUS I do not think't.

LAERTES And yet it is almost against my conscience.

HAMLET Come, for the third, Laertes. You do but dally[1].
I pray you pass with your best violence.
I am afeard you make a wanton of me[2].

LAERTES Say you so? Come on.

Play

OSRIC Nothing neither way.

LAERTES Have at you now! *[Wounds Hamlet]*

In scuffling they change rapiers

CLAUDIUS Part them. They are incensed[3].

HAMLET Nay, come again. *[Wounds Laertes]*

[Gertrude falls]

OSRIC Look to the queen there, ho!

HORATIO They bleed on both sides. How is it my lord?

OSRIC How is't Laertes?

LAERTES Why, as a woodcock to mine own springe[4], Osric.
I am justly killed with mine own treachery.

HAMLET How does the queen?

CLAUDIUS She sounds[5] to see them bleed.

GERTRUDE No, no, the drink, the drink – O my dear Hamlet –
The drink, the drink – I am poisoned. *[Dies]*

HAMLET Oh villainy! – Ho, let the door be locked!
Treachery! Seek it out!

[Laertes falls]

LAERTES It is here Hamlet. Hamlet, thou art slain,
No medicine in the world can do thee good,
In thee there is not half an hour of life –
The treacherous instrument is in thy hand,
Unbated and envenomed[6]. The foul practice
Hath turned itself on me; lo, here I lie,
Never to rise again. Thy mother's poisoned –
I can no more – the king, the king's to blame.

Hamlet wounds Claudius and forces him to drink from the poisoned cup. Claudius dies. Laertes forgives Hamlet, then dies. Hamlet prevents Horatio from suicide, and asks him to report his (Hamlet's) story.

剧情简介：哈慕雷刺伤了克劳迭，并强迫他喝下酒杯中的毒酒。克劳迭死去。雷厄提原谅了哈慕雷，随后死去。哈慕雷阻止何瑞修自杀，请他把自己的故事告诉世人。

1 Key moments

a Staging the death of Claudius The killing of Claudius is often a savage affair. Hamlet runs him through with his sword, then, without pity, forces him to drink poison. The courtiers cry 'Treason, treason!' but do nothing. Some productions have Hamlet chasing a terrified Claudius, who tries to hide behind the courtiers. Others have portrayed Claudius facing death with calm dignity. How would you stage lines 301–6? Write notes on how Hamlet, Claudius and the courtiers behave (in line with your view of Hamlet's and Claudius's characters).

b Treachery! Seek it out! In line 292 of this scene, Hamlet's final act appears not to be a vengeful one, but an act for his country's honour. In pairs, talk about how this affects your view of him.

c 'Wretched queen adieu' Hamlet's three-word farewell to his mother at line 312 is often turned into a poignant (辛酸) moment in performance. In one production, Hamlet crawled across to Gertrude and kissed her as he spoke. Write notes on how you would turn those three words into a memorable theatrical episode.

d 'Exchange forgiveness with me' Laertes turns against Claudius, asking Hamlet for mutual forgiveness. Discuss how Laertes's last speech relates to *Hamlet* as revenge tragedy.

e 'A wounded name' Hamlet forbids Horatio to take the poison and commit suicide, because he wants Horatio to 'report me and my cause aright / To the unsatisfied' (those who do not know the full story). Hamlet wants to ensure that his 'name' (reputation) is remembered. List six words you think Hamlet would wish to be included in Horatio's description of him. Then list six words of your own to describe how you see Hamlet. Do the two lists match?

f *'March afar off, and shot within'* This stage direction heralds the arrival of the Norwegian force and the ambassadors from England, and with a single offstage sound effect takes the action back into a wider political frame. It is a reminder that this scene marks not only the death of Hamlet but also the end of the reign of Hamlet's entire line. Decide whether you wish to make the sound effect small scale and intimate, or large scale and epic.

g Act it out Lines 302–40 constitute a tremendous part of the scene to act out. In groups of four or five, take parts and rehearse the lines for presentation to the rest of the class.

1 is justly served 罪有应得
2 tempered 掺入，调制
3 chance = mischance 不幸
4 mutes 无言的（旁观者）
5 fell sergeant death = fell sergeant, death 死神，这个索命军曹
6 the unsatisfied 欲知真相的人
7 antique Roman 古罗马人（宁死不苟活）
8 ha't = have it
9 wounded name 受损的名声
10 Absent thee from felicity awhile 把你的解脱先往后推推

HAMLET The point envenomed too! Then, venom, to thy work!
Hurts the king

ALL Treason, treason!

CLAUDIUS Oh yet defend me friends, I am but hurt.

HAMLET Here, thou incestuous, murderous, damnèd Dane,
Drink off this potion. Is thy union here?
Follow my mother. *King dies*

LAERTES He is justly served[1],
It is a poison tempered[2] by himself.
Exchange forgiveness with me, noble Hamlet.
Mine and my father's death come not upon thee,
Nor thine on me. *Dies*

HAMLET Heaven make thee free of it! I follow thee.
I am dead, Horatio. Wretched queen adieu.
You that look pale, and tremble at this chance[3],
That are but mutes[4] or audience to this act,
Had I but time, as this fell sergeant death[5]
Is strict in his arrest, oh I could tell you –
But let it be. Horatio, I am dead,
Thou livest; report me and my cause aright
To the unsatisfied[6].

HORATIO Never believe it.
I am more an antique Roman[7] than a Dane.
Here's yet some liquor left.

HAMLET As th'art a man,
Give me the cup. Let go, by heaven I'll ha't[8].
O God, Horatio, what a wounded name[9],
Things standing thus unknown, shall live behind me!
If thou didst ever hold me in thy heart,
Absent thee from felicity awhile[10],
And in this harsh world draw thy breath in pain
To tell my story.
March afar off, and shot within
What warlike noise is this?

Before dying, Hamlet declares Fortinbras to be his choice as king of Denmark. Fortinbras wonders at the sight of so many dead bodies. The English ambassador reports that Rosencrantz and Guildenstern are dead.

剧情简介：哈慕雷死前宣布他选择福庭布拉当丹麦王。这么多的死尸令福庭布拉感觉触目惊心。英格兰来的使者报告，柔森克阮茨和吉尔顿斯登已死。

1 'the rest is silence' (in pairs)

Hamlet dies – seemingly undramatically, although his death is soon followed by the entrance of Fortinbras and the English ambassadors – and his final words are as much political as personal. He wishes Fortinbras, whom he prophesises will take over as king, to know what has led up to this moment. But characteristically, he entwines the personal with the political.

- Discuss the nature and impact of Hamlet's death. Compare your thoughts with the rest of the class.

▼ In the 1990 Zeffirelli movie, Hamlet dies beside his mother. How would you stage Hamlet's death?

1 warlike volley 礼炮齐鸣
2 o'ercrows = overcrows 战胜
3 prophesy … Fortinbras 预见福庭布拉将被推选为丹麦王
4 he has my dying voice 临死前我表示支持他
5 th'occurrents more or less 发生的所有事情
6 solicited 促成，引起
7 *drum, colours* 鼓手，旗手
8 quarry 成堆的死尸（字面义为"打猎打来的成堆的鹿"）
9 cries on havoc 声嘶力竭地喊着大屠杀
10 toward 准备着

OSRIC Young Fortinbras, with conquest come from Poland,
To the ambassadors of England gives
This warlike volley[1].

HAMLET Oh I die, Horatio,
The potent poison quite o'ercrows[2] my spirit.
I cannot live to hear the news from England.
But I do prophesy th'election lights
On Fortinbras[3]; he has my dying voice[4].
So tell him, with th'occurrents more and less[5]
Which have solicited[6] – the rest is silence. *Dies*

HORATIO Now cracks a noble heart. Good night sweet prince,
And flights of angels sing thee to thy rest. –
Why does the drum come hither?

Enter FORTINBRAS *and* ENGLISH AMBASSADORS, *with drum, colours*[7] *and Attendants*

FORTINBRAS Where is this sight?

HORATIO What is it you would see?
If aught of woe or wonder, cease your search.

FORTINBRAS This quarry[8] cries on havoc[9]. O proud death,
What feast is toward[10] in thine eternal cell
That thou so many princes at a shot
So bloodily hast struck?

I AMBASSADOR The sight is dismal,
And our affairs from England come too late.
The ears are senseless that should give us hearing,
To tell him his commandment is fulfilled,
That Rosencrantz and Guildenstern are dead.
Where should we have our thanks?

Horatio asks for the bodies to be placed on view, and says he will tell how the carnage came about. Fortinbras claims the throne of Denmark. He commands that Hamlet be carried with due ceremony to the platform.

剧情简介：何瑞修命手下把尸体摆放好，供人瞻仰，并说他会讲述这一场杀戮是如何发生的。福庭布拉宣布即丹麦王之位。他命令按照应有的仪式把哈慕雷抬上高台。

1 Tell Horatio's story (in small groups)

In lines 359–64, Horatio lists seven incidents he proposes to relate. In role, and moving from person to person in the group, tell the story Horatio intends to tell, in any of a number of ways: as an anecdote; as an epic tale; as a tragedy; or as a murder mystery.

Stagecraft 导演技巧

'The end is everything'

Aristotle, the ancient Greek philosopher and critic, commented that in Greek tragedy 'the end is everything'. The suggestion is that in any story, the end reflects back on the story as a whole. Comedies in Shakespeare often end in marriage, dance and jollity; tragedies end in despair, downfall and possible renewal. Undertake the following activities, leading towards a presentation of the final two pages of the script (and perhaps continuing the final activity on p. 234).

a The moment captured in the script opposite is one of transition: from the past, which Horatio will tell 'to th'yet unknowing world' (line 358), to the future, represented by Fortinbras, whom we know is a young soldier of honour. Work out positions on stage and postures for Horatio and Fortinbras, either in a tableau or in a more dynamic performance, and write notes in your Director's Journal.

b There is a calmness and shocked silence at the close of the play, perhaps echoing Hamlet's dying words, 'the rest is silence'. How sinister is this silence? Even though there are words from Horatio and Fortinbras, and 'a peal of ordnance are shot off', what part does silence play towards the end?

c Why are Hamlet's last words (331–7) so seemingly modest? And what does he mean by them?

d What image and soundscape would you wish to leave in the audience's mind as the play ends and people leave their seats?

e What part will lighting play in the final moments? Most of the play has been dark, much of it in the castle. Do the final moments bring some light and fresh air to the stage, or does the sombre atmosphere continue to the end?

f When you have considered the points above, work in groups to stage the final moments of the play.

1 jump … question　紧随这场血腥事件之后
2 carnal　肉欲
3 judgements　惩罚
4 put on　带来，造成
5 forced cause　人为的原因
6 upshot　结局
7 purposes … heads　阴谋出了差错，阴谋者送了性命
8 have some rights of memory　记得有些权利
9 claim my vantage　认领这份好运气
10 And … more　而且这话出自哈慕雷本人之口，权当他还有一口气可以残喘
11 wild　冲动
12 put on　推上那个位置（王位）
13 passage　下葬仪仗
14 rite　仪式
15 Becomes the field　与战场相配
16 *peal of ordnance*　礼炮轰鸣

HORATIO
Not from his mouth,
Had it th'ability of life to thank you;
He never gave commandment for their death.
But since, so jump upon this bloody question[1],
You from the Polack wars, and you from England,
Are here arrived, give order that these bodies
High on a stage be placèd to the view,
And let me speak to th'yet unknowing world
How these things came about. So shall you hear
Of carnal[2], bloody, and unnatural acts,
Of accidental judgements[3], casual slaughters,
Of deaths put on[4] by cunning and forced cause[5],
And in this upshot[6], purposes mistook
Fallen on th'inventors' heads[7]. All this can I
Truly deliver.

FORTINBRAS
Let us haste to hear it,
And call the noblest to the audience.
For me, with sorrow I embrace my fortune.
I have some rights of memory[8] in this kingdom,
Which now to claim my vantage[9] doth invite me.

HORATIO
Of that I shall have also cause to speak,
And from his mouth whose voice will draw on more[10].
But let this same be presently performed,
Even while men's minds are wild[11], lest more mischance
On plots and errors happen.

FORTINBRAS
Let four captains
Bear Hamlet like a soldier to the stage,
For he was likely, had he been put on[12],
To have proved most royal; and for his passage[13],
The soldier's music and the rite[14] of war
Speak loudly for him.
Take up the bodies. Such a sight as this
Becomes the field[15], but here shows much amiss.
Go bid the soldiers shoot.

Exeunt marching, after the which a peal of ordnance[16] are shot off

Looking back at the play 本剧回顾

Activities for groups or individuals

1 Love in *Hamlet*

'forty thousand brothers / Could not with all their quantity of love / Make up my sum' cries Hamlet as he rages against Laertes beside Ophelia's grave. In all the writing about *Hamlet*, 'love' is less discussed than 'revenge' or 'madness'. Yet it plays a vital part in the tragedy in many ways.

- Consider each major character and identify who (or what – Polonius loves the sound of his own voice) they love, and if that love is returned or if it changes. Use your findings to write an extended essay: 'The importance of love in *Hamlet*'. Remember to back up your observations with quotations.

2 What caused the tragedy?

Write at least a paragraph on each of the following, analysing how it contributes to the tragedy of *Hamlet*:

- the personality of Hamlet (perhaps a fatal flaw; see pp. 254–8)
- the personality of Claudius (see p. 259)
- fate – the inevitability of destiny, and whether it comes from 'outside' or is a flaw of character
- the supernatural – ghostly intervention
- Denmark (a corrupt society is perhaps the major cause of the tragedy)
- chance and accident (e.g. the encounter with the pirate ship).

3 Modern relevance

Write down all the factors you would include in an argument that *Hamlet* is relevant to today's world. Discuss this as a whole class, and move the discussion to a formal debate if you wish.

4 'the rest is silence' – an 'early' ending

Some productions have ended at Act 5 Scene 2, line 337: Hamlet's 'the rest is silence.'

- Give your view on that practice, identifying what is lost or gained dramatically by ending the play at that line; and what an early ending would mean for our view of Horatio's role in the play.

5 The structure of the whole play

Hamlet is Shakespeare's longest play. If we look at the relative length of the scenes, we can see that, in this edition, Acts 1 and 3 take up about twenty-five pages each and Acts 2, 4 and 5 about twenty each. You might like to undertake a more granular (细致) analysis, and work out the balance of the play scene-by-scene within each act.

a What do you think are the reasons for the length, and are they justified? Is it principally to do with Hamlet's procrastination, or do the complexities of the plot and the personal/public dimensions require such length?

b If you were asked, as a director, to cut the play, where would you make the cuts and why?

c See if you can stage or present the whole of *Hamlet* in two minutes. Use your inventiveness to compress the action (and inaction) into the timeframe. Afterwards, watch Tom Stoppard's *15-Minute Hamlet*.

These images from a 2006 production by the Royal Shakespeare Company show the intimacy and passion of the final struggle between Claudius and Hamlet. Compare them to any production(s) you have seen, to your imagined ending, and/or to images you can collect from the Internet.

Perspectives and themes 视角与主题

What is the play about?

Millions of words in thousands of books and articles have been written on *Hamlet*. They stand in ironic contrast to Hamlet's final words: 'the rest is silence.' The character of Hamlet himself has attracted most critical commentary. In the nineteenth century, he appealed to the romantic melancholic mood and was interpreted as the noble doomed hero. From the second half of the twentieth century, more attention has been given to his contradictions and unpleasantness: a man who can speak great poetry yet revile (辱骂) a young woman, stab her father in a sudden violent moment and send two old friends to their death without a twinge of conscience.

There is something universal about *Hamlet*. It absorbs the interests and anxieties of any culture and any age. When manifested in performance and criticism, it renders back those interests and preoccupations as 'abstracts and brief chronicles of the time'. Just as Hamlet described the purpose of playing as to show 'the very age and body of the time his form and pressure', so every society reproduces *Hamlet* to mirror itself. Thus a German production in the 1970s presented Ophelia as a Baader–Meinhof terrorist. A Romanian production in the late 1980s portrayed Denmark as a totalitarian (极权主义) police state in Eastern Europe. And in 2004, London's Old Vic Theatre presented Hamlet as a contemporary disturbed, neurotic adolescent. In a Lithuanian production at Shakespeare's Globe in London's 2012 World Shakespeare Festival, the director's interpretation was described as 'engag[ing] with the diversity of human nature, at once funny and violent, visceral and light-hearted, and always deeply compelling'.

One way of answering the question 'What is *Hamlet* about?' could be to think of it as the dramatisation of a story. Denmark is under threat of invasion by Fortinbras of Norway. Young Hamlet, Prince of Denmark, is deeply depressed. His father, the king, has recently died in mysterious circumstances. His mother Gertrude has quickly married his uncle Claudius, whom Hamlet detests. Claudius, not Hamlet, has become king. Hamlet's father returns as a ghost and tells Hamlet that Claudius is responsible for his murder. Hamlet desires revenge and pretends to be mad to achieve that end. But he is uncertain whether the Ghost is honest, or is an agent of the devil, tempting him to do evil.
He delays taking revenge.
The visit of a group of

travelling actors gives him an idea: he will have them perform a murder before Claudius. If Claudius reacts guiltily, it will prove the Ghost has spoken the truth. And that is what happens.

But Hamlet's assumed madness has disastrous consequences. He violently insults Ophelia, the young woman we suppose that he had loved. Then, confronting his mother, he kills Polonius, Ophelia's father, thinking him to be Claudius. The result is that Ophelia is actually driven mad, and Hamlet is sentenced to be exiled to England, where Claudius plans Hamlet's execution. But a chance encounter with a pirate ship enables Hamlet to return to Denmark, where he learns that Ophelia has drowned. Ophelia's brother Laertes plots with Claudius to kill Hamlet deceitfully in a duel using a poisoned sword and drink. Their plan backfires, and Gertrude drinks the poison and dies. Laertes, fatally wounded, reveals the truth. Hamlet, wounded by the poisoned sword, kills Claudius, and then he too dies. Fortinbras arrives, to become king of Denmark.

Such a brief telling of the story, however, seems inadequate to answer the question 'What is *Hamlet* about?' It has become customary to attempt to answer the question by considering the themes of the play. Themes are ideas or concepts (such as 'delay' or 'surveillance') that recur throughout the play. They suggest that Shakespeare was preoccupied by such ideas as he wrote, and sought to explore them through drama that would entertain his audiences – and make them think. Major themes include: the relationship between the individual, politics and society; revenge in relation to honour and justice; madness and melancholia; sin and salvation; acting and theatre; confinement, responsibility and freedom; the nature of existence; sexuality; and connections between all of these.

- **Look back at the diagram that you began on page 12, showing how the different themes are interconnected. Is there one dominant theme? In small groups, discuss whether you think there is a hierarchy of themes.**

Politics and society – 'Denmark's a prison'

The play is set in a politically and culturally interconnected Europe: Denmark, Norway, Poland, France, Germany, England. Elsinore is not a remote backwater, but a vital strategic place in European political and social life. Its young aristocrats are educated at Wittenberg University and it claims England as one of its dependent states, subdued by bloody combat (Act 4 Scene 3, lines 54–60).

But Claudius's Denmark is insecure. When the play opens, it is a country feverishly preparing for war. The nervous anxiety of that preparation is evident in the very first words spoken: 'Who's there?' Barnardo, the relieving sentry, mistakenly challenges Francisco, when military discipline requires Francisco to challenge the newcomer. When the Ghost appears, it may be a visitor from the supernatural world, but its meaning is political: it 'bodes some strange eruption to our state' (Act 1 Scene 1, line 69).

There are echoes of an older, feudal world of the dead fathers (old Hamlet and old Fortinbras) who settled disputes by personal combat guided by a chivalric code ('law and heraldy'). But that older society of honour is giving way to the new world under Claudius. He is a smooth negotiator, an efficient, unscrupulous schemer who prepares for war but settles territorial quarrels by dispatch of ambassadors and formal treaties. He is truly a 'politician' of the type Hamlet reviles in the graveyard: 'one that would circumvent [outwit] God' (Act 5 Scene 1, line 67).

The people of Denmark barely appear in the play, but Claudius increasingly sees them as a threat to his rule. They are 'the distracted multitude', 'the rabble', 'false Danish dogs' who favour Hamlet, or who call for Laertes to be king. All such unreliable people must be closely watched, even more so those who are a direct threat to Claudius's rule, such as Hamlet. It would be dangerous to allow Hamlet to return to Wittenberg, so Claudius refuses permission. He keeps Hamlet under surveillance at home, with the devious words: 'Here in the cheer and comfort of our eye' (Act 1 Scene 2, line 116). That comforting eye will shortly employ two of Hamlet's close friends to spy on him. When Hamlet tells Rosencrantz and Guildenstern 'Denmark's a prison' (Act 2 Scene 2, line 234), he is not simply speaking metaphorically.

The chief minister of state, Polonius, is a willing instrument of Claudius's desire to keep his subjects under surveillance. In the England of Queen Elizabeth I, Polonius's equivalent was Lord Burghley, who also believed in close surveillance to maintain order.

▼ Lord Burghley was the chief advisor to Queen Elizabeth I for most of her reign.

Just as Burghley maintained an extensive network of spies, so Polonius is infected by the desire to overhear in secret, to keep all potential dissidents (持不同政见者) under surveillance. He spies on Hamlet, using his own daughter as bait. Even his own family must be watched. Although Polonius utters conventional decencies to Laertes ('these few precepts'), he sets a spy on his own son. It is hardly surprising that rumours circulate in Denmark. After the death of Polonius, there is no shortage of 'buzzers' (rumour-mongers) to infect Laertes's ears.

For all the ordered formalities of Claudius's court and the seemingly close domesticity of Polonius's family, a sense of corruption grows throughout the play. 'Something is rotten in the state of Denmark' says Marcellus (Act 1 Scene 4, line 90), and the stench of decay at the heart of personal and social life increasingly infects the language. The madness that Hamlet displays and into which Ophelia descends is the individual symptom of a deeper social malaise. Hamlet projects his disgust onto a variety of targets: Claudius, his mother's and Ophelia's sexuality, death itself. But his words mirror the deeper social corruption that pervades Denmark: 'foul deeds', 'maggots', 'carrion', 'offal', 'rank corruption, mining all within', 'the ulcerous place', 'an unweeded garden'. However civilised outward appearances are, the routine oppressions of a police state prevent natural social interaction.

The two women in the play are little more than pawns in a patriarchal world of sexual exploitation. Gertrude has been 'taken to wife' by Claudius. Just as he has seized Denmark, so too he appropriates her body. She has no real power, but is a possession to be fought over by king and prince, husband and son. Ophelia is even more of an object manipulated by men. Her brother lectures her, seeking to control her sexuality. Her father uses her as bait in a spy trap: 'I'll loose my daughter to him' (Act 2 Scene 2, line 160). Hamlet takes out on her a misogynistic (women-hating) side of his character. The masculine brutalities of Denmark quite literally drive Ophelia mad.

Hamlet, with his reflective self-questioning, is as much a modern man as a Renaissance prince. His preoccupation with notions of sin and salvation (see pp. 249–50) shows he is the product of a feudal world where religion is used as an instrument of control. But his style of thought marks him out as a true individual. He is trapped in this changing world and subject to its contradictions. Hamlet can both reflect 'What a piece of work is a man!' (Act 2 Scene 2, line 286) and casually dismiss Rosencrantz and Guildenstern to their deaths.

As well as being a personal quest for justice and/or revenge, Hamlet's vendetta (积怨) against Claudius is also a struggle for political power, just as Claudius's murder of old Hamlet was a political assassination. Such political struggles mirrored the anxieties of Shakespeare's England. Elizabeth's reign might have seemed on the surface to be stable and secure, but it was always subject to threats of overthrow by a powerful faction of the nobility. At the end of the play, Fortinbras and his army take over. This is not the harmonious end of a domestic tragedy, with order restored by a benevolent ruler. Rather, it is the brutal realpolitik (politics based on practical or material reasons rather than theoretical ideas) of a society that, at base, rests on the dominance of a state by a small but militarily powerful minority.

The *quietus* (peace in death) that Hamlet finally achieves might represent private fulfilment, but it is politically empty and futile. Such a way of coming to terms with death might be seen as a weak submission that masks the harsh realities of political and social life in Hamlet's Denmark.

◆ **Use the information in this section as the basis for an extended essay that answers this question: 'In what ways might a production of *Hamlet* explore the political and social implications of the play?'**

Revenge, and revenge tragedy – 'Oh, vengeance!'

Today, many people consider revenge immoral because it means taking the law into one's own hands. It is seen as a profoundly unsocial act. But it seems to be a very human impulse: to exact retribution from someone who has done wrong to you or your family. Revenge follows the Old Testament maxim 'an eye for an eye, a tooth for a tooth'. Revenge is still central to some criminal codes of honour (e.g. the vendetta [仇杀] among the Sicilian mafia [黑手党]).

In Shakespeare's time, revenge was a crime in law and was also an irreligious act. For the Church of the late sixteenth century, revenge was a sin. The revenger's soul was damned, condemned to suffer everlasting torment in hell. That thought preoccupies Hamlet for much of the play. (See the image on p. 44.)

Francis Bacon, a contemporary of Shakespeare, called revenge 'a kind of wild justice'. He wrote in 1625 in an essay on revenge:

> *The most tolerable sort of revenge is for those wrongs which there is no law to remedy, but then let a man take heed the revenge be such as there is no law to punish; else a man's enemy is still beforehand, and it is two for one. Some, when they take revenge, are desirous the party should know whence it cometh. This is the more generous. For the delight seemeth to be not so much in doing the hurt as in making the party repent … This is certain, that a man that studieth revenge keeps his own wounds green, which otherwise would heal and do well. Public revenges are for the most part fortunate, as that for the death of Caesar. But in private revenges it is not so. Nay rather, vindictive persons live the life of witches, who, as they are mischievous, so end they infortunate.*

◆ **Write a reply to Bacon. Begin 'In Hamlet's case …', and argue the points Bacon makes in his essay. You could also write a reply that argues with Bacon's position from your own point of view.**

◆ **Write a brief outline of a modern revenge story or play. Then write the opening chapter of the story, or the first scene of the play.**

◆ **Write a paragraph responding to each of the following statements:**

- **Revenge is always wrong.**
- ***Hamlet* is not so much a revenge play as a play about revenge.**
- **The play suggests that revenge does not pay.**
- ***Hamlet* is more a tragedy than a revenge play: its focus is on the fall of a hero rather than on the execution of a pledge to revenge.**
- **The revenge plot of *Hamlet* is one of the least important elements in the play.**

Revenge tragedy was hugely popular when Shakespeare began his playwriting career. The central feature of each revenge play was a hero (or villain) who sought to avenge a wrong. Elizabethan playwrights served up a rich diet of madness, melancholy and retribution. In the ten years before *Hamlet* was performed, enthusiastic crowds flocked to see Thomas Kyd's *The Spanish Tragedy*, Christopher Marlowe's *The Jew of Malta*, and Shakespeare's *Titus Andronicus*.

Shakespeare also knew a twelfth-century revenge story about Amleth, Prince of Denmark. In the tale, a brother murders the king and marries his wife. The son, Amleth, pretends to be mad to pursue revenge. He slays one of his uncle's spies, forges a letter to have the king's two accomplices executed in England, and finally kills his uncle and becomes king.

Elizabethan revenge tragedy contained typical ingredients:

- a melancholy hero/avenger
- a hesitating avenger (without hesitation the play would be over too quickly)
- a villain who was to be killed in revenge
- complex plotting
- murders (usually from sexual motives) and other physical horrors
- a play-within-a-play
- sexual obsession and lust related to the passion for revenge
- a ghost who calls for revenge
- real or feigned madness
- the death of the revenger.

The plays were usually set in Italy or Spain, but the Elizabethans seemed able to relate the wider themes of each play to their own world.

The typical revenge tragedy had five parts:

- **exposition** usually by a ghost (providing motivation for revenge)
- **anticipation** in which detailed planning of the revenge takes place
- **confrontation** between avenger and intended victim
- **delay** as the revenger hesitates to perform the killing
- **completion** of the revenge (often with the death of the revenger).

Hamlet has four revenge plots. Hamlet vows to revenge his father's death at the hands of Claudius. Laertes swears to avenge his father's death at the hands of Hamlet. Fortinbras seeks to avenge his father's death at the hands of King Hamlet. Another son seeking revenge is Pyrrhus in the play-within-a-play: he slaughters Priam, whose son had killed Pyrrhus's father.

Hamlet has many elements of Elizabethan revenge tragedy. Merely telling the story makes it sound very sensational: eight deaths, a mad woman, a fight in a grave, and so on. But *Hamlet* has outlived most other revenge plays and is still immensely popular. Why?

◆ **Use the information given above to identify in what ways *Hamlet* can be regarded as an Elizabethan revenge tragedy. Then suggest reasons why *Hamlet* continues to hold great appeal after 400 years.**

For more on *Hamlet* as a tragedy, see the section on 'The nature of tragedy' on page 259.

Madness and melancholia – 'This is mere madness'

Today, doctors and psychiatrists rarely use the words 'mad' or 'lunacy'. Instead, they use such expressions as 'manic depression' (violent mood swings), 'schizophrenia' (deranged perceptions and emotions), 'suffering from a nervous breakdown', 'psychotic' (suffering from delusions, dangerously out of contact with reality), 'emotionally disturbed' and 'mentally ill'. Shakespeare's audiences had few qualms (顾虑) about using the term 'mad'. Often, when people were considered mad they were thought to be possessed by devils, and were confined to asylums (精神病院). Visiting such places to watch the behaviour of 'mad' men and women was considered a source of amusement.

Madness was one of the conventions of revenge tragedy. Following that convention, Hamlet proposes to 'put an antic disposition on' (Act 1 Scene 5, line 172). From then on, the question of whether he is merely feigning madness, or has indeed descended into real mental derangement, has divided critics and audiences alike. Every new production of the play raises the issue afresh.

▲ **Albrecht Dürer's engraving of *Melancholia* (1514). Dürer's engraving has often been used in programmes for stage productions of *Hamlet*. Give some reasons why you think it is frequently chosen as a powerful picture to illustrate the play.**

Some of Hamlet's behaviour, particularly his verbal assault on Ophelia in Act 3 Scene 1 ('To a nunnery, go'), is extreme. Ophelia's lament 'Oh what a noble mind is here o'erthrown!' seems a well-judged comment on what she has experienced, and she thinks Hamlet 'Blasted with ecstasy [madness].' But her earlier description of his behaviour, 'Pale as his shirt, his knees knocking each other' (Act 2 Scene 1, line 79) makes him sound rather like a man putting on an act. Yet as he prepares for the duel with Laertes, Hamlet offers an apology – apparently sincere – in which he claims he was indeed mad: 'His madness is poor Hamlet's enemy' (Act 5 Scene 2, line 211).

The one person in the play who is without doubt driven to mental breakdown is Ophelia. Her two 'mad episodes' (in Act 4 Scene 5) are both poignant and bizarre, 'A document in madness'. The terrible blow of her father's death has tipped her over the edge, and her songs display a curious mixture of innocence and sexuality, sense and nonsense.

Her evident dementia stands in contrast to the constant puzzle that attends all instances of Hamlet's 'madness': is he just 'putting it on'?

- Step into role in turn as Claudius, Gertrude, Polonius, Ophelia, Horatio, Rosencrantz and Guildenstern. Give each character's response, with reasons, to the question 'Is Hamlet mad?' Then speak Hamlet's own answer to that question.

- An Elizabethan medical text described the symptoms of melancholy: 'sad and fearful … distrust, doubt, diffidence or despair, sometimes furious, and sometimes merry … sardonian [sardonic], and false laughter … every serious thing for a time, is turned into a jest, and tragedies into comedies' (Timothy Bright, *Treatise on Melancholy*, 1586). How accurately does each of these words or phrases describe Hamlet?

▼ Use these images of Ophelia to help you define the nature and manifestation of her own madness. She is often depicted as a helpless victim – but madness can present itself in many ways.

Sin and salvation – 'What form of prayer / Can serve my turn?'

In Shakespeare's day, the threat of hell and eternal damnation was much more sharply felt than it is today. Most Elizabethans cared passionately about their religion and the state of their souls. They were obsessed by what would happen to them after death. They believed that one of three possibilities awaited them. If they died in a state of grace, with all their sins confessed, they would go to heaven and enjoy eternal peace. If none of their sins was confessed and forgiven, they would go to hell and endure eternal suffering. The third possibility was purgatory, where those who had not made full confession would go. There they suffered until their unconfessed sins were burnt away (purged). Suicides were bound for hell in whatever state they died.

Hamlet explores this obsession with the afterlife. In his first soliloquy Hamlet longs for the peace of death ('O that this too too solid flesh would melt'), but recognises that suicide is forbidden by God ('Or that the Everlasting had not fixed / His canon 'gainst self-slaughter'). In his 'To be, or not to be' soliloquy, he broods on the uncertainty of what will happen after death. It is 'the dread of something after death' that makes us endure the oppressions of life (Act 3 Scene 1, lines 56–88).

Later in the play, the consequences of religious attitudes to suicide are highlighted as the gravediggers' talk reveals that suicides are normally denied the right to 'Christian burial' in a churchyard. Ophelia should be denied the full rites of such burial because it is thought she has taken her own life ('Her death was doubtful'). The Priest at her funeral says that only Claudius's command prevented what she should properly receive as a suicide: not 'charitable prayers', but 'Shards, flints, and pebbles should be thrown on her'. Such was the pronouncement of the Church on suicides.

The Ghost tells how he suffers in purgatory: 'confined to fast in fires, / Till the foul crimes done in my days of nature / Are burnt and purged away' (Act 1 Scene 5, lines 11–13). Because he died without having a chance to confess his sins, he must undergo torment before he can earn a place in heaven, reconciled to God. But Hamlet cannot be sure whether the Ghost is good or bad: 'Be thou a spirit of health, or goblin damned' (Act 1 Scene 4, line 40).

The question of whether the Ghost is to be trusted or not haunts Hamlet for much of the play. It reflects the Elizabethan view that some ghosts were benign, others evil, tempting humans to behave badly and so damn themselves to an afterlife of torment in hell. Hamlet fears what he has seen may be a devil who 'Abuses me to damn me'.

To test whether it is a 'damned ghost' sent to lure his own soul to eternal damnation, Hamlet contrives the play in which he hopes to 'catch the conscience of the king'. When Claudius reveals his guilt by his reaction to the Mousetrap play, Hamlet is convinced the Ghost has spoken true: 'I'll take the ghost's word for a thousand pound' (Act 3 Scene 2, lines 260–1). And in the play's final scene, Hamlet declares his conviction that heaven guides him (Act 5 Scene 2, lines 10–11).

Hamlet's delay in avenging his father's murder can be partly explained by his beliefs about sin and salvation. Shortly after the play-within-the-play, Hamlet finds Claudius at prayer, hoping God will pardon him. The fact that Claudius is praying stops Hamlet from instantly killing him. Hamlet's own father suffers after death because Claudius killed him at a moment when he was unprepared for heaven, not having confessed his sins. Now Hamlet wishes Claudius to experience the same horrible suffering after death. He therefore sheathes his sword and decides to wait, to catch Claudius at a moment 'That has no relish of salvation in't'. That moment will be when Claudius is committing a sin: 'drunk asleep, or in his rage, / Or in th'incestuous pleasure of his bed, / At game a-swearing' (Act 3 Scene 3, lines 89–91). Killing him at such a moment, when he has no thoughts of heaven in his mind, will surely send Claudius to hell, to eternal damnation. Ironically, as Claudius reveals, he has not been successfully praying at all: 'My words fly up, my thoughts remain below. / Words without thoughts never to heaven go' (Act 3 Scene 3, lines 97–8).

Dr Johnson, an eighteenth-century essayist, poet and Shakespeare critic, believed Hamlet's thoughts when he found Claudius at prayer 'too terrible to be read or uttered'. Johnson's view influenced productions for over 100 years. Hamlet's speech (Act 3 Scene 3, lines 73–96) was either cut in performance or interpreted as not expressing Hamlet's real intentions, but simply an excuse to procrastinate, to delay the action.

- **Talk together about what you think of Dr Johnson's view in the preceding paragraph.**

- **Imagine you are Hamlet and write a paragraph about each of the following characters: Polonius, Rosencrantz and Guildenstern, Ophelia, Laertes, Gertrude, Claudius. Say whether you feel responsible for their death, whether each one deserved to die, and what you think will happen to each character after death.**

Acting and theatre – 'The play's the thing'

Hamlet richly displays Shakespeare's interest both in his own profession as actor and playwright, and in the London theatres at the end of the reign of Queen Elizabeth I. *Hamlet* is an intensely theatrical play, with many references to playing and acting. Play-acting is part of a puzzle that obsesses Hamlet: the difference between appearance and reality, truth and falsehood. Hamlet uses a company of travelling players to perform a stage murder. The performance traps Claudius into revealing his guilty conscience: a fiction has discovered the 'truth' of the Ghost's story.

The play resonates with the language of theatre: 'play', 'act', 'show', 'perform', 'applaud', 'prologue', 'shape' (costume), 'part' and 'stage' (see p. 265). Hamlet's soliloquies are like those of an actor reflecting on the part he has to play.

He sees the players as 'the abstract and brief chronicles of the time', and the purpose of acting as holding 'the mirror up to nature'. For Hamlet, the function of drama is to portray the nature of society: 'to show virtue her own feature, scorn her own image, and the very age and body of the time his form and pressure' (Act 3 Scene 2, lines 19–20).

On Hamlet's first appearance he denies he is playing a part: 'I know not seems.' His grief is real. But he puts on 'an antic disposition', and throughout the play muses (or rages) about deceptive appearance: 'Smiling, damned villain!' Other characters dissemble, most obviously Claudius. Rosencrantz and Guildenstern put on an act of friendship, and even Ophelia is instructed to 'show' to enable her father and Claudius to eavesdrop on Hamlet.

The play is filled with highly dramatic scenes: the Ghost's five appearances; Hamlet's raging at Ophelia and Gertrude; the dumb-show; the fight in the grave.
The final scene has abundant theatrical opportunities and references: the duel between Hamlet and Laertes; the many deaths, witnessed by 'mutes or audience to this act'; the entry of Fortinbras (preceded by 'March afar off, and shot within'); Horatio's 'give order that these bodies / High on a stage be placed to the view'; Fortinbras's order that 'four captains / Bear Hamlet like a soldier to the stage'; and the final stage direction: '*Exeunt marching, after the which a peal of ordnance are shot off*'.

The 'tragedians of the city'

Shakespeare's own company of players was sometimes forced to tour when plague closed the London theatres. The players' appearance at Elsinore echoes the experience of troupes of London actors as they toured the English provinces or Europe. On tour, they performed in the great halls of country houses or on makeshift stages in inn-yards or town squares.

Around the time Shakespeare wrote *Hamlet*, an acting company of boy players was enjoying great success in London. For a short time, these 'little eyases' (unfledged hawks) threatened the livelihood of some adult professional acting companies. The adult players were forced to tour because they could not attract London audiences. Hamlet's exchanges with Rosencrantz and Guildenstern in Act 2 Scene 2, lines 295–333, are thought to be about these boy players and the 'war of the theatres' (see p. 84). There was a brief but intense rivalry between adult companies as their resident playwrights mocked each other in their plays ('much throwing about of brains').

The members of Shakespeare's acting company (The King's Men, originally The Lord Chamberlain's Men) worked together closely for over twenty years. They knew each other very well and may have contributed to Shakespeare's script. Because of his fascination with acting, Shakespeare may have put into *Hamlet* private jokes and theatrical references that would have amused his fellow players at the Globe Theatre on London's Bankside:

- 'you hear this fellow in the cellarage' (the space under the Globe stage?) Act 1 Scene 5, line 151
- 'this distracted globe' (the Globe Theatre? Hamlet's head? The world?) Act 1 Scene 5, line 97
- 'I did enact Julius Caesar' (the actor who played Polonius may well have created the title role in *Julius Caesar*, written by Shakespeare shortly before *Hamlet*.) Act 3 Scene 2, line 91
- 'this majestical roof fretted with golden fire' (the sky, or the painted 'heavens' of the Globe's stage?) Act 2 Scene 2, lines 284–5
- 'thy face is valanced [bearded] since I saw thee last'; 'Pray God your voice ... be not cracked' (was Shakespeare joking at his fellow actor's changed appearance, and the thought that the boy actors who played the female parts would all too soon grow up?) Act 2 Scene 2, lines 386–90

- ◆ **Collect quotations from the play about actors, acting or the theatre. Use them to write an essay (or written dialogue in question-and-answer form) in response to the following: '*Hamlet* is a tragedy dominated by the idea of the play. Discuss.'**

Further themes

In addition to the themes discussed above, ideas of confinement, responsibility and freedom, attitudes towards sex, and the nature of existence pervade the play.

Confinement manifests itself in terms of the prison-like nature of Denmark for Hamlet, who seems trapped and shackled by his presence there. He is back from university, and finds the transition to home difficult ('For your intent / In going back to school in Wittenberg / It is most retrograde to our desire', Act 1 Scene 2, lines 112–14) – particularly because his mother has married Claudius and the Ghost indicates that his father has been murdered. Some productions of the play emphasise Denmark's dark, prison-like nature and the sense that Hamlet has limited choice in his actions. His stature as prince of Denmark also constrains him.

Responsibility and freedom are closely related to Hamlet's position as prince. On the one hand, Hamlet has freedoms and privileges – he appears not to have to work or account for his time, and can afford to sink into melancholy with only gentle chiding from his mother ('Good Hamlet cast thy nighted colour off', Act 1 Scene 2, line 68). But at the same time, he has responsibilities weighing upon him as successor to the throne of Denmark. The sight of Fortinbras passing through the country with his army reminds Hamlet of his inaction and his need to put things right.

Hamlet's attitude towards sex (Act 3 Scene 1, Act 3 Scene 2 and Act 3 Scene 4) has been described as Oedipal, warped, frustrated and cruel. He treats Ophelia with impunity, urging her to 'Go thy ways to a nunnery'. Freudian analyses of Hamlet's state of mind might suggest that his horror of the sexual relationship between Claudius and Gertrude, his solitude, his obsession with his mother, and even his inability to act until late in the play, are evidence of imbalance – perhaps also contributing to his 'madness'. (For more on this, see p. 255)

The nature of existence is a theme that recurs through the play. First, the appearance of the Ghost raises questions of perception and the afterlife for Horatio and the Watch; once verified by Horatio, it threatens doom and inspires revenge. Second, and in contrast, the very existence of the physical self in the world preoccupies Hamlet, who muses on the relationship of life and death. Third, the loneliness of the human on the planet ('existentialism') creeps into Hamlet's consciousness, as does a sense of the inevitability of – and preparedness for – death: 'There is special providence in the fall of a sparrow … the readiness is all' (Act 5 Scene 2, lines 192–5).

- Take three or four themes as identified in this section, and work out how they are related to each other in the play. You might find it helpful to discuss their relationship in groups first, then as a class, as you will touch on some complex philosophical issues. Then, using appropriate evidence from the script, write an essay on the relationship between your chosen themes.

What relevance does *Hamlet* have to a young, contemporary audience?

The part of Hamlet is often played by an actor in his late twenties or early thirties – perhaps to suggest Hamlet himself is around that age, maybe also because it is a long and difficult part for a younger actor to take on. But Hamlet as a character appeals to younger age groups (those in their teenage years or early twenties) because of his rebelliousness, his shifting moods, his anger and frustration at oppression and confinement, and his complicated sexuality and identity (or his search for some sense of solid identity).

- Look at the photographs of Hamlet in this edition of the play, and in pairs discuss which of them you find the most appropriate for your own vision of how he should appear. Rank the best three and the worst three, from your point of view, and then debate your preferences with the rest of the class.
- Look at the photographs from a young persons' workshop on the opposite page. Which moments from the play do you think are being enacted?
- Imagine you are producing *Hamlet* for an audience younger than you. What parts would you cut? Which themes would you emphasise? How can you ensure that the audience will be engaged by the play, and that they will see something of their own lives, problems and preoccupations in your production? Juliet in *Romeo and Juliet* can be played as a thirteen-year-old, according to the script. How young can you play Hamlet and Ophelia? You could put on a performance as a community play for a younger year group, a partner school or a young people's group in your area.

▶ *Hamlet* in workshop performance with the Royal Shakespeare Company's Young People's Shakespeare in 2010. Can you identify the characters in each photo?

Characters 人物分析

▼ **Which of Hamlet's characteristics do you think are most evident in this 2010 performance?**

Hamlet

Hamlet's words to Guildenstern – 'you would pluck out the heart of my mystery' – describe what thousands of books and articles have tried to do since *Hamlet* was first performed. But Hamlet's character remains elusive. He plays many roles throughout the play: alienated outsider, potential suicide, actor, swordsman, joker, friend of Horatio, angry son, bloodthirsty revenger, lacerating self-critic. His mood swings from depression to elation, from extreme self-loathing to quiet acceptance of his fate in 'the readiness is all'.

Hamlet has been seen as an ironic commentator on mortality and sin, a man with acute sexual problems, a genuine madman, a clever impersonator of madness, a man tortured by irreconcilable moral dilemmas, an unhappy adolescent, a puritanical fundamentalist, a dreamer, a philosopher and a truly noble prince.

The script shows that Hamlet is a great listener. He listens intently to what is said to him and often seizes on a word or phrase to construct his own reply. His very first words: 'A little more than kin, and less than kind' (Act I Scene 2, line 65), imply that Claudius is too presumptuous in calling him 'son' (kin), and that his nature (kind) is unlike Claudius's. His next line 'I am too much i'th'sun' puns on Claudius's 'son'. His following two replies to Gertrude pun ironically on her use of 'common' and 'seems'.

In many ways, Hamlet is something of a chameleon – he changes colour in relation to those he is with, and/or in relation to the situation in which he finds himself. Another way of putting this is in modern social-psychological

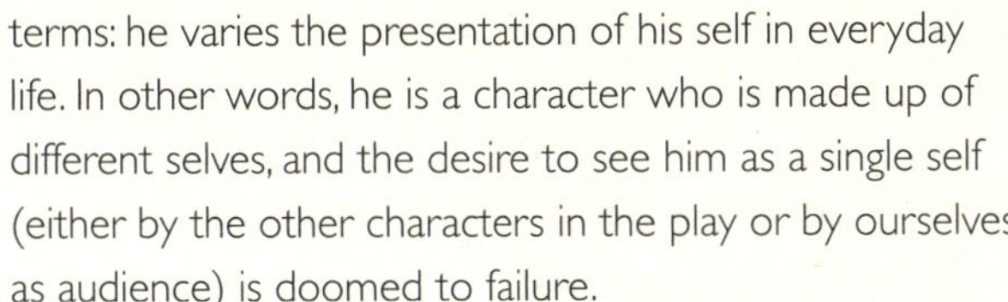

terms: he varies the presentation of his self in everyday life. In other words, he is a character who is made up of different selves, and the desire to see him as a single self (either by the other characters in the play or by ourselves as audience) is doomed to failure.

Hamlet revels in how the slipperiness of language gives potential for bitter or comic puns or ironic retorts. He uses puns to great effect, picking up a speaker's words and giving them back with a different meaning (look at Act 3 Scene 2, 82–113 for an example). The Clown/ gravedigger is the only other character in the play to use this style of deliberate misunderstanding. He gives Hamlet a taste of his own medicine.

- Identify examples of this linguistic technique of Hamlet's. Against which characters does he use it most frequently?

- Hamlet not only listens carefully to others, he also listens intently to himself and comments on his own thoughts. Identify passages in his soliloquies in which he comments on his own thoughts and feelings (e.g. with self-disgust or reproof).

- Use your findings in the two activities above to compile an assignment on what aspects of Hamlet's character are revealed by how he listens to others and to himself.

- Track Hamlet's appearances throughout the play. Identify one or two moods from each appearance, and then create a graph of his changing states of mind across the play as a whole. Does he present the trajectory of a typical tragic hero – the rise and fall of a great person? Or is his trajectory different? If so, in what respects and why? (See the notes on tragedy on p. 258.)

- What is the significance of Horatio for Hamlet? At a simple level, he is a trusted friend in a world of deceit, intrigue and falsity. But there is more to Horatio. Identify the scenes in which Horatio and Hamlet appear together. Highlight their dialogue, and examine how they talk together. What does a friendship with Horatio tell us about Hamlet – how is Hamlet reflected in Horatio?

Hamlet's sexual identity

What is Hamlet's attitude towards the two women in the play? Some productions have suggested that Hamlet is sexually obsessed by his mother. Other productions imply that he truly loves Ophelia. Almost every possibility about Hamlet's sexuality has been explored on stage, on film and in print.

- **An Oedipus complex?** Hamlet is in love with his mother and is violently jealous of Claudius, his stepfather. This Oedipus complex makes him unable to have a loving relationship with Ophelia, whom he treats badly. His hatred for Claudius is based on sexual jealousy, since Claudius has usurped not only his father's crown but also his mother's bed.
- **A Puritan?** Hamlet is severely puritanical about love and sex. He is appalled by what he sees as the lust that drives the relationship between Claudius and Gertrude (see Act 3 Scene 4, lines 92–4). His disgust at his mother's sexuality makes him despise all women. Hamlet therefore subjects Ophelia to violent verbal abuse, full of sexual innuendo.
- **A true lover?** Hamlet genuinely loves Ophelia. He urges her to go to a nunnery to escape the torturous, prison-like nature of love in the world that Denmark represents. His harsh words cover his deep love for her, and he is being 'cruel only to be kind'.
- **An immature boy?** Hamlet is not ready for love. His sexual bantering with Polonius, Rosencrantz and Guildenstern is immature male behaviour. He is unable to understand his mother's sexual life or to appreciate Ophelia's innocent and more mature affection for him.
- **A split personality?** Hamlet both loves and hates Ophelia, and simultaneously admires and abhors his mother. His sexual feelings for Ophelia and his mother fight against his other feelings. His rational mind attempts to reconcile these sexual and emotional tensions, but thought itself makes him unable to act.
- **Private love versus public office?** Hamlet's sexual confusion arises not from his personality but from his position as prince of Denmark. He may not choose for himself in marriage but must think first of his responsibility to the country.

▼ 'I loved Ophelia'. In this Royal Shakespeare Company production, Hamlet displayed his genuine love for Ophelia by leaping into her grave for a final embrace.

- Find two or more quotations from the script to support each of the viewpoints listed on page 255. Arrange the six interpretations in order of which you find the most convincing, using the evidence in the play.
- Undertake some research into Freud's theories of sexuality and depression, and then do a Freudian analysis of Hamlet. You can do this in two stages: a dramatised analysis of Hamlet as a client of Freud's in his clinic in Vienna or London; and a written set of case notes on Hamlet, compiled after a number of sessions with him.
- Step into role as Hamlet. Imagine, just before you die, that you have the chance for a longer, cooler and more reasoned reflection on your behaviour and attitudes to Gertrude and Ophelia. Either write this out as a prose or verse soliloquy, or respond to questions and accusations from Gertrude, Ophelia and Horatio.
- In another possible world, or different story (one in which the present play stops before the 'closet' scene), imagine that Hamlet, after the erratic behaviour of the first half of the play, marries Ophelia. You can stage the marriage and perhaps the reception afterwards with as many characters as you wish (six, to include Gertrude, Claudius, Polonius and Laertes; or a larger wedding party to include the other characters in the play). In particular, write the best man's speech (Horatio?); the father of the bride's speech (Polonius); and the groom's and bride's speeches.

▼ Do you think that Hamlet shows an unhealthy, negative attitude towards the women in the play? In this production, Ophelia was visibly upset when Hamlet insulted her.

Hamlet: a tragic hero?

'Tragedy' is the conventional description of a play that portrays human suffering and the decline and death of a hero or heroine. Traditionally the hero or heroine is of high status, and the fall from grace immense. But some modern tragedies, like Arthur Miller's *Death of a Salesman*, have an ordinary person as their tragic hero. To help your thinking about Hamlet's character, consider the following interpretations of Hamlet as a tragic hero.

- **Tragic flaw?** The hero's downfall is caused by a tragic flaw or blemish in his character. Hamlet's weakness may be that he 'thinks too much' and cannot make up his mind. The resulting inaction leads to his death. But Hamlet's tragic flaw ('vicious mole of nature', Act 1 Scene 4, line 24) may be some other feature in his character responsible for his downfall.
- **A tragedy of fate?** The hero has no real control over his destiny. Once the spring of *Hamlet*'s tragic narrative is released, it unwinds inevitably towards its conclusion: the death of Hamlet. His fate is predetermined. As Hamlet says, 'There's a divinity that shapes our ends'.
- **A tragedy of chance?** Accident and bad luck determine the fate of the hero. The unplanned chance encounter with the pirate ship, for example, brings Hamlet back to Denmark. Hamlet accidentally kills Polonius. The tragic hero is the victim of random events.
- **Irreconcilable opposites?** The hero's character comprises sets of irreconcilable forces. Hamlet's mind and feelings are filled with such tensions: reason battles with passion, love is contrasted with lust, action is inhibited by thought. Hamlet struggles with a wish to die and an urge to live. *Hamlet* can be read as the tragedy of a man trapped between such contraries.
- **Hero as paragon?** The tragic hero has an excess of virtues. This nineteenth-century Romantic view of Hamlet as a Renaissance prince suggests that he is more noble and refined than ordinary people, and that his nobility and purity carry the seeds of their own destruction. Hamlet cannot live in the world because he is too 'good' for it. His sensitivity and noble qualities lead to his downfall.

◆ **Find evidence (quotations or actions in the play) to support each of the above viewpoints. Decide which interpretation you favour most. Rank the rest in order, dismissing any you think are not plausible or not supported by evidence. Then write your own view of Hamlet as a tragic hero.**

The nature of tragedy

Aristotle's *Poetics* contains some ancient Greek insights into tragedy, which was then emerging as a major new genre to challenge the epic form. For example:

> *Tragedy is an imitation of an action that is admirable, complete and possesses magnitude … [it effects] through pity and fear the purification [or* ***catharsis****] (心灵清洗，净化) of such emotions*
>
> *The events, i.e. the plot, are what tragedy is there for, and that is the most important thing of all.*
>
> Translated by Malcolm Heath, Penguin, 1996

According to Aristotle's theory, a tragic character needs four qualities: to be moral, to behave appropriately, to be realistic and to be consistent. He defines four kinds of tragedy:

- a simple tragedy with a straightforward plot of the rise and fall of a great person
- a complex tragedy, depending entirely on reversal and recognition, so that there is some degree of self-knowledge gained by the protagonist
- a tragedy of suffering, which often marks the slow decline of a person who experiences loss, despair and hopelessness
- a tragedy of character that identifies the 'tragic flaw' mentioned above.

These refer to different types of plot, and at least three may be present in any one play.

◆ Use these definitions from Aristotle to shed light on *Hamlet* and on its eponymous hero. Which of them apply to Hamlet?

◆ Which of the following characteristics and dramatic devices of tragedy might apply to *Hamlet*? Give reasons and evidence for your answers.

- **Hubris (鄙视神灵):** pride or arrogance in the over-estimation of one's powers, usually followed by a fall and humiliation.
- **Catharsis:** the revelation brought about by purgation, clarification and/or purification; a moment of insight and release from emotional tension, usually in an audience but sometimes in a character.
- **Anagnorisis (识破):** a critical discovery by a character in a play.
- **Peripeteia (剧情急转):** a reversal and turning point for a key character in a play.

Claudius

Claudius has committed an evil deed to become king, murdering his own brother. He plans similar evil as the play unfolds, plotting to have Hamlet killed in England. When that fails, he lures Laertes into a scheme to kill Hamlet in a deceitful duel. He lies about his 'love' for Hamlet and tells Gertrude that he tried to calm Laertes, when in fact he deliberately fuelled Laertes's rage. Hamlet condemns Claudius as a drunkard and sees him as the source of corruption in Denmark: 'this canker of our nature'.

Claudius's hypocrisy is evident throughout the play (see p. 14 on the devious eloquence of his first speech). But he seems a competent king, intelligent and quick witted. There is no hint that the nobles of Denmark challenge his right to the throne. He appears to love Gertrude and to respect Polonius, willing to accept his advice. He knows that he does wrong, and is racked by conscience, struggling unsuccessfully to pray to find some way of absolving his murderous guilt: 'Oh my offence is rank, it smells to heaven.' He bravely stands up to Laertes's threats, but his noble words 'There's such divinity doth hedge a king' are hypocritical, because he himself has killed a king, his own brother.

◆ Write a character study of Claudius, describing in particular how Shakespeare portrays his hypocrisy. Consider ways in which Shakespeare complicates the view that Claudius is simply 'a villain' in order to make him sympathetic and human.

▼ Glenn Close as Gertrude in Franco Zeffirelli's 1990 film. What aspects of her character are suggested by this image?

Gertrude

A puzzle that all productions of the play face is the question of whether Gertrude knows that Claudius is a murderer. She seems in thrall (受控制) to Claudius for the first half of the play, and is genuinely distressed by her son's bizarre behaviour. But Shakespeare gives Gertrude lines in and after her encounter with Hamlet in her chamber that suggest she progressively distances herself from her second husband.

Critics have often judged Gertrude as a weak, selfish and innocent woman, caught up in conflicts she does not fully understand. Her hasty marriage to Claudius so soon after her first husband's death disgusts Hamlet, and seems to indicate her pliability or perhaps her powerlessness as the widow of a dead king. That capacity to be easily persuaded is evident when she allows Polonius to use her private chamber to spy on Hamlet.

Gertrude feels compassion for both Polonius and Ophelia, and she may well love Claudius, at least for the first half of the play. She tries to protect him from Laertes's aggression. But what are Gertrude's feelings towards Hamlet? Ever since Laurence Olivier's film portrayed Hamlet's incestuous desire for his mother, productions have to decide just how to present her affection for Hamlet.

Polonius

Polonius is the king's counsellor, Claudius's chief minister of state. He is evidently filled with a sense of self-importance, and is proud of the service he has given to the king. Claudius acknowledges him as 'a man faithful and honourable'.

Polonius seeks to control public life. He also wishes to control his family. He hands out good advice to his son Laertes ('these few precepts in thy memory'), but then sends Reynaldo to spy on him in France. He orders Ophelia to avoid Hamlet and to return his love tokens. He even uses her as an accomplice to eavesdrop on Hamlet, an action that results in his daughter being savagely insulted by Hamlet. Polonius offers no word of comfort to the distraught Ophelia.

He conceals himself behind the arras in Gertrude's chamber, only to be killed by Hamlet, who mistakes the hidden figure for the king.

In spite of his pomposity and authoritarianism, Polonius is loved by his children. Shakespeare enables the actor to play Polonius not simply as a spymaster and over-strict father, but also as a character who can gain audience sympathy as a well-meaning father and loyal counsellor.

- **What aspects of parenthood are embodied in Polonius? Use the theme of the father-son relationship to explore how Polonius's relationship with Laertes mirrors or contrasts with that of Claudius and Hamlet.**
- **As a comparison, talk about the father-daughter relationship. How does Polonius interact with Ophelia?**

Ophelia

Many critics have judged Ophelia as a beautiful, innocent but essentially passive character. Increasingly, however, actors have sought to bring out her strength and knowledge of the world. In the past, she was often played as obedient to her father, and touchingly poignant in her madness. Modern productions tend to emphasise how she rebukes Laertes after his long catalogue of advice, and show her unwillingly or resentfully following her father's instructions.

Ophelia feels deeply for Hamlet, and his apparent rejection affects her grievously, 'Oh woe is me / T'have seen what I have seen, see what I see.' When he jokes with her at the play scene, she seems fully aware of his sexual meanings. The songs she sings in her madness reveal not simply the depth of her love for her father, but also an uninhibited sexual awareness that her mental derangement has allowed to surface.

There are parallels between Ophelia and Hamlet. Both have fathers who have been violently killed. Both feel let down by a person they deeply love. Both suffer the distress of madness, whether it is real and/or assumed.

- **Use the photographs of Ophelia in this book to explore her character. Is she the passive victim of her father, brother and lover as she is often portrayed? What evidence can you find in the script to show that there is more to her than passivity?**

- **As the only young woman in the play (without a foil or friend that she can define herself against), what clothes and look would you provide for her as a costume/make-up designer for your production? Does Ophelia obediently follow court custom, as Polonius's daughter; or is she more rebellious?**

- **In relation to Hamlet, and in her own development as a young woman, how would Ophelia account for herself? Write her diary, or her version of a psychiatric appointment with Freud (see activity on p. 256), before her death.**

Laertes

From his first speech (Act 1 Scene 2, lines 50–56), Laertes seems straight, honourable, dutiful and a potential foil to Hamlet – who is not the opposite embodiment of these traits, but is a darker, more complex character burdened by melancholy. Laertes does not dwell on his feelings inwardly, but manifests them in direct expression. Interestingly, he 'bookends' the play by appearing near the start and near the end, and so provides a frame of reference for Hamlet's procrastination. He also provides his own revenge motives in response to Hamlet's treatment of Ophelia and the killing of Polonius.

Despite this, there is something hypocritical about Laertes. His invocation to his sister to be wary of Hamlet's approaches (Act 1 Scene 3) while she retorts that he himself must live by his own precepts (lines 45–51); his willingness, in Act 4 Scene 7, to go along with Claudius's devious scheme to poison the rapiers for the duel with Hamlet; and his thrust at the apparently off-guard Hamlet with the poisoned rapier in Act 5 Scene 2, line 280. All these instances point to a character who is not entirely honourable and who, like all the characters in the play – with perhaps the exception of Horatio and Ophelia – is tainted somewhat by the corruption of Denmark.

- **Do you see Laertes as merely representative of certain values (honour, duty, loyalty) or as a rounded character in his own right? Take sides in a debate. One side argues that Laertes is a victim of circumstance, a largely honourable young man (without a mother) whose sister and father fall prey to a disturbed and reckless prince. The other side argues that he is a corrupt, weak-minded, easily angered and hypocritical character who pales in comparison to Hamlet.**

- **Imagine the play without Laertes. Would it work?**

The language of *Hamlet* 《哈慕雷》的语言

Imagery – 'the morn in russet mantle clad'

Hamlet abounds in **imagery**: vivid words and phrases that conjure up emotionally charged pictures or associations in the mind. When Hamlet thinks of how the First Player would perform if he had suffered such grief as Hamlet, he declares, 'He would drown the stage with tears'. The image passionately conveys the depth of Hamlet's feelings. Similarly, Polonius abruptly dismisses Hamlet's 'holy vows' of his love to Ophelia as 'springes to catch woodcocks': merely traps to snare innocent and foolish birds.

Imagery carries powerful significance, far deeper than its surface meanings. Images enrich particular moments, as when Claudius agonises that his hand is stained with his brother's blood: 'Is there not rain enough in the sweet heavens / To wash it white as snow?' Imagery repeatedly illuminates the themes of the play such as revenge or madness (as when Gertrude describes Hamlet as 'Mad as the sea and wind, when both contend / Which is the mightier.').

Imagery stirs the audience's imagination and deepens the impact of particular moments or moods. It provides insight into character, and intensifies meaning and emotional force. In *Hamlet* the imagery is sometimes so brilliantly complex that, although it can be analysed and understood, it defies any final 'explanation', as in Hamlet's words:

> *Whether 'tis nobler in the mind to suffer*
> *The slings and arrows of outrageous fortune,*
> *Or to take arms against a sea of troubles,*
> *And by opposing end them.*
>
> Act 3 Scene 1, lines 57–60

All Shakespeare's imagery uses metaphor, simile or personification. All are comparisons that in effect substitute one thing (the image) for another (the thing described).

A **simile** (明喻) compares one thing to another using 'like' or 'as'. Ophelia describes Hamlet's derangement as 'Like sweet bells jangled, out of time and harsh'. The Ghost tells how the poison spread through his body 'swift as quicksilver'.

A **metaphor** is also a comparison, suggesting that two dissimilar things are actually the same or have something in common. The distraught Hamlet speaks of his head as 'this distracted globe'. He describes one play as 'caviary to the general' (caviar to ordinary people – too good for them). To put it another way, a metaphor borrows one word or phrase to express another.

Personification (拟人) turns all types of things into persons, giving them human feelings or attributes. In the quotation from Act 3 Scene 1, 'fortune' is personified. The dying Hamlet memorably personifies death itself as a cruel officer of the law: 'this fell sergeant death / Is strict in his arrest'.

Certain image clusters recur through the play, notably those of corruption and disease, the theatre and acting.

Corruption and disease

In the play's opening moments Francisco's 'I am sick at heart' is the first indication of the many images of infection that pervade *Hamlet*. Marcellus declares that 'Something is rotten in the state of Denmark.' Hamlet is haunted by the corruption of his mother's incest, seeing it as an infectious disease: 'the ulcerous place / Whiles rank corruption, mining all within, / Infects unseen.' Claudius thinks of Hamlet as a fever: 'like the hectic in my blood he rages'. Hamlet describes Claudius as 'a mildewed ear' and as 'this canker of our nature'.

Watching Fortinbras's army marching towards death, Hamlet reflects that 'This is th'impostume [abscess] … That inward breaks, and shows no cause without / Why the man dies' (Act 4 Scene 4, lines 27–9). This final image refers to an inner problem, like the development of cancerous cells, that cause death without there being any visible signs of the disease.

Theatre and acting

Page 250 describes how the language of theatre and acting recurs in the play: 'play', 'act', 'cue', 'prompted', 'mutes' and so on. Shakespeare's fascination with his own professional world is evident in *Hamlet*: the players, the play-within-a-play that reveals Claudius's guilt, the talk of the 'little eyases' (boy actors). In Hamlet's first appearance he uses 'actions', 'play' and 'show' as he angrily denies that his grief is reflected only in his outward appearance (Act 1 Scene 2, lines 84–5):

For they are actions that a man might play,
But I have that within which passes show –

The notion of acting as a pretence that somehow convinces finds expression in Hamlet's amazement that an actor can weep for a fictional character: 'And all for nothing? / For Hecuba!'

Lastly, imagery is intimately and deeply connected with the themes in the play. In many ways, it operates to indicate the themes, as in the clusters of images mentioned immediately above – along with what the actors explicitly say and do (the plot). It points towards unconscious connections in the play, and the preoccupations of the characters who express their thoughts.

- **Identify a dozen images in the play that especially appeal to you. Write an analysis of how they operate, both for immediate effect in the scene and in the play as a whole, reinforcing and complicating its themes.**

Antithesis

Antithesis is the opposition of words or phrases against each other, as in 'To be, or not to be', and 'I must be cruel only to be kind'. This setting of the word against the word ('To be' versus 'not to be', 'cruel' versus 'kind') is one of Shakespeare's favourite language devices. He uses it extensively in all his plays. Why? Because antithesis powerfully expresses conflict through its use of opposites, and conflict is the essence of all drama. In *Hamlet*, conflict occurs in many forms. Claudius versus Hamlet, revenge versus justice, son versus mother, and dark shadows versus a more colourful presence (for example, in the acting troupe that visits Elsinore). Antithesis intensifies the sense of conflict and definition.

Claudius's many antitheses in his first speech (Act 1 Scene 2) suggest a man attempting to balance conflicting emotions and values as he tells of his marriage to Gertrude – for example, lines 11–13:

With one auspicious and one dropping eye,
With mirth in funeral and with dirge in marriage,
In equal scale weighing delight and dole

For an Elizabethan audience the antithesis 'With one auspicious and one dropping eye' implied deviousness, because a contemporary proverb held that a false man looked up with one eye and down with the other. The other antitheses imply a similar two-facedness: someone who can simultaneously express joy and sorrow, or show an inappropriate emotion at a funeral or a marriage. In Act 3 Scene 1, lines 51–3, Claudius uses an image full of antitheses to acknowledge that a prostitute's use of make-up is similar to how he hypocritically conceals his evil deed behind a mask:

The harlot's cheek, beautied with plastering art,
Is not more ugly to the thing that helps it
Than is my deed to my most painted word.

Laertes's passionate desire for revenge on Hamlet ('To cut his throat i'th'church') is given additional emotional power by the opposition of the bloodiness of the action with the sanctity of the holy place. In the very last moments of the play (Act 5 Scene 2, lines 380–1), Fortinbras opposes the appropriateness of dead bodies on the battlefield ('field') with their inappropriateness in the court ('here'): 'Such a sight as this / Becomes the field, but here shows much amiss.'

- **Collect between ten and twenty examples of antithesis in the play script. Use them in an essay showing how antithesis helps create a sense of conflict and paradox in *Hamlet*.**

Verse and prose

Just under three quarters of the play is in verse, and just over one quarter in prose. How did Shakespeare decide whether to write in verse or prose? A rough rule of thumb is that aristocrats speak verse, and low-status and comic or mad characters speak prose. But context is very important. Thus the players (low status) speak verse in the Gonzago play to emphasise that they are playing aristocratic characters. Hamlet and Ophelia (high status) express madness in prose.

Verse was thought more suitable than prose to moments of high dramatic or emotional intensity. So 'serious' scenes are likely to be in verse, 'comic' episodes in prose. Hamlet uses prose with Rosencrantz and Guildenstern, the Gravedigger and Osric. Hamlet's 'What a piece of work is a man' speech (Act 2 Scene 2, lines 286–90) is also in prose, but has all the qualities claimed for poetry.

Hamlet is written mainly in **blank verse**: unrhymed verse written in **iambic pentameter** (抑扬五音步). This is a rhythm, or **metre** (韵律), in which each line has five unstressed syllables (/) alternating with five stressed syllables (×) (often expressed as da-DUM da-DUM da-DUM da-DUM da-DUM), as in Act 3 Scene 2, line 196:

/ × / × / × / × / ×
But die thy thoughts when thy first lord is dead

By the time he wrote *Hamlet*, Shakespeare had become very flexible in his use of iambic pentameter. He often uses **enjambement** (跨行)(running on), where one line flows on into the next, seemingly with little or no pause. Lines may have more or fewer than ten syllables.

◆ Choose a verse speech and speak it to emphasise the metre. Then speak it as if it were prose, then as you feel it should be delivered on stage. Finally, write eight lines of your own in any form of verse.

◆ Choose a passage of verse from the play and 'translate' it into prose. What is gained or lost in translation? How do the effects of each differ? (See also the activities on pp. 92 and 184.) Why is this exercise not so satisfactory or useful if you are asked to convert prose to verse?

Questions

Hamlet is full of questions. Barnardo's opening challenge 'Who's there?' sets the questioning tone that characterises the whole play. Virtually every character wishes to find out something. On almost every page questions are asked. Hamlet is often self-questioning.

◆ Turn to any page of the script. Identify the questions on that page, and check how many are answered. Repeat for several more pages. Decide which questions can be answered, and which cannot. Then make up a few questions of your own about the play. Try to answer them in a small group. Put any you cannot answer to the class as a whole – and to the teacher!

Soliloquies

Hamlet is famous for his **soliloquies**. A soliloquy is a kind of internal debate spoken by a character who is alone on stage (or believes themselves to be alone). Soliloquies reveal the character's true thoughts and feelings. Hamlet's soliloquies, in parts, give the impression of a man discovering what he thinks as he speaks.

◆ Hamlet's soliloquies appear at the following points in the play:
- Act 1 Scene 2, lines 254–7
- Act 1 Scene 5, lines 92–112
- Act 2 Scene 2, lines 501–58
- Act 3 Scene 1, lines 56–90
- Act 3 Scene 2, lines 349–60
- Act 3 Scene 3, lines 73–96
- Act 4 Scene 4, lines 32–66

Select one and work out a dramatic presentation. You could share the lines around your group, and have several people echoing key lines or phrases. Try speaking it as a conversation, or to the audience, or to a portrait of another character, or to a stage prop. Experiment with styles of delivery (for example, as an observer disgusted with the human condition, or as a bloodthirsty revenger).

- ◆ Divide the class into seven groups. Each group takes one soliloquy. First, in your groups, enlarge a copy of your text so that you can see the whole speech in one poster or banner. Annotate it with verbal commentary and with images. Have two of the group stand by the poster while the others in your group visit the other posters/banners and pose questions about the nature of the soliloquies.
- ◆ If you wish to explore the meaning differently and perhaps in more depth, perform a dialogic version of the soliloquy using more than one voice, and employing techniques such as choral presentation, question and answer, and emphasis of key words and phrases.

Doubling language: a cause of delay?

All kinds of 'doubling' go on in *Hamlet:* the two sentries at the play's beginning; Rosencrantz and Guildenstern; Cornelius and Voltemand; two English ambassadors; two kingly brothers, Claudius and old Hamlet. Furthermore, Hamlet and Laertes are both students, sons, revengers and opponents.

Such doubling is strikingly reflected in the play's language. It appears in repetition of words and phrases: 'Tush tush', 'Speak, speak', 'this too too solid flesh', 'To be, or not to be' and so on. Polonius seems to say everything twice: 'You have me, have you not?' Most commonly the doubling is by means of the conjunction 'and'. When Laertes requests Claudius for permission to return to France, he uses 'leave and favour', 'thoughts and wishes', 'leave and pardon'.

Hamlet contains around 250 examples of such 'doublings'. In Act 3 Scene 1, lines 144–55, Ophelia's lines lamenting Hamlet's treatment of her ('Oh what a noble mind is here o'erthrown!') includes doubling of single words (observed/observers, quite/quite, seen/seen, see/see), together with six examples of doubles using 'and':

- expectancy and rose of the fair state
- glass of fashion and the mould of form
- deject and wretched
- noble and most sovereign reason
- out of time and harsh
- form and feature.

A special type of such doubling is known as **hendiadys** (pronounced hen-die-a-dees), a technical term meaning 'one through two'. Here, the two words express a single idea. They duplicate the sense rather than amplify or modify each other, as these few examples from the script show:

- food and diet
- grace and mercy
- spark and fire
- cheer and comfort
- lecture and advice
- flash and outbreak
- pith and marrow
- duty and obedience
- native and indued
- book and volume
- heat and flame
- strange or odd.

This tendency to use two words when one would be sufficient to convey meaning contributes to dramatic effect. It lengthens the play, adding to the sense of delay. In its suggestion of 'one through two' it echoes the play's concern with marriage and incest (the union of separate or *like* selves).

- ◆ **Search through the play for examples of these 'doubling' devices. Talk together about their dramatic effect and how they provide insights into character and situation.**

What did Shakespeare write?

Shakespeare probably wrote *Hamlet* around 1601. But there are problems in knowing exactly what he wrote (let alone what he intended). First, he was a playwright, and undoubtedly had second thoughts as he worked with the actors rehearsing and performing the play. Second, there are three versions of the play, from which all editors make their choices as they prepare their own edition for publication.

- **The First Quarto** (Q1: the 'bad quarto'), published in 1603 and thought to be a pirated (unauthorised) version, put together by some actors and sold for a quick profit. It has 2154 lines.
- **The Second Quarto** (Q2: the 'good quarto'), published in 1604 and thought to be Shakespeare's response to the 'bad quarto', in order to establish the 'correct' version. It has 3674 lines.
- **The First Folio** (F1), published in 1623. This is thought to be Shakespeare's version of the play to make it even more suitable for the stage. But remember that Shakespeare died in 1616, and the First Folio was compiled seven years later by two actors in his company. It has 3535 lines (including 83 that do not appear in Q2).

Some lines of the script are in square brackets [ ]. These are the lines in Q2 that were cut out of F1. It is thought that Shakespeare cut these lines to make a more actable version of the play.

◆ **Find several examples of lines in square brackets (for example, Act 1 Scene 4, lines 17–38, Act 3 Scene 4, lines 203–11 and Act 4 Scene 7, lines 113–22). Discuss possible reasons why Shakespeare cut them. But remember – no one can be certain that Shakespeare himself did so. Would you cut the lines in performance? Give reasons for your decision.**

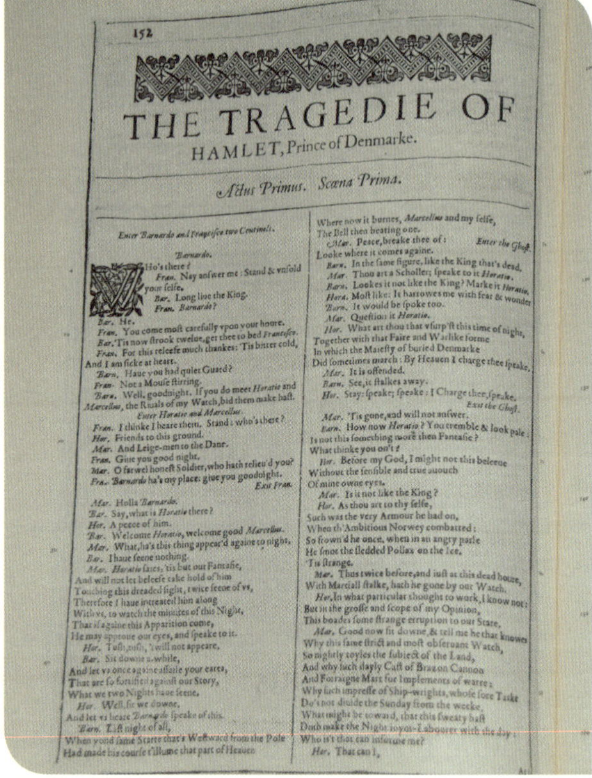

152

THE TRAGEDIE OF
HAMLET, Prince of Denmarke.

Actus Primus. Scœna Prima.

Enter Barnardo and Francisco two Centinels.

Barnardo.
Who's there?
Fran. Nay anſwer me: Stand & vnfold your ſelfe.
Bar. Long liue the King.
Fran. Barnardo?
Bar. He.
Fran. You come moſt carefully vpon your houre.
Bar. 'Tis now ſtrook twelue, get thee to bed *Franciſco*.
Fran. For this releefe much thankes: 'Tis bitter cold,
And I am ſicke at heart.
Barn. Haue you had quiet Guard?
Fran. Not a Mouſe ſtirring.
Barn. Well, goodnight. If you do meet *Horatio* and
Marcellus, the Riuals of my Watch, bid them make haſt.
Enter Horatio and Marcellus.
Fran. I thinke I heare them. Stand: who's there?
Hor. Friends to this ground.
Mar. And Leige-men to the Dane.
Fran. Giue you good night.
Mar. O farwel honeſt Soldier, who hath relieu'd you?
Fra. *Barnardo* ha's my place: giue you goodnight.
Exit Fran.
Mar. Holla *Barnardo*.
Bar. Say, what is *Horatio* there?
Hor. A peece of him.
Bar. Welcome *Horatio*, welcome good *Marcellus*.
Mar. What, ha's this thing appear'd againe to night.
Bar. I haue ſeene nothing.
Mar. *Horatio* ſaies, 'tis but our Fantaſie,
And will not let beleefe take hold of him
Touching this dreaded ſight, twice ſeene of vs,
Therefore I haue intreated him along
With vs, to watch the minutes of this Night,
That if againe this Apparition come,
He may approue our eyes, and ſpeake to it.
Hor. Tuſh, tuſh, 'twill not appeare.
Bar. Sit downe a-while,
And let vs once againe aſſaile your eares,
That are ſo fortified againſt our Story,
What we two Nights haue ſeene.
Hor. Well, ſit we downe,
And let vs heare *Barnardo* ſpeake of this.
Barn. Laſt night of all,
When yond ſame Starre that's Weſtward from the Pole
Had made his courſe t'illume that part of Heauen
Where now it burnes, *Marcellus* and my ſelfe,
The Bell then beating one.
Mar. Peace, breake thee of: *Enter the Ghoſt.*
Looke where it comes againe.
Barn. In the ſame figure, like the King that's dead.
Mar. Thou art a Scholler; ſpeake to it *Horatio*.
Barn. Lookes it not like the King? Marke it *Horatio*.
Hora. Moſt like: It harrowes me with fear & wonder
Barn. It would be ſpoke too.
Mar. Queſtion it *Horatio*.
Hor. What art thou that vſurp'ſt this time of night,
Together with that Faire and Warlike forme
In which the Maieſty of buried Denmarke
Did ſometimes march: By Heauen I charge thee ſpeake.
Mar. It is offended.
Barn. See, it ſtalkes away.
Hor. Stay: ſpeake; ſpeake: I Charge thee, ſpeake.
Exit the Ghoſt.
Mar. 'Tis gone, and will not anſwer.
Barn. How now *Horatio*? You tremble & look pale:
Is not this ſomething more then Fantaſie?
What thinke you on't?
Hor. Before my God, I might not this beleeue
Without the ſenſible and true auouch
Of mine owne eyes.
Mar. Is it not like the King?
Hor. As thou art to thy ſelfe,
Such was the very Armour he had on,
When th'Ambitious Norwey combatted:
So frown'd he once, when in an angry parle
He ſmot the ſledded Pollax on the Ice.
'Tis ſtrange.
Mar. Thus twice before, and iuſt at this dead houre,
With Martiall ſtalke, hath he gone by our Watch.
Hor. In what particular thought to work, I know not:
But in the groſſe and ſcope of my Opinion,
This boades ſome ſtrange eruption to our State.
Mar. Good now ſit downe, & tell me he that knowes
Why this ſame ſtrict and moſt obſeruant Watch,
So nightly toyles the ſubiect of the Land,
And why ſuch dayly Caſt of Brazon Cannon
And Forraigne Mart for Implements of warre:
Why ſuch impreſſe of Ship-wrights, whoſe ſore Taske
Do's not diuide the Sunday from the weeke,
What might be toward, that this ſweaty haſt
Doth make the Night ioynt-Labourer with the day:
Who is't that can informe me?
Hor. That can I,

▲ **The first page of *Hamlet* from a facsimile edition of the First Folio of Shakespeare's plays, published in 1623.**

Quick-fire dialogue

As well as seven soliloquies, there is a great deal of (potentially) fast dialogue in the play, usually associated with Hamlet's wit. For example, Hamlet's dialogue with Polonius in Act 2 Scene 2, lines 169–212, or with Gertrude, Claudius and Ophelia in Act 3 Scene 2, lines 210–30.

◆ **Find other examples, and divide the class into the same number of groups as the total number of quick-fire dialogues you can find (including the two examples listed here). Each group (or members of the group) tries acting out a section at various paces – with both or all characters talking at speed; with Hamlet as the fastest; and with some variation within the dialogues.**

- Can you find any examples of 'stichomythic' (针锋对话式的) dialogue, when single alternating lines, or half-lines, are given to alternating characters? What is the effect of such rapid-fire exchanges?
- When you have experimented with pace, ask yourselves (and answer the questions as best you can): which versions work best, and why? What do we learn about Hamlet's mind and his impatience and/or wit as a result of these dialogues?

The language of the First Player

When the players first arrive at Elsinore, Hamlet asks the First Player to recite a speech that he 'chiefly loved' in which Aeneas speaks of Priam's slaughter (Act 2 Scene 2, line 405 onwards). Hamlet starts the speech (lines 410–22) then asks the Player to continue it (lines 426 onwards). Shakespeare's contemporary, Christopher Marlowe, writes in this grander style in some of his plays (e.g. *Tamburlaine*, *Dido Queen of Carthage*), and it is possible that Shakespeare is both mocking the style and appreciating it at the same time. The style is characterised by archaic diction ('couchèd in the ominous horse', line 412); epithets ('hellish Pyrrhus', 'reverend Priam', lines 421 and 437); an excess of doubling ('wrath and fire', line 419; 'Baked and impasted', line 417); numerous classical references (Pyrrhus, Priam, Ilium); circumlocution ('th'Hyrcanian beast', line 408); and over-dramatic grandeur ('anon the dreadful thunder / Doth rend the region', lines 444–5). It is a far cry from the colloquial language of much of Shakespeare's prose.

- From line 410 to 475, divide the speech into constituent sentences (there are twelve in all). Individually, in pairs or in threes, take a sentence and compare it to sentences in any of Hamlet's soliloquies – choose two or three from Hamlet's speeches that you think will make a good comparison. Undertake a close analysis of Hamlet's and the Player's 'acting' language on the one hand and that of Hamlet in his soliloquies on the other. See if you can characterise the similarities and differences in style. As a starting point, think of how the Player's performance demonstrates epic as a form of narrative (an epic is a lengthy story in the grand style, involving heroism and adventure); and how Hamlet's soliloquies follow his thoughts. There are different functions here – but how are those functions revealed in the language used?

Hamlet's last lines

Between the wounding of Hamlet at line 280 in Act 5 Scene 2, and his death at line 337, there are over fifty lines spoken, more than half by Hamlet himself. And yet as Hamlet becomes aware that he is soon to die, his language is not epic or dramatically 'tragic' or over-imbued with emotion. Rather, it is measured, conscious of his fate and his reputation ('report me and my cause aright / To the unsatisfied' and 'tell my story'), dignified and, finally, political ('I do prophesy th'election lights / On Fortinbras; he has my dying voice').

In some ways, it is surprising that Shakespeare did not give Hamlet some grander lines to end with, reflecting on human nature, existence, his father's revenge and his own relation to death and the 'divinity that shapes our ends'.

- Write the 'missing' speech by Hamlet in which he does reflect on the grander themes, and as a misunderstood, wronged and complex figure, takes his leave from the world.
- Perform that speech, inserting it where you see fit in the closing part of the play.

Hamlet in performance 《哈慕雷》的演出

Hamlet through history

Hamlet has always been a popular play. Since it was written around 1601, it has rarely been absent from the stage for long. There is even a record of a version acted on a ship off the coast of Sierra Leone in 1608. Quotations from the play (such as 'To be, or not to be') have become utterly familiar, even to those who have never seen the play. But in every age the text has been cut, altered and added to. For over 400 years audiences have watched and heard very different versions of *Hamlet*. For example, throughout the eighteenth and nineteenth centuries Fortinbras disappeared from most productions – this tradition still influences modern productions. Also, performances occasionally end with Hamlet's death: 'the rest is silence'.

The example of the famous eighteenth-century actor-manager David Garrick shows there is no such thing as the 'authentic' *Hamlet*. Garrick wanted to portray Hamlet as a truly noble prince, and to make the play into what he saw as a genuine tragedy. He therefore cut anything that detracted from a heroic image of Hamlet, and removed what he called 'the rubbish of the fifth act': Ophelia's funeral and the gravediggers. Garrick's audiences did not hear how Hamlet sent Rosencrantz and Guildenstern to their deaths, nor the 'Now might I do it pat' speech (in which Hamlet wishes for Claudius to suffer in hell), because Garrick thought both speeches diminished Hamlet's noble nature. Laertes did not poison his sword, or Claudius the drink. Gertrude died off stage in guilt-ridden insanity, Fortinbras did not appear, and Laertes survived to rule over Denmark jointly with Horatio.

Productions in the nineteenth century usually presented romantic interpretations of Hamlet as a sane, intellectual, sensitive prince, unable to sweep swiftly to revenge. Sets often attempted to create the illusion of a historically accurate castle of Elsinore. For example, Edmund Kean played Hamlet between 1814 and 1833, removing much of the blank verse and replacing it with prose. His attitude to the Ghost was more one of welcome than of terror, and he also treated Ophelia with tenderness rather than bitterness. In the USA, Edwin Booth performed the part in a production at Burton's Theater in New York in 1857: apparently an introspective and mild performance, eschewing (避开) the more melodramatic style that was popular at the time.

Modern productions have increasingly portrayed Hamlet as disturbed and alienated, and have abandoned realistic sets. They rely more on 'symbolic' settings or bare stages with a minimum of scenery. This can be seen as a return to the conditions of Shakespeare's own Globe Theatre stage, which was not dependent on theatrical illusion. The first mention of Hamlet in the play is as 'young Hamlet' and, from what the gravedigger says, he seems to be about thirty. But for over 400 years Hamlet has been played by actors of all ages.

▼ Christopher Eccleston as Hamlet in a production at the West Yorkshire Playhouse, Leeds, 2002.

Notable productions

In 2004, a twenty-three-year-old Ben Whishaw played Hamlet at The Old Vic in London (see right). One reviewer said: 'Far from being a robust young man, haunted by anger and revenge that is only held back by uncertainty, this Hamlet [was] skinny and frail in stature, raw and idealistic in nature', considering suicide with a penknife and a bottle of pills as he recited 'To be or not to be'. The youthful appearance of Hamlet's mother in this production dramatically heightened his confused feelings towards her. Alongside this, nineteen-year-old Samantha Whittaker played Ophelia as a teenage girl with a crush on Hamlet. It is possible, as has been suggested in this edition, to play Hamlet as an even younger character, and for younger actors to play him – though the demands are considerable.

Richard Burbage, the first actor ever to play Hamlet (in 1601), was thirty-four when he filled the role. Other actors have played the part when they were well past forty. Sarah Bernhardt, a French actress, played him when she was fifty-six. In the eighteenth century, Thomas Betterton played the part when he was over seventy.

A number of features create the impression of a youthful Hamlet. He faces familiar problems of adolescence: relations with the opposite sex, coming to terms with responsibility, finding one's own personality. He seems rebellious and misunderstood, and is constantly self-questioning, unsure whom to trust, and feeling betrayed by former friends. He has problems with his mother and stepfather, and with coming to terms with the death of his own father.

In 2001, Sam West took the title role in the Royal Shakespeare Company's uncut four-hour version of *Hamlet*, which emphasised the bleak, modernistic dimensions of the play. In 2008, another RSC production of the play starred David Tennant as a witty, graceful Hamlet who compulsively mimicked other characters rather than looking inwards at his conflicted self.

In 2012, *Hamlet* was produced at the Utah Shakespeare Festival, directed by Marco Barricelli and characterised as a 'powerful examination of the human psyche … [Shakespeare's] most mature, and chilling, revenge tragedy'. In London in the same year, the play was performed in Lithuanian as *Hamletas* in the Globe World Shakespeare Festival. This production's frantic pace was set by the jerky, deranged physical movements of the characters, and Hamlet displayed his madness by lying completely still in the midst of this manic scene.

Hamlet at the Globe Theatre

In Shakespeare's lifetime, *Hamlet* was almost certainly performed at the Globe Theatre. It was a round theatre, open to the sky. The audience standing in the pit, the 'groundlings', got wet if it rained. Those in the galleries (who paid more), and the actors on stage, were protected from the worst of the weather.

The original Globe Theatre audiences expected and enjoyed a noisy display of drums, trumpets and the firing of cannon. *Hamlet* richly fulfils that expectation. In the play's second scene, Claudius promises that 'the great cannon' will sound to heaven itself to celebrate his drinking. That boastful ritual is heard as Hamlet awaits the Ghost's appearance ('The kettle-drum and trumpet thus bray out'), and in Act 5 Scene 2 before the duel Claudius orders 'let the kettle to the trumpet speak, / The trumpet to the cannoneer without, / The cannons to the heavens'. His order is obeyed as '*Drum, trumpets sound, and shot goes off*'.

In Shakespeare's day, Gertrude and Ophelia were played by boys. Although there were no elaborate sets on the bare stage of the Globe Theatre, the actors dressed in attractive and expensive costumes, usually the fashionable dress of the times. Only a few props were used – swords, goblets and so on.

The 2000 production of *Hamlet* at Shakespeare's Globe presented the play in that 'authentic' style. Actors were dressed in the fashion of the Danish court in the late sixteenth century (similar to Elizabethan costume). The royal family wore red and gold, and their coat of arms was visible on stage. To suggest the freezing cold on the gun platform, sheepskin cloaks were worn. The players in the play-within-a-play wore what Elizabethans would have thought of as Roman dress.

In Dominic Dromgoole's stripped-down and touring production of *Hamlet* at Shakespeare's Globe in 2012, the emphasis was on 'political intrigue and sexual obsession, philosophical reflection and violent action, tragic depth and wild humour'.

Performing *Hamlet*

Consider what your own production of *Hamlet* would be like. There are various aspects to putting on a performance, and you can choose from the following activities – whether you work on *Hamlet* as a full production, whether you create a stripped-down version, or whether you simply undertake some of the activities as a way of engaging with and interrogating the script itself.

- Take the whole script (which, as we have seen, can take four hours and more if performed in its entirety). Cut it down, either to half its length or to a minimal version that would take forty-five minutes to an hour to perform. What would you retain and what would you cut?
- Look at examples of set design, in the images throughout this book and on the Internet. Decide whether you wish to have an elaborate design set in a particular period, or whether you prefer the more minimal approach. You can work with a shoebox for your initial designs, or you can construct a more ambitious model.
- Costume design often follows the stage and set design. Traditionally, *Hamlet* is performed in dark colours to reflect the sombre, melancholy mood of the play. But there is room for contrasts, eccentricity and extravagance in parts of the play. Choose a section where the action is particularly exciting, and draw designs for the costumes of one or more characters on stage at this point.
- On the left-hand pages of this book, there has often been reference to a Director's Journal in which you have been encouraged to write guidance for actors, notes about stage directions and other reflections about performing *Hamlet*. As a director, look back at your notes and sketch out your grand plan as to your conception of the play and how you would like to see it performed.

All-female and all-male performances

In an article in the *Guardian* newspaper on 20 November 2012, the actress Harriet Walter stated, 'When you play Hamlet, you become, as it were, humanity. You stand for humankind.' Yet women are not often given the centrality and status of Hamlet in Shakespeare's plays (Rosalind in *As You Like It* may be the exception). The practice of having women play Shakespeare's male roles seeks to explore and interrogate this issue and its related assumptions.

In November 2012, there was an all-female production of *Julius Caesar* at the Donmar Warehouse, London, directed by Phyllida Lloyd. The drive to an all-female cast in the professional theatre is partly a feminist wish to redress imbalances in casting over centuries, and to provide a counterpoint to the frequent all-male casts in Shakespearean productions. Of the 900 and more characters in Shakespeare, only fifteen per cent are female.

▼ Asta Nielsen as Hamlet in the 1920 movie version of the play.

In some all-girl schools, an all-female cast presents an opportunity and a challenge. Why not attempt plays like *Julius Caesar* and *Hamlet*, which look male dominated, but in which an all-female production would give a very different perspective? The Sydney Theatre Company cast a female Hamlet for their 2010 production. As their notes to the production stated:

> *The 'female Hamlet' has become an enigma. Ever since the late eighteenth century, leading actresses such as Sarah Bernhardt (also the first Hamlet on film, 1899), Sarah Siddons, Asta Neilsen and more recently Diane Venora (1983) and Angela Winkler (1999) have played the role of Hamlet. Many of these performers have been involved in radical politics and theatre movements in Stalinist Russia, Poland, and Germany.*
>
> *In theatre, film, and radio, women have challenged the notion of Hamlet as exclusive to the male gender. The opportunity to play this cultural icon for many is viewed as a political act drawing attention to gender inequity, the lack of substantial roles for women and the often unspoken 'femininity' of Hamlet.*

◆ **Think of the major male characters in *Hamlet*: Hamlet himself, Claudius, Polonius, Horatio. What challenges, and what particular characteristics would need to be addressed and considered carefully if casting only women in the play? What would it mean to the dynamic of the play as a whole?**

Women can also play female roles in Shakespeare in ways that subvert the traditional associations of passivity and marginalisation. In a Canadian production of *Hamlet*, Ophelia was played by a woman dressed in black – like Hamlet himself – and her madness was represented by violent movements with a sword, presaging the duel between her brother and her lover.

All-male productions have been common since Shakespeare's day. Single-sex schools tend to choose the plays that give the boys or girls the most accessible parts to play. And yet an all-male version of *Hamlet* presents interesting problems for those playing Gertrude and Ophelia, as consideration of sexuality is never far from the surface.

Hamlet on the radio

Think of a production of *Hamlet* on the radio. In many ways, it is well suited to the medium: its dark, inactive (until the final act) nature; the speaking Ghost on the battlements; the clanking chains of the prison that is Denmark; the doors opening and shutting, or remaining half-opened as spies keep account of the developing behaviour of Hamlet himself. All these qualities lend an air of internal mental anguish to the play, and are ideal for the interior soundscape of radio. There are many great recordings of *Hamlet*, but why not make your own?

- **Split into groups, and have each group take a scene or two of the play to work with – there are twenty scenes in the play as a whole, of uneven length. Larger groups could take an act each. Record a radio version of the selected play section, with each member of the group taking responsibility for a certain element – direction, voice acting roles, sound effects and so on. Mood can be created by emphasising variations in speech (tone, volume, spoken asides, soliloquies, public statements), sound effects and atmospheric background soundtracking.**

Hamlet in the movies

Laurence Olivier's 1948 movie of *Hamlet* began with the statement, 'This is the tragedy of a man who could not make up his mind', and strongly implied that Hamlet felt incestuous desire for his mother. Another famous black-and-white film of *Hamlet* is the 1964 version by the Russian director, Grigori Kozintsev, which stresses the political aspects of the play.

In 1990, Mel Gibson played Hamlet in a colour movie that used only about one third of Shakespeare's script. Fortinbras is cut from this version, as well as scenes with Claudius as a political diplomat. In contrast,

Kenneth Branagh's 1996 film lasted four hours, using virtually all the script, although a shortened two-hour version is available. Branagh's use of late nineteenth-century costumes contrasts with a 2000 modern-dress American movie in which Hamlet is a New York businessman. In 2010, David Tennant played Hamlet in a BBC production in which surveillance was the key motif, and in which the madness was emphasised.

Films provide close-ups, tracking shots and cinematic spectacle not available on stage. In the 1964 Russian movie Fortinbras's army marches along a real sea coast (see p. 166). The sea symbolises the possibility of freedom from Elsinore's prison-like atmosphere. Movies can even suggest moral perspectives, as when Olivier uses high-angle shots to look down on Claudius's court as if in moral judgement.

▲ Modern films sometimes make sly or obvious reference to *Hamlet*, as in Arnold Schwarzenegger's *Last Action Hero* from 1993.

◄ This image and the one on page 210 both show how Ophelia's funeral has been presented in stage versions of *Hamlet*. How would you adapt the funeral scene for a film version of the play? Think about how you could use different shots and camera angles to show the characters' reactions at this point to the greatest effect.

▲ The poster for the 1948 movie.

Some final activities in relation to *Hamlet* in performance

- Consider in detail the different design and content elements of the poster shown on this page. Source other posters of movies or stage productions of *Hamlet*. Then create your own poster, perhaps using inspiration from the existing posters you think are most striking and effective.
- Write programme notes for a production, including the usual features in programmes: a narrative of the action of the play; background thematic material; and some character analysis.
- Create a list of props you will need for an actual or imagined production, and write a note for the stage manager as to how they will be used.
- Go to see a stage production of *Hamlet* – or more than one, if possible. Write reviews of each production you see.
- Take one of the soliloquies from the play (e.g. 'To be or not to be') and compare clips of performances online. Rate the different versions and justify your decisions.
- Write a comparative review of as many movie productions of *Hamlet* as you can see. In addition to those mentioned so far, there is a 2000 movie directed by Michael Almereyda with Ethan Hawke as Hamlet, Diane Venora as Gertrude, Bill Murray as Polonius and Kyle MacLachlan as Claudius. This version is set in corporate, urban America, with Hamlet as an independent filmmaker trying to find his way through the corruption of contemporary culture.
- Write or produce a satirical and subversive version of *Hamlet* that compresses the play into a very short space of time – at most, ten minutes.

Several such works exist, ranging from *The Skinhead Hamlet* (1982), which reduces the play to a series of grunts, exclamations and expletives, to the *Bouncy Castle Hamlet* performed at the Edinburgh Festival.

- There are productions of *Hamlet* worldwide, in movies and on stage. One example is *The Banquet* (《夜宴》)(also known as *Legend of the Black Scorpion*, directed by Feng Xiaogang, China, 2006), a Kung Fu movie adaptation. The opera *Revenge of the Prince* (《王子复仇记》), produced by the Shanghai Peking Opera, is set in ancient China, complete with acrobatic and dance elements. Eastern European productions of *Hamlet* have often accentuated the play's political significance.
- Several manga editions of *Hamlet* exist, as well as other comic book versions. Seek them out and carry out a comparison to determine which is the best.
- Several puppet versions of *Hamlet* are available on the Internet; watch a few, and decide whether you think the play is suitable for this approach. Not all these puppet versions are light-hearted. See, for example, kabuki (Japanese dance-drama), which sometime includes puppetry, or bunraku, which involves puppets of about half-life-size. You might like to produce your own puppet version of a shortened *Hamlet* in the style you think appropriate (or inappropriate!).

▼ A scene from the kabuki version of *Hamlet*, Mermaid Theatre, London, 1991.

Writing about Shakespeare 笔论莎士比亚

The play as text

Shakespeare's plays have always been studied as literary works – as words on a page that need clarification, appreciation and discussion. When you write about the plays, you will be asked to compose short pieces and also longer, more reflective pieces like controlled assessments, examination scripts and coursework – often in the form of essays on themes and/or imagery, character studies, analyses of the structure of the play and on stagecraft. Imagery, stagecraft and character are dealt with elsewhere in this edition. Here, we concentrate on themes and structure. You might find it helpful to look at the 'Write about it' boxes on the left-hand pages throughout the play.

Themes

It is often tempting to say that the theme of a play is a single idea, like 'death' in *Hamlet*, or 'the supernatural' in *Macbeth*, or 'love' in *Romeo and Juliet*. The problem with such a simple approach is that you will miss the complexity of the plays. In *Romeo and Juliet*, for example, the play is about the relationship between love, family loyalty and constraint; it is also about the relationship of youth to age and experience; and the relationship between Romeo and Juliet is also played out against a background of enmity between two families. Between each of these ideas or concepts there are tensions. The tensions are the main focus of attention for Shakespeare and the audience; this is also how the best drama operates – by the presentation of and resolution of tension.

Look back at the 'Themes' boxes throughout the play to see if any of the activities there have given rise to information that you could use as a starting point for further writing about the themes of the specific play you are studying.

Structure

Most Shakespeare plays are in five acts, divided into scenes. These acts were not in the original scripts, but have been included in later editions to make the action more manageable, clearer and more like 'classical' structures. One way to get a sense of the structure of the whole play is to take a printed version of the play (not this one!) and cut it up into scenes and acts. Then display each scene and act, in sequence, on a wall, like this:

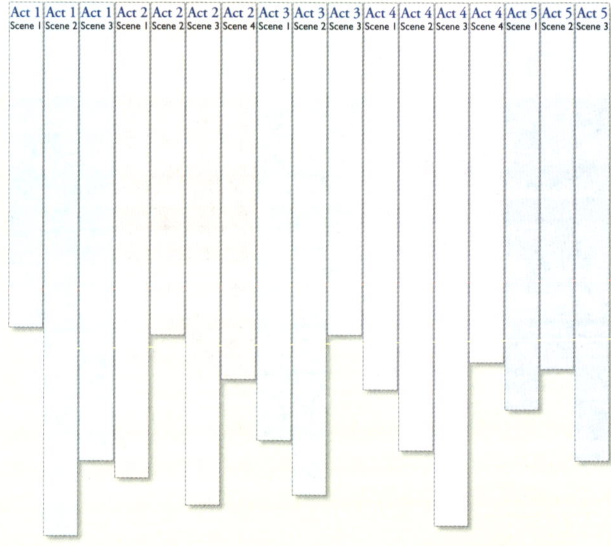

As you set out the whole play, you will be able to see the 'shape' of each act, the relative length of the scenes, and how the acts relate to each other (such as whether one of the acts is shorter, and why that might be). You can annotate the text with comments, observations and questions. You can use a highlighter pen to mark the recurrence of certain words, images or metaphors to see at a glance where and how frequently they appear. You can also follow a particular character's progress through the play.

Such an overview of the play gives you critical perspective: you will be able to see how the parts fit together, to stand back from the play and assess its shape, and to focus on particular parts within the context of the whole. Your writing will reflect a greater awareness of the overall context as a result.

The play as script

There are different, but related, categories when we think of the play as a script for performance. These include *stagecraft* (discussed elsewhere in this edition and throughout the left-hand pages), *lighting*, *focus* (who are we looking at? Where is the attention of the audience?), *music and sound*, *props and costumes*, *casting*, *make-up*, *pace and rhythm*, and other *spatial relationships* (e.g. how actors move around the stage in relation to each other). If you are writing about stagecraft or performance, use the notes you have made as a result of the 'Stagecraft' boxes throughout this edition of the play, as well as any information you can find about the plays in performance.

What are the key points of dispute?

Shakespeare is brilliant at capturing a number of key points of dispute in each of his plays. These are the dramatic moments where he concentrates the focus of the audience on difficult (sometimes universal) problems that the characters are facing or embodying.

First, identify these key points in the play you are studying. You can do this as a class by thinking about what you consider to be the key points in small groups, then debating the long-list as a whole class, and then coming up with a short-list of what the class thinks are the most significant. (This is a good opportunity for speaking and listening work.) They are likely to be places in the play where the action or reflection is at its most intense, and which capture the complexity of themes, character, structure and performance.

Second, drill down at one of the points of contention and tension. In other words, investigate the complexity of the problem that Shakespeare is exploring. What is at stake? Why is it important? Is it a problem that can be resolved, or is it an insoluble one?

Key skills in writing about Shakespeare

Here are some suggestions to help you organise your notes and develop advanced writing skills when working on Shakespeare:

- Compose the title of your writing carefully to maximise your opportunities to be creative and critical about the play. Explore the key words in your title carefully. Decide which aspect of the play – or which combination of aspects – you are focusing on.
- Create a mind map of your ideas, making connections between them.
- If appropriate, arrange your ideas into a hierarchy that shows how some themes or features of the play are 'higher' than others and can incorporate other ideas.
- Sequence your ideas so that you have a plan for writing an essay, review, story – whichever genre you are using. You might like to think about whether to put your strongest points first, in the middle, or later.
- Collect key quotations (it might help to compile this list with a partner), which you can use as evidence to support your argument.
- Compose your first draft, embedding quotations in your text as you go along.
- Revise your draft in the light of your own critical reflections and/or those of others.

The following pages focus on writing about *Hamlet* in particular.

Writing about *Hamlet* 笔论《哈慕雷》

More has been written about *Hamlet* than about any other work in literature. It is sometimes said that at least one article or review about this play is published per day. Given its popularity as a play for study in schools, colleges and universities, there are probably many essays and other types of writing produced in academic contexts every day. What can you write about that will make your piece distinctive; and how will you go about expressing that new perspective? First, here is some guidance to help you in the preparation for your writing on *Hamlet*.

Look back over the writing you have done in the course of reading, acting and studying the play – in particular at your Director's Journal and your responses to the 'Write about it' activities. You may already have a good deal of material in the form of paragraphs, notes and reflections on the play.

In addition, some of the work you have undertaken in relation to the 'Themes', 'Characters' and 'Language' boxes will contribute to the substantial and reflective writing you might now do.

◆ This edition has emphasised the importance of embedded quotations in your writing. You will have already collected quotations that illustrate your sense of the complexity of themes and character in the play. Go back over the play to see if you can add to that collection of quotations.

Second, an important stage in preparing to write about *Hamlet* is standing back and looking at the play as a whole. The activity on page 278, which involves cutting out the play and displaying it on a wall, is one way of achieving a sense of the whole play. This act of standing back is particularly important in *Hamlet*, given its length.

◆ Here are some short statements about the play to help you decide your own perspective on it. Rank these in order of importance to you. Gather supporting evidence for the issue you have ranked as most important; also consider how you could structure an argument for this issue – based on cause (why you believe it to be true) and effect (how it is represented in the play). Then discuss your order with a partner or with a larger group.

a Hamlet is clearly central to the play. He is the eponymous hero (i.e. the play is named after him) and that makes his actions and his inner psyche the main focus of attention.

b The play is principally a political drama in which the succession to the throne of Denmark is the paramount concern. The line of succession from old Hamlet through Claudius, bypassing young Hamlet and moving on to Fortinbras, is the main strand.

c Essentially, this is a revenge tragedy with an extra dimension: that dimension is the procrastination that Hamlet experiences throughout the play – the result of a combination of reason, humanity, impulsiveness, feigned madness and conscience.

d The women in the play are victims: Ophelia is subject to her father's, brother's and lover's bullying; Gertrude is often in the dark about what is going on around her. They are caught up in a male-dominated world of confinement and corruption.

You can also disagree with these statements; amend their wording to suit your own perspectives; and adapt them as titles for your own writing as you see fit, and in discussion with your peers and teacher.

Third, you can decide which genre or type of text you wish to use in writing about *Hamlet*. Here are some alternatives to the conventional essay that might suit *Hamlet* in particular:

- An extended review of film or stage or radio productions (to do all three would require a dissertation or thesis). Such a review should be done with close reference to the script, using quotations as you would in a conventional essay. You can collect resources for such a review online, in libraries and via other means. Remember to consider the nature of the medium (the hardware, the context, the frame) as well as the modes of expression (sound, the spoken word, action) and the affordances of the medium you have chosen (what does it allow, what are its characteristics, and what aspects of *Hamlet* does it foreground?).
- Dialogues, in question-and-answer format, between the characters and an interrogator. For example, as has been suggested, Hamlet or Ophelia could be interviewed by a psychiatrist; Horatio could be interviewed by a judge and/or panel that is investigating the death of Hamlet, Laertes, Gertrude, Ophelia and Laertes.
- A Socratic dialogue, in which an interrogator (like Socrates – look up an example) has a thesis that he or she wishes to prove via questioning. Often the questions are designed to catch out the person or character being questioned – who could be an actor, a character in the play, a director or some other figure who will need to draw on the script to provide evidence.

Finally, some examples of essay questions that you are likely to encounter in writing about *Hamlet*:

- 'Hamlet has a split personality, which makes it difficult for him to put revenge into action.' Discuss this statement, considering whether Hamlet's personality is split into two, or whether there are more sides to him. To what extent is he a typical revenge hero?
- In Denmark's corrupt world, Hamlet is too naïve, too full of the better sides of human nature, to survive. Discuss.
- Write an essay on the links between the private and the public in *Hamlet*, focusing on one or more of the main characters.
- The prevailing imagery of the play is that of confinement, prisons, chains and the physicality of the human body. This suggests the play is essentially about the struggle between the mortality of the flesh on the one hand, and the desire for freedom of the spirit and soul on the other. Discuss.
- At the core of the play is the struggle between free will and fate. But fate is divided into two kinds of determination: divine intervention and the machinations and deliberations of a corrupt political state. Is this a fair reflection on *Hamlet*?
- Write a study of Gertrude and/or Ophelia that argues that, far from being victims of circumstances, they have a power and self-determination that often goes unrecognised in commentary upon *Hamlet*.
- *Hamlet* is principally a play in which language dominates. It charts the interior life of a central character, and is more suited to radio than to television, film or the stage. Discuss.
- Is the plot of *Hamlet* secondary to a) the characterisation, and b) the creation of a fictional world of despair, gloom and corruption?

William Shakespeare 莎翁年表 1564–1616

1564 Born Stratford-upon-Avon, eldest son of John and Mary Shakespeare.
1582 Marries Anne Hathaway of Shottery, near Stratford.
1583 Daughter Susanna born.
1585 Twins, son and daughter Hamnet and Judith, born.
1592 First mention of Shakespeare in London. Robert Greene, another playwright, described Shakespeare as 'an upstart crow beautified with our feathers'. Greene seems to have been jealous of Shakespeare. He mocked Shakespeare's name, calling him 'the only Shake-scene in a country' (presumably because Shakespeare was writing successful plays).
1595 Becomes a shareholder in The Lord Chamberlain's Men, an acting company that became extremely popular.
1596 Son, Hamnet, dies aged eleven.
Father, John, granted arms (acknowledged as a gentleman).
1597 Buys New Place, the grandest house in Stratford.
1598 Acts in Ben Jonson's *Every Man in His Humour*.
1599 Globe Theatre opens on Bankside. Performances in the open air.
1601 Father, John, dies.
1603 James I grants Shakespeare's company a royal patent: The Lord Chamberlain's Men become The King's Men and play about twelve performances each year at court.
1607 Daughter Susanna, marries Dr John Hall.
1608 Mother, Mary, dies.
1609 The King's Men begin performing indoors at Blackfriars Theatre.
1610 Probably returns from London to live in Stratford.
1616 Daughter Judith, marries Thomas Quiney.
Dies. Buried in Holy Trinity Church, Stratford-upon-Avon.

The plays and poems

(no one knows exactly when he wrote each play)

1589–95 *The Two Gentlemen of Verona, The Taming of the Shrew, First, Second* and *Third Parts* of *King Henry VI, Titus Andronicus, King Richard III, The Comedy of Errors, Love's Labour's Lost, A Midsummer Night's Dream, Romeo and Juliet, King Richard II* (and the long poems *Venus and Adonis* and *The Rape of Lucrece*).
1596–99 *King John, The Merchant of Venice, First* and *Second Parts* of *King Henry IV, The Merry Wives of Windsor, Much Ado About Nothing, King Henry V, Julius Caesar* (and probably the Sonnets).
1600–05 *As You Like It*, **Hamlet**, *Twelfth Night, Troilus and Cressida, Measure for Measure, Othello, All's Well That Ends Well, Timon of Athens, King Lear.*
1606–11 *Macbeth, Antony and Cleopatra, Pericles, Coriolanus, The Winter's Tale, Cymbeline, The Tempest.*
1613 *King Henry VIII, The Two Noble Kinsmen* (both probably with John Fletcher).
1623 Shakespeare's plays published as a collection (now called the First Folio).

Acknowledgements 鸣谢

Cambridge University Press would like to acknowledge the contributions made to this work by Rex Gibson.

Picture Credits

p. iii: Royal Shakespeare Theatre 2001, © Donald Cooper/Photostage; p. v: Hackney Empire 1995, © Donald Cooper/Photostage; p. vi: Old Vic, 2004, © Donald Cooper/Photostage; p. vii: Barbican Theatre 2004, © Donald Cooper/Photostage; p. viii top: Royal Shakespeare Theatre 1997, © Donald Cooper/Photostage; p. viii bottom: Royal Dramatic Theatre Stockholm 1987, © Donald Cooper/Photostage; p. ix top: Mermaid Theatre 1991, © Donald Cooper/Photostage; p. ix bottom: Greenwich Playhouse 1999, © Donald Cooper/Photostage; p. x top: Royal Lyceum Theatre Edinburgh 2003, © Donald Cooper/Photostage; p. x bottom: Hackney Empire 1995, © Donald Cooper/Photostage; p. xi top: Tobacco Factory Bristol 2008, © Donald Cooper/Photostage; p. xi bottom: Bouffes Du Nord 2000, © Jean-Pierre Muller/Getty Images/AFP Images; p. xii top: Royal Dramatic Theatre Stockholm 1987, © Donald Cooper/Photostage; p. xii bottom: Barbican Theatre 1992, © Donald Cooper/Photostage; p. 10: National Theatre 2010, © Johann Persson/ArenaPAL; p. 18: Sadler's Wells 2003, © Marilyn Kingwill/ArenaPAL; p. 22: Royal Shakespeare Theatre 2004, © Donald Cooper/Photostage; p. 24: Young Vic 2011, © Donald Cooper/Photostage; p. 26: still from 1948 *Hamlet* film, © ITV Global/The Kobal Collection/Wilfred Newton; p. 32: still from 1996 *Hamlet* film, © Castle Rock Entertainment/The Kobal Collection; p. 36: Royal Shakespeare Company Tour 1988, © Clive Barda/ArenaPAL; p. 42: still from 1990 *Hamlet* film, © Paramount/The Kobal Collection; p. 44: section of 'The Garden of Earthly Delights' by Hieronymous Bosch; p. 48: Swan Theatre 2006, © Tristram Kenton/Lebrecht Music & Arts; p. 54: Royal Shakespeare Theatre 2013, © Donald Cooper/Photostage; p. 57 top: Bloomsbury Theatre 2000, © Donald Cooper/Photostage; p. 57 bottom: Barbican Theatre 1992, © Donald Cooper/Photostage; p. 58: Royal Shakespeare Theatre 1981, © Donald Cooper/Photostage; p. 62 Old Vic 2004, © Donald Cooper/Photostage; p. 66: National Theatre 2010, © Donald Cooper/Photostage; p. 72: National Theatre 2010, © Johann Persson/ArenaPAL; p. 76: Donmar West End 2009, © Donald Cooper/Photostage; p. 84: Royal Dramatic Theatre Stockholm 1987, © Donald Cooper/Photostage; p. 90: Royal Shakespeare Theatre 1984, © Donald Cooper/Photostage; p. 99 top left: Swan Theatre 2006, © Marilyn Kingwill/ArenaPAL; p. 99 top right: Barbican Theatre 1998, © Colin Willoughby/ArenaPAL; p. 99 bottom left: Swan Theatre 2006, © Marilyn Kingwill/ArenaPAL; p. 99 bottom right: Royal Theatre Northampton 2005, © Donald Cooper/Photostage; p. 100: National Theatre 2010, © Donald Cooper/Photostage; p. 102: Shakespeare's Globe 2000, © Colin Willoughby/ArenaPAL; p. 108: Shakespeare's Globe 2011, © Donald Cooper/Photostage; p. 114: Courtyard Theatre 2008, © Donald Cooper/Photostage; p. 118: Barbican Theatre 1992, © Donald Cooper/Photostage; p. 122: Annotated *Hamlet* prompt book, © University of Virginia; p. 124: Yvonne Arnaud Theatre 2005, © Marilyn Kingwill/ArenaPAL; p. 128: Half Moon Theatre 1979, © Donald Cooper/Photostage; p. 130: National Theatre 2010, © Donald Cooper/Photostage; p. 138: Royal Shakespeare Theatre 1984, © Donald Cooper/Photostage; p. 142: Drawing of Hamlet killing Polonius, © Leonard de Selva/Corbis; p. 146: Royal Opera House 2003, © Clive Barda/ArenaPAL; p. 148: Royal Shakespeare Theatre 2001, © Donald Cooper/Photostage; p. 152: Royal Shakespeare Theatre 1997, © Donald Cooper/Photostage; p. 155 top: Riverside Studios 1992, © Donald Cooper/Photostage; p. 155 bottom: Yvonne Arnaud Theatre 2005, © Donald Cooper/Photostage; p. 160: Young Vic 2011, © Donald Cooper/Photostage; p. 162: National Theatre 2010, © Donald Cooper/Photostage; p. 166: *Hamlet* from 1964 film, © Lenfilm/The Kobal Collection; p. 172: Royal Lyceum Theatre Edinburgh 2003, © Donald Cooper/Photostage; p. 180: Barbican Theatre 2011, © Donald Cooper/Photostage; p. 182: Swan Theatre 2006, © Donald Cooper/Photostage; p. 186: Tobacco Factory Bristol 2008, © Donald Cooper/Photostage; p. 196: 'Ophelia' painting by John Everett Millais; p. 199 top left: New Ambassadors

Theatre 2006, © Marilyn Kingwill/ArenaPAL; p. 199 bottom left: Royal Shakespeare Company Young People's Tour 2010, © Donald Cooper/Photostage; p. 199 right: Shakespeare's Globe 2011, Pete Jones/ArenaPAL; p. 202: National Theatre 2000, © Donald Cooper/Photostage; p. 208 top: Royal Shakespeare Theatre 2001, © Donald Cooper/Photostage; p. 208 middle: Donmar Warehouse 1993, © Donald Cooper/Photostage; p. 208 bottom: Swan Theatre 2006, © Donald Cooper/Photostage; p. 210: Barbican Theatre 2011, © Donald Cooper/Photostage; p. 222: Tobacco Factory Bristol 2008, © Donald Cooper/Photostage; p. 230: Royal Shakespeare Theatre 1984, © Donald Cooper/Photostage; p. 236: still from 1990 *Hamlet* film, © Paramount/The Kobal Collection; p. 241 left: Swan Theatre 2006, © Marilyn Kingwill/ ArenaPAL; p. 241 right: Swan Theatre 2006, © Marilyn Kingwill/ArenaPAL; p. 242 top: Courtyard Theatre 2008, © Geraint Lewis; p. 242 bottom: Edinburgh Festival Theatre © Clive Barda/ArenaPAL; p. 244: Painting of Lord Burghley by unknown artist; p. 247: 'Melancholia' engraving by Albrecht Dürer; p. 248 top: Round House 1969, © Donald Cooper/ Photostage; p. 248 middle: National Theatre 2010, © Johann Persson/ArenaPAL; p. 248 bottom: Shakespeare's Globe 2011, © Donald Cooper/Photostage; p. 253 top: Royal Shakespeare Company Young People's Tour 2010, © Donald Cooper/ Photostage; p. 253 bottom: Royal Shakespeare Company Young People's Tour 2010, © Donald Cooper/Photostage; p. 254: Crucible Theatre 2010, © Donald Cooper/ Photostage; p. 256: Barbican Theatre 1992, © Donald Cooper/Photostage; p. 257: Shakespeare's Globe 2000, © Donald Cooper/Photostage; p. 258: Yvonne Arnaud Theatre 2005, © Donald Cooper/Photostage; p. 260: Still from 1990 *Hamlet* film, © Paramount/The Kobal Collection/ Elizabeth Zeschin; p. 261: National Theatre 2000, © Fritz Curzon/ArenaPAL; p. 263: Royal Lyceum Theatre Edinburgh 2003, © Donald Cooper/Photostage; p. 268: First page of *Hamlet* folio; p. 270: West Yorkshire Playhouse 2002, © Donald Cooper/Photostage; p. 271: Old Vic 2004, © Donald Cooper/Photostage; p. 273: still from 1920 *Hamlet* film, © ullsteinbild/TopFoto; pp. 274–5: Royal Shakespeare Theatre 1992, © Donald Cooper/Photostage; p. 275 inset: Still from 1993 *Last Action Hero* film, © Columbia/The Kobal Collection/Zade Rosenthal; p. 276: poster for 1948 *Hamlet* film, © ITV Global /The Kobal Collection; p. 277: Mermaid Theatre 1991, © Donald Cooper/Photostage.

Produced for Cambridge University Press by
White-Thomson Publishing
+44 (0)843 208 7460
www.wtpub.co.uk

Project editor: Alice Harman
Designer: Clare Nicholas
Concept design: Jackie Hill